A HEART FOR TRUTH

The story of Nicodemus
An Unlikely Believer

A HEART FOR TRUTH

The story of Nicodemus
An Unlikely Believer

Joyce Cordell

...everyone who exalts himself will be humbled,
and he who humbles himself will be exalted.
Luke 18:14

...whoever lives by the truth comes into the light...
John 3:21

ISBN-13: 978-0-9893714-6-9
ISBN-10: 0989371468

Home Crafted Artistry and Printing
1252 Beechwood Avenue
New Albany, IN 47150
HomeCraftedArtistry@yahoo.com

Dedicated
To
Norma Watkins
My mother, supporter,
and cheerleader

Acknowledgments

As with my first book, *Ears to Hear,* I stand amazed at God's provision in writing this work. He led me in the most astounding ways at every turn.

On challenging days, two quotations carried me through.

"*The task ahead of us is never as great as the Power behind us.*"

"*Make your life a mission rather than an intermission.*"

On other days, I couldn't wait to get to the computer to see what would happen next in the story. I had the general direction in mind, but at times, I was on as much of an adventure as my characters were.

Many people stood with me in this journey. Mary Gaskins, my dear friend and encourager, provided overall observations that were very helpful. My pastor, Dr. Greg Barr, declared it reasonably possible to the culture and Scripture.

Many thanks to Bonnie Abraham who did the red-ink make-over from one end to the other. I am greatly indebted to her gifted eye for punctuation, unnecessary words, and general fine tuning.

Others who cheered me on include the members of my Louisville Christian Writers' group who listened every month to my victories and woes. Thanks to Crystal Murray, president of LCW, who helped me with all things technical.

I am grateful to Michael McCormick who graciously posed for the front cover. Mike was a chemist before he retired. He, like Nicodemus, searched for truth and found it in Jesus. Cancer took over the last years of his life, but he served the youth of our church as long as he was able. He posed for the front cover toward the end of his bout with the cancer and passed away a few months later.

Thanks also to Candy Ailstock who used my photo and beautifully designed the front cover.

Finally, a big thank you to my husband, Jim, who has encouraged me and supported me all along the way.

The many readers of my first book were always asking, "How's Nicodemus coming along?" "Have you finished the book yet?" And so, dear readers, after another seven years, book two has at last come to pass. Thank you for all your support.

Contents

Characters

Abigail — the shepherd's wife
*Annas — the previous high priest
Argus — contrary classmate of Nicodemus
Benjamin — the shepherd's son
Bramble — the lame sheep
*Caiaphas — the present appointed high priest
Deborah — the wife of Joseph of Arimathea
Rebecca — Nicodemus' cousin in Capernaum
Ebed — servant to the next door neighbors of Nicodemus
Ethan — a priest-in-training
*Gamaliel — friend and classmate of Nicodemus, grandson of Hillel
Hakkoz — the spoiled son of Nicodemus' next door neighbor
*Hillel — an important spiritual leader. The house of Hillel opposed many opinions of the house of Shamai.
Jeremias — middle brother of Nicodemus
*Joseph — of Arimathea, a close friend to Nicodemus and fellow member of the Sanhedrin
Malia — mother of the family next door to Nicodemus
Marida — one of Nicodemus' servants
Martha — mother of Nicodemus
Michael — the shepherd who rescues Nicodemus
Neziah — oldest brother of Nicodemus
Pethahiah — friend of Argus
Rabbi Judah — Nicodemus' teacher of the law
Ruth — mother of Michael, the shepherd
*Sanhedrin — the ruling body of religious leaders in Jerusalem, like a Jewish "supreme court"
*Shammai — an important spiritual leader. The house of Shammai opposed many rules of the house of Hillel.
*Yeshua — the Hebrew name for "Jesus"
Zilia — Martha's servant

*These are biblical historic people or groups. All others are fictional.

1

CHAPTER 1

The Census

In those days Caesar Augustus issued a decree that a census should be taken of the entire Roman world. And everyone went to his own town to register.   Luke 2:1, 3

Crowds line the dusty Bethlehem road and anxious voices fill the air.

"Another census. Can you believe it?"

"Caesar just wants to see how the population has grown so he can tax us all the more."

"Doesn't he have enough money in his coffers?"

"Rulers never have enough."

"How long is this line anyway?"

"You should have seen the line yesterday. It extended way down the road."

"Well, there's only one more day so I guess everyone is trying to get registered before tomorrow."

The grumbling persists as Jews make their way to Bethlehem, the city of David, to register for the census.

"Where are you staying tonight?"

"We have relatives in Bethlehem. What about you?"

"We have friends in Jerusalem. Oh well, at least it gives us a good excuse for a visit."

"You're right. We have to find something good in all this mess the Romans make of our lives."

❦❦❦❦

Meanwhile in Jerusalem, Nicodemus, a twenty-year-old student of the law, joins a gathering of old friends. Some are in town for the census; others live in Jerusalem. All afternoon Nicodemus gazes down the main road hoping to catch a glimpse of his friend from Arimathea.

Where is that man, anyway? A trip from Arimathea is a bit of a journey, but Joseph should have arrived by now.

"Have you seen Joseph today?" Nicodemus asks a fellow student.

"No, but he should be here soon."

Nicodemus' eyes dart from one face to another as he scans the crowd once more. *Maybe Joseph slipped in trying to be unnoticed. It would be just like him.*

Nicodemus feels a gentle shove against his arm.

"Looking for someone?"

"Joseph, you old bird, it's good to see you." They hug and slap each other on the back.

"What took you so long?" Nicodemus asks.

"Oh, it was crowded on the road. Everyone coming for the census, I guess."

"And your family, how are they?"

"Doing fine," says Joseph. "They're over at my uncle's house."

"Are you still studying with your rabbi?"

"Of course." Then, with his chest puffed up, his nose pointed in the air, and a gleam in his eye, Joseph adds, "I'll soon be a rabbi myself."

"Sure you will. You'll be studying the next few years just like the rest of us." They both have a hearty laugh, knowing how true it is.

Glancing around to be sure no one is in earshot, Joseph whispers behind the back of his hand, "Don't you know I have those ten thousand Pharisee laws memorized already?"

Nicodemus remembers their last talk about how the Pharisee rabbis teach the basics of the Torah, but dwell on such minute detail of the additional oral laws that it leaves even the best of students bewildered.

Their friend, Gamaliel, greets Joseph warmly. "Joseph, it is so good to see you again."

Gamaliel is about to ask a question when Argus, another student of the law, approaches the threesome. "Ah, it's our well-dressed friend from the hills of Arimathea," Argus says as he bows with a dramatic flip of his hand.

4

Nicodemus flinches. Argus has a way of putting conversations on edge. In truth, Joseph does come from a well-to-do family, but he never flaunts his wealth as Argus would surely do if the circumstances were reversed. *Jealousy shows itself in many ways,* reflects Nicodemus.

"Greetings from the hills," Joseph responds enthusiastically, not to be put down.

✧❀✧❀✧❀✧❀

That evening, Nicodemus, Joseph, Gamaliel, and Argus engage in conversation with their other friends who have gathered. They enjoy a hearty meal with light debate. Inevitably at these get-togethers, these young students discuss the law, trying to impress one another with their latest insights, each one attempting to out-do the other.

At one point, their discussion moves beyond the details of the law. They bemoan Roman domination and long for Israel to be restored. "Perhaps the promised Messiah will come soon to deliver us," one student offers.

On into the night these young men ramble with their enlightened and not-so-enlightened talk, serious and pious for a time then bursting into good-natured laughter. They enjoy being together in spite of the fact that they don't always agree.

Gamaliel reminds them that with so many visitors in town for the census, their morning classes are postponed. "This will give us plenty of time to resume our discussion tomorrow."

The hour is late; many have traveled long distances, so the students stand to say their parting words to one another.

As Nicodemus ambles along in the chilly night air, he pulls his cloak up around his neck. Unusually bright stars punctuate the clear dark sky. He has farther to go than the others, but he doesn't mind. He often walks after dark. Somehow he can think more clearly in the solitude of the night. Besides, the moon lights his way and the sky boasts such an array of stars that he finds himself lost in its beauty.

5

Nicodemus is deep in thought when, without warning, a flood of light flashes to his left. He jerks his head around quickly. The light seems to be coming from the direction of Bethlehem, about five miles away.

Strange. He squints his eyes trying to see what it could be. *Perhaps a large group of people are out with beaming lanterns.* But it is so late and the light appeared so abruptly. Nicodemus stares in that direction for several moments. He feels an unusual sense of holiness. Does he hear voices or singing? He can't quite tell—too far away. The light lingers a while longer, and then suddenly disappears as quickly as it had come.

"Strange," he says out loud.

Reluctantly, he turns and continues the walk to his house, glancing back occasionally just to be sure the light is truly gone, but the valley that cradles the little town of Bethlehem is quiet and dark.

His thoughts turn to the conversation he had with his friends earlier. He tries to remember what had led them into the discussion of the Messiah. *Perhaps it was because of the Roman ruler, Caesar Augustus, who has once again reared his ugly head of dictatorship. When will the Redeemer ever come? How long must we be under the burden of Rome?*

He remembers that just a couple of years ago a "would-be" messiah appeared on the scene. *The young fellow had claimed he would lead Israel into freedom from Roman rule. Most likely an over-zealous zealot. That one suddenly disappeared, probably at the hand of a Roman soldier.*

Nicodemus contemplates the great deliverer, Moses. *Now that's who we need, another Moses,* he decides. To be sure, the people of Nicodemus' day are not suffering the extreme bondage that their Israelite ancestors endured. He and his friends are not slaves making bricks under the hot sun like the Israelites in Egypt of long ago.

No, they have their businesses and moderate means. They enjoy freedom to come and go, even to rule themselves within the confines of their faith. But they live always under the umbrella of Roman domination, expectation, and taxation.

This is our promised land. Maybe we need a Joshua to lead the battle and claim our land anew. "Pax Romana," the Romans declare— Roman peace. It may feel like peace for Rome, but it is not peace for us in our pagan-infested land.

Soon Nicodemus arrives at his house and snuggles in his bed. The thoughts of deliverance and law, even the Bethlehem light, fade into his slumber.

CHAPTER 2
A Shepherd Report

But the angel said to them, "... I bring you good news of great joy that will be for all people. Today in the town of David, a Savior has been born to you; he is Christ the Lord." When they had seen him, they spread the word concerning what had been told them about this child, and all who heard it were amazed at what the shepherds said to them.

Luke 2:10, 11, 17, 18

The next morning, Nicodemus lazily dresses, says his morning prayers, and stumbles to the table to have breakfast with his father. He stretches and rubs his back.

"Martha, I believe our son had a late night."

"It seems so," Nicodemus' mother says as she pats his shoulder and sets two boiled eggs in front of him.

"Yes, we had many topics to discuss," Nicodemus yawns.

"Discussion is good. And did you lead them all to truth?"

"I tried, father, I tried," Nicodemus says with a smile. "Of course Argus is always a bit of a challenge."

"Ah, yes, Argus. He takes after his father, you know." *I hope I take after mine*, Nicodemus ponders as he lovingly watches his father chew on a piece of bread. "Did you see Joseph?" his father asks between bites.

"Yes, he finally came strolling in from the hills."

"The hills?"

"Yes, that's what Argus says as though Joseph were from Nazareth or Cana or some other obscure town in Galilee."

"Don't forget, we have relatives in Galilee."

"Oh, you know what I mean."

"You allow Argus to cloud your thinking."

"Perhaps I do," shrugs Nicodemus. "What did you mean that Argus is like his father?"

"Argus' father, Hiram, is arrogant and head strong. His temper has gotten him in trouble more than once. How he ever made it to the Sanhedrin, I'll never know." He stares out the doorway for a moment, as though in another world, and then he continues.

"Well, perhaps I *do* know. You see, Argus' family struggled financially for a few years and then came into a sizeable inheritance on his mother's side. His father, Hiram, spent this newfound wealth with reckless abandon. He made sure the chief priests knew of his rise to financial prominence. Apparently, his persistence paid off. The next year he received his appointment to the Sanhedrin."

Nicodemus detects a slight edge in his father's voice. Jealousy perhaps? No, more like sadness.

"Argus' family doesn't seem to be all that well off." Nicodemus prods him on.

"No, Hiram wasted much of the wealth and now the family just barely gets by."

Nicodemus has often wondered why his father was never appointed to the Sanhedrin. *He is favored with great respect among the leaders. He is known as the best physician in all of Jerusalem. Why has he been overlooked? Did someone like Hiram usurp his potential appointment?*

Anxious to get on with his day, this doesn't seem to be the time to pursue the discussion, so Nicodemus stands to leave.

"Well, I must be off. We're meeting at the Temple today."

"Speak the truth in love, my son."

They bid one another "Shalom."

Nicodemus picks a fragrant flower from a bush near his house and sniffs the pleasant scent. He is well aware that his family lives in above-average means, but he never thinks about being wealthy. Perhaps it is because his father never makes it an issue. *Father is a wonderful physician, bringing healing herbs to many-a sick one; wrapping wounds and setting broken bones. He is always steady—always the same; true, honest and faithful to the core. Why then has he never been chosen to be in the Sanhedrin?*

9

Turning his attention to the day at hand, Nicodemus picks up his pace and tosses the flower aside as he hurries along to meet his friends.

Nicodemus mirrors the grin on his friend Joseph's face when they greet each other for the new day. Conversation flows freely while they make their way to the Temple. Nicodemus contemplates asking Joseph if he knows why his father has never been accepted in the Sanhedrin, but thinks better of it. Some things should stay in the family.

Soon the two friends climb the steps to the Temple. They are just in time for the Levites' morning call to prayer and readings.

After worship, Nicodemus and Joseph stroll over to Argus, Gamaliel, and a few more friends who have gathered. They are ready to pick up their thoughts from the night before, when suddenly, their discussion is interrupted by two local merchants.

"What's all the commotion?" asks Argus.

"I don't know." Nicodemus studies the men.

The Bethlehem merchants dart from group to group in the Temple court telling about something with animated gestures. Nicodemus picks up the word "shepherds." The merchants point to the sky and look up as they say something about "angels." Then with a sweep of their arms, he hears them say, "running through the town".

On the third telling of the story, Nicodemus edges close enough to get more details from this excited pair. It seems that two or three Bethlehem shepherds claim to have had a visitation from angels in the night. In fact, they say that a great host of angels appeared, proclaiming the birth of the Messiah. The shepherds had been told that they could find the *baby* wrapped in swaddling clothes and lying in a manger.

"The shepherds came running down the hill where they had been tending their sheep," one merchant exclaims. "Sure enough, they found a newborn baby in one of the stables over there." He points toward Bethlehem.

"This morning, the shepherds ran everywhere telling their news!" the second merchant chimes in.

At the first news of the report, Nicodemus has a flashback to the light from the night before. Could the Deliverer possibly have come and so soon after he and his friends had just been discussing it? Does that explain the light he saw? And angels? Even a host of angels appearing and praising God? He thought he heard voices or singing.

Nicodemus remembers a visitation as recorded in the sacred Scripture. Angels came to Abraham to share the news that Abraham's wife, Sarah, would bear a son. But Abraham's angel visitation can't compare to this story.

Joseph steps beside Nicodemus just as the two merchants finish their story for yet a fourth time. The merchants move on to retell their story to another group. Argus joins Joseph and Nicodemus.

"What's going on?" Argus asks again.

Nicodemus tells the story, trying to remember all the details.

"That's the most ridiculous tale I've ever heard," scoffs Argus.

They all agree that even if such a proclamation were made by angels, it wouldn't be announced to a motley group of shepherds, and the Messiah would certainly not be placed in an animal's feeding trough. When the excitement dies down, they dismiss the whole notion.

Nicodemus doesn't tell Joseph about the Bethlehem light from last night. He figures that if Joseph had seen it he surely would have said something about it this morning. Joseph always blurts out whatever is on his mind. Even if Nicodemus were to mention the light, he isn't quite sure what to say about it. Anyway, he fears Joseph would only make fun of him.

꧁꧂꧁꧂꧁꧂꧁꧂

That night, Nicodemus probes his father's keen mind. He relays the story once again complete with angels declaring praise to God and giving instructions to *shepherds* to find the Savior as a baby in a *manger*. "What do you think of that, Father?"

"And did they find a baby—in a manger?"

'Well, they *said* they did. Imagine delivering that kind of news to smelly old shepherds."

"Hmm," he says, stroking his beard thoughtfully. "Shall we call our father, Abraham, a smelly old shepherd? Or our deliverer, Moses, whom God called out of his *shepherd* duties to lead the nation? What about Jacob's greatest son, Joseph, who spent his early years as a shepherd, as did King David? Were all these, our ancestors, *smelly old shepherds*?"

Nicodemus' frown turns to a smirk. "I see what you mean, Father, but surely you don't believe the Messiah would come in such poverty."

Ignoring his comment, Nicodemus' father continues. "Angels, did you say? My, we haven't had a visitation of angels in centuries. A couple of men—angels—came to Abraham to proclaim that Sarah would bear a son. Two angels went to Sodom to spare Lot before the cities of Sodom and Gomorrah were destroyed. Angels brought messages to Moses and Joshua, to Samuel and King David. They protected our ancestors in battle and spoke to the prophets, but we have had no visitation in recent years.

"Ah, but what am I thinking? Just last year a priest, uh, let me see, I believe his name was Zechariah. Yes, it was Zechariah. He is an older priest, well past his years for fathering a child. When he took his turn officiating in the Temple, he claimed that an angel spoke to him and declared that his wife would have a baby. Zechariah doubted and questioned the messenger. Because of his doubt, he was struck mute, unable to speak a word, I am told.

"He went back to his home, somewhere in Galilee, I believe it was, or west in the mountains, I don't quite remember. We recently received word that, after the birth of the baby, Zechariah could speak again. Now that's pretty remarkable, don't you think?"

"Yes, now that you mention it, I recall that incident. And are you connecting it with this baby?"

"God reveals His plans in mysterious ways, my son. We must be ever alert."

12

Nicodemus can see that he isn't going to receive the same reaction from his father that he had encountered with his friends, so he bids his father goodnight.

✐✐✐✐✐

The next day, Nicodemus catches up with Joseph as he is packing his donkey for another trip. "Where are you off to this time?" Nicodemus asks.

"My father is obsessed with bronze at the moment." Then in Joseph's best imitation of his father's voice, he mimics, "The Romans like to use bronze, *and* bronze materials are in demand for Jews and Gentiles alike."

"What is he going to do?" Nicodemus asks.

Joseph throws a blanket over his donkey's back. "Well, since copper and tin are the components of bronze, Father has decided to explore these industries. One prime mining location is far away to the northwest, but the materials are shipped into the ports of Phoenicia. My father is considering the possibility of sending his ships there to bring tin and copper to the shores of Joppa. He always has an eye for finding and matching available materials with the needs of the people."

"That's a great gift for a business man. How does this affect you?" Nicodemus hands Joseph a bag to load. Joseph throws it over the donkey's back.

"Father keeps asking me to assist more and more in his businesses. He is careful not to interfere with my studies, but he does want me to make a trip to the shore to oversee some of these deliveries. I enjoy my Mediterranean visits. I like traveling from my home in the mountains to the sea shore or to the rocky hills of Jerusalem, always something interesting to see and hear. Always something to do and learn."

Nicodemus still has the shepherd and angel incident on his mind, so he relays part of the conversation he had with his father.

Joseph stops packing for a moment. "I know of the incident with Zechariah and his wife, Elizabeth."

"You know her name?"

"Yes, their village is over the mountain from ours. News like that spreads quickly. When Elizabeth gave birth, Zechariah's voice returned. Some reported that the child would be the forerunner of the Promised One. I'm not sure about that, but the circumstances of his birth were mysterious indeed."

Joseph loads a final bundle on his donkey. "So, I must be off once again." Joseph sees the disappointment in Nicodemus' face. "I will return for Passover," he says. "Study well, my friend, but don't get too far ahead of me." He winks at Nicodemus.

Nicodemus hates to see him leave. It seems they are never able to totally catch up during these intermittent visits. Another hug, a good slap on the back and Joseph is gone.

For several days, Nicodemus thinks about Joseph and his travels. He ponders the shepherd's story, his father's comments, and Joseph's observations. No more is said about the shepherds among his friends or even by his father, so Nicodemus pushes the whole thing to the back of his mind as the days slip by.

CHAPTER 3
40-Day Purification

When the time of their purification according to the Law of Moses had been completed, Joseph and Mary took him to Jerusalem to present him to the Lord. Luke 2:22

Nicodemus is passing through the Temple area one morning when he runs into a long-time friend. "Ethan, my friend, I haven't seen you for a while. Where have you been?"

"I've been spending the majority of my time in the Holy Place under the tutelage of my chief priest, Simeon. This week, he's been teaching me about the care and lighting of the candelabra."

"What else have you been doing?"

"Well, among other things, I assist with purification rites. We had 15 new mothers come just this week for their 40-day purification. And of course, I still tend to the needs of visiting priests—a new set of twenty-four priests every week. I help with the assignment duties. Where have you been? I haven't seen you either."

"I've been pouring over the ancient scrolls of the Torah and studying at the south steps of the Temple with my teacher."

"I guess we've just missed each other coming and going."

In spite of the fact that the young priest is a Sadducee and Nicodemus a Pharisee, they have known each other from childhood and exchange ideas occasionally.

༄ེ࿎ེ࿎ེ࿎ེ

Over a month has gone by since their last conversation. Nicodemus is about to pass the doors to the Temple Sanctuary, when he notices Ethan staggering down the steps, looking unusually pale.

"What has happened?" Nicodemus asks, in concern.

"I… I can't believe what I've just heard," Ethan says in a daze.

"Heard? What have you heard?" Nicodemus is fearful that Ethan will faint. He gives an arm for support. "Who have you been talking to?"

The young priest talks on, oblivious to Nicodemus. "What does Simeon mean? What does he mean?" Ethan seems to be in a world to himself.

Trying to bring Ethan to reality, Nicodemus continues to question him. "Ethan, what did Simeon say?"

Ethan takes a big gulp of air and heaves a shoulder-sagging sigh. He stares out of glazed eyes with furrowed brow trying desperately to remember Simeon's words.

Slowly he speaks. "Simeon gave purification rites to a young couple with their baby, but he said the strangest things about the child. It wasn't the usual ritual. Not the usual routine."

Ethan pauses for a moment. Nicodemus waits patiently for him to continue. "Simeon said, 'My eyes have seen God's salvation and a light for revelation to the Gentiles.' The *Gentiles!* What revelation could there possibly be for the Gentiles? And what does God's salvation have to do with this child?" Ethan hangs his head, slowly shaking it back and forth.

Isaiah's words, Nicodemus thinks to himself.

Ethan looks up and frowns as he remembers something else. "Simeon said, 'This child is destined to cause the falling and rising of many in Israel, so that the thoughts of many will be revealed.' What does it all mean? He said other things to the child's mother, strange things."

Ethan focuses on the people passing by and then looks at Nicodemus as if he suddenly becomes aware of where he is. He shakes his head as though shrugging off Simeon's mystifying words. He seems embarrassed that he has divulged this intimate encounter.

"Oh you know old Simeon; he's always a bit strange. Nothing to be concerned about." Off he goes, apparently not wanting to be questioned further.

Nicodemus stands there puzzled by the encounter with the young priest. He reasons that Simeon is highly respected among the leaders of the Temple and he remembers Simeon's claim that the spirit of God had revealed to him that he would not die until he saw the Messiah. *Are these strange words meant for the Messiah? For this child?*

Hmm, let me see—40 days before purification rites. With his methodical Pharisee mind, he figures up the days since the Bethlehem shepherds' report. *It has been about forty days*, he calculates. *Oh I'm imagining things*, he mumbles to himself. Kicking a stone, he agrees with the young priest. Simeon *is* a bit odd. Still, Nicodemus is very fond of him. Simeon seems so genuine, not haughty like some of the other Temple elders and priests.

His curiosity gets the best of him, so Nicodemus lingers long enough to catch a glimpse of the young couple as they come from the Temple with their baby. *Very ordinary looking.* He hears them say a few words to each other. By their accent they appear to be from the north, somewhere in Galilee.

Simeon comes out as if to have a final look at the couple and the young mother turns to have a last glimpse of the priest. Simeon raises his upturned hand in a combined gesture of farewell and blessing. She smiles slightly and bows her head humbly in gratitude.

Nicodemus follows for a time thinking he will catch up with them, but what would he say? He keeps a moderate distance to see which way they go. They seem to be headed toward Bethlehem, but with the press of the crowd, he loses track of them.

Why would they head to Bethlehem if they are from the Galilee? Are they visiting? Were they here for the census? Of course, that must be the reason—and in her condition she would not be fit for traveling back to Galilee yet. He determines to check further with Ethan about this incident.

Nicodemus can hardly concentrate on his morning lesson because he is most anxious to tell this news to his father. He hurries home and thankfully finds his father eating lunch.

"So the child was born in Bethlehem?" his father questions.

"It would seem so."

"That would follow the Scripture according to Micah the prophet."

"Yes, I know."

His father leaned back, arms crossed. "I've known Simeon a long time. He is very devoted. I cannot imagine him making up such a thing. Perhaps he will share it with the other priests."

CHAPTER 4
Studying with the Rabbi

*These are the commands, decrees, and laws the Lord your God
directed me to teach you to observe in the land you are crossing
the Jordan to possess.* Deut. 6:1

The sun warms the day as Nicodemus and his fellow
students gather on the south steps of the Temple to begin
their morning discussion. Nicodemus' rabbi sits on the higher
step in the shade of the wall as the rabbi's disciples settle in
on lower steps at his feet.

"You recall that yesterday we concluded our lessons
on Sukkoth, the Festival of First Fruits. Today we shall begin
our study of Shabbat, our holy day of rest. You know that the
Lord used six days to create our world and everything in it,
but on the seventh day?"

"He rested," the students respond automatically.

"Of course, and He commands that we, too, must
rest on the seventh day, Shabbat. Our labor must cease. We
use this holy day to worship and rest.

"Today, we focus on the laws handed down from our
forefathers through the centuries. The oral laws help us fulfill
God's commandments given to Moses long ago at Mt. Sinai."

"Rabbi Judah," Argus interrupts.

"What is it, Argus?" Rabbi Judah responds with
controlled patience.

"Rabbi, would it not be helpful to have the oral laws
written down in topical order rather than scattered through
our minds even as the original commandments and laws are
scattered through the Torah? We find references to the
Shabbat in various places throughout the Torah. If we had all
the references written together with the oral law
accompanying, it would be much easier to study them."

"Our laws and commandments were written as they
were received," says Rabbi Judah with icy rebuke. "We are
not to tamper with the sacred scrolls."

The rabbi's jaw clenches as he looks away from his interrupter. He shifts slightly with shoulders at attention. "Our interpretations have been handed down from one generation to another. They are taught verbally so that careful instruction and discussion can be given by teachers of the law. You will do well to listen so that you will be prepared to pass them on to the next generation and to explain them with integrity and accuracy."

Gamaliel looks at Argus and adds gently, "Perhaps that's why we call it the 'oral law', my friend."

Ah, Gamaliel, always the one to try to diffuse strained discussions. Nicodemus swallows a smile at this interchange. *When will Argus ever learn his place?*

Argus squirms a bit, but appears to be unaffected by the rabbi's rebuke. He smirks with a side-glance to his friend, Pethahiah.

Nicodemus ponders the exchange. While he, too, would appreciate a categorized record in order of topics, he realizes that he learns more by digging it out for himself. He also learns from his teacher who not only reveals the oral laws but allows for discussion. Argus, on the other hand, would prefer not to do so much digging. After all, a person who considers himself privileged should not have to work so hard.

Dear Gamaliel. He is a bit older than Nicodemus. Perhaps that is why he admires him. That and the fact that Gamaliel is the grandson of Hillel, the most prominent Pharisee of the Sanhedrin. Old Hillel and his adversary, Shammai, have been at odds for years. Still, Hillel commands great respect among the elders. Yes, Gamaliel has a rich heritage. *Does that also give him a heavy load to carry? A reputation to uphold?*

Rabbi Judah's aggravated voice pulls Nicodemus from his contemplation.

"As I was saying, we will proceed with our oral law regarding transfer on the Sabbath. There are two acts constituting transfer of movable things over the dividing line of adjoining premises on the Sabbath. The two acts, however, increase to four on the inside and to a like amount on the outside of the premises." The rabbi looks into the blank faces of his disciples knowing full well that he will be repeating this law several times before they understand it.

He presses on. "How so? The mendicant (visitor) stands outside and the master of the house inside. The mendicant passes his hand through a window or door and puts something in the hand of the master, or he takes something out of the master's hand and draws it back toward him. In such a case, the mendicant is guilty of transfer and the master of the house is free.

"Likewise, if the master of the house passes his hand outside and puts a thing in the hand of the mendicant, or takes something out of the mendicant's hand and brings it into the house, the master of the house is culpable and the mendicant is free."

The wrinkled foreheads of the rabbi's disciples make it clear to him that his students are concentrating.

"In the second act, the mendicant extends his hand into the house and the master takes something out of it, or puts something into it which is drawn outside by the mendicant, they are both free. Likewise, if the master of the house extends his hand outside and the mendicant takes something out of it, or puts something into it which is drawn to the inside by the master, they are both free."

Rabbi Judah pauses for a moment to let the rule settle in their minds. All is silent as the students try to process the things their teacher has just told them.

Nicodemus recalls a Sabbath long ago when a visitor brought a basket of fresh figs to the door. As the visitor started to offer the basket to him, Nicodemus reached out the door to take the figs. His father touched his arm. "Wait to receive the gift, my son," he had said. The visitor passed the basket through the doorway. Nicodemus looked at his father who gave a slight nod of approval. Nicodemus had then lifted the basket from the visitor's hand.

Nicodemus begins to make sense of this law. Reaching out to take, deems him guilty of transfer; but waiting to receive, and then taking it makes him free of guilt.

Nicodemus also recalls that by the next Sabbath his mother had been ill for a few days. Just as Sabbath was beginning, a neighbor had knocked at the door. Nicodemus remembered his father's reprimand and waited for the neighbor to pass the bread through the door.

"How is your mother faring, Nicodemus?"

"She is improving each day, Samuel."

"My wife thought you might need some bread for Sabbath."

Nicodemus had been careful not to reach out. "You're very kind."

Finally Samuel, his neighbor, passed the bread through the door. Nicodemus held his hands out to receive the bread. The neighbor continued to hold the bread. In a soft voice, Nicodemus' father had said, "Take the bread thankfully, my son."

Nicodemus took the bread from his neighbor' open hand. "Thank you for your generosity."

"Goodnight, my friends. Shalom."

Nicodemus remembers that when he had closed the door, he looked at his father. "I don't understand. I waited to receive the bread as you taught me last week. What did I do wrong this time?"

"You must take the bread from his hand once it is offered, lest you be guilty of transfer." His father had left the room leaving Nicodemus to scratch his head.

Nicodemus realizes that all the students as well as the rabbi had been sitting in silence for a few moments; each trying to understand the conditions of this law.

Nicodemus shares his insight. "Can we say that the giver must be the one to reach out first? The receiver must wait until it is offered and then take it from him so that both are involved in the transfer rather than only one?"

Rabbi Judah turns to Nicodemus, pausing to consider his explanation. "Yes, I believe you could say that."

"And can we say that unless an object is offered it must not be taken?"

Another pause, and then the rabbi answers enthusiastically, "Why yes, that's exactly correct."

The others glance at Nicodemus in gratitude for his interpretation. Nicodemus catches Gamaliel's smile and is elated to have offered a worthy comment.

Argus begins a debate as to how the two acts become four acts and why it could actually be eight acts when you count all the possibilities. Nicodemus is content to have understood the essence of the law and not get mired down in these number details.

After a lengthy laborious discussion, Gamaliel and Nicodemus stroll across the Temple courts together. Nicodemus sighs. "To think, this is but one of a multitude of debates we will have about our Sabbath laws."

"True, but we must learn them all," answers Gamaliel, ever aware of his heritage and the expectations it carries.

The following day the discussion drags on with questions of clarification on the minute points of the same oral law they discussed the day before, all of which point back to Nicodemus' original summations. Much of the debate centers on the point about this law being two acts, four acts, or more.

The next day—more discussion. And the next, and the next. Nicodemus is ready to move on to a new law.

At last, on the fifth day, Rabbi Judah gives another law for consideration. "One school of thought states that, on the Sabbath, one is not allowed to negotiate marriage engagements for children, nor to engage teachers or artisan masters for children, nor to pay visits of condolence to mourners, nor to visit the sick." Rabbi Judah glances at Gamaliel knowing that these statements are of Beth Shammai (the house of Shammai) who is the opponent of Gamaliel's family, Beth Hillel (the house of Hillel.)

Gamaliel waits to speak until the others have an opportunity to give their thoughts. It is obvious by their comments that they are not aware of the schools of thought on these matters and speak only out of their own experience and practices.

One student reasons that they are not to conduct business contracts on the Sabbath and, in a sense, negotiating marriage engagements could fall under that heading. Another protests that marriage is not a business.

Argus objects. "Marriage arrangements and engaging teachers for children would certainly fall under the category of contractual agreements and thus be conducting business on the Sabbath." Another argues that it isn't business unless money is exchanged.

Less time is spent debating the issues of visiting mourners or visiting the sick other than how much energy it could expend or the distance to travel. Nicodemus reminds his fellow students that if they are allowed to help an ox out of the ditch on the Sabbath, surely deeds of mercy should be permitted.

Finally, Gamaliel speaks up. "All of these matters are matters of relationship, not work. Beth Hillel allows these acts, but reminds us to say to the sick, 'It is the Sabbath and we are not to cry, but relief is drawing nigh.'"

All eyes turn to Rabbi Judah who nods agreeably to Gamaliel, not only for his knowledge of the Beth Hillel school of thought, but also for his patience in allowing the students to think through and discuss this rule. With that the debate ends.

Nicodemus finds greater admiration for Gamaliel and for his teacher in permitting his students to talk and reason among themselves—a quality he intends to demonstrate with his own followers one day.

For a moment, Nicodemus day dreams of having a head full of knowledge with disciples sitting at his feet. He will teach with patience and compassion. He will encourage discussion but bring them to the essence of the law, the spirit of the law, and the *truth* of the law.

Ah, but the knowledge must come first, so Nicodemus pulls out of his reverie to focus again on the lessons at hand.

In the ensuing days, he and the other students thrash out the fine points of the oral law that states, "A tailor shall not go out with his needle when it is *nearly* dark, (that is, almost Sabbath) lest he go out carrying it about with him *after* dark; nor a scribe with his pen. No one is to dye material on Sabbath eve, nor bleach bundles of linen thread, nor set traps for animals, nor wash clothes unless all these things can be brought to conclusion by sundown."

Nicodemus worries, *"How will I ever remember all these laws, much less be able to teach them one day?"*

CHAPTER 5
Sabbath Eve

Remember the Sabbath day by keeping it holy. For in six days the Lord made the heavens and the earth, the sea and all that is in them, but he rested on the seventh day. Exodus 20:8, 11

With Sabbath preparations in mind, Nicodemus turns down the street to his house. The servants will have the washing done and the bread made. So often he drifts through Sabbath as just one more day, one more ritual. His mind has been saturated in the minutia of Sabbath laws and rules. He has been mired down in detail and debate for much too long. He raises his eyes to the skies to focus on the beauty of the pinks and oranges of the setting sun. How long has it been since he focused on anything beyond his studies?

Nicodemus sees children laughing and playing in the street; a mother calls them in to prepare for Sabbath. He watches their reluctance, remembering his own dawdling attitude from childhood days gone by. The smells of fresh bread and chicken soup waft through the air. He sighs audibly. *Come, sweet rest. Come, Queen Sabbath,* he cries in his heart.

"Come, O bride! Come, O bride," his father used to say, as Sabbath approached. Nicodemus smiles in remembrance of his happy childhood.

With his house in view, Nicodemus slows his steps to savor the moment. *Thank you, Holy One of Israel, for commanding us to rest. Help me to celebrate the joy of the Sabbath.*

Nicodemus enters his house and plants a kiss on his surprised mother's cheek. "Nico," she blushes, using her childhood pet name for him. "What do you have stirring in that heart of yours?" He chuckles and pats her shoulder.

As Nicodemus bathes, he recalls his rabbi's words from yesterday, "Making distinctions and separations permeate our religious life. We distinguish between holy time and ordinary time. We declare certain books holy or others mundane and distinguish the way we study and treat these books. The Torah teaches us that Elohim, our creator, created the world by distinctions, light and darkness, water and empty space, earth and water. To mark the beginning of sacred time, we light two candles."

Nicodemus dries himself and dons the special outfit saved for Sabbath. Jeremias, his next older brother is bathed and ready as well. The two brothers move to the living area where Mama has two candles ready along with the Kiddush cups of wine and the challah loaves of bread.

The family gathers for Kabbalat Shabbat, the evening prayer, which welcomes the Sabbath.

"Come, O bride! Come, O bride!" Papa calls out, as he once did. Nicodemus smiles, wondering why Papa has spoken these long-remembered words from time past, but glad to hear them again.

Mama lights the two candles representing the dual commandments to *remember* and *observe* the Sabbath. She waves her hands over the candles to welcome the Sabbath, but she covers her eyes so as not to see the candles before reciting the blessing:

> "Blessed are you, Lord, our God,
>   King of the Universe,
>   who sanctifies us with his commandments,
>   and commands us to light
>   the candles of Shabbat. Amen."

The candles cast a warm glow about the room. They sing together the psalm:

> "Ascribe to the Lord, O mighty one,
>   ascribe to the Lord glory and strength,
>   ascribe to the Lord the glory due his name;
>   worship the Lord
>   in the splendor of his holiness."

Nicodemus sings on with renewed energy and praise as he and his family finish the final refrain:

> "The Lord gives strength to his people;

the Lord blesses his people with peace."

Nicodemus, Jeremias, and their father hold the Kiddush cups of wine as their father recites the blessing:

> "And there was evening and there was morning,
>   a sixth day.
> The heavens and the earth were finished,
>   the whole host of them.
> And on the seventh day God ended his work
>   which he had made.
> And he rested on the seventh day
>   from all his work which he had made.
> And God blessed the seventh day,
>   and sanctified it because in it he had rested
>   from all the work which he had created
>   and done."

The family continues their familiar celebration of the Sabbath. Though Nicodemus has gone through this routine every week for years, it has taken on fresh delight tonight.

༄ ༄ ༄ ༄

The following morning, Nicodemus and his family go to their nearby synagogue to continue their Sabbath celebration.

The priest invites Nicodemus' father to come to the altar for the reading of the Holy Scroll. On this particular Sabbath, Nicodemus is called on to carry the Sepher Torah to the bimah, the table. Carefully, Nicodemus removes the sacred scroll from its holder, unrolls it, and holds it up for all to see. When he lays it down on the table, his father reaches for the yad, the pointer, to follow the words as he reads. His father counts it a privilege to take his turn at this holy task.

Friends join Nicodemus and his family as they go to his home to spend time together for the afternoon.

At sundown of Sabbath day, as three stars appear in the sky, the family gathers for Havdalah to mark the end of the sacred day. Mother sets the braided candle on the table as Father brings the Kiddush cup and the spice box.

As Father lights the braided candle, the strands remind them of the many Jews around the world all of whom form a unified people. Father fills the Kiddush cup full of wine as an expression of hope that the coming week will be a good one. He says,

> "Behold, God is my unfailing help;
>> I will trust in God and will not be afraid.
> The Lord is my strength and song;
>> God is my deliverer."

Nicodemus, Jeremias, and their mother say,

> "There is light and joy, gladness and honor
>> for the Jewish people.
> So may we be blessed."

Father raises the Kiddush cup.

> "I will lift the cup of salvation,
>> and call upon the name of the Lord.
> Blessed are you, Lord, our God,
>> King of the Universe,
>> who creates the fruit of the vine.

Father places his hands over the box of sweet smelling spices to pronounce a blessing.

> "Blessed are You, our God,
>> Creator of time and space,
>> who creates a potpourri of spices."

Father passes the spice box around for Nicodemus, Jeremias, and their mother to inhale the sweet scent. Father places his hand near the light to pronounce a blessing over the Havdala candle.

"Blessed are You, our God,
> Creator of time and space,
> who creates the light of fire."

They all raise the back of their hands to the light, seeing the shadow on their palms. It reminds them of the distinction between light and darkness. Father pronounces the final blessing.

"Blessed are You, Lord our God,
> ruler of the world,
> who separates the holy
> from the mundane,
> light from darkness,
> Israel from the other peoples,
> the seventh day of rest
> from the six days of work."

Father takes a sip of the wine from the Kiddush cup and passes it to Jeremias and Nicodemus who take a sip remembering the joy of the Sabbath. Nicodemus pours the remaining wine in a plate and his father douses the flame of the candle in it and so ends the Havdala.

✿✿✿✿✿

Nicodemus peers through the window to check the night skies. Yes, a clear evening, plenty of stars, and a half moon. That should be enough for walking without a lantern. He dislikes carrying a lantern—it spoils the mood. He throws his cloak around his shoulders and sets out for his evening walk.

Lantern light spills out of many houses, further illuminating his way. A few homes still have the flicker of candle light as they conclude their Havdala celebration. It was a good Sabbath. He breathes deeply. It is always a good Sabbath. *Why do we clutter the blessed day with so many rules?*

Nicodemus remembers the early days of learning. He had feared he simply could not remember all the laws. Each night he walked the streets of Jerusalem thinking about the law for that day; rehearsing it over and over in his mind, making up situations of how the law could play out in real life. *If I practice, I will remember,* he had reasoned.

Week by week, Nicodemus had concentrated on the laws, the discussion of his fellow students, and the teachings of his rabbi. As the weeks stretched into months, his mind became so sharp that he anticipated the remainder of the law before the rabbi completed his sentence. He knew his fellow students so well that he could predict their comments and questions.

Ah, but tonight, no laws. I will just contemplate the goodness of the Lord. Your power is as vast as the spacious heavens above, Oh Lord. Your mercy never fails. Help me as I seek truth. Teach me your commands that I might serve you in obedience.

Nicodemus looks up at the Temple across the city with its white façade and gold trim, glistening, even in the moonlight. He passes the house of Joseph's uncle. Thoughts of his friend, Joseph, bring a smile. *Always the bold one. I wonder what new adventure he will seek next.* Nicodemus compares his own life—methodical, predictable, but just the way he likes it.

His path takes him down the alley where Argus and his family live. The narrow street, lined by a series of connected dwellings on each side, is like a dark tunnel that has blocked out the moon. *Dare I compare this darkness to the dark nature of Argus? No, I will not let his negative attitude cloud my thinking tonight.*

Ten more steps, and Nicodemus is back in the moonlight again. He passes through the marketplace. Though tables stand empty, the passing of Sabbath day has not erased the smells of busy market days. A hint of onion and dried fish still penetrate the air.

Content that he has had a blessed Sabbath and a good walk, Nicodemus turns toward his own path that leads home, ready for whatever tomorrow may hold.

CHAPTER 6
The Magi from the East

After Jesus was born ...Magi from the east came to Jerusalem and asked, "Where is the one who has been born king of the Jews? We saw his star in the east and have come to worship him." When King Herod heard this he was disturbed, and all Jerusalem with him. Matthew 2:1-3

Several months pass as Nicodemus continues studying with his rabbi. He begins asking many questions about the prophecies concerning the Messiah.

"We will come to that all in good time," his teacher says patiently. Nicodemus decides that he will have to study the subject himself—only after he memorizes today's lesson, of course.

Nicodemus walks alongside Gamaliel as they leave the group. Gamaliel notices Nicodemus' sagging shoulders and the burdened look on his face. "You must be patient, my friend. Rabbi Judah has much to teach us."

Nicodemus nods his head reluctantly.

Gamaliel glances over to the palace of Herod. "I've heard that King Herod is in town this week. I think he has come to Jerusalem to check on the progress of the Temple. My father remembers when the preliminary work began on the Temple mount over fifteen years ago. Once the foundation and courtyards were in place, work on the Temple itself began. Herod should be pleased with the way it is taking shape. It is about the only thing that endears him to our leaders."

As Nicodemus and Gamaliel come down the steps to the court of the Gentiles, they catch sight of strange looking men in bright, striped colors leading their camels. "Easterners," whispers Gamaliel. Everyone at the Temple stares at this unusual scene. The leaders frown with disgust at the sight of these intruders. Others just stand gawking, unable to understand what in the world is going on.

A team of Levites scurry over to the strangers, fearful that they will unknowingly proceed beyond the court of the Gentiles. It appears that the foreigners have a translator with them. After much pointing and gesturing, the Levites lead the strangers and their entourage out of the Temple area and head toward the palace of Herod. Nicodemus and Gamaliel stand transfixed by the scene.

Out of breath, Argus rushes over to Nicodemus and Gamaliel. "Who are they? Where are they from? What are they doing here?"

Nicodemus grabs Argus by the arm. "Slow down. We know as much as you do. It looks like they are headed to Herod's palace. I suppose *he* will figure out the situation."

Anxious to get the latest word, Argus hustles over to the Levites who had talked to the visitors. The Levites appear annoyed both with the situation and with Argus' persistence. Argus seems satisfied that he has learned enough to be at least somewhat knowledgeable and ambles back toward Nicodemus and Gamaliel. Obviously pleased with the fact that he knows more than they do, he savors his nuggets of information as long as possible.

He stops along the way to inform an expectant group what he has learned. His animated face and his dramatic gesturing draw them in to catch his every word. As he points to King Herod's palace, they turn that way and then immediately lean back in to Argus to hear every little bit of gossip.

In spite of Argus' antics, Nicodemus and Gamaliel wait patiently to hear what Argus knows and when Argus is ready to tell. He glances toward Nicodemus and Gamaliel and offers a knowing smile. Casually, he meanders their way.

"Well, my friends, it seems that these men are from the east; stargazers or Magi of some sort. They claim they have seen a star in the East that represents the birth of a new Jewish king and they have come to worship him. You are right. The Levites are taking the strangers to King Herod."

Nicodemus shakes his head. "Can you imagine Herod's surprise and displeasure at hearing that this group wants to inquire where the *newborn* king of the Jews can be found? He will be furious."

Within the next hour, four of Herod's servants come seeking the teachers of the law. Nicodemus' teacher is one of those who is escorted back to Herod's palace.

"Now what?" Argus throws up his hands in frustration.

࿐࿐࿐࿐

The next morning, the students huddle around their teacher, anxious to know what had occurred the day before. Their rabbi reports, "Those *men of the east*," he emphasizes, "were seeking the newborn *king of the Jews*," he emphasizes again, carefully checking each student's response to see if they fully understand the impact of the situation. Asking King Herod where to find a new king is volatile to say the least.

Rabbi Judah presses on, "Evidently these astrologers thought they saw a star that led them to our land. Herod wondered if the astonishing circumstances might be related to the Promised One, our Messiah, because Herod inquired of us as to where the Messiah is to be born. We informed him that Messiah's birthplace is to be Bethlehem, according to the prophet Micah."

The students nod their heads knowingly.

He continues on. "Herod asked the Magi to report back to him if they found the child because he wanted to *worship him* as well." Their teacher's eyebrows rise as he nods his head to emphasize the words.

Well, of course everyone can see through that. Nicodemus also raises a doubting eyebrow, rolls his eyes, and gives a tilt of the head toward Gamaliel. Gamaliel responds with closed eyes and a slight shake of his head.

They all know that Herod worships no one but himself. Undoubtedly Herod is upset and when Herod is upset so are all in Jerusalem. He makes sure of that. No one ever knows what he might do on a whim.

To add to the turmoil, the Jewish leaders themselves are troubled with the very idea that God would reveal the Messiah to some eastern Gentiles rather than to upright Jews. Such a notion borders on blasphemy.

Rabbi Judah concludes, "I'm not sure what these foreigners have to do with our Jerusalem concerns. It seems that they would have plenty to do in their own country. Their pagan practices are not tolerated by our laws."

It is quite obvious that the whole incident is very disturbing to Rabbi Judah. He dismisses the class early for the day.

That afternoon, Nicodemus studies the ancient scroll of the prophet Micah. He finds the prophecy. "Yes, there it is," he says out loud.

"But you, Bethlehem Ephrathah, though you are small among the clans of Judah, out of you will come for me one who will be ruler over Israel, whose origins are from of old, from ancient times."

That's the prophecy concerning Messiah. It sounds like King David, born in Bethlehem; but David had already lived and died when Micah prophesied. Yes, it must be about the Messiah.

Nicodemus reads on:

"He will stand and shepherd his flock in the strength of the Lord, in the majesty of the name of the Lord his God. And they will live securely, for then his greatness will reach to the ends of the earth, and he will be their peace."

Ah, to have that peace! But how will that peace reach "to the ends of the earth"? Does this mean beyond the boundaries of Israel? Certainly this must apply only to the hearts of the chosen ones scattered about and not Gentiles. But what was it that Ethan quoted Simeon? A light for the Gentiles? Oh, I have so much yet to learn.

Looking again at the Scriptures, he repeats, "He will shepherd his flock in the strength of the Lord." *Hmm, "shepherd his flock."*

A pensive mood hangs over Jerusalem the next few days. Nicodemus spends many evenings walking under the stars contemplating these things. Bethlehem again, shepherding, revelation to absolute strangers, most perplexing. *How would these eastern men know or even care about a king of the Jews? They look Persian. Could Esther and Mordecai's influence or Daniel and his friends' influence along with other captured Jews so long ago, have possibly carried down through these many centuries?*

In spite of this puzzling disturbance, nothing more is heard from the Magi. The whole episode could have been disregarded, but Herod refuses to let it go that easily. A rumor spreads that Herod is so obsessed, that in one of his typical tirades, he gave orders to kill all boy babies in the vicinity of Bethlehem, two years of age and younger, just in case a potential king *had* been born.

Nicodemus and his friends deduce that Herod, so fearful that his throne is being threatened, has given in to one of his usual tactics—simply kill those who might get in his way. After all, he had done the same to his mother-in-law and brother-in-law, even one of his own wives and three sons.

Nicodemus longs even more for Messiah to come and deliver them from the bondage of Rome and Roman-appointed kings such as Herod.

CHAPTER 7
Joseph's Intentions

*Now there was a man named Joseph [of Arimathea]
...a good and upright man...*
Luke 23:50

Each time Joseph comes from Arimathea for the festivals, he and Nicodemus review the laws together. They catch up on each other's lives. Nicodemus looks forward to each visit. Just that day, one of the students brought up a point Nicodemus wants to probe with him. Maybe Joseph will have another viewpoint.

On this visit, Nicodemus realizes Joseph has covered more laws than Nicodemus' class in Jerusalem. However, Joseph discovers that his group of three students in Arimathea does not generate nearly the discussion that Nicodemus' group does.

As they talk, Nicodemus says, "Joseph, I wish you could study here. We could be together more and have post discussions."

Joseph smiles. "Nicodemus, I would truly like the opportunity of studying under a Jerusalem teacher, perhaps Rabbi Judah. In fact, I have spoken to my father about this very thing. Surprisingly, father seemed open to the idea. I waited a few days and brought it up again. He had been thinking about another man who could possibly take over my jobs in our business, but my father wants me to make a trip to Phoenicia before I move to Jerusalem."

"Joseph, this is great news. This is wonderful news! How long will it take you to go to Phoenicia? When can you move? Where will you live?"

"Hold on, Nicodemus. One question at a time."

"Okay, when can you move?"

"Well, first I must train the new man to do my jobs. He has worked with me to some extent, so that shouldn't take too long. The trip to Phoenicia will be another matter. It will take a good while to sail there and a few days to do the business my father desires, plus the trip back. Hopefully, I can make the move here by Pentecost."

"But that's months away."

"Better than not at all, my friend."

"Yes, yes that's true." He pauses. "What exciting times you have ahead of you."

"Yes, I have traveled to Cyprus many times, but never as far as Phoenicia."

"Be careful of those foreign ladies."

"My Deborah frets about that too."

"And how does *your* Deborah fit into all these plans?"

"If it were up to my mother, Deborah would already be in the family."

"So?"

"We will definitely marry, but I want to have my life a bit more steady and in order when I bring her into it. Perhaps next year."

"What will she think of moving to Jerusalem?"

"If I am here, I suppose she has no choice in the matter, eh?"

"I suppose not." They laugh together.

"It will be good to have you here, Joseph, and where will you stay?"

"I'll probably stay with my uncle until I get settled enough to find a place. I imagine Deborah would want us to have a place of our own."

"Most likely. Most likely," Nicodemus grins.

CHAPTER 8
The Twelve-Year-Old Boy

Every year his parents went to Jerusalem for the Feast of the Passover. When he was twelve years old, they went up to the Feast, according to the custom.   Luke 2:41, 42

Nicodemus has had a particularly meaningful Passover. As he walks and reflects on his way to the Temple the next morning, he contemplates the past twelve years. *Dear Joseph and his wife, Deborah; I will miss them greatly. It seems only yesterday that Joseph moved to Jerusalem to complete his studies. Now he is off on a business adventure of his own.*

Nicodemus passes the marketplace, purchases a handful of almonds to munch on as he walks to the Temple. *I have studied well and my future looks bright. Now that I have become a teacher myself, I must study all the more to prepare for my student followers.*

He roams through the Temple, observing servants and other Temple helpers as they clean up the court where the massive crowds of Passover week worshippers have come and gone.

Nicodemus notices a group of teachers gathered on the east side of the court. He wanders that way, curious to see what is going on. Much to his astonishment, the teachers are clustered around a boy. He cannot be more than twelve years old. *Has the boy been caught in some wrong doing?*

As Nicodemus approaches, he realizes the teachers are not condemning the boy at all. Quite the contrary, they are *listening* to him with rapt attention.

Gamaliel listens from the outer edge of the group. He notices Nicodemus approaching. "It's been like this all morning."

"Who is he?"

"We're not sure. Sounds as if he is from Galilee. The lad asks highly intelligent questions. Even more amazing are his perceptive answers."

Nicodemus observes the discussion to the end, but wishes he had come earlier.

"Thank you for your time," the boy says as the group begins to disperse.

Nicodemus watches the boy walk across the Temple court and wonders where he lives and to whom he belongs. He looks around to see if anyone knows anything about the boy, but all have gone, even Gamaliel. *Will the boy return tomorrow?*

The next day, Nicodemus hurries to the Temple court in anticipation. Sure enough, when he reaches the discussion spot of yesterday, there stands the boy with the rabbis encircling him. Nicodemus listens for a short while as the teachers impart their wisdom to the lad, and then he notices that Gamaliel and a few others are missing.

"Where is Gamaliel?" he asks one of his friends.

"He and three others went to get Hillel."

"Why?"

"They want to see Hillel's response to the boy."

"Do you think he will come?"

"I don't know. He doesn't get out much these days."

❧❧❧❧

Gamaliel and his friends do meet with resistance when trying to persuade Hillel to come and observe the boy. After all, Hillel complains, why should one of his age and prominence trouble himself with a mere lad? Besides, it takes great effort for him to move anywhere these days. But the teachers are insistent. Gamaliel, his favorite grandson, also encourages him and offers to help him to the Temple. Reluctantly, Hillel agrees.

The boy is still engaged in dialogue with the teachers when Hillel is brought into their midst. All the men watch in quiet respect as Hillel slowly limps to the gathering place on the arms of his grandson, Gamaliel, and another friend. They carefully seat the revered teacher on the first step. The boy notices the group's diverted attention and waits for Hillel to be settled into his place. Hillel breathes heavily and then glares at the boy, the source of all this aggravation and disruption to his ordinarily peaceful morning. Not deterred, the boy nods politely and resumes asking his questions.

"In our holy Scriptures, Isaiah says, 'arise, for thy light has come.' To what light do you think he is referring?"

The teachers shift nervously on the steps above the boy as he looks up at them expectantly. They look to Hillel, so the boy turns to Hillel as well.

"The light represents the Lord's holy presence," Hillel says sternly.

"Does it represent the light of the Almighty or the One to come?" the boy asks.

Hillel raises an admiring eyebrow. "Why, both, I would say."

"Is the light to shine *on* man or to illuminate *through* man?"

"Hmm." Hillel lowers his head, deep in thought. He slowly raises his eyes, focusing intently upon the boy. "Once again, I would say both. The light of God's laws shine upon us, but as our father David prayed, 'Renew a right spirit *within* me.' We are to understand God's laws and speak in truth."

"Do we speak in truth or in love?" the boy persists.

Hillel's eyes narrow upon the lad's face. "Truth and love," concedes the old man.

The boy is about to ask another question when Hillel interrupts him.

"And now, let me ask *you* a question."

"Yes, sir," the boy responds expectantly.

"Our law forbids us to do work on the Sabbath. Does that disallow us to pay visits of condolence to mourners or visit the sick on the Sabbath?"

Without a pause, the boy answers. "Man was not made for the Sabbath; the Sabbath was made for man, that he might have rest. Yet deeds of mercy are always fitting. Bearing words of encouragement is always needed."

Nicodemus smiles, knowing that this answer will please Hillel who opposes Shammai on this point. The smile in Hillel's eyes confirms his approval. He continues questioning.

"And what say *you* concerning the light Isaiah speaks of?"

The boy responds, "The light of God's favor shined upon our ancestors who were in captivity in Babylon. Even while they were held captive, He promised release from their darkness. He would rescue them even as he had rescued our forefathers from Egypt."

The boy continues. "Likewise the Redeemer will come to Zion, to those in Jacob who repent of their sins. The light comes into the world, but men love darkness instead of light because their deeds are evil. Everyone who does evil hates the light, and will not come into the light for fear that his deeds will be exposed.

"But whoever lives by the truth comes into the light, so that it may be seen plainly that what that person has done has been done, not through his own deeds, but through God."

"Well said, my son."

Nicodemus stands there astonished by the boy's depth of understanding and observes the same amazement in the faces of the other teachers.

The next day, the same teachers of the law gather once again. Others have come to see and hear this remarkable boy. Even Hillel has returned. Shortly, the boy comes across the Temple court seeking the rabbis.

Hillel is the first to speak.

"You have returned, I see."

"Yes sir."

"Yesterday, my son, you asked about the light of Jehovah shining on man or illuminating through man. You also asked about truth and love. What have you to say?"

"Anyone who claims to be in the light but hates his brother is still in darkness. Whoever loves his brother is in the light, and there is nothing in him to make him stumble. But whoever hates his brother walks around in darkness; he does not know where he is going, because the darkness has blinded him."

"Yes," Hillel says as he frowns in deep concentration. He has not heard this kind of talk before. "Yes, go on."

"Jeremiah reminded us that the pride of our hearts deceives us. We pray every day, 'Love the Lord your God with all your heart.' The good man does good things out of the good things stored up in his heart, and the evil man does evil out of the evil things stored up in his heart. Out of the overflow of the heart, the mouth speaks."

"True enough, but we must also consider the law, being obedient to the law," Hillel emphasizes.

"The Lord says, through the prophet Isaiah, 'These people come near to me and honor me with their lips, but their hearts are far from me. Their worship of me is made up only of rules thought up by men.'"

Out of the corner of his eye, Nicodemus catches a glimpse of a man and woman rushing across the Temple court. They have a hurried conversation with one of the elders who points to the boy. They slow their steps as they cautiously approach those in discussion. The boy looks up, obviously recognizing the couple. It becomes clear that these are his parents. Apparently they had left Jerusalem, thinking the boy was with their group only to discover he was missing.

They are simple people, apparently from somewhere in Galilee, Nicodemus surmises. The boy talks to his parents, reminding them that he has to "be about my Father's business." *What a strange thing to say.*

The boy turns to the teachers, thanking them for their instruction and time. The parents bow slightly. The mother puts her arm around his shoulders and timidly ushers him away. She glances back with an expression that seems familiar. It's as though Nicodemus has seen her before.

The boy obediently goes with his parents, leaving Nicodemus and the others to contemplate these astonishing three days.

"What an outstanding young man," says Gamliel.

"Unusual questions and answers," comments another rabbi.

"Extraordinary insight," says Hillel.

They all sit in stunned silence watching the young family walk across the Temple court and out the gate.

❧❧❧❧

That night as Nicodemus takes his evening walk, he reflects back to the night, yes twelve years ago, when he saw the bright light from Bethlehem. He gazes over the valley toward Bethlehem remembering the report from the shepherds. They told that angels had appeared to them proclaiming, "Unto you a Savior is born."

He recalls that forty days later, the young priest, Ethan, staggered down the steps of the Temple after participating in a ceremony of purification with a new mother. The old priest, Simeon, had been jubilant over the child. Suddenly Nicodemus stops. He remembers thinking that the parents were probably from Galilee. Here, twelve years later, a couple comes from Galilee who belongs with this remarkable boy. *Was the young mother I saw years ago, the same mother I saw today?*

Nicodemus sinks down on a stone nearby. His self-talk tells him that this is merely a series of coincidences. It was so long ago that he even questions the light from Bethlehem. Had he just imagined it?

Simeon *was* very old. The Magi *were* just stargazers. But what of the astounding questions and answers he has heard the past three days from this young boy?

Even in his secret thoughts he cannot bring himself to ask plainly, "Is this the Christ, our Messiah?" This isn't the way the Messiah should come. He should ride in triumphantly; ready to lead the Jewish nation out from under the political yoke of Rome. At least that's what he had always been taught to think.

Surely the prophets made it clear. He must study further. He must also talk to his father about this. Ah, the thought of his father brings sadness. Will he find his father feeling better this afternoon?

CHAPTER 9
A Visit to the Neighbors

The rod of correction imparts wisdom,
but a child left to himself disgraces his mother.
Proverbs 29:15

Nicodemus' father seems to have recovered from his recent bout with coughing because Nicodemus finds the patriarch of the household rushing from his room with great ease and his mother also darting from one room to the other as if in preparation for something.

"What is going on?" Nicodemus asks his mother.

"Don't you remember, dear? Malia, from next door, invited our family to dinner tonight."

"Sorry, mother, I forgot."

"Dear Nicodemus, you study way too hard; your mind always tied up in the law. You haven't even time to acknowledge the young women of Jerusalem. Now, freshen up and prepare for our visit."

"Yes, mother," he answers with little enthusiasm.

Why is it that I am well recognized and respected among my peers but feel like a child in my home? Maybe I should purchase my own home!

He walks toward the basin of water in the next room then turns and calls out to his mother from the door. "Is that little Hakkoz going to be there?"

She grunts. "Well, of course he's going to be there. He lives there, doesn't he? He's a part of the family."

"I wish they'd feed him in another room," Nicodemus mumbles.

"I heard that."

No response.

She rounds the doorway, peering at her son, not ready to let his comment go. "Remember, they *are* our neighbors. Neighbors take care of one another. They honor each other. You mind your manners."

"Yes, mother."

Fortunately for Nicodemus, his head is hovering over the water basin so his mother can't see his grimace. He feels for the towel. While wiping his face, he inhales deeply and exhales noisily. He doesn't relish the idea of an evening with that spoiled boy next door.

He thinks about his older brother, Neziah, who married and decided to move to lower Jerusalem near his work. *He's the fortunate one.* The only thing that makes this visit worthwhile is the fact that the neighbors' family servant is a wonderful cook. *At least we will have a tasty meal.*

"Are you ready?" calls Jeremias, the middle brother.

"Ready as I will ever be," sighs Nicodemus.

The family parades next door, bearing a gift of sweet grapes from the small vineyard in their courtyard. Not many use their courtyards for such, but Nicodemus' mother has a particular fancy for grapes and wants them available at all times.

Little Hakkoz is the first to the door, just behind the servant, as Nicodemus' family enters. He jumps up and down with squeals of excitement. Nicodemus rolls his eyes at his brother, Jeremias, who cocks his head and raises his eyebrows right back. The mother comes, leans over the little fellow's shoulders from behind, and criss-crosses her arms over his chest to contain him.

"Hakkoz, I know you're so pleased to have our dear friends to dinner." She giggles nervously in an attempt to cover her son's over exuberance.

Nicodemus' mother bends over. "Hakkoz, we're glad to see you, too."

Hakkoz wriggles out of his mother's grip and goes running into the other room.

His mother giggles again. "Do come in everyone," she says, as she leads them into the sitting room. They all follow her to a room fitted with richly covered chairs and sofas. "We're glad you were able to visit this evening. Have you had a busy day?"

"The men have been about their businesses and Nicodemus his studies. I've been tending my flowers in the courtyard," says Nicodemus' mother, trying to look at ease.

"You do have such lovely flowers, but why don't you let your servants tend to them?"

"Oh, but I love doing it myself. It brings me such joy to take care of them and watch them grow."

"Indeed." Malia sits and motions for the men to be seated.

"I almost forgot," Nicodemus' mother exclaims. "I brought you a basket of grapes from our garden. Jeremias, do you have them?"

"Yes, of course."

He picks up the grape-laden basket and hands it to Malia.

"Thank you. I always enjoy having your famous grapes." She leans forward as if sharing a secret. "Little Hakkoz loves them, too."

Malia's husband enters and greets the visitors. "Shalom, friends."

Malia hands off the grape basket to a servant and whispers to her husband. "Where is Hakkoz?"

He answers in a low voice, "I think he's hiding in the courtyard, waiting for you to come find him."

"Oh, dear. What shall we do with him?"

Malia's husband and the men discuss their businesses, while Malia fidgets with her hands and keeps glancing toward the courtyard. A servant appears in the doorway, giving the sign that dinner is ready. Malia motions to her guests to rise.

"I believe our dinner is ready to be served," she says, grateful for the opportunity to check on her son.

Malia hastens to the courtyard in search of Hakkoz while the others find their places around the table. She knows his favorite spots to hide and finds him right away.

"Guess what, Hakkoz," she bribes. "Our neighbors brought those wonderful grapes you like so well." Her voice is soft, and wooing.

Hakkoz willingly comes to the table to claim his share of grapes.

"Where's the grapes?" he says, as he comes running into the dining area.

"We will have our meal first and then you may have your grapes," his father says sternly.

"I want them now."

"After the meal, Hakkoz."

Hakkoz makes a disgruntled face at his father and pouts as the blessing is pronounced before the meal.

At least his pouting is quiet, Nicodemus muses.

The aroma of onion-cooked lamb floats in the room as the fine dishes are brought in. *At last, the best part of the evening.*

Hakkoz has not begun to give up the fight though. "I want my grapes now," he pronounces defiantly.

His father glares at his wife, Malia, and then at Hakkoz. With affected patience, he says, "Hakkoz, you will eat your meal first and then you may have your grapes."

Hakkoz huffs and puffs and twists all about. His mother whispers something in his ear, but it has little effect on him. He simply turns away from her in another huff.

She dishes out small bites of food on his plate, but he totally ignores the food as he sits slumped over, arms folded, and showing his best mad face.

Others at the table try to carry on a conversation, but all are aware of the tension, wondering when the next outburst will come. No amount of encouragement or coaxing will persuade him to eat.

Finally, Malia calls a servant in and whispers for her to take him to the kitchen (where the grape basket is waiting.) Hakkoz has won.

At least, we can now have our dinner in peace, Nicodemus decides.

Only an occasional outbreak from the kitchen reminds the guests that Hakkoz is still around.

When Nicodemus' family reaches their home, Hakkoz is the first subject of conversation.

"Well, I'm sorry I took grapes to them," sighs Nicodemus' mother. "I didn't know it would be the source of such disturbance."

"If it hadn't been the grapes, it would have been something else," chimes in Nicodemus' father.

"What does 'Hakkoz' mean anyway?" asks Jeremias.

"It means nimble," answers his mother. "Malia said that when he was born, he came very quickly and was so bright-eyed and nimble."

"The name also means 'the thorn,' " declares Nicodemus.

They all go to their rooms shaking their heads with a smirk.

CHAPTER 10
The "Thorn" Continues to Grow

Even a child is known by his actions,
by whether his conduct is pure and right.
Proverbs 20:11

Hakkoz grows into a rather handsome young twelve-year-old. He often greets Nicodemus when he passes the boy's house on the way home from the Temple. Nicodemus tries to be congenial and the boy does have his agreeable moments, but lately Nicodemus notices Hakkoz fraternizing with some questionable characters.

I hope Hakkoz' companions will not influence him into further mischief. Come to think of it, maybe it is the other way around. Hakkoz might be the instigator of mischief.

One spring afternoon, as Nicodemus comes home from his teaching responsibilities, Hakkoz is standing by the door of his house.

"Shalom, master Nicodemus."

"Shalom, Hakkoz."

"Did your class go well today, sir?"

"Yes, my students learn well. And you, are you studying successfully in your Yeshiva?"

"Yes, perhaps you can help me if I have questions."

"I would be glad to."

Maybe there is hope for this spoiled boy after all, but why is he fidgeting so and moving about?

Hakkoz pulls a small wooden piece out of his cloak.

"Did you see the new dreydl my friend made for me?"

"Ah, that is a nice one. Well crafted."

"I'll show you how it works." Hakkoz squats to the ground to twirl the toy. With hands on knees, Nicodemus bends over to watch. Each time the dreydl twirls, it spins a little closer to Nicodemus causing him to back up. Hakkoz continues spinning it over and over until Nicodemus sits on the stone wall behind him.

Shortly, Hakkoz ends his spinning game and bids Nicodemus another "Shalom" as he walks down the street.

Nicodemus walks on to his house amused by the friendliness of his young neighbor. As he enters, he is faintly aware of talking and laughter down the street. Turning to glance down the street, he catches sight of Hakkoz and his friends dashing around a corner.

"Nicodemus, is that you?" calls his father from inside.

"Yes, father. Did you need something? How is your cough today?" Nicodemus finds his father propped up on his bed.

"I'm okay. Only a few coughing spells this afternoon. I'm just resting before our evening meal."

Nicodemus walks closer to his father's side.

"What is that awful smell?" sniffs his father. Nicodemus smells a slight scent. He twitches his nose this way and that. When he turns to walk toward the door to sniff in that direction, his father gasps.

"What's wrong, father?"

"Nicodemus, what is that on the back of your robe? It's dreadfully dirty." Nicodemus pulls his robe around and takes a look at the back.

"Oh my," he says, discovering the smudged brown spot. About that time, he gets a good whiff of the odor. "Whew!" He cautiously takes another sniff and wrinkles up his nose. "Oh my, that's donkey dung if I ever smelled it."

"Where in the world did you go to be with donkeys today?"

"I think I have an idea and if I'm right, it is just one donkey."

Out the door Nicodemus rushes in a huff. He marches out the gate and straight to the neighbor's front door. Sure enough, a strategically placed patch of donkey dung is smudged on the very rock where Nicodemus was coerced into sitting moments earlier.

Nicodemus knocks furiously on the door. A servant comes rushing to answer and looks startled to see Nicodemus.

"May I speak with your mistress, please," he sputters impatiently.

"Yes, yes of course. One moment, please."

Malia comes hastily to the door. "Master Nicodemus, what is it?"

"Malia, can you step outside a moment?" Without giving her time to respond, he exclaims, "Do you see this mess at your front door?" She looks in the direction where his finger is pointing.

"Oh my, but where did…"

"Well, I suggest you have it cleaned up and I suggest you have your *son* do the cleaning—*not* a servant." With that, Nicodemus stomps off. As he does so, Malia spies the telltale spot on the back of his robe.

"Oh dear," she gasps. "Oh my. Oh dear," she whispers to herself, as she begins to surmise what has happened, but wrinkles her forehead in puzzlement as to what her son has to do with it.

Nicodemus does not see Hakkoz for a very long time after that incident, which suits him just fine.

CHAPTER 11
A Loving Father

A good name is better than fine perfume…
… death is the destiny of every man.
Ecclesiastes 7:1, 2

Two months later, Nicodemus awakes early before his daily teaching duties begin. He takes a brief walk down the street to refresh himself from a troubled sleep. Worry over his father cuts deep furrows in his forehead. As he returns home and pushes open the gate, he wonders, *What will I find this morning? Will father rally from this illness that has overtaken him? Will he succumb into deeper coughing fits until he breathes his last?* Literally shaking his head, Nicodemus tries to push away thoughts of the inevitable.

Before entering the house, he reaches up, as he has done so many times, and touches the small cylinder attached to the doorframe. Usually, it is a quick, routine touch, but this time his hand lingers on the Mezuzah. He thoughtfully whispers the words contained inside.

"Hear, O Israel, The Lord our God, the Lord is one. Love the Lord your God with all your heart and with all your soul and with all your strength."

His head falls into his raised arm as he continues his grip on the Mezuzah. *Your strength, O Lord, grant me your strength.* He opens the door, but when he sees his mother's emotionally drained face, his heart sinks.

"It doesn't look good, my son," she says softly, her eyes cast down farther than her sagging shoulders.

His father, confined now to bed, responds to Nicodemus' footsteps. Unable to move his head, he can only turn his eyes toward the doorway. He doesn't have the strength to hold out his hand to Nicodemus, so he weakly motions with his fingers. "Come," he whispers hoarsely. His eyes close; his mouth forms a faint smile.

Nicodemus cautiously draws near to his father's side. He doesn't want his father to strain any more than necessary. "You are a good Jewish son," says his ailing father, over a half-cough.

How many times has Nicodemus heard that loving phrase? Somehow it sounds more endearing at this moment.

"We have had many good talks," the old man says as he coughs again.

"Many good talks," whispers Nicodemus, choking back tears. Nicodemus' mind instantly flips through years of memories. Indeed, conversations with this loving father have been more valuable to him than all the sessions with his rabbi. In many ways, his father has been his true teacher.

On one hand, Nicodemus wants his father to rest to conserve his strength because each time he speaks, it brings another round of coughing. On the other hand, Nicodemus wishes for yet one more "good talk." He knows these significant words might be the last. He bends down on one knee beside the bed, touching his father's arm gently, his heart breaking.

Closed eyes open slowly as the struggling father looks at his son. "I have always tried to speak the truth to you," he says.

Nicodemus nods his head in agreement. "Yes, Papa."

"You have learned well, my son."

"I have tried," smiles Nicodemus.

With an ever-so-slight burst of energy, he continues, "You must always seek the truth, Nicodemus. When you enter the council, seek truth. You must have a heart for truth." His voice trails off.

"Yes, Father, I will."

With that, his father closes his eyes and seems at rest. Nicodemus has a thousand more things to say, questions to ask, hopes to share, but his father appears so at rest that Nicodemus simply sits quietly, holding his father's arm.

Seek truth. What is *truth?*

Nicodemus gently rubs his father's arm. His father is peaceful, but is he still breathing? Nicodemus' eyes dart to his father's chest. *Yes*, he sighs, *he's still breathing.*

The council. Father always envisions me being chosen for the Sanhedrin, the great high council of Israel. The fact is, he wanted to be a part of our high court himself. Why did he never make it to that position? Why didn't I ask him? So many questions.

Nicodemus watches the good man for several moments then eases himself to the floor from his kneeling position and gently lowers his head to the side of the bed.

He wants to cry like a baby. He wants his father to take him in his arms as he did in childhood days. He longs to hear more stories of their Jewish ancestors and hear his father read from the Sefer Torah in the synagogue. He yearns to hear his father quote Scripture around the Passover table just one more time, but he knows the end is near. These things will not be.

This trusted physician drew from his storehouse of herbs and spices and lovingly treated so many patients over the years. Now he is the patient. Gradually, a sense of peace envelopes Nicodemus as he sits there in silence; peace that this has been a life well lived, and gratitude that he has been privileged to be a part of it.

He keeps vigil at his father's side for a long while, thinking and praying. His mother comes in and tenderly pats his shoulder. "He must rest now," she whispers. She holds both his arms as if lifting him up. Slowly he stands and puts his arms around his mother, partly holding her, partly being held. They walk from the room.

Nicodemus treads wearily into the street. The bright sunshine almost blinds him after having been in the darkened room. His heavy heart rejects the brilliance. Anger, despair, and gratitude well up inside him simultaneously. Where can he go? To whom will he turn? He has always turned to his father. And now...

He finds himself at the steps of the Temple. A few people are milling about; priests preparing for the day, Levites opening the massive doors, worshippers gathering.

Nicodemus is glad not to be near anyone. He doesn't want to feel obliged to engage in conversation.

The steps, where he usually meets with his class, provide a quiet, secluded place to sit and think. Strange that he should come to the Temple instead of his usual retreat spot under a favorite tree. The holiness of this place seems to woo him.

He mulls over his father's last words. *The council.* Yes, that has been Nicodemus' goal for some time now.

Could it be my *goal because it is my* father's *goal?* He wonders.

And then it dawns on him that indeed, he could best *honor* his father by being chosen for the Sanhedrin. *Yes, that is what I must do.* Energized by these thoughts, he moves into the rest of his day with new determination. He resolves to talk with his father about it later.

But that evening, as Nicodemus nears his parent's house, he sees five women gathered around the doorway, weeping and wailing. *No,* he cries out from deep within his soul. *No, Papa, I'm not ready yet. One more talk. Just one more word. Did I tell you how much I love you? Did I thank you for your love and care through the years? No, Adonai, don't take him yet!*

He picks up his pace. The women sense the rush of his steps and part to make way for him. Nicodemus rushes into his father's room to find his mother and a friend. She turns to him and shouts, "Nico, oh Nico, he's gone."

Nicodemus throws off his robe and rends his tunic. He cries out with uplifted arms. "Adonai, have mercy!" He tears his tunic once again and falls to his knees before his father's bed, weeping uncontrollably; his mother weeping behind him. The friends at the door begin wailing once more.

Nicodemus sinks down farther; elbows on the floor, holding his head in his hands. "No, no," he cries out again. He runs his fingers through his hair and tucks his head in his own lap, rocking forward and back.

His mother, her friend, the women outside, and Nicodemus continue moaning with intermittent bursts of loud cries.

Nicodemus finally gains control and stands to embrace his mother, finding strength in trying to comfort her. In a few moments, the women outside become quiet as Nicodemus' two brothers enter the room. They, too, tear their tunics with much wailing. Nicodemus sits slumped in the corner of the room, his heart filled with despair.

The brothers, Neziah and Jeremias, embrace. They turn to their mother and hold her between them, groaning with intermittent gasps of air and audible sighs. The mood of the dark room hangs heavy with grief.

As their emotions settle, they ask their mother if anyone was with her when their father died.

"No," she says. "I had poured some soup and brought it in to Papa. I called to him, but he didn't answer. When I touched him there was no response. I called louder. I said, 'You must eat something, my darling,' but he said nothing." She heaves gulping cries into the shoulder of Neziah, her eldest son. "I knew he was gone," she cries with muffled voice. Neziah holds her as her shoulders shake.

Jeremias glances over at Nicodemus, slumped on the floor in the corner of the room. He sits down by him with an arm around his shoulder. The family continues to mourn over the loss of their dear one.

They are comforted that Nicodemus will be with their mother for the night. As they say their goodbyes, Neziah places two pieces of broken clay pots on his father's eyes, as is the custom and the two brothers depart.

⚜❦⚜❦⚜❦⚜❦

The following morning Neziah's wife accompanies him. She greets Martha without words, only an embrace and helps her gather a few things. After a final glance at her beloved husband, Martha walks out the door with her daughter-in-law, leaving the men to take care of the body.

Neziah looks at Nicodemus as if to ask how things went through the night.

"Mama cried herself to sleep, but I think she did get some rest."

"And you?"

Nicodemus lowers his head with moist eyes. "It is hard."

"I know, my dear brother. I can hardly believe it is not as it always has been. It seems he should have come to the door to greet us."

Jeremias arrives to check on everybody. He leaves shortly saying that he will take care of the coffin and coffin bearers.

Neziah, being the oldest brother, stays to prepare their father's body for burial and perform the *Tahara*, purification. He and Nicodemus still wear their torn shirts from the *keriah*, rending of garments, of yesterday. Nicodemus insists on staying to help.

"Very well," concedes Neziah. "I *will* need help. Fetch me a basin of water and two cloths."

While Nicodemus is gone, Neziah cuts their father's hair and trims his nails according to custom. Nicodemus watches as Neziah covers their father's body except for one arm. Stretching the arm out, Neziah gently rubs his father's arm with the cloth dipped in water.

"I will also need a *pitcher* of water," he says.

Nicodemus leaves and comes back with a pitcher full of water.

Neziah holds the basin under his father's arm. "Pour the water over Papa's arm," he instructs. Nicodemus hesitates but his brother only looks at him until Nicodemus follows his command. The water trickles over his father's arm and into the basin. Neziah takes the dry cloth to lightly pat his father's arm and gently places the arm back against his father's body under the covering.

They go to the other side to repeat the process with his other arm. As they continue, they move slowly, lovingly to cleanse and sprinkle water over each part of their father's body. Neziah softly quotes scripture as they work.

"We will need the myrrh." Neziah nods toward the storage pantry.

Nicodemus goes to the pantry where his father kept ointments, spices, and other medical supplies for his patients. He reaches up to the top shelf to pull down the special jar and takes it to Neziah.

"Rub the salve on his skin. I'll get the aloes," Neziah tells him.

The strong scent of the myrrh erupts immediately. Nicodemus is tenuous about touching his father, but gradually he begins to feel at ease and develops a sense of peace and purpose—even reverence as the sweet fragrance permeates the room.

Neziah carries the aloes to their father's bed. He breaks the leaves apart, allowing the milky substance to ooze out. With tender touch, he rubs it on his father's legs.

"We need the linen," Neziah says, with a slight catch in his voice. He knows this is the final step. Nicodemus goes to the special wooden box which holds the precious shroud they purchased a few weeks ago.

Nicodemus recalls the trip he and his brothers made to the Galilee, all the way to Sepphoris, to purchase the finest linen available. He knew the intent for the linen. His brothers were preparing even then for their father's death. Somehow it felt to Nicodemus that by making this trip it would bring on death, but his brothers had convinced him that it is better to be prepared. After all, death could come to any one of them at any time.

"While we've traveled this distance, we may as well purchase enough linen for five shrouds," Neziah had suggested. Nicodemus knew Neziah was trying to make it seem less pointed that the shroud was for their father, but in reality, Neziah's suggestion did make sense.

With those memories in his head, Nicodemus carefully slides the box from the shelf and slowly opens it. He touches the linen that has been folded to fit exactly in the wooden box. A tear slips out the corner of his eye. Breathing deeply, he continues his assigned task. He retrieves the needed linen and drapes it over his arm, closes the box lid, and replaces it on the shelf.

The pungent aroma draws his attention as he reenters the room. Neziah is finishing with the aloes. Without a word, they look at each other, sharing the feeling of finality that sweeps over them. Lovingly, they unfold the linen and wrap their father's face and body.

They stand on each side of their father, satisfied that their work is complete. Neziah raises his eyes to the ceiling and lifts his arms in blessing.

"He ruleth below and above; He ordereth death and restoreth to life; He bringeth down to the grave and bringeth up again."

"Amen," whispers Nicodemus.

They turn as they hear wagon wheels rolling down the street and to the front door. "It is Jeremias with the coffin," Neziah says, as he walks to the door.

Jeremias and four of his friends bring the coffin-borne cart to a stop. The four friends release their hold of the corners as Jeremias lowers the handle of the cart and looks intently at his brothers.

"We are ready," Neziah tells him.

The four friends bring the coffin in the house and lower it to the floor. Jeremias nods his thanks and dismissal to his friends. They wait quietly outside the door.

Jeremias stares at his father with moist eyes. The other two spontaneously walk over to him; one places an arm over his shoulder, the other an arm around Jeremias' waist.

After a few moments the three brothers lovingly lower their father into the coffin.

❧❧❧❧❧❧❧

The coffin bearers are called into the room. They carefully lift the coffin and carry it out to the cart. Hundreds of mourners have lined the street to mourn with Nicodemus, his mother and brothers.

Slowly, the four friends turn the cart around. All process behind the coffin with slow steady steps; some in silence, some weeping softly, others wailing loudly. A friend steps in line with Jeremias to relieve him of pulling the handle of the wagon. He gratefully joins his family.

At one juncture the procession stops as a Levite friend comes forth to lead the mourners in singing a psalm.

"The Lord is my shepherd," they chant.
"I shall not be in want.
He makes me lie down in green pastures,
    he leads me beside quiet waters,
    he restores my soul.
He guides me in paths of righteousness
    for his name's sake."

Some voices drop out as grief overtakes them. This good physician had brought many of them out of pain. Others continue the singing.

"Even though I walk through the valley of death,
    I will fear no evil, for you are with me,
    your rod and your staff, they comfort me."

More voices join in with the hopeful ending.

"Surely goodness and love will follow me
    all the days of my life,
    and I will dwell in the house
    of the Lord forever."

Some of the mourners disperse at this point. The procession resumes and weaves a path down the streets, through the gate, and outside the city. They approach the family burial cave, where the stone has already been rolled away to receive this dear loved one. They stop before the entrance. Rabbi Judah steps before the mourners who have continued with the procession. He raises his eyes and begins his prayer.

"The Rock," he calls out in rich resonant tones.
"His work is perfect, for all his ways are judgment:
  A God of faithfulness and without iniquity,
  just and right is He.

"The Rock, perfect in every work,
  who can say unto Him,
  'What workest Thou?'
He ruleth below and above,
  He ordereth death and restoreth to life:
  He bringeth down to the grave,
  and bringeth up again.

"Just in all Thy ways art Thou, O Rock.
Slow to anger and full of compassion.
  Spare and have pity on wife and children,
  For Thine, Lord, is forgiveness and compassion.

The Lord gave and the Lord hath taken away;
  Blessed be the name of the Lord."

The coffin bearers lift the coffin and carry it to the entrance where Nicodemus and his brothers lovingly place their hands under their father and carry him into the burial cave to recline on a shelf. Neziah adjusts the linen shroud. They stand respectfully before their father in silence. With bowed heads, they walk backwards through the entrance. Friends roll a rock across the opening.

As the family returns to their home in silence, friends have gathered to console, bear friendship, and provide a bountiful meal.

꧁꧂꧁꧂꧁꧂꧁꧂

Joseph receives the news the morning of the funeral while visiting back in Arimathea. He leaves immediately and arrives in Jerusalem that evening and quickly makes his way to the house of Nicodemus. Words are not necessary as their eyes meet. Their usual frivolity is replaced with a long, gripping embrace. After a few moments, Joseph speaks softly, "He loved you and you served him well, my friend."

"He was a loving father and a wonderful teacher," answers Nicodemus, with tearful eyes.

Joseph spends the evening with Nicodemus and stays nearby throughout the *Shiva*, the seven-day mourning period.

CHAPTER 12
A Disciple in the Sanhedrin

The Lord said to Moses, "Bring me seventy of Israel's elders who are known to you as leaders and officials among the people. They will help you carry the burden of the people."
Numbers 11:16, 17

After his father's death, Nicodemus immerses himself in his studies, asking many questions, observing the walk, the talk, and the ways of the Pharisees, especially the ones who are members of the Sanhedrin. He takes on their austere posture, their dignified gait, and their deliberate, deep-toned speech. He smiles less and offers opinions more. He spends greater periods of time in solitude; practicing the piety he has been taught. He carefully rehearses the laws in his mind determined to demonstrate the laws in full action and obedience.

Joseph comes by one day, walking briskly up the path to Nicodemus' house. "I have good news," he announces with bubbly enthusiasm. "My uncle tells me that we may be included in the group of disciples who are invited to the next meeting of the Sanhedrin. They will choose the new student disciples soon. He will put in a good word for us."

"That *is* good news. That's *great* news!" says Nicodemus, his old sense of enthusiasm returning. "How many will they choose? When will we know for sure? Do we need to make our request known?"

"Whoa, hold on there. I know about as much as you do. I don't think the decision will be made until at least two more Sabbaths have passed."

Perhaps this will prove to be the opening he has been looking for, the next step toward the goal Nicodemus has set for himself. He teaches with enthusiasm and anticipation during the following days.

Sure enough, a couple of weeks later, Joseph and Nicodemus *are* invited to participate in the gathering of the Sanhedrin.

Nicodemus can hardly sleep. He recounts the suggestions that his teacher had made in a private conversation. "You are there to observe, not to speak," Rabbi Judah had warned. "Treat this invitation with the dignity that it deserves."

"Yes sir," Nicodemus had said.

"Listen carefully to the arguments in civil cases. Observe the questions of the members and their demeanor in asking their questions. You will learn much from the experts who know how to get at the heart of a matter."

"Yes, I understand."

"If the council is trying a case, the members of the council can speak for or against the one being accused. However, those in your group can only speak if you have something to say in favor of the accused."

"I see."

"When the council interviews potential priests, notice the testimony of those the council accepts and the way the young men answer the inquiries. You won't be voting, merely observing, but be a keen observer, even as you were in my class."

"Yes, rabbi. Thank you, sir."

As he lay in his bed that night, Nicodemus envisions himself strolling slowly and piously up to the meeting place, bowing slightly as the elders pass in front of him. He drifts in and out of sleep, playing the scene over and over in his mind. In his dream, he can never quite make it into the great hall. He just keeps walking there, bowing to the members as they pass by.

Nicodemus rouses the next morning realizing that he had finally drifted off to sleep after his fretful night. He splashes water onto his face to wake himself fully, for he wants to be as fresh as possible for the big day. He glances at his reflection in the brass water pot, seeing, as always, his father's nose.

He dries his face and dresses, then searches high on a shelf for the old leather box his mother gave him after his father's death. His father's red phylactery box bares delicate

66

designs on the outside, faded with years of use. Nicodemus gently lifts the phylacteries out of the box and unwinds the well-worn brown leather straps. "This will be the special morning I will use father's phylacteries for my morning prayers," he whispers to himself. "Papa would like that."

As he turns one of the two small phylacteries over in his fingers, he thinks about the scriptures from Exodus and Deuteronomy contained inside. He quotes the *shema* and the verses that command faithful Jews to remember the way God has provided for them and to teach their children, *just as Papa taught us.* As he winds the leather straps around his finger and seven times around his left arm, he recalls the Scriptures that instruct Israel to tie these commands on their hands and their foreheads. After tying the second phylactery to his forehead and flipping the strap over his shoulder, he wraps the *tallith*, his prayer shawl, around his shoulders and pulls the front edge over his head. In humility, he begins his morning prayers.

His heart beats rapidly as he utters his praise and petitions to God. Memories flood his mind as he touches the knotted cord falling from his prayer shawl. The shawl is like a holy blanket enveloping him in this quiet moment as he bows in gratitude for the prospect of what this day will bring.

With great care, he packs his father's phylacteries back in the box and wears his own set for the day.

When he emerges from his prayer room, his mother asks, "Are you ready, my son?"

"I'm ready," he smiles back. Far too excited to eat his morning meal, he kisses her good-bye and marches off to meet Joseph. Between his own leather straps, he can still feel the imprints of his father's phylacteries. He touches them, feeling his father's presence, jubilant that the day has finally come.

"Search for truth my son," his father would have said.

"Yes, father, I will search for truth," Nicodemus says out loud.

He picks up his pace and soon sees Joseph in the road, ready and waiting.

"It's about time," laughs Joseph.

"We have plenty of time, you impatient one," jousts Nicodemus.

They give each other shoulder pokes while they traipse down the road like two school boys instead of men in their late forties. As they near the Temple gate, their demeanor changes, and their conversation falls silent. Both spontaneously stare up at the massive archway to the Temple mount. They come this way nearly every day, but it is as though they are passing through for the first time. When they step under the arch, a new chapter of their lives will open.

Both men arch their backs and stand just a little bit taller. They slow their gait with an air of dignity to fit the occasion.

They are greeted at the entrance of the meeting area by one of the chief priests.

"Shalom, sons of Abraham," nods the chief priest.

"Shalom," they nod back.

An elder shows them to their seats in the large hewn stone room. A few priests, rabbis, and elders have gathered and nod to the two newcomers. Their weak knees welcome the opportunity to sit in a designated area to the side, reserved for new disciples. Each inhale and exhale audibly as they settle in and look around, attempting an air of assurance. Nicodemus muses that in spite of his dream, he *did* make it into the great hall.

Argus comes strolling in as though he did this every day. He speaks to the elder who had seated Nicodemus and Joseph. "Not necessary," they hear him say. "I see my friends over there." He strides across the room with a flourish and stops in front of Nicodemus and Joseph. With a side tuck of his chin, he says, "Good morning, gentlemen, Shalom."

"Shalom," says Nicodemus.

"Shalom," mutters Joseph.

"I wonder what cases we will hear today," says Argus, as he sits beside Nicodemus, giving a dramatic swish of his robe around his legs.

Soon, all the members of the Sanhedrin gather for the morning session. The members form a semicircle while the younger disciples sit in three rows to the side of the council in the great hall. A moderate rumble of chatter fills the room bringing a level of comfort to the new ones.

"Can you believe we're sitting here in this prestigious group?" whispers Joseph.

Nicodemus smiles, reminded how Joseph usually says what Nicodemus is thinking. *Always the bold one to give voice to my thoughts.*

The session begins. Three priests are brought in for questioning and consideration for becoming chief priests. Nicodemus' friend, Ethan, is one of them. *Interesting that we are both here on the same day for new phases in our lives. Simeon would have loved to see this.* Simeon had passed on shortly after the incident with the young couple and their baby.

After the three are made chief priests, a discussion ensues about a man who has come out from the wilderness and is drawing crowds to gather near the Jordan River. He preaches repentance and baptizes several every day. The Sanhedrin decides to select a contingent of leaders to make a trip to find out more about this wild baptizer and determine his real purpose. Nicodemus is chosen to represent the new disciples of the Sanhedrin.

A shabbily dressed young man is brought in who is accused of murder. Two witnesses, the required amount, give their account. A member of the council knows the man's father and comments on his negative reputation.

Argus squirms a bit as though he wants to say something. Nicodemus and Joseph had both previously decided that they would not comment until they had made several visits to the meetings. Not so with impetuous Argus. Clearing his throat, he speaks up, "I know the manager who hired this young man. I feel sure he would only hire someone with impeccable character."

A few priests frown at Argus for what seems like an interruption. They continue to discuss the case, all but totally ignoring Argus' comment.

A few months pass. Nicodemus and the other new disciples have attended several meetings of the Sanhedrin. They have endured many heated discussions between the members; the Pharisees want to add to the law and the Sadducees want to leave the laws "as is" in the Torah.

One day, a young man, barely twenty years old, is accused of stealing. Nicodemus leans forward when the accused is roughly brought in and given a shove by the Temple guard. The lad loses his balance and falls to his knees. Immediately, Nicodemus recognizes Ebed, the son of his next door neighbor's servant.

What on earth is Ebed doing here? he wonders. Nicodemus has always found him to be a kind, obedient boy who worked diligently for his master. Two other young men enter—friends of Nicodemus' neighbor, Hakkoz. The friends look a bit intimidated by the great host of priests, scribes, and teachers of the law.

Next, with a grand entrance, comes Hakkoz himself. He stretches up as tall as possible seemingly to make himself appear more than his twenty years of age. Visions of endless ordeals of bad behavior with this spoiled boy, flash through Nicodemus' mind.

Hakkoz, *the thorn*, pronounces his caustic accusation against the despicable thief in front of him. "This *servant*," he spews, pointing with a finger, "has stolen three of my mother's jewels." To add more drama, Hakkoz claims, "One of these was a special, precious jewel from my mother's wedding." He details the presumed deed in his whiny "I want my way" voice. *The results of a lenient father and an indulgent mother*, Nicodemus concludes.

Nicodemus asks to speak. He rises slowly, facing the semicircle of scribes, Pharisees, and Sadducees. Ebed's gaze shifts quickly to the familiar voice. "I personally know this young man, Ebed. I have had the advantage of observing him over several years. He is kind and helpful, hard-working and diligent. I have found him to be honest and responsible. I have also observed that a certain young lady seems to have taken a liking to young Ebed."

Ebed lowers his head with a blush. Hakkoz contorts his face in scorn.

Turning to the accuser, Nicodemus continues, "Hakkoz, is it possible that you have mistaken a jewel for a young lady?" A slight ripple of laughter makes its way around the semicircle.

More angry than embarrassed, Hakkoz flies into a fit of rage. "He has no right to take her from me. What has he to offer but soup and rags? No name, no home, no comforts."

The more Hakkoz speaks, the more he digs his own grave. The members begin to murmur as it becomes evident that Nicodemus has struck a revealing nerve.

Hakkoz only makes it worse. "He is only scum. Scum, I tell you! She has been set apart for me. Me, not him!" He has to yell now over the chatter and chuckling of the group. "It isn't fair. It just isn't fair," he whines. Hakkoz lunges toward Ebed.

The whole Sanhedrin sucks in a collective gasp. The so-called witnesses cower in fear. Ebed's eyes blink in disbelief. Quickly, the accuser and his false witnesses are escorted out of the council. Young Ebed's shoulders slump in relief. His grateful eyes seek out Nicodemus. Nicodemus smiles and nods his head in acknowledgement. Walking up to the boy, Nicodemus whispers in his ear. "You may leave now."

"Thank you, Rabbi Nicodemus, thank you." Ebed reaches out his hands as though he wants to hug Nicodemus and then kneels at his feet. He continues bobbing his head in quick bows as he makes his exit.

Another slight mumble of the members of the Sanhedrin is interrupted by Caiaphas, the high priest. "I believe we have had quite enough for today," he says. Turning, he continues, "Thank you, Rabbi Nicodemus, for your expedient perception in this matter." Nicodemus nods. "We are dismissed."

71

The members linger and gather in small clusters to rehash the day's excitement.

Argus makes numerous attempts to divert the conversations, but the men of this high court continue commenting on the finesse of Nicodemus that brought on such an open confession from the young accuser.

Spying a group of Pharisees gathered around Nicodemus, Argus decides if you can't overcome the situation, you might as well join in. He motions his friends to join him as they strut across the court. "Nicodemus," he declares jovially. "You were quite spectacular this morning!"

"Only seeking the truth, Argus."

"You have everyone singing your praises, my friend."

"I didn't want to see an innocent boy accused."

"Yes, yes, but you might have been wrong. The young accuser had two witnesses lined up ready to testify."

"I knew this young man's nature. A man's true character always shows itself eventually, Argus."

"Hmm, I'm sure that's true," he mutters, with a flip of his garment. He ushers his two friends off and continues chatty conversation with them, totally oblivious to the implications of the previous comments.

"Well said, my friend," murmurs Joseph under his breath to Nicodemus.

As they watch Argus saunter off, another friend comments. "Argus never changes, does he? Look how he fraternizes with the chief priests."

Another chimes in, "One would hardly know he is a Pharisee the way he seems to be spending more and more time with the chief priests and other Sadducees."

"Vying for a permanent position on the high court, no doubt."

"His theological bent may be like ours, but his political tendency grows more like the Sadducees every day." Others nod their heads in judgmental agreement.

CHAPTER 13
Trip to Capernaum

*In those days John the Baptist came preaching
in the Desert of Judea.*   Matthew 3:1

Another trip to Galilee. Nicodemus is reminded of his last trip with a contingent of other Pharisees to check on John the Baptizer. John had many followers. Nicodemus' frown turns to a scowl as he remembers that day.

What a scrappy pack of Galileans they were, gathered together in one big crowd. They hung on the words of the baptizer who shouted curses on all those who did not repent, reducing them to mindless puppets. No wonder they all flocked to the water to be baptized.

Nicodemus is repulsed by the idea of possibly running into that madman again. But his mother has been hinting for some time to go to Capernaum to visit her sister, Leah. At this point, his mother practically *insists* on going.

Nicodemus has noticed how lonely and sad she has been since his father's death. He knows time with her sister would be refreshing and comforting to her, but oh the dread of seeing that baptizer again.

To make matters worse, rumor has it that another preacher is going about the countryside, turning things upside down as well. *A bunch of ignorant, foolish people—that's what they are. How did my gracious mother and her sister ever come from the Galilee?*

In spite of his protests, here he is, packing his clothes and traveling gear to take his mother to see Aunt Leah.

"It's bad enough to go to Galilee, but why couldn't it at least be southern Galilee?" he complains wiping the sweat from his brow. "Capernaum is all the way to the northern tip of the sea."

"Well, at least we can take a boat part of the way," his mother chimes in, trying not to let anything spoil her excitement.

If the sea remains calm, he reasons, but the Sea of Galilee is well known for sudden squalls. *A storm at sea—now that would be just great.*

In spite of his reluctance, Nicodemus has to admit his mother has been so happy the past few days. Why, he even heard her singing as she worked in her garden. No, he can't disappoint her. He will just have to swallow his pride, gather his wits about him, and head to Galilee.

They plan to depart the day after the Sabbath so they will be able to arrive before the following Sabbath. One of his mother's servant girls, Zilia, is going along with them. Nicodemus reminded his mother that her sister, Leah, will have servants to help her, but Martha loves Zilia and is determined to take her along. Zilia has never been to Galilee and talks excitedly about making the trip. *I suppose Zilia is like the daughter she never had. Thankfully, mother is leaving the better cook at home for me when I return.*

The dreaded day arrives. Nicodemus' brothers, Neziah and Jeremias, said their goodbyes the night before. Nicodemus loads his mother's last bag. "Now, how long are you going to stay in Capernaum?" he asks again.

"I told you, Nicodemus, I will return to Jerusalem with Leah's family when they come for the Festival of Booths."

"But that's two months away."

She sighs audibly, "Nicodemus, we've been through this over and over. Now let's get started."

He helps his mother onto a donkey he had purchased from a good friend. He swings the water jugs the other way so they won't be banging into her.

"Oh, I feel like a young girl again—off on an adventure!" Martha exclaims.

Nicodemus turns his head to hide the smile on his face. Somehow he finds it hard to think of his mother on an "adventure." Her life is so routine and predictable. *I suppose this will indeed be an adventure for her.*

He helps Zilia onto her donkey and adjusts the food baskets on the donkey's back.

74

"Thank you Master Nicodemus."

"Are you on secure, Zilia?"

"Yes sir. Quite secure. I've ridden many-a donkey in my time."

In her time? Somehow that sounds humorous as well, coming from such a young woman, a rather attractive young woman at that. Even with her drab servant clothes, she has a beautiful smile.

Put away such thoughts, you old man. You're pushing fifty, don't forget. Why she's young enough to be your daughter.

He shakes his head as he thinks back on the many times his mother has tried to match him up with one young lady after another, with no success. With his head in the scrolls and his serious memorization of the law, he'd had no time for the young women of the community.

Now I'm quite past the marrying age. Surely mother has finally given up on further matchmaking.

Nicodemus mounts his donkey and holds the rope tied to the fourth beast of burden, heavy laden with all the other bags and baskets. "I should have brought a cart," he grumbles to himself.

At last the anxious travelers are on their way, through the city streets, out the gate, and on the rocky road toward the Jordan.

As they head east, they follow narrow winding paths. Nicodemus stays on the lookout for robbers. Fortunately several others are on the road today. Hopefully, this greater number of travelers will serve as a deterrent to any would-be thieves.

After riding for a couple of hours, Nicodemus notices that the women are getting bent over with fatigue. The late morning sun is stirring up quite a thirst in him, so he is sure they are dry as well. He finds a tree with sufficient shade and pulls his little traveling caravan under its protection.

"Time for rest and a drink."

"That sounds wonderful," mutters his mother wiping a stray strand of hair with the back of her hand. Zilia flings her limp, moist robe off and spreads it on the ground for Martha to sit on. Zilia straightens up to get the water jugs, but Nicodemus already has them in hand. They sip the cool water, grateful for the shade and a break from the lumpy back of the donkey.

"How much further?" His mother's voice sounds weary.

"By lunchtime, we should be to the cooler streams of the Jordan."

"Hmm, cooler. That sounds inviting."

"Would you like to stretch out and rest awhile?" Nicodemus asks.

"No, let's keep going. I think I will walk along side my donkey for a while, though." They all agree that it will be good to walk a bit to exercise their legs.

As they gradually descend the hills and near the Jordan River, they welcome the cooler air. Mounting their donkeys again, they ride until it is time for lunch.

Munching on dates and walnuts, Martha studies her maturing son. "You know, I was just thinking," she says in her coy tone.

"Yes, mother," he responds begrudgingly, sure that he isn't going to like what she has to say.

"Wouldn't it be wonderful for you to stay awhile with us in Capernaum? It would be a nice rest for you. You could teach students there just as you do in Jerusalem."

"Mother, you know I have my work in Jerusalem and can't be gone indefinitely."

Besides, why would I want to be in that place when my life and work are so tied to my beloved Jerusalem? Mother probably has another woman for me to meet there. Dear mother, will she ever understand how important my work is?

This small band of travelers continues their journey along the east side of the Jordan River. A slight breeze tempers the blazing sun. An occasional cloud provides additional relief. They are making good time on their journey with no mishaps, but the ever vigilant Nicodemus finds himself gazing over the river to the western side, glad for the watery border between them and the Samaritans. They certainly wouldn't want to be near those people.

On the Samaritan shores, donkeys carry heavy burdens; a few travelers plod behind them, farmers plow what little fields they have, three fishermen sit on the bank. *Half-breeds*, he scowls. He deliberately looks the other way as if to discount their existence. On his side of the bank, a shepherd leads his sheep in search of another field of grass; a carpenter works on a wooden yoke for his oxen.

This is such a different, slow-paced existence from the busy life of learning and teaching in Jerusalem with its crowds of people in the marketplace and the Temple. His mind drifts to his students. He has some promising ones, but none like Gamaliel's new student, Saul. Gamaliel reports that this young upstart is full of questions and opinions. Nicodemus amuses himself imagining how Gamaliel might be handling this curious prodigy. "Firm and fair;" that would be Gamaliel's motto.

A starling darts across the sky, catching Nicodemus' attention. It flies up the river and lands in a tree. With searching eyes, Nicodemus scans the northern length of the river, wondering again about the baptizer. *Tomorrow we will be at the place where he baptizes. Ah, well, I will just wait until then to worry about that wretched man. Besides, he may have moved to a new location.*

The sun settles lower in the western sky. Nicodemus knows of an inn not far away; one that is cleaner than most, though none are much to speak of. *Nothing outside of Jerusalem is much to speak of.* The proprietor usually provides a small meal for the evening, so Nicodemus decides they will stop there for the night.

Soon the small village comes into view. Nicodemus points toward it. "Our rest is in sight, dear ladies."

"Thanks be to the Lord our provider," says his mother. They pick up their pace in anticipation.

"It isn't much to look at, but weary travelers can't be choosey," Nicodemus reminds them. They unload their things for the night. The meal is simple—lentil soup and bread, but it tastes good to them and they are ready to lie down for a night of rest.

CHAPTER 14
Day Two

...the word of God came to John... He went into all the country around the Jordan, preaching a baptism of repentance for the forgiveness of sins.
Luke 3:2, 3

Up and ready for the second day, Nicodemus buys more food and drink and reloads the donkeys. When the women are ready he helps them onto their beasts of burden. "We will reach the sea by day's end," he says, mounting his own donkey.

The farther they travel, the more Nicodemus fidgets. He looks right and left; he pats his donkey; he adjusts the pouch behind him; he audibly sucks in his breath and blows out.

Martha notices his anxious behavior. "Is something wrong, Nicodemus?"

"No, no. Are you both comfortable?"

"I'm fine, Master Nicodemus," Zilia calls from behind.

Martha sits up a little straighter. "I wouldn't say I'm comfortable riding on a donkey for miles on end, but I'm managing well. Better than *you* seem to be."

Nicodemus knows he must give some explanation to his mother; she knows him too well. "There may be a crowd of people up ahead soon. We will move out and around to avoid the confusion."

"But there aren't cities of any size between here and the sea."

"No, but do you remember that I traveled here with others from the Sanhedrin last month?"

"Yes, you seemed upset when you returned. Is this going to be a dangerous crowd?"

"Well, probably not. They seemed peaceful before, but it's the leader that I don't trust."

"Is he a wicked man?" His mother's voice sounds frightened.

I wish I had never started this conversation. Annoyed with her inquiries and frustrated with his own dread of seeing John the Baptizer again, he blurts out, "Mother, it will be fine, just fine."

She knows his limits and refrains from further discussion.

In the next couple of hours, his dread is realized. Up ahead, he sees the crowd assembled near the river. Out in the middle of the river stands the baptizer with his arms waving in the air. The number of people seems to have increased.

Nicodemus pulls the donkey's rein to the right, gradually leading his entourage around the throng. Even at a distance, the baptizer's voice booms out over the mass of people.

"It is written in the book, the words of Isaiah," he shouts to the crowd.

> "A voice of one calling out in the desert,
>   'Prepare the way for the Lord,
>   make straight paths for him.
>   Every valley shall be filled in,
>   every mountain and hill made low.' "

Nicodemus begrudgingly mouths the closing lines of the quote with the baptizer.

> "The crooked roads shall become straight,
>   the rough ways smooth.
> And all mankind will see God's salvation."

Who does he think he is? He claims not to be Elijah returned, but he speaks as though he is the one to proclaim the Messiah's coming. What does he know? He even uses the sacred Scripture to his advantage. Blasphemy, that's what it is—blasphemy!

Nicodemus attempts to move the donkeys along faster, but they stubbornly stay at the same lazy pace. *When*

<u>will</u> *we get past this madman?* Try as he may, he cannot get his small band of travelers out of earshot of the preacher.

"You brood of vipers! Produce fruit in keeping with repentance. Do not begin to say to yourselves, 'We have Abraham as our father.' I tell you that out of these stones God can raise up children for Abraham. Judgment is near for those who give no evidence of repentance. The ax is already at the root of the trees, and every tree that does not produce good fruit will be cut down and thrown into the fire."

Nicodemus glances back to the two women, wishing he could cup his hands over their ears so as not to expose them to this ranting and raving. To his dismay, both women are captivated by the scene before them. Martha stretches her neck straining to hear every word, while Zilia crouches in timidity and fear.

"We'll soon be past this frightful man," he assures them.

"Sh-h," hisses his mother. "Someone is asking him a question."

They miss the question, but the answer is broadcast loud and clear. "Repentance shows itself in the way we treat one another. The man with two tunics should share with him who has none, and the one who has food should do the same."

Nicodemus notices three Jewish soldiers. *Probably some of Herod's soldiers, hired to protect tax collectors. What a despicable bunch of humanity.*

One of those next to a soldier appears to be asking a question. John's answer rings out. "Don't collect any more than you are required to." A few listeners nod their heads in agreement.

Must be a tax collector. Now that is actually good advice.

Unbelievably a *soldier* asks a question. John's answer comes swiftly. "Don't extort money and don't accuse people falsely—be content with your pay." More approving nods bobble through the crowd.

"All have fallen short of obedience to Almighty God," the preacher proclaims once again. "All must come before him in humility. All need to come to the water to be baptized." He motions as if trying to draw them in. "Everyone!"

A few kneel in honor of John's comments. Others join in. The people seem to be ready to accept John himself as their Messiah. John hastens on. "But remember, I baptize you with water." He raises his arms, ready to emphasize his next point. "One more powerful than I will come, the thongs of whose sandals I am unworthy to untie; He will baptize you with the Holy Spirit and with fire." Several more men go to the water's edge for baptism.

John continues to preach and baptize, but Nicodemus finally puts enough distance between his travelers and the crowd so that John's words are now but a faint echo. The women are silent, leaving Nicodemus to wonder what they are thinking. He knows his mother will need time to mull it over. He, too, tosses the baptizer's words over in his head.

"Another is coming," John said, "more powerful than I am." What will the next one be like? Probably another Galilean. And here we are, going deeper into this backward country.

A breeze flutters across Nicodemus' face, but he is too steeped in bitterness to enjoy it, or to notice the lush green grass and vegetation coming into view.

They have traveled for a while when his mother breaks his train of thought. "Oh, look, Nicodemus. What a lovely grape arbor. Let's stop to buy a few clusters. They would be so tasty and fresh for our lunch. The farmer is right there in the second row. Oh, Nicodemus, let's do stop."

Reluctantly, Nicodemus pulls the donkeys to a stop. *Humph, you old donkeys will stop, but you couldn't be persuaded to go faster back there in the crowd. Stubborn old beasts.*

He walks down the vine row to approach the arborist. Half alarmed, the farmer swings around with a start. To ease the man's mind, Nicodemus quickly calls out.

"Shalom. You have a fine looking arbor."

The man frowns, as though a bit uncertain. He tilts his head, examining Nicodemus up and down.

Nicodemus continues to approach the vine grower. "We are traveling from Jerusalem. My mother is quite impressed with your healthy vines. She insisted that I stop and buy some grapes from you. Do you have a few clusters to spare?"

By now, Nicodemus is at the man's side. The farmer seems eased by the compliment and the prospects of a sale. He leans around Nicodemus to wave at the women who are taking in the whole scene.

"Why certainly." He breaks into a toothy grin. "I will find the most perfect grapes for a lady of such good taste. Oh, but what am I thinking? My baskets are all so large. Do you have a smaller basket to put them in?"

Nicodemus walks back to the donkeys to retrieve a small basket with just a few figs and one wrapped loaf of bread. "I think we can fit several grapes in here."

They agree on a price. Nicodemus thanks him, mounts his donkey and once again, they are on their way. Of course the women cannot wait and just have to have a few grapes to munch on as they continue the journey. Nicodemus likewise slips a small bunch into the fold of his tunic.

Well, at least they do grow good grapes out here. He chews two at a time. The sweetness of the fruit begins to sweeten his thoughts as well. *Ah, mother and her grapes. She'll be able to have all the grapes she desires in this productive land.*

For the first time, he relaxes and enjoys the countryside. He amuses himself with the memory of that night long ago when they visited with Hakkoz' family and Hakkoz threw his little temper tantrum over the grapes. Then there was the donkey dung incident with young Hakkoz. Not to mention Hakkoz' embarrassing behavior in the courtroom of the Sanhedrin. *Dear Hakkoz, what will ever become of him?*

Nicodemus wipes his sticky fingers on his tunic. He senses that they are drawing near to the sea. Is it the smell of fish or the lay of the land? Maybe it's the small roadside markets selling their baskets of fish. Yes, they must be getting closer to the sea.

Shielding his eyes, he looks for the sun. *It's directly overhead. Time for lunch.*

"This looks like a good place for lunch." He slows his donkey to a stop, dismounts, and leads the donkeys and women to a shady tree away from the fish stand. A few large stones will make a fine place to sit and rest while they eat.

"How would you ladies like some tasty dried fish for lunch?"

"Sounds delicious," smiles his mother, glad to hear her son's cheerier tone.

While the women retrieve the food basket and drink, Nicodemus purchases the fish.

They settle in, eating their lunch. "I wish we had more trees and plants and lush green land like this in Judea," says his mother.

"And fresh fruits and vegetables, not ones that are brought into the market," chimes in Zilia.

"But we have the Temple," says Nicodemus, defending his beloved Jerusalem.

"Yes," the ladies say together in plaintive tone.

Obviously, having the Temple nearby is not as dear to the women as it is to him. After a short silence, Nicodemus tries to pick up the conversation.

"The fish vendor tells me that we should reach the sea by late afternoon. We'll stay overnight and find a boat that sets out first thing in the morning. We should arrive in Capernaum just in time for lunch tomorrow. How does that sound?"

"I'm so excited. I haven't been back here for a long time. Let me see ..." Martha wrinkles her forehead, trying to think back. "How long *has* it been, Nicodemus?"

"Hmm. Well, I had just started as a disciple in the Sanhedrin—I guess it has been nine or ten years ago."

"Too long," she sighs wistfully.

Zilia speaks up. "I can't wait to meet your sister. I was ill when she came to the last Passover. Is your sister anything like you?"

Nicodemus and his mother look at one another, and then break out in laughter. Bewildered, Zilia looks from one to the other, wondering what she has said to evoke such a response.

Nicodemus gets control enough to speak. "My aunt Leah *looks* a lot like mother, but she is quite different in temperament. She is very, uh… outspoken. You never have to wonder what she is thinking. You might say she is ready to tell *you* what to think."

"Now, Nicodemus," his mother gives him a "shame-on-you" look.

"Well, you'll have to admit it's true."

His mother just smiles and lowers her head, slowly shaking it back and forth.

Zilia begins gathering things up and soon they are all ready to travel again. As they ride past the fish vendor, Nicodemus nods. The man calls out "Shalom, my friends."

Hmm, always "friends" when you cross their palms with money. Ah, but I mustn't be so negative. I mustn't ruin this time for Mother; besides, I'm rather looking forward to visiting my Aunt Leah, Uncle Laban, and Cousin Rebecca.

Traveling this last leg of the day's journey sparks a remembrance of times in Nicodemus' childhood when they used to go to Capernaum to visit his aunt and uncle and their crippled daughter, Rebecca. *Ah, dear Rebecca.*

His cousin is a few years younger than Nicodemus. He remembers her sweet smile when he used to bring in a handful of wild flowers to her. Nicodemus always felt like she favored him over his brothers. He paid attention to her. Once she said, "Nicodemus, you talk to me like I'm a real person, not like a stool to be ignored."

Nicodemus remembers the time he made her a little crutch. *I was determined to help her walk. She tried very hard to use it. One leg wasn't exactly crippled, but she sat so long because of the crippled leg that the "good" leg had little strength.*

He smiles as he remembers the days when he would carry her out to the big tree so she could enjoy the sunshine and fresh air. One of those days was when he showed her the crutch he had fashioned. Tears filled her eyes as she tried to express her gratitude to Nicodemus for his thoughtfulness. He helped her stand on the good left leg and placed the crutch under her right arm. He was so delighted that it fit perfectly.

"Now, put your crutch forward then hop on your other foot," he had said. But she would have fallen had he not caught her. As he supported the other side, he realized she needed not one, but two crutches for balance.

The next morning he found another sturdy walking stick and whittled it down just as Uncle Laban had taught him. He compared it to the other crutch and beamed with pride as he presented it to her by mid-afternoon.

Rebecca spoke words of gratitude, but he could hear discouragement in her voice. *She has to be persuaded to try again,* he had thought. *She's so frail, but I have to help her try.*

During the rest of their visit that summer, Nicodemus carried her outside and worked with her, exercising her legs, supporting her, and encouraging her. She didn't have the strength to lift the lame leg. She had to drag it along. Rebecca made some improvement and actually walked by herself with the crutches for a few feet, but the dragging limb slowed her down and took great effort.

What she really enjoyed were the times Nicodemus sat with her under the tree and talked. He pretended to be a great teacher of Israel and expound on the lessons he had learned in his yeshiva classes. She asked questions that made him feel very important.

Pondering childhood memories softens his furrowed brow and makes the journey pass quickly. *Perhaps I, too, will enjoy this visit, just as much as Mother.*

"The Sea of Galilee!" Martha shouts. "Oh, I feel like we are almost there."

Nicodemus can't help but chuckle at his mother's enthusiasm. *She really is excited about seeing her sister and friends from her childhood town. I'm happy for her. She has been gracious at home, but since Father's death, I know she has suffered in loneliness.*

He has a twinge of nostalgia as he remembers his father. He misses him too. In fact, he has a pang of dread as he realizes that both Father and Mother will be gone when he returns to Jerusalem. But enough of that. He must tend to the next set of duties for this trip.

"Did you sleep well, my ladies?"

"It's not like home, but quite adequate. And you, my son?"

"Likewise. I have two of our donkeys sold and two stabled for my return trip. An available boat awaits us on shore after we eat a bite. Looks like we have a lovely morning for sailing."

"Sounds like you've been quite busy this morning." His mother yawns.

After their breakfast, they walk the short distance to the shore. Martha takes Nicodemus' arm. "Thank you for taking such good care of us. This trip means a lot to me and you're a dear for leaving your work in Jerusalem to bring me here."

Nicodemus pats his mother's hand in acknowledgement. No further words are necessary.

Soon they are off on this "adventure." The morning wind blows in their faces, whipping their tunics here and there. No sitting on the knobby back of a donkey or sweating in the hot sun. Nicodemus leans back on the side of the boat, closes his eyes, and faces the morning sun.

He has to admit this is a refreshing change from his routine at the Temple. No civil cases to decide. No oral laws to describe and decipher. No immature, lazy students to contend with. Just enjoy the wide open space and the swirling waters of the sea.

He gazes across the boat stern to the shore where vendors tend their fruit and vegetable stands and children splash through the water. He watches fishermen gather and sort their fish from a night's catch; their nets spread out ready to be dried and mended. In the distance a couple of camels carry travelers into the desert.

The noisy wind makes it impossible to have conversation, except for necessities, so Nicodemus and the others sit back for the ride, lost in their own thoughts.

Nicodemus remembers other rides on this sea when, as a child, Uncle Laban used to take him on a boat ride to Tiberias where his uncle had business. One time they sailed to Magdala to purchase material for Aunt Leah and then on to another uncle's house for an overnight visit. Uncle Laban always had stories to tell. Nicodemus sat with wide-eyed wonder taking in every word, for his uncle had a way of spinning a story that made you see it come to life.

Another time, the wind blew so strong that it nearly tossed the boat over. Uncle Laban turned that one into quite a tale that he told over and over.

A strong gust turns one of the food baskets on its side. Nicodemus grabs the handle just in time to save its contents. He secures the basket as well as the other boxes and wrapped packages from blowing away.

The women seem at rest, so he leans back on a stack of blankets and looks up at the sails whipping in the wind. His mind drifts into oblivion as the monotony of the waves and gentle rocking of the boat lulls him into a lazy nap.

The boat suddenly tips up as it takes an extra wave from the wake of another boat. Nicodemus rolls around and catches his mother before she falls over. She cries out in astonishment at the jolt. Zilia rolls onto a pile of blankets and baskets. When they realize that everyone has survived the spill, all three have a good laugh and then settle in for the remainder of the trip.

Nicodemus realizes they are already in the wide part of the sea. Hills and mountains line the shore along the east and west. The wind felt good at the beginning of the trip, but now they feel whipped to death. It will be good to walk on land and escape the sun.

At last the north shore comes into view. Excitement builds as they make out houses and markets and the synagogue. It's as though the town is floating to them. For a moment, Nicodemus is the little boy anxious to relive long-ago memories, but as they glide toward land, he straightens up, adjusts his garments, and strikes his Pharisaic posture.

The synagogue in Capernaum is one of the better ones in the Galilee. The elders will insist on having Nicodemus teach them. They requested it even before he became a member of the Sanhedrin. They will be doubly honored to have him there now.

They disembark and Nicodemus pays a servant boy to load a cart with their belongings and pull it to the house of Laban and Leah.

CHAPTER 15
Visit in Capernaum

They love the place of honor at banquets and the most important seats in the synagogue; they love to be greeted in the marketplaces and to have men call them "Rabbi."
Matthew 23:6, 7

"Martha, my dear sister, you've come at last."

"Leah, oh Leah, I can hardly believe I'm actually here!"

A warm, emotional embrace helps both of them express what words cannot. To be together again in their growing-up place brings tears of joy. Nicodemus' mother turns to her brother-in-law. "Laban, it's so good to see you again."

"I'm glad you made it safely," beams Laban as he gives a big hug. "And you, my fine Nicodemus. Just look at you."

Nicodemus joins in the hugs. "It's been too long, Uncle Laban." As the two sisters catch up on their news, Nicodemus looks around for Rebecca. "And where is my favorite cousin?"

Leah motions, "She's waiting for you in the other room."

Nicodemus quickly searches for Rebecca. He finds her sitting on a pile of cushions. Her eyes brighten as Nicodemus enters the room, but he is struck by her pale, drawn face. She has aged drastically in these past ten years. He takes her outstretched hands and kisses them. He kneels beside her. "Rebecca, Rebecca. It's been way too long since I've seen you. We must get you out in the sunshine to enjoy God's creation."

"That sounds delicious," she says, her eyes sparkling with gratitude.

"I will clean up and be back to get you." Rebecca's dry, wrinkled face breaks into a familiar smile.

Nicodemus walks back to the room of happy noisy voices. After another round of hugs, Leah looks over at Zilia. Martha explains, "This is my sweet servant, Zilia. I hope it is all right for her to come, too."

"But of course. The more the better." Leah claps her hands. "Come, come Zilia, set your things in there." She whisks Zilia to an adjoining room and continues talking as she moves back and forth. "You must all be exhausted from that dreadfully long trip. That sea wind can whip you to pieces. Laban loves it, but I avoid it except when absolutely necessary. Zilia, I'm sure that long hair will be beautiful when you get it all untangled. Nicodemus, Laban will take you to get a bath. Ladies, come with me and we'll get you out of those terribly dirty clothes. When everyone is fit to be seen, we'll have a delicious lunch."

As Leah passes the kitchen, she calls out to her cook, "Gather up something for lunch, my dear; we have weary travelers to feed."

Zilia suppresses a soft giggle as they scurry off to clean up. "You see, Zilia," Nicodemus whispers. "Aunt Leah may *look* like her sister, but she is far more, hmm…what would one say?

"Unrestrained?" laughs Zilia.

By the time Leah is done with them, they do indeed feel refreshed and ready for lunch.

Nicodemus returns to Rebecca's room and sweeps her up in his arms as he did so long ago. He is startled by her feather-light frame. She seems so frail.

"We must fatten you up, my dear cousin." She smiles, delighted to have his attention once again. He carefully seats her at the table, fearful he might break her delicate bones.

Martha greets her with a hug and kiss. Nicodemus sees the same concern in his mother's eyes that he feels in his heart.

"Fried fish, fresh from the sea this morning. How does that sound?" Leah announces.

"Wonderful," they all agree.

91

They all dig into the fish and salad of lettuce, onion, and chives.

Laban dips his flatbread into a bowl of honey. He reminds them of his old joke about looking for his "Rachael." With the Bible names of Laban and Leah, he has always teased that Rachel must be somewhere. "Ah, but I have decided to be content with my Leah," he says, looking fondly at his wife.

Leah smiles at him, shaking her head in only mild amusement, for she has heard his quips many times before. "Perhaps we can find a Rachael for our Nicodemus," she says. "It is high time he has a wife. Maybe a good Galilean girl."

"Aunt Leah, I'm not a young man. I believe my time is past for such thinking."

"Nonsense. You need a good wife."

Nicodemus thinks she has gone to meddling now, so he decides to move this conversation in another direction. "Does this fish come from the fleet of Zebedee?"

"Indeed, and Zebedee's young son, John, is old enough to join the fishermen now," Leah answers.

"I remember him. Smart little boy—active too. He used to ask me all kinds of questions about the law, the prophets, why I dressed like I did." Nicodemus chuckles. "So, Uncle Laban, what do you hear from my Uncle Zeriah? Is he well?"

"I'm not so sure. I haven't been up to traveling the sea for some time nor is he up to making the walk to the sea from his village. How long has it been, Leah, since we saw Zeriah?"

"Too long," she sighs, pushing up a stray wisp of hair with the back of her hand, just like Nicodemus' mother does. She passes a bowl. "Do have some nuts. We'll have a melon later. And I haven't forgotten your precious grapes, my dear," she smiles at her sister. "Our neighbor said we could pick fresh bunches from his vines this afternoon."

"I've been thinking," continues Nicodemus avoiding Leah's banter, "I might pay a visit to Uncle Zeriah after the Sabbath."

"I think that would be wonderful," Laban responds. "He would be delighted to have you come to see him."

Leah sadly shakes her head. "You know, of course that his wife died two or three years back. We'll have to load you up with good things for him to eat. Poor man, so lonely." As soon as the words are out of her mouth, she glances up at Martha. Leah touches her sister's arm. "I know you've had such heart ache as well."

Nicodemus' mother lowers her eyes as she nods her head.

Leah breaks the awkward silence. "I'm sure you all would like a nice nap after your tiring journey."

"I promised Rebecca a breath of fresh air in the sunshine," says Nicodemus.

Rebecca looks up. "Thank you, Nicodemus, but a bit of a rest would be most welcome, and then we can have a good talk outside."

Leah fusses about, stacking the plates. "Come, ladies, I'll show you to your rooms. Laban, you help Nicodemus."

"I'm sure he knows where his room is. It hasn't moved in fifty years."

Nicodemus grins at the long-time antics of his aunt and uncle and plods up the steps. Yes, he is tired. He steps into the old familiar room once shared with his two brothers and looks out the small window, over the houses, to the lush countryside. It *is* quite lovely here he has to admit, even if it *is* Galilee. The thought crosses his mind that he has never been any farther north. *Perhaps someday.* He removes his outer cloak and stretches out on the prepared bed.

Ah, it feels so good to stretch out in a clean home with the joy of family nearby. He ponders the prospect of striking out across the sea to Magdala just like he and Uncle Laban used to do and then walking due west to his Uncle Zeriah's house. Would he remember the way on his own? Surely he would. He's been there many times before.

He drifts off, thinking of his uncle, but in his dream, he walks and walks and can't seem to get there. Finally, he goes into a deep sleep.

Nicodemus is aroused by talking and commotion downstairs. He looks out the window and realizes the shadows from the houses mean that the sun has moved farther west than he thought. He flings on his cloak and hurries down the stairs.

"What's going on?" he questions.

His mother is perfectly giddy as she chatters away. "We just returned from the orchard. The vines are so thick and healthy. I just can't grow them that way in Jerusalem. Look at these grapes, Nicodemus. They're huge. And taste. M-m-m, so sweet."

"I wish she went on about me that way," Nicodemus teases.

Uncle Laban chuckles. "Maybe you can grow some thick vines and turn a little sweeter, Nicodemus."

"Oh, Laban," Martha responds, patting his shoulder. "Here try one, and see for yourself."

"Uh-m, not bad," he says, acting surprised in spite of the fact that he tastes these grapes about every other day. "By the way, Nicodemus, you know the elders will expect you to teach in the synagogue on the Sabbath. Can we count on you?"

"Yes, of course." He strikes his Pharisaic posture on command.

"What will you speak about?"

"I'll have to think about it."

I must warn these people about John the Baptizer and whoever this other fellow is that is about to take his place. But I don't want to spoil our lovely visit with these concerns right now.

Nicodemus looks around for Rebecca.

"Your cousin is out on the back porch," Laban says with a knowing smile. Nicodemus wonders how Laban is still able to carry her about in his old age. Then he remembers how frail and featherlike she was when he picked her up earlier.

Nicodemus finds her sitting at the back of the house, gazing at the trees up the hill, the afternoon sun shining on the side of her thin face. *How content her demeanor. Oh, that we all could live such simple, uncluttered lives.*

"And what might you be dreaming of this fine summer afternoon?" he offers. Her face lights up at his voice. She turns to him with a ready smile.

"Nicodemus. Did you have a pleasant nap?"

"Very pleasant. You appear rested as well. How would you like to sit under that tree you have been watching?"

"That would be fine indeed," she says expectantly.

"Then it is done." He sweeps her up in his arms and carries her to their favorite tree. He nestles her carefully in a little hollow spot that just fits her where she can lean back on the tree.

"How is that?"

"Just perfect. Thank you, Nicodemus."

He finds a grassy spot to sit nearby, crossing his legs, and settling in for a good chat, just like they used to do as children.

"I remember many good talks under this tree," he says contentedly.

"Yes," she answers wistfully.

"I'm sorry it has been so long."

"Tell me about your work in Jerusalem."

"Well, I've been a member of the Sanhedrin for a while now."

"Yes, I heard about that."

"But the bulk of my work is teaching. I am on my seventh round of new disciples."

"Tell me about them."

He told of the smart, insightful students and the stubborn, cantankerous ones. He gave examples of their discussions, ways in which they followed the rules, and ways in which they failed miserably. Then it dawned on him that she had done what she always did—she had him talking about himself.

"And you, tell me about yourself."

"Oh, there's not much to tell. I do my sewing. Mama puts me at the table so I can help prepare the vegetables. Papa teaches me Hebrew lessons and teaches me the Torah." She looks up at Nicodemus, a bit embarrassed because such lessons are usually given only to the sons. "Well, you know, Papa never had a son to teach."

Nicodemus is careful not to show disapproval. "I'm sure you are a fine student."

"Tell me about Aunt Martha," she says.

They talk about Nicodemus' mother, and the death of his father and how his mother has coped.

Nicodemus entertains Rebecca with stories about Hakkoz and all his antics. She laughs at his tales and asks about Nicodemus' brothers and their children. She speaks of a good friend who visits her regularly and reports on others in the town that Nicodemus might remember from years past.

"Zebedee's sons are quite grown up," she tells him. "John is always off on some adventure."

"It's hard to think of him grown up. He was just a boy last time I was here."

"James takes more responsibility with the fishing fleet, along with Simon. Simon is married, you know."

"No, I didn't know that."

"Yes, his mother-in-law has a large home in town, so Simon and his wife have been living here now."

Nicodemus notes the western sky. "I believe the night is upon us."

"What a beautiful sunset. Let's stay just a few minutes longer." She takes in the gorgeous pinks and yellows as the sun slowly drops to a half circle beyond the grassy hill.

They join the others in the house who have already lit the lanterns for an evening of discussion and banter between Uncle Laban and Aunt Leah.

Yes, mother will thrive in this lively household. She will be good for Rebecca and it will make mother feel needed. Zilia will be good company for Rebecca as well.

On Sabbath evening, Nicodemus finds it gratifying to be in the home of his aunt and uncle. They celebrate in much the same way, but being in a different place with these loved ones makes it special.

The next day, Nicodemus dons his Pharisee garb and gives a stately nod to the town's people on the way to the synagogue. He secretly delights in their admiring glances and the snippets of conversation he hears about himself as he passes by. Laban enjoys the attention as well, smiling and nodding knowingly to friends and neighbors.

With the synagogue in view, Nicodemus' heart beats a bit faster. He has always enjoyed the small group of worshippers here. It feels so much more intimate than his synagogue near the Temple. Today, the synagogue seems smaller than he remembered; perhaps because he has grown taller and older. He is reminded that Father is not with them on this visit, but he must not think about that right now; he must stay focused on his lesson for the day.

"There's John, Zebedee's son," Laban whispers with surprise. "He and his father have had a parting of ways ever since John began to follow..."

The local rabbi stands to pronounce the beginning prayer, and then he leads the people in singing a psalm of prayer and devotion. Nicodemus glances at John. *I wonder what Laban was going to tell me about John.* Centering his attention back to the rabbi, Nicodemus leads out with his voice on the singing.

> "Teach me your way, O Lord,
> and I will walk in your truth;
> Give me an undivided heart,
> that I may fear your name."

Laban stands to read the sacred Scripture. He unrolls the scroll to Deuteronomy and reads slowly, squinting over the ancient words.

> "If a prophet, or one who foretells by dreams, appears among you and announces to you a sign or wonder, and

if the sign or wonder spoken of takes place, and he says, 'Let us follow other gods' (gods you have not known) 'and let us worship them,' you must not listen to the words of that prophet or dreamer. The Lord your God is testing you to find out whether you love him with all your heart and with all your soul. It is the Lord your God that you must follow, and him you must revere. Keep his commands and obey him; serve him and hold fast to him."

Ah, this will lead perfectly into what I need to say today. Nicodemus parades to the most visible location and sits in his teaching position. Straightening his back and scanning the group of worshippers with a dramatic pause, he begins his lesson.

"You have sung, as did King David, a psalm of praise and petition. You sang, 'Teach me your way, O Lord, and I will walk in your truth.' Indeed, today we speak of truth. What is true? What is false? What builds up? What tears down? How do we discern truth?

"Moses makes it clear in the reading we have just heard. Prophets or imposters may come to deceive you. They may even do special signs before your eyes, but it is a test, a test to see where your heart lies. We say, 'Hear, O Israel: The Lord our God, the Lord is one. Love the Lord your God with all your heart, and with all your soul, and with all your strength.'

"There are those who will come to deceive and lure us to serve other gods. We must not bend to their deception. We must not succumb to their evil power. Instead we must seek truth. We must revere the Lord our God, keep his commands, and obey him."

The people sit spell bound by Nicodemus. His delivery captivates them. His way with words impresses them. Their pride in him as "Martha's boy" is evident as they smile with approval.

Then Nicodemus begins to delineate the commands of God, the laws of Torah, the oral laws. Some look at the floor; some stare out the window. They fidget. Their shoulders sag. Their eyes glaze over. No matter how eloquently or how loud Nicodemus speaks, their faces betray their boredom.

Why aren't they paying attention? Why are they not thrilled to have a great teacher of Israel right here in their midst to bring enlightenment? This may be my mother's childhood home, but they are just as backward as any other small town inhabitants in the Galilee.

Nicodemus finally concludes his teaching. They sing a hymn and depart to their homes.

As they leave, the local rabbi comments. "Thank you for your fine teaching, Rabbi Nicodemus." But Nicodemus knows that his words fell, for the most part, on deaf ears.

He overhears one man mumble to another. "Yeshua of Nazareth is much easier to understand. He speaks with such authority."

Humph! Who is this one they speak of? Did they not listen to my warning? "Many will come to deceive."

Nicodemus marches out of the synagogue and down the path, Laban scampers to try to keep up with him.

Why did I think they could comprehend, much less appreciate my teaching? Ignorant, that's what they are, just ignorant farmers!

Nicodemus arrives at the house first. He storms up the stairs, and throws his robe on the bed. Laban comes tottering in trying to catch his breath after his brisk walk home. Martha and Leah catch up shortly, huffing and puffing themselves.

Martha slips into her room, but overhears the whispered tones of Leah and Laban.

"Why was he in such a hurry, Laban?"

"I don't think he received the praise he expected. Our people are simple folk, you know that. They work hard. They try to do the right thing. They help their neighbors. They can't be burdened down with all the laws that the Pharisees want to impose on them."

"Well, I think he did a fine job."

"Of course you do. He's your nephew." Laban grins.

Martha smiles as well, but her heart is breaking for her son. She is used to him and his ways as well as the ways of Jerusalem: the rabbis, the priests, the Roman soldiers tramping around. It is all so different here. Maybe she doesn't belong here either. A tear slips out the corner of her eye. "I must go to him," she whispers to herself.

Meanwhile, Nicodemus is trying to get control of his temper. He sinks to the bed and runs his fingers through his slightly graying hair. He hangs his head, trying to sort out his feelings. He hears soft footsteps coming up the stairs. *Mother.*

She enters quietly and sits beside him on the bed.

"You're upset, my son."

"I don't think I belong here."

"That's strange. I was just thinking the same of myself."

"My dear mother, you would fit in wherever you go. Everyone loves you."

"Nico, you make me blush."

"It's true. I think you will thrive here in your hometown. Don't even think of going back just yet. Of course, I hope you'll return sometime."

The corners of her mouth turn up slightly.

He pats her hand and continues, "Tomorrow, I shall set out for Uncle Zeriah's. When I return, you will have adjusted quite well. I'm sure of it."

CHAPTER 16
An Unexpected Turn

Pride goes before destruction, a haughty spirit before a fall.
Proverbs 16:18

Laban rises early the next morning to arrange a place for Nicodemus on a ship going to Magdala while Aunt Leah makes sure that her nephew is well fortified for his journey to visit Uncle Zeriah. Nicodemus pushes a cart of his belongings to the shore.

Laban reminds him, "I have many friends in Magdala. Just tell them you are the nephew of Laban from Capernaum. One of them will be glad to loan you a donkey. Now do you remember the way to your Uncle Zeriah's house?"

"Yes, Uncle, you reminded me of the way. Remember, I used to go there with you."

Laban pats his nephew on the back. "We will take good care of your mother. Leah and Martha will be good for one another."

"Yes, I'm sure you're right. Thank you for your hospitality."

"Shalom, dear nephew."

"Shalom, Uncle Laban."

With that, Nicodemus is off on another "adventure" as his mother would say. As the boat bobs along in the waters of the Galilee, Nicodemus amuses himself with thoughts of Aunt Leah and his mother chatting over breakfast, Rebecca enjoying the activity, and Uncle Laban pushing his empty cart home.

He leans back in the boat, satisfied that all is well. Even the debacle of his synagogue teaching lesson is already fading in his mind. Uncle Zeriah's village is too small to have a synagogue so he won't be "boring" anyone there.

The gentle lapping of the waves and rocking of the boat soon have Nicodemus dozing away. Before he knows it, the other passengers chatter about landing on the shore as they gather up their belongings.

The seashore at Magdala is teeming with activity—fishermen unloading their boats and market stands busy as beehives as buyers and sellers bargain with each other. Nicodemus remembers arriving here as a young man, intrigued by all the enterprise going on.

He sees no one with a donkey, but he spies a boy with a cart. He pays the boy to load his things and to help him find someone with a donkey. When the boy sees the shiny coins, he is much obliged to be helpful.

When a man with a donkey comes in view, Nicodemus decides he will drop Uncle Laban's name to see if it gets him anywhere.

"Shalom. I'm in need of a donkey for a few days. My Uncle Laban of Capernaum says I might find someone to help me."

"Laban? From Capernaum?"

"Yes. Yes, I'm his nephew."

"Well, how is the old man? I haven't seen him for some time." He bursts out with a hearty round of laughter. "His nephew, you say?"

"Yes. I just came from a visit. Uncle Laban hasn't made the trip for a couple of years. He doesn't think he's up to it."

"He's a good friend, a long-time friend. You tell him you saw 'Old Bones.' He'll know what you mean."

Nicodemus can't imagine the story behind that, but he's sure Uncle Laban will tell him later.

"You're not from around here, are you?"

"No. Jerusalem. Uncle Laban said someone might loan me a donkey?"

"Sure. I can do that." He turns to look at three of his donkeys. "Here's ole Hemlock. He's not much to look at but he's sure and steady."

"Thank you. I should have him back in three or four days."

Nicodemus loads two baskets on "Hemlock's" back and heads off for the two-hour walk to Uncle Zeriah's village.

The first little bit is easy because the land is fairly flat out from the shore, but as he plods along, the incline grows steeper—more rocks, too. The higher he climbs, the bigger the rocks.

I don't remember this. I hope I'm going the right way. Hemlock doesn't seem to be having any trouble. Surely I can do anything a donkey can do.

About that time, Nicodemus twists his ankle and bumps into Hemlock. The old donkey stumbles a bit but catches himself.

"I guess you *are* steady and sure, old fellow." Nicodemus pats his trusty steed. Across on the other hill are some grassy areas. A shepherd prods his sheep along.

"Why can't we be going that way? It sure would be better on the feet than these jagged rocks."

He breathes heavily with each step as he talks to Hemlock.

"Uncle Laban said 'due west.' I think we're still heading that way. I know I can do this," he gasps.

Every step on Nicodemus' twisted ankle causes him pain, making his steps less sure.

And then it happens. He turns to adjust a sagging basket on the donkey's back and doesn't see the pointed rock in front of him. He trips and falls with full force into Hemlock who staggers, regains his footing, and staggers again. The old donkey finally loses control and tumbles over, rolling down the hillside with Nicodemus cascading behind him. He hears himself screaming out as he rolls over and over down the rugged rocks.

Tumbles and screams are his last memories, and then—everything goes blank.

After what seems like hours, Nicodemus slowly becomes aware of a sound, someone close to him. *What is that sound? Someone breathing?* Nicodemus' head throbs with pain. He feels a dribble running down his cheek. He tries to reach up, but he can't seem to move his arm. The slight effort to do so causes his leg to shift. A sharp pain shoots up his right leg. His mind whirls.

Where am I? What's happening to me? Why can't I open my eyes? Why am I in so much pain?

One eye feels swollen shut but he manages to open the other eye just a slit. He sees a bit of blue sky with streaks of pink. *Is the sun setting? Will I lie here and die? Will wild animals come and tear me to pieces?*

He feels something touch his arm. Afraid and startled, he jerks, which arouses all the painful spots.

"Don't be afraid. I found you. You'll be okay. I'll stay with you."

Nicodemus grunts. He can't seem to form any words.

"I wasn't sure you were going to come back to the land of the living," the comforting voice says. "Apparently, you fell. I heard your call from the next hill. Your donkey didn't fare as well. I've washed your wounds and found an extra tunic in your bag. I had to tear some strips to make a bandage for your head. I need to get more strips. You've had a lot of bleeding."

The voice goes away. *Where is he?* Nicodemus tries to think, but his mind is a muddle. *Fallen... donkey... wound... blood. What is he talking about? Where am I?*

The voice returns. "I will wash the wound again."

Nicodemus feels the cool water running over his forehead. It stings, but it numbs the pain at the same time.

"Oil will help the blood congeal."

Nicodemus feels the thick oil. He makes a soft sighing sound.

"I will have to lift your head just a bit to wrap the cloth around your wound."

Nicodemus let out a groan.

"I know you're in pain, but I must wrap it to keep out the flies and insects."

The only thing that eases the pain is the gentle, soothing voice.

"Now your leg is another story. You have a broken bone or a bad sprain under that wound. I must set it. We don't want to leave it like this too long. I'm putting a rag in your mouth for you to bite down on. I'm sorry. It will be painful, but I must reset your leg."

He doesn't know how I feel. It can't be any worse than it already is.

Oh, but it could.

The kind voice moves to Nicodemus' leg. The man takes hold of the lower shin with one hand and just below the knee with his other hand and then he twists and pulls. Nicodemus bites down on the rag in his mouth which re-initiates the throbbing in his head.

"I'm so sorry, but I must do it one more time."

"No," Nicodemus tries to say, but the words won't come and even if they did, he has this rag in his mouth. Again, he feels the hands on his ankle and knee, the twist, and the pull."

He stiffens; he grunts, he feels faint. *Please don't tell me you have to do it again.* Nicodemus fades in and out of consciousness. He "comes to" long enough to realize he is being moved.

"My friend has come to help me move you closer to me for the night and get you off of the rocks. We will fix you a soft bed."

At last he is settled on a soft wool hide. Something is propping up his leg. Another soft thing provides a pillow to elevate his head. Finally the pain eases enough that he sleeps.

CHAPTER 17
A Miserable Night

Day and night your hand was heavy upon me;
my strength was sapped.
Psalm 32:4

In the night, Nicodemus rouses enough to realize that it is dark. His whole body feels racked with pain—throbbing here, sharp darts there, dull aches everywhere else. Once again he tries to reconstruct what has happened and where he is.

In the midst of his suffering, he becomes aware of a foul smell. *Is it me? My wounds? Something nearby?*

He can't seem to get awake enough to reason, much less think straight. He weaves in and out between a dream world and reality.

The break of day, along with animal noises, and a man's voice arouse Nicodemus. The voice is high pitched with a slight nasal tone. *Not my man's voice.* For a fleeting moment he panics. *Where's my man?*

Nicodemus hears movement and baa-ing. *Sheep. I'm lying right next to sheep!*

The nasal-sounding man calls out to his sheep. The sheep move out. Their hooves gather momentum. *Are they stampeding? Will I be trampled along with all my other troubles?* He feels the reverberation of their stamping hooves, but none touch him. He's able to raise his head slightly and open his one-slit eye enough to see their wooly hides moving past him.

Oh the smell. Yes, that is the foul smell he remembers from in the night. He rolls his head over the other way. *I've slept next to a sheep pen all night. Oh, dear Adonai, where am I? How have I ended up in this nightmare? Please let me go to sleep and wake up with all this behind me.*

The rhythmic pounding of sheep hooves fades like an echo in the distance. Before Nicodemus can relax, he hears more baa-ing, more movement, but they aren't going anywhere, just moving around. Nicodemus senses that there is a wall between him and the sheep. He hears a voice, a quiet voice, talking to the sheep. *It's my man! He hasn't left me. Oh, what comfort.*

The man talks to his charges as though they are his friends, as though they understand him. Their baa-ing grows softer. Nicodemus hears a creaking sound. A gate perhaps?

"I see you are awake, my friend. I won't ask if you slept well. I know you are in much pain."

Nicodemus opens his mouth and tries to find words, but all he can manage is a pitiful grunt. The kind man bends over him.

"You need to drink water. I have just a little left."

Nicodemus feels the container against his parched lips. It tastes good to him. *How can something so simple taste so good?*

"Not too much, sir. I must use a bit of it to clean your wounds."

Nicodemus feels the strip around his head loosen. The man lifts Nicodemus' head to unwrap the bandage. With the last layer, the cloth pulls at the dried blood. Nicodemus grunts. The man soaks the bandage with a few drops of water and eases the bandage away.

"It looks better. The gap is closing a little. The Lord made our bodies in a miraculous way to heal themselves."

The man dribbles a few more drops of water on the wound and uses the middle layers of cloth strips to wipe it off. He wipes Nicodemus' "good eye" with the damp cloths to remove the crustiness.

"We'll wrap you up with a new bandage today."

Nicodemus forces his eye open a little farther to have a first look at his benefactor. A young man; brown, curly hair, maybe you could say bushy hair, hangs just above his shoulders. A short curly beard as well. The man tightens his lips as he tears the cloth in long strips.

A shepherd. A smelly shepherd. Nicodemus smiles to himself as he thinks of his words to his father that day so long ago. *Well, father, this smelly ole' shepherd has saved my life.*

107

The shepherd looks over at Nicodemus. His eyes are as gentle as his voice.

"I'm Michael," he smiles. "You took quite a fall down that mountain. Perhaps you are ready to be propped up so you can see the sheep and the hillside. It will do you good."

Squatting down on Nicodemus left side, Michael slides his right arm around Nicodemus' back to help him sit up. Michael pulls him up and back to lean against the wall of the sheep fold.

For a moment, Nicodemus feels light headed. Michael holds him in place until the world stops spinning, then releases him slowly.

Nicodemus grunts his gratitude, though his throat is dry and his voice raspy.

Michael nods to him. "My sheep are anxious to get out of their sheep fold. I put you on the east side of the wall so you could enjoy the warmth of the morning sun. By afternoon, you will welcome the shade of the wall. A running stream is about an hour away. I will bring back some fresh water for you after the sheep have settled and grazed a while. Here's a piece of bread and one more swallow of water."

Michael digs in his pouch as he talks and brings out a small piece of bread. It is all Nicodemus can do to choke down the bread, but he is hungry and it tastes good to him. He savors the remaining drops of water and eases back to his propped up, sitting position.

Nicodemus manages a half smile and nods his head in gratitude to Michael. Michael adjusts Nicodemus' leg and walks back to the gate. The shepherd talks as he moves so as not to frighten the sheep. He taps on the gate as he opens it and continues talking to them while calling out their names.

They have names?

Nicodemus can't see them but he feels the movement of their hooves on the ground. Slowly, methodically, they follow the shepherd out the gate and up the hill like a mother hen with her chicks.

CHAPTER 18
A Day in the Sun

The Lord is my shepherd. I shall not be in want.

Psalm 23:1

Nicodemus watches the shepherd lead his flock to the green pasture just beyond the sheep pen. The sheep spread out and find their own little patches of grass in which to graze, munching awhile here and there. Michael moves among them, talking, petting them on the head, bending over to examine one more closely.

A psalm comes to Nicodemus' mind.

The Lord is my shepherd; I shall not be in want.

He makes me lie down in green pastures.

A sense of peace flows over Nicodemus for the first time since his fall. He sits mesmerized by the sheep and their shepherd. Out of his good eye, he looks up to the blue, blue sky. Billowy clouds drift lazily as the morning sun rises. He leans his head back and closes his eye. The warmth of the sun feels soothing on his face as it dries out the moist, chill air of the morning.

Nicodemus thinks about his mother, Uncle Laban, Aunt Leah, and dear cousin Rebecca. *They think I'm already at Uncle Zeriah's house by now.* He relives the non-eventful ride across the Sea of Galilee and the talk with the man about his donkey.

"Old Bones," is that what he told me to tell Uncle Laban? No telling what that story is all about.

He thinks about walking with the donkey. *Hemlock? Was that his name? Yes, Hemlock. Well, at least I can remember something; I haven't lost my mind completely.*

Then came the fateful walk to his uncle's house. *What went wrong? Did I take a wrong turn? I thought I was going due west, just like Uncle Laban told me, but I didn't remember that rocky mountain from years gone by.*

The turn of his ankle, the trip, the fall—it all comes back to him. Rolling over and over, falling, falling, jagged rocks, bruises, pain. Suddenly Nicodemus jerks and opens his eye. He looks around. *The sheep. Where are the sheep?* He scans the hillside. Two last sheep go leaping out of sight.

He must have drifted off to sleep. How long? He looks at the sun. It must be about four hours since sunrise. *What was it that Michael said? A running stream is about an hour away? An hour there, an hour back. What's taking him so long? Haven't those sheep settled and grazed enough by now?*

He takes a deep breath and lets it out nosily. The thrust of it hurts. Must be some broken ribs too, or bruises. Nicodemus realizes he hasn't really taken an inventory of his injuries. No one is in sight so he pulls open his cloak and stares at his blood-stained tunic and his hands and arms. Yes, plenty of bruises and scrapes.

Fingering the bandage on his head, he traces the wrapping all the way around, angled just above his left eye. He touches the spot on his forehead where he imagines the wound to be located. It feels dry. That's good—no more blood oozing out.

He tries to lean forward, inching slowly. He can almost reach the sheep hide thrown over his legs, but his fingers can't quite grasp it. Placing the heels of his hands on the ground near his hips, he makes great effort to scoot his hips backward so he can sit up straighter. It takes nearly all the strength out of him. Something in his leg lets go with a sharp pain. He grimaces and spontaneously lets out a cry, then stops midstream to catch his breath and rest for a moment.

He is determined to throw that sheep hide off and have a look. Besides he's getting hot from the sun. With renewed effort, he leans forward. Victory! He clutches the hide and pulls it to the side.

He stares at his leg in disbelief. His right leg has swollen almost twice the size of the other leg. Blood soaked bandages encircle the wound and more strips of cloth hold two sticks tight on either side of his leg and foot to hold it in place and keep it from twisting. His foot is dark from bruising or lack of blood flow, he isn't sure which. For a moment, he feels nauseous. He looks away and tries to breath. Repositioning himself, he straightens his back in an effort to open the air flow. Gradually, he lowers himself back to his propped up position, heaving a great sigh of relief.

He dozes again and awakes with the sun directly overhead. His tunic is wet with perspiration. Beads of sweat break out across his scalp and run through his hair. His arms feel wet, his lips dry and parched. Flies and gnats swarm around his head and mouth. He swats them away but they come back.

Where is that shepherd? He promised me water. Where's my water?

"Where's my water?" he mumbles.

"Where's my water?" he cries out.

"Where's my water?" he croaks.

"Water, water, water," he moans in near delirium.

He looks up the hillside and sees someone coming. Is it a mirage? Has he gone completely mad?

The figure comes closer. He swats at more gnats and rubs his eye, straining to see the man coming. At last, he can tell—it's his shepherd!

The shepherd picks up his pace when he sees Nicodemus suffering.

"Where have you been, man?"

"It's a long way," pants Michael from his sprinting effort, "and I must have the sheep settled before I leave them." He hands Nicodemus the water jug. "I can't be gone long. Some want to stray and then they get in trouble."

And what about my trouble? Nicodemus wants to say, but thinks better of it. This man is his only source of water.

Michael glances at the exposed leg. His forehead burrows into serious wrinkles as he assesses the swelling. He reaches in a bag not far from Nicodemus and pulls out another piece of fabric. For the first time, Nicodemus is aware that all these strips of bandages have come from one source—his own extra tunic. *I guess I won't need it anyway. Good thing I had it along.*

Studying the bag, Nicodemus realizes it is the one Uncle Laban loaned him. He wonders if anything else is left.

"Any food in that bag?" he asks Michael.

"A couple of figs," he answers. "Most everything else fell out."

Michael is still fumbling around with the fabric piece, folding it this way and that.

"This is my water jug. Was it left in the basket, too?"

"No, I found it down the hill a little farther."

Michael works to loosen the leg bandages. He takes his own wineskin from around his neck and carefully drips wine on the cloth with which he had been working until it is saturated. He places it on Nicodemus' leg and tucks it under gently.

"Isn't that a waste of wine?" Nicodemus asks.

"We need to get the swelling down." Michael studies it seriously. He glances up at the head wound and seems satisfied that it needs no more attention. After refilling Nicodemus' water jug, Michael pulls a large piece of bread from his cloak and picks up the two figs from the basket. "These will need to last you until sunset. Eat them sparingly. I will be back with the sheep just before the setting of the sun. Rest if you can." And off he goes.

Nicodemus stares as his shepherd walks off and leaves him, *again*. The image grows smaller and smaller the farther he goes. Nicodemus sits there stunned.

My servants would never leave me like this. They would be attending to my every need. I'm so weary. I'm hungry. I'm tired. I'm dirty and smelly, just like those sheep, just like their shepherd, just like this stinking sheep pen. Another big sigh.

He looks down at the bread in one hand and the figs in the other. He takes a big bite of bread, and then remembers that it must last all afternoon. He chews slowly, trying to savor every bite. Where can he protect the rest of the bread to keep for later? *Some place where those incessant flies won't eat it first.* He finds a spot in his cloak to stash the bread and wraps it up tightly with one of the figs.

Now to savor the other fig. Studying this one fig, he ponders the fact that when he was at home in his luxurious house, he had all the figs he wanted and someone to serve him. In Jerusalem, he had plenty of water to ceremonially cleanse his hands, and abundant food to go with his figs. *Here I am languishing over this one puny, shriveled fig.* He takes very tiny bites to make it last longer

Sparingly, he sips water from his water jug. Closing his eyes, he relishes the trickle that moistens his dry throat and parched lips.

His hunger moderately satisfied, he continues to contemplate his condition. His hands are dirty from the fall, blood stained like everything else. *I should have washed before I ate.*

If the other Pharisees could see me now, they would be clicking their tongues at my disobedience to the law. You must wash before you eat, be ceremonially clean. Always. For an instant he considers pouring drops of his precious water on his hands. *Well, my "friends" haven't been injured and left in a sheep field to fend for themselves. Besides, the damage is done, I've already eaten.*

Laws—he hasn't thought about the law in days. *Days? Wait, what has it been? Only a day and a half? No, not even a whole day. It seems like I've been sitting in this spot for weeks.*

He contemplates what his friends would be saying if they saw his plight. "What wrong have you done, Nicodemus? For what sin are you being punished, Nicodemus?"

Just like Job, he would sit in condemnation. But also like Job, he would assure them that he had done no wrong. Or had he done some misdeed? Had he failed in keeping one of the laws? After all, he prided himself in keeping *every* law.

His body is stiff and sore. Lying in this position so long has made him numb. *I have to move again.* He tries bracing himself on his hands as before and scooting back. *It's easier this time—not so dizzy, didn't take my breath away.*

Slowly, painfully he leans toward his knees. So far, so good. With all the strength he can muster, he pulls his shoulders up, straightens his back and holds the position until his breathing eases. He rounds his back again, reaching for his knees. Up and down, each time stretching a tiny bit farther. *That's probably enough for now,* he sighs. His head throbs.

Nicodemus eases back against the wall, glad for its shade, for now the sun has moved to the west casting shadows across his legs. The rolled-up blanket or sheep hide, or whatever it is behind him, has shifted. With great effort he pulls and pushes it this way and that to find a comfortable position. At last, he leans back and closes his eyes, welcoming a time of rest.

His fitful sleep comes and goes. Every time he rouses, he is reminded of his plight. A flock of starlings overhead stirs him enough to open his eye and become fully awake. Hunger pangs gnaw at his stomach. Thirst scratches at his throat. He eases himself up on his elbow enough to reach for his water jug. The water runs down his throat in refreshing gulps and dribbles through his beard. He remembers the precious bread and fig. Are they still there? Have insects beaten him to them? Or in his fuzzy mental state, has he already eaten them?

He sees the bulky lump in the spot where he had stored his treasures. Carefully he unwraps the precious supplies. "Yes," he sighs in gratitude. "Thank you for supplying." It dawns upon him that this is the first time he has invoked the Lord Almighty. Not only has he not washed, he has not even given thanks nor said his three daily prayers. *Wretched man that I am.*

He whispers a prayer of thanks from the Psalms and breaks the bread in small pieces, once again savoring every morsel. He thinks about the poor blind beggar at the Temple. *Is this what his life is like each day? Does he grapple for every morsel he eats?*

He glances at his legs and realizes that the shade has not only covered his legs, but also has covered a large patch of ground beyond him. The sun is setting low in the sky.

Where is that shepherd? Will he leave me alone for the night? What am I to him? He has no idea of my importance in the Temple. Humph, he could probably care less for Jerusalem or its "important" people. I'm no better than these sheep. In fact, I seem to be less than his sheep. He's been off with them all day, leaving me to rot away in this filthy place.

Readjusting his position reminds him that in his injured situation, he could not easily be moved anywhere. *Will I have to stay here indefinitely?*

It dawns on him that he no longer smells the putrid dung of the sheep pen. *I smell the same as the sheep, I suppose. I've just blended in.* A disgusted snort from his nose releases his pent-up disgust with his situation and makes him imagine he is ridding himself of these smells.

Loneliness is about to overtake him when suddenly, he hears an unusual sound coming over the hill. He tilts his head trying to listen more intently. *Something rolling and rumbling. What could it be? Not an animal. No thunder clouds in the sky.*

He raises himself up enough to have a look up the hill. He sees nothing, but the sound continues. Finally, an object appears on the top of the hill. He can't quite make it out. Whatever it is, it's coming his way.

Soon a man appears, pulling something. Is it his shepherd? But what is that thing he is pulling? The rolling, rumbling thing? At the top of the hill, the shepherd moves around behind the thing and follows it. The closer he comes, the better Nicodemus is able to make out some kind of cart. Yes, it's his shepherd; he's pushing a cart. Along behind him comes another person, a shorter person.

Nicodemus squints his one good eye to see the images coming toward him. He presses his hands on the ground as before to pull himself up into a sitting position. His heart beats a bit faster with the excitement of seeing another living being and the puzzlement about the cart. And who is this other young person?

As they draw near, Nicodemus can feel the rolling of the cart and the pounding of sheep hooves. The shepherd shouts something to the young boy and the boy turns to the sheep, slowing their fast pace. The shepherd stops the cart, takes an object out, and hands it to the boy. The shepherd throws a quick wave to Nicodemus while holding on to the would-be runaway cart. He holds it steady as he rolls it down the hill.

Shepherd and cart arrive first. "Shalom, my friend," he calls as he rolls the cart in place. He is out of breath and places his hands on his knees until his heavy breathing eases. The boy arrives with the object that turns out to be a water skin, apparently a full skin by the way he labors in carrying it. The boy bends over, also taking in big gulps of air.

About the time they both get in control, the sheep begin to arrive. The shepherd quickly walks out to them, once again slowing their pace and speaking gently to them.

The boy shyly studies Nicodemus from afar. He looks back at the shepherd who is busy with the sheep, and then looks down as though pondering what to do next, casting side glances at this strange injured man. Finally, he saunters over to the shepherd to say something. The shepherd motions to the sheep; the lad gathers in a few strays.

The shepherd leads the flock closer, just outside the sheep fold where Nicodemus lies. "I see you're still alive, my friend," he says, smiling.

"Just barely." Nicodemus raises his eyebrows which reminds him of his bandaged head injury.

"I brought you a cart. Well, actually my son brought the cart from our house. Oh, and this water skin. We filled it with water from the stream. Plenty of water to drink and to wash your wounds."

The thoughts of "plenty of water" is music to Nicodemus' ears. Never did he think he would ever want for water in this way.

The boy walks over to his father. "This is my son, Benjamin." Benjamin lowers his chin. He can't be more than ten or twelve years old, but strong and handsome under his dirty face. He rolls only his eyes over to acknowledge Nicodemus.

"Shalom, Benjamin."

"Hello, sir," the boy mumbles.

Nicodemus watches patiently as shepherd and son examine each sheep before sending them in to the sheep fold. Michael gives instruction to his son as they pick briers and pesky insects out of their wool. They examine every hoof and anoint each cut with oil. Michael and Benjamin continue to talk to the sheep, pat them on the back, and watch them trot obediently through the gate.

"We brought more wool skins," the shepherd reports to Nicodemus as he pulls out a thorn from one sheep leg. "Benjamin, after our friend has a last drink, you can refill his water jug for him."

Nicodemus has been so enthralled with having company and watching all that has transpired that he had forgotten about his water. He reaches for his water jug and enjoys the last drops.

The boy cautiously approaches Nicodemus, carrying the water skin.

"I'm sure you're a great help to your father, Benjamin." No response.

Benjamin tips the water skin to refill Nicodemus' jug. He turns his head toward Nicodemus' leg.

"I fell down that hill over there, the rocky one." Benjamin nods his head in acknowledgment and glances over at the craggy hill.

"Thank you for bringing the water, and the cart, too," says Nicodemus, though he has no idea why they have brought this cart. He certainly can't pull it and doesn't have anything to put in it, even if he could pull it.

The shepherd stands up and rubs his back after being bent over the sheep so long. "Now to attend to you, my friend."

Nicodemus is suddenly aware that he has not told the shepherd his name. *Will he know who I am if I tell him my name? Will he give me greater honor, tend to me more carefully or will it change his calm, friendly attitude? Will he be intimidated to be in my presence?*

Who do I think I am? I look like anything but a dignified member of the Sanhedrin. A great Jerusalem teacher of the law would not be lying in the mud, bandaged and bruised. Oh, well. Why not? Let's see, what did he say his name is? Michael? Yes, that's it, Michael.

"Michael, I don't think I have told you my name."

"No, sir." Michael unwinds the bandage from Nicodemus' forehead.

In his most prestigious voice, Israel's great teacher says, "I'm Nicodemus."

"Yes, sir."

Well, that was uneventful. Why did I think he would know me? He's out here in these hills all the time. He probably lives in an obscure little village, totally oblivious to great teachers and great teachings.

Michael unwinds the last bit of cloth, carefully examines the wound, and declares it improved. "I think I will wash it and apply more oil. It's looking better."

Michael walks over to Benjamin who has the water skin flung around his neck, and brings it back to his patient. He reaches in Nicodemus' borrowed bag and pulls out what's left of his spare tunic, tearing another strip from it. Using this as a wiping cloth, Michael tips the water skin and douses the cloth with a bit of water. Gently he wipes away the dried blood.

"And so, Master Nicodemus, have you had a good day?"

It was good to hear his name, even "Master" Nicodemus. Perhaps this backward shepherd does know his fame. *But good day? I think not!*

"Well, I've been burning in the mid-day heat and practically dying of thirst and hunger. Every muscle in my body is aching and I've been left here in this filth. If you call that a good day, then I guess I could say, 'Yes, I've had a delightful day.' "

Michael is unaffected by Nicodemus' sarcasm.

"Your muscles are working better. You are able to sit up by yourself. That is a good sign."

He continues working as he talks. He daubs oil on Nicodemus' forehead.

Nicodemus studies the shepherd as he tends to the wound. *Young man—can't be more than thirty. Concerned expression in those deep-set eyes. Handsome face like his boy, tanned from days in the hillside sun. Definite Galilean accent, but such a gentle voice.* Nicodemus is reminded of the comfort of that voice, shortly after the fall, when he couldn't get his eyes open enough to see.

"I think we will leave the bandage off tonight. The flies will not bother you so much at night and it will be good for the air to heal your wound." He casts the blood-stained cloth aside and stands up to tear another piece of cloth.

"Now let's have a look at that leg." Michael's soothing voice and focused caring attention confuses Nicodemus somehow. This shepherd is so in charge of the situation that it renders Nicodemus feeling helpless, out of control. What choice does he have but to succumb to the care of this smelly shepherd of Galilee?

Nicodemus has been sitting up, supporting himself on his hands for a while now. He feels weary and weak. "I need to lie back down." Michael helps him as he eases onto one elbow. He feels himself shaking and lies back in exhaustion.

Michael waits until his patient is settled and then he unwraps the bandage from around the leg. Nicodemus feels some discomfort with the manipulation of his leg, but he is so weary that he doesn't even have the strength to complain, other than a soft moan. He flinches when he feels the cool water washing directly on his leg. Now the shepherd wipes it tenderly around the edges and pats the wound itself.

'The swelling is some better," he mumbles, almost to himself. After he sprinkles the wound with wine, he pats it dry and daubs it with oil.

"I'm making a poultice with some herbs I gathered. It will help it to heal."

Nicodemus hears him tear more strips of cloth and re-bandage the leg. He remembers his father using poultices with patients. Nicodemus would comment but doesn't have the strength to talk anymore.

"I think we'll wait on the cart until morning," Michael says to his son, Benjamin.

Nicodemus fades in and out while Benjamin and Michael settle the sheep. He hears Benjamin's high-pitched voice talking to the sheep.

"Benjamin, my son."

"Yes, Papa."

"Tomorrow, I need you to take the sheep on this hill to graze for a while. You've been with me several times now. The sheep know your voice. You are good with them. You have learned well. I'll take care of the poisonous weeds in the morning."

"Where will you be while I watch the sheep, Papa?"

"I'll take the cart around the base of the hill and meet you on the next hill. We'll refill the water jug and the water skin at the stream again. I'll be within sight."

Nicodemus hears bits and pieces of their conversation. It reminds him of the talks he used to have with his father. The thought of his father touches a soft, vulnerable place in his heart. His eyes moisten. He feels so alone.

CHAPTER 19
A New Day

*Who may ascend the hill of the Lord? Who may stand in his
holy place? He who has clean hands and a pure heart.*
Psalm 24:3, 4

In the early dawn, Nicodemus rouses just enough to
remember his plight. Muscles ache and joints are stiff. He
rolls his head over to see the shepherd walking up the hill. In
his half-drowsy state, Nicodemus wonders if Michael is
leaving him, but he has enough sanity to realize that the sheep
aren't with him. Their soft baa-ing and shuffling around give
signs of their presence in the sheepfold.

*Surely he won't leave his sheep, but where is that shepherd
going? What could he be doing at this unearthly hour of the morning?*
Nicodemus' mind is too weary to think clearly and he drifts
back into a light sleep.

"Master Nicodemus," he hears his name. He opens
his eyes to see the face of his shepherd. It seems like only a
short moment ago that he saw Michael walking up the hill. He
looks around once again, trying to get his bearings.

"It is morning, my friend. Time for you to join us on
our journey today." Nicodemus frowns, unable to
understand. "You will travel in the cart. We'll pack blankets
under your leg to soften the rough ride."

Nicodemus can't imagine trying to get up and move
himself. Even if he could, how demeaning, riding around in a
cart! *Ah, well, nothing could be more demeaning than to have spent two
nights on the dirty ground next to a sheep pen with their confounded
noises and smells.*

"But first, I'm sure you would like to clean up and
feed your hungry stomach."

Now that sounds good. With closed eyes, he raises his
eyebrows and grunts while he nods his head.

When the shepherd goes to the cart to gather
supplies, Nicodemus makes every attempt to get himself into

a sitting position as he did yesterday. Every muscle feels tight and bruised. It's like starting all over again. With great effort, he finally succeeds in sitting up. The shepherd stuffs something behind his back to give him support.

"Now, if you will hold your hands over this way, I'll pour water on them and you can clean up a bit."

Nicodemus very willingly reaches out, allowing the water to pour over his hands and on up his arms. He rubs them vigorously in an attempt to remove the dirt and blood stains. He splashes the water on his face, being careful with the cut to his forehead. Michael pours water one more time to give him a final rinse.

"Is there water left to drink," Nicodemus asks, remembering his low supply from yesterday.

"Yes, I filled all our water skins and we will be to the stream by lunchtime."

Michael reaches in his pouch and pulls out the fresh bread, dried fish, and grapes that Benjamin brought the day before. *A feast for the eyes!* Nicodemus' joy does not go unnoticed.

"This looks good to you?" Michael says.

"Aye, indeed." Nicodemus smiles for the first time, feeling genuine gratitude. He is suddenly aware that he can open his bad eye slightly now.

"Come join us, Benjamin." Michael motions. "After all, you brought us these fresh supplies."

Nicodemus wonders how Benjamin knew to bring more food and the cart "How did he know of our need?" Nicodemus asks.

"I sent word by my shepherd friend who was with us the first night."

He thinks of everything.

Benjamin sits beside his father. Michael closes his eyes, lifts his head, and prays. "We give thanks, Oh Lord, for your bountiful blessings."

A simple prayer, but Nicodemus is grateful.

Michael breaks the bread and hands pieces to Nicodemus and Benjamin. Nicodemus savors every bite. Fish

122

has never tasted so good. As he looks down at the grapes, wonderful memories of his mother flood over him. At the thought of her, he feels sudden panic. *Mother will worry where I am and what has happened to me. How can I get word to her that I'm safe?*

Then he remembers that this is only the third day since his departure. She won't expect him until just before Sabbath. He sighs in relief until he reasons that he might not be able to return until after Sabbath. *Oh, well, I can't think about that right now.* He munches another grape, enjoying its sweet flavor and thinking of his mother. *"Grapes will help you feel better," she would say.* His eyes smile.

After they feast on the delicious fare, Michael checks Nicodemus' forehead. "It looks good this morning. We'll wrap it only one time around, just to keep the flies away."

Nicodemus has forgotten about the impossible task of trying to get in the cart, but he is reminded when Michael and Benjamin start pulling wooly skins and blankets out of it. They bring the cart over right next to Nicodemus and lay a large sheep skin in it.

"You can rest a moment while I tend to the sheep. They are usually out of the sheepfold by now. They're getting anxious," he tells Nicodemus.

Michael opens the gate to talk kindly to his sheep; patting this one, rubbing the ears of that one. The sheep crowd in toward the gate, anticipating their departure. The baa-ing grows louder. Benjamin tries to assist, talking to the flanks toward the back. He draws them away from the gate to alleviate the crowded exit.

Michael pushes the lead sheep back gently, talking to them continuously. "Hold on, my dears. You will be grazing shortly. We have other business to take care of. Easy, old girl. Back up a bit. Yes, we'll go soon." He continues patting them as he and his son ease out the gate and close it.

They walk back to Nicodemus and adjust the position of the cart.

"Can you sit up again?"

Nicodemus dreads the thought of trying to get onto the cart, but he pulls up in obedience. Michael bends down behind Nicodemus.

"Okay, Benjamin, my man, you take care of Master Nicodemus' leg and I'll lift his body."

Michael slides his arms under Nicodemus arms and lifts him up. Nicodemus is able to balance on the heel of his good foot as Michael swings him onto the edge of the cart. Benjamin carefully lifts the injured leg as Michael helps Nicodemus scoot back into the cart. Michael quickly rolls up a blanket to place behind Nicodemus head and back. Nicodemus collapses onto the blanket. Benjamin and Michael both help situate Nicodemus and prop up the injured leg.

Nicodemus' heart races wildly, while his head and leg throb, sending him into a dizzy frenzy. If he had the slightest notion of getting up and walking around any time soon, this episode certainly squelched that idea.

Michael pats his arm. "We'll give you a moment to rest, my friend."

Nicodemus listens with his eyes closed as Michael calls the sheep. "Ah, yes, my impatient ones, it is time for us to depart. Slowly, slowly. Come, we will find some good grasses for you to munch on. Watch yourself, Buck. Bramble, come on, don't get behind."

Oh, yes, the sheep have names, he remembers.

"Benjamin, you lead them on, I'll get the cart. We'll meet around on the next hill."

By this time, Nicodemus is feeling better. The throbbing has subsided. He is able to open his eyes without the world spinning around.

"You look much improved. Are you ready for the ride?"

Do I have a choice? Nicodemus grunts a response. Michael checks the blankets, readjusts the packing under Nicodemus' leg, and off they go.

Nicodemus watches as the sheep pen grows smaller in the distance. On the one hand, he feels like he's leaving his safe home, his harbor in the time of storm. On the other hand, he laughs at himself for even considering a sheep pen his "home." At least it was sure. Now, he moves into the unknown.

CHAPTER 20
A Day with the Sheep

He makes me lie down in green pastures,
he leads me beside the quiet waters, he restores my soul.
Psalm 23:2, 3

The cart, carrying Nicodemus, jiggles and joggles this way and that over the grass and rocks. At last they make it around the base of the hill with the next hill in sight. Michael stops the cart. They can still see the sheep grazing up on the first hill. Michael smiles proudly as he gazes up at Benjamin. The young shepherd moves among the sheep, bending over this one and that one.

"You have taught him well," Nicodemus says.

"Thank you. He's a good boy."

"Yes, a good Jewish son," Nicodemus whispers to himself, reflecting on his father's words.

"Uh-oh, Bramble is straying again. She's headed for the ravine. Your water jug is there in your bag on the blanket. I'll be awhile." He grabs his staff.

Nicodemus starts to comment, but Michael is already off to take care of the stray. *He certainly tends to those sheep. What about me? Alone again.*

Nicodemus watches Michael running up the hill. Bramble strays farther and farther from the flock. Two lambs follow not far behind her. Nicodemus is caught up in the drama playing out before him.

Benjamin spots his father running up the hill. Puzzled, he stands and looks around unaware of the lost sheep. When Benjamin walks toward his father, he realizes the danger. Michael waves at his son to let him know that things are under control, but Bramble is also watching Michael and not paying attention to where she is going. Before Michael can get to her, she disappears.

She must have fallen into the ravine just as Michael feared. Nicodemus leans forward, anxious to see how this will play out.

Michael shoos the other would-be strays back toward the flock. Benjamin calls them and they head back his way. "But what about the other one? What are you going to do for *Bramble*?" Nicodemus says out loud. He is amazed by his own interest in this one lone stray.

After Michael is sure the other wayward sheep have rejoined the flock, he returns to the place Nicodemus last saw Bramble. Michael turns his shepherd's staff upside down and lowers it into the ravine. He scoops her up in the crook of his staff. Nicodemus lets out a sigh of relief, but then he watches Michael do a frightening thing. He flips the staff back over and swings the straight end of his staff striking Bramble on one leg. She bleats in pain and collapses on the grass. The shepherd picks her up in his arms and carries her. He walks with her to the shade of a tree and holds her in his lap, rubbing her wooly coat. Pulling a long strip of cloth out of his bag, he wraps it round and round her injured leg.

Now that's a strange thing—rescue her from the ravine, break the poor creature's leg, and then coddle her and treat the wound. Puzzling.

Nicodemus strains to see what else the shepherd will do, but he appears to just be sitting and talking to the fallen one while keeping an eye on the other sheep. Nicodemus is transfixed by the scene before him—the shepherd, the son, the lame stray, the sheep nibbling on grass, a few lying in the sun, all contented.

All seems well, so Nicodemus shakes his head, lies back to relax, aware of how tense he has been. *Such a different life. How much longer will I be stuck out here with shepherds and sheep, wooly hides and blankets?*

The sun is in full force but feels comforting in the cool morning breeze. He props the blanket under his head, trying to release his tight muscles. When he closes his eyes, all he can think of is the swing of the shepherd's staff striking the sheep. *Why would he do such a thing?*

He opens his eyes and rolls his head over to check on everyone. Still the same scene—and quite a peaceful scene, actually. More of the sheep are lying down. He closes his eyes again and feels content as well, breathing deeply to take in the fresh air, away from that filthy sheep pen. Never mind that he is still surrounded by sheep skin in his cart. He drifts off to sleep like his fellow companions.

In his dreams he sees himself walking up the rocky mountain of a few days ago, straining, out of breath, rocks poking around his sandaled feet. He trips and falls and falls....

Nicodemus wakes up with a start. He looks at the cart and his splinted leg. Oh, yes, the fall, the sheep pen. He glances up the hill to check on the flock. Still resting.

Hmm, I'm thirsty. Ah, there's my water jug right where Michael said it would be. He reaches over, aware that his hands look cleaner than they did before. He takes slow sips of water, fearful of being without.

Michael hasn't moved from the tree. The wounded ewe lies beside him, munching what grass she can reach. Michael picks her up, motions to Benjamin and points to the next hill. He walks down the hill toward the cart. Halfway down, he lifts Bramble up, placing her around his shoulders.

When he arrives, he reports, "We will head around the next hill and meet the flock at the stream. Bramble will have to ride with you." Placing Bramble in the cart beside Nicodemus, Michael lifts the handle to pull the cart.

What? No explanation as to why you purposely injured this poor animal? It was no accident. It was absolutely intentional. I saw it with my own eyes. Two witnesses needed. Bramble and me. That's enough. (Though he knew full well an animal can't be a witness.) He sighs. *Why am I so concerned about this common animal? It's only a sheep.*

"Baa." Bramble expresses her feelings softly. Nicodemus turns away from her soulful eyes, not to be taken in by a smelly sheep, though he is regrettably aware that he can hardly smell her now.

He looks up the hill to see if the flock is following their young shepherd. Benjamin has them up and going.

As they bounce along, Bramble makes her dissatisfaction known, getting louder by the moment. Nicodemus checks her lame leg, which is thumping up and down with the rhythm of the bouncing cart. He pulls the remaining blanket out of the basket and props up the sheep's leg to pad it with the blanket. Bramble looks up at Nicodemus in gratitude with a soft "baa."

"You're welcome." *Oh, no. Now I'm talking to them! What has become of me? I'm being pulled around in a cart and now I not only have to share it with a sheep, I'm talking to her!*

Unexpectedly, Nicodemus thinks about his friend, Joseph. *Joseph would not be pointing a finger of accusation at me, he would be doubled over in laughter. He has always said I take things way too seriously. Perhaps he's right.* He stares at his "traveling companion." *There's still the matter of that shepherd mistreating you, my wooly friend.*

Nicodemus feels the cart gradually slanting upward. He holds on to the side of the cart with one hand and Bramble with the other, fearful they will both go sliding out the foot.

"We're here," announces their gallant cart-puller.

"It's about time," grumbles Nicodemus. "We about went sliding right out of this cart."

"Sorry, I wanted to get you as far upstream as possible. The water is better here."

Michael maneuvers the cart around where Nicodemus can see the flow. Plentiful water gurgles down the wide stream. Lush green grass carpets the hillside—a sight to behold.

Michael removes Bramble from the cart. "If you're up to it, I can help you out of the cart. You can sit by the stream, wash yourself, and drink all the water you can hold,"

Nicodemus is feeling stronger, but the thought of getting in and out of the cart is not particularly appealing. Reluctantly, he agrees to give it a try.

Michael strategically places large rocks behind the wheels and steadies the slanting cart while Nicodemus scoots to the edge. He balances as before on the heel of his good foot.

Michael holds Nicodemus under his arms, swivels him, and lowers him to the ground. While Nicodemus' heart pounds faster, he is not as light-headed as before. Pleased, he reaches over to the rushing stream, relishing the cool water as it flows through his hand. He casts off his hot cloak and rolls over enough to get both hands in the water. He splashes it up to his arm pits, rubbing vigorously up and down his arms.

"Would you like for me to help you out of your tunic?"

Modesty to the wind, Nicodemus agrees. Free of the stench of his dirty clothes, Nicodemus splashes himself all over in childlike abandon. Michael looks away, but Nicodemus hears him chuckling to himself.

Michael takes Nicodemus' tunic and cloak downstream and washes them, attempting to rub the blood stains. He spreads Nicodemus' clothes across the cart to dry and takes Bramble to another area to graze.

Once Nicodemus has his fill of washing himself, he sprawls out in the soft grass to rest and dry off. *Another new experience—lying bare in the grass. My life seems full of new experiences these days.* He has an uncanny sense of freedom like nothing he has known before. Instead of being in the crowded close atmosphere of Jerusalem's buildings and people and pavement, here he is alone in these wide open spaces with a gurgling brook and lush green grass tickling his back.

He dozes for a while, dreaming of little lambs frolicking on the hillside. They playfully butt heads before they graze peacefully in the grass. Then in his dream, Nicodemus sees a dangerous ravine not far away. He tries to warn them. "Run away, little lambs." But they can't hear him.

He awakens in a sweat. When his eyes pop open he sees the deep blue sky above and hears the babbling stream next to him. His body is dry from the bath, but he is sweating from the sun. Gnats buzz around his face. What happened to his beautiful oasis? Back to reality. He wonders how long he has slept and *where is that shepherd?* Propping up on his elbows, he spots Michael climbing up the hill toward him, Bramble in hand. Here's his chance to ask about the incident with Bramble's leg.

Michael checks Nicodemus' clothes. "Dry," he proclaims. He grabs them off the cart and hands them to Nicodemus. Nicodemus pulls the tunic over his head and inches the bottom of his tunic under himself.

"Did you rest well?" Michael asks as he sits beside Nicodemus. A perfect opening.

"Well, actually, I dreamed."

"Yes?"

"I dreamed about two little lambs leaping and playing in the grass. They were about to fall in a ravine."

"That wasn't a dream. It happened today."

"That's right, and what I want to know is why you pulled Bramble out of the ravine and then *intentionally* broke her leg." He is sure his justified condemnation will bring immediate repentance.

Michael smiles slightly and nods his head knowingly. "Yes. It does seem cruel and unwarranted, but you see, Bramble has had a bad habit of straying from the flock lately, which constantly pulls me away to rescue her. And now, as you have seen with your own eyes, she leads her lambs to do likewise. Others will follow suit if I do not discipline her. I broke her leg to train her to depend on me, to stay close to the flock. It may save her life and the lives of others."

Nicodemus sees the wisdom in Michael's explanation, but he is miffed that his condemnation was unmerited. He doesn't comment.

"Bramble's leg will heal," Michael goes on to say, "and she will be all the better for it. She's a strong ewe. She brings forth quality lambs."

About that time, Benjamin and the flock come over the hill. He moves them on down toward the lower part of the stream.

"Why aren't they drinking from the stream?"

"Sheep won't drink from a moving stream; they like still water. Benjamin is taking them down where the stream pools in that flat area."

Nicodemus stretches to look down stream and spies the spot that Michael has pointed out. The rams are rushing down the hill faster than the others. A few more are on their tail. When they reach the water, the rams begin butting the ones behind them. The butted ones move back and butt the ones behind them. Benjamin intercedes with his staff, rebuking them and talking to the others.

"A family argument?" Nicodemus asks.

"You might say that. Sheep have a butting order; kind of like chickens have a pecking order. The rams butt heads with the younger ones and they in turn butt heads with the next ones in line. They're kind of like people." Michael smiles and allows that thought to settle. Then he adds, "The prophet Ezekiel had it right. The Lord said to him, 'I will judge between the fat sheep and the lean sheep. Because you shove with flank and shoulder, butting all the weak sheep with your horns until you have driven them away, I will save my flock, and no longer be plundered. I will judge between one sheep and another.'"

Nicodemus' ire rises up. *How dare this common Galilean shepherd purport to teach me!* He turns his head away, nose in the air. *I may be weakened by a sprained leg, but I am still a great teacher of Israel. If he only knew who he was talking to, he would have more respect.* Although he would have to admit that he doesn't recall that Scripture.

Michael comments on Benjamin's fine handling of the flock, oblivious to Nicodemus' anger and demeanor, which annoys Nicodemus even more.

Nicodemus remembers that Michael went up the hill early this morning and questions him about it.

"Oh, I went up to the pasture where the sheep would be grazing today and pulled up the poisonous weeds growing wild on the hill. I set the weeds up on rocks out of reach. The weeds dry up and wither by the time the sheep arrive. They will eat anything, so I have to watch for the harmful weeds. The Lord does the same for us. 'You prepare a table before me in the presence of my enemies.'"

Is there anything this shepherd leaves undone in the care of his sheep?

Michael nervously tilts his head this way and that, studying the sheep. "The sheep seem a bit restless." He sounds concerned. "Benjamin is doing a good job. He has been helping me more and more lately, but sheep don't like changes. I think I better go and help him calm them down." He stands and pulls a stick-like thing out of his pouch. As Michael walks away, he glances back and calls, "Is it okay if Bramble stays with you? She'll be fine."

"*She'll* be fine? What about me?" But Michael is already half way down the hill. He slows his pace and puts the stick up to his mouth. *Ah, so it is a flute.* A haunting tune floats across the meadow. It does seem to calm the sheep. It even mesmerizes Nicodemus for a little while.

As Nicodemus and Bramble sit there on the quiet hillside, Nicodemus is reminded again of the psalm that was sung at his father's funeral. Maybe it's the flute that jogged that memory.

> *The Lord is my shepherd, I shall not want,*
> *he makes me to lie down in green pastures,*
> *he leads me beside still waters,*
> *he restores my soul.*

Nicodemus looks down at Bramble who rolls her sleepy eyes up at him. "Well, it's just you and me, old girl. Your shepherd may have treated you cruelly, but he says he's doing it for your own good. He takes care of all your needs, even the things you don't know you need."

Nicodemus gazes back at the flock. Most have finished drinking from the still water. Michael weaves his way through the flock and they soon lie down in their green pasture—calm and restored.

Nicodemus recalls the afternoon of his fall. The first conscious thing he remembers is the shepherd's calming voice. "Your master saved my life, Bramble. He used his own water skin to wash my wounds and bandage them. He set me on the east side of the sheep pen wall so I would be shielded from the afternoon's hot sun. He had his son make a long trip from home just to bring this cart for me. He has cared for me with the same attention he gives you." Nicodemus looks down at Bramble, but her eyes are closed peacefully.

Nicodemus feels tired, but when he turns on his elbow to lie down, he sees his traveling bag behind him. As he fumbles around in the bag, he discovers something that feels like leather. Pulling the bag closer, he sits up again to get a good look inside. Down in the bottom lie the curled up straps of his phylacteries. Slowly, respectfully, he draws the cherished treasure out of the bag.

Turning the straps and phylactery boxes over in his hands, he carefully examines them. Tiny bits of rock are embedded in the leather. Dirty scuffs mar the straps, but oh, the thought of having this sacred part of his identity to clutch in his hands once again. He thrusts the precious phylacteries to his heart, hangs his head over and rolls back and forth. His shoulders shake as he weeps.

> "My God, my God, why have you forsaken me?
> Why are you so far from saving me,
>> so far from the words of my groaning?"

He continues to quote David, the psalmist:

> "O my God, I cry out by day,
>> but you do not answer,
>> by night, and am not silent.
>
> Yet you are enthroned as the Holy One;
>> You are the praise of Israel.
> In you our fathers put their trust;
>> they trusted you and you delivered them.
> They cried to you and were saved;
>> in you they trusted and were not disappointed.
> But I am a worm and not a man."

134

Nicodemus sobs all the more. His whole body trembles in the despair of this moment. He holds his handful of straps and boxes up to the sky and cries out;

"I am poured out like water,
        and all my bones are out of joint.
My heart has turned to wax;
        it has melted away within me.

My strength is dried up like a potsherd,
        and my tongue sticks to the roof of my mouth;
You lay me in the dust of death."

Having claimed the psalmist agony and expressed it openly, he lowers his hands, gently rocking back and forth once again.

At last, he breathes deeply and utters the psalmist's final words;

"But you, O Lord, be not far off;
O my strength, come quickly to help me."

After another moment of silence, Nicodemus finds his jug, fills it in the cool stream, and drinks from its refreshment. With his head tilted up to the sky, he is thankful to see a cloud cover giving relief from the sun. Bramble's head is up and alert, watching him intently. "Time to rest old girl," he says, as he rubs her head. He eases himself down on his back in exhaustion with his phylacteries draped across his chest. He succumbs to a welcomed deep sleep.

Nicodemus dreams of the Sanhedrin. He is about to enter the chamber when a few Pharisees block his entrance. "Are your hands ceremonially washed, Nicodemus? Have you prayed three times a day? Do you follow the laws you teach, Nicodemus? Why has the Lord chastised you with an injury? What wrong have you done, Nicodemus?"

Their voices mount in thunderous chorus. Their faces turn grotesque as they tower over him until he hunkers down in shame. He turns to find escape and there stands John the

Baptizer. "Repent," he cries. "Repent for the kingdom of God is at hand."

Nicodemus suddenly arouses from his restless sleep. He quickly looks around. No Pharisees, no John, just Bramble and the rippling stream. The sun has moved farther in the west. He must have slept for a good while. When he starts to move his hands, he is reminded of his phylacteries. His mind flashes back to his emotional prayer.

When he manages to sit up, he puts his phylacteries and jug back in his bag. *The shepherd retrieved my things after the fall. He knows. He knows I am a Pharisee. Surely he knows that we are the righteous ones to faithfully wear our phylacteries. Why has he not treated me with more respect? How dare him leave me stranded and alone so often and then leave me to watch over a lame sheep. Why doesn't he take me back to town to see a doctor, instead of just patching me up out here in the country side? If he could see how richly I live in Jerusalem, he would honor me more.*

Nicodemus' self-pity session is cut short, for he hears the bark of wild dogs or wolves or something that frightens the sheep. They all come stampeding up the hill to escape. Benjamin runs up ahead of them, moving his staff back and forth, talking as calmly as possible in this upsetting commotion. The sheep finally begin to slow their pace.

Meanwhile, Michael is downhill, aggressively using the straight end of his staff to ward off and attack three wild dogs. Two go running off and one limps away having been struck by Michael's rod.

By the time the sheep reach Nicodemus, they have stopped but stare warily back down the hill at their shepherd, bleating their angry "baa's" at the enemies. Benjamin walks patiently among them, copying the gentle words of his father, petting this one and that. At last the sheep seem to relax as they see their shepherd coming up the hill to them.

> *"I will fear no evil, for you are with me;*
> *your rod and your staff, they comfort me."*

How hard it is to be angry with this shepherd. My job is to teach. His job is to care for sheep. Can I guilt him for doing his job and still trying to care for an injured man at the same time?

Once Benjamin has the sheep settled, he sits beside Nicodemus.

"Is Bramble okay?" Benjamin asks.

"She's fine and, thanks to you, the rest of the flock seems to have settled down, too."

"Whew!" Benjamin shakes his head as though relieved that it is all over.

"Your father has taught you well and you have been a good student."

Benjamin smiles shyly before he turns his head away, wiping a stray tear. They sit in silence. "And does your father teach you about our Holy Scriptures?"

"Oh, yes," Benjamin responds with a bit more enthusiasm and control. "When he comes home from his grazing days, we have lessons."

"And what things are you learning?"

"Well, last time, we talked about King David. Before he was a king, he was a shepherd you know?"

"Yes, yes."

"He tended sheep just like we do." Benjamin's eyes begin to sparkle for the first time.

"And you like tending sheep, do you?"

"Yes, just like David. My father is taking me out with him more and more. Sometimes when the sheep are resting, I practice my sling."

"Just like David." Nicodemus smiles, thinking what it would have been like to have had a son.

"But I don't know the harp, only the flute—like my father."

"We can praise the Lord with many instruments. Have you heard the instruments at the Temple in Jerusalem?

"No, but next year my father said I could go with him."

"Ah, that will be a special year for you."

"Have you been to the Temple?"

Nicodemus smiles. "Oh, yes. I go every day. I live in Jerusalem."

"You *live* in Jerusalem?" Nicodemus nods his head. Benjamin thinks about that. "Then why are you here?"

"I came to Capernaum to bring my mother for a visit."

"But why are you here?" He gestures his upturned palms to the hillside.

"Well, I was on the way to visit an uncle when I fell down the hill and was injured. I certainly didn't plan to be *here*." Nicodemus copies Benjamin's gesture.

Nicodemus realizes his tone is a bit more sarcastic than he intended. *This innocent boy isn't a Sadducee. I'm just not use to talking to young boys.*

"I'm sorry you were hurt. Are your wounds healing?"

"Yes, I think there's improvement." Nicodemus looks away. He doesn't know how to react to thoughtfulness and gentleness. It isn't the way of his world.

Michael comes toward them.

Nicodemus calls to him, "Your protection is appreciated, shepherd—by your sheep and also by me."

"You never know when wild animals will show up. The rod comes in handy." Michael holds his staff up. "And you, my fine young shepherd, you did a responsible job of settling the sheep. They would have stampeded if it hadn't been for your capable control."

Benjamin beams at his father's compliment and then rolls his eyes over to Nicodemus, who nods his head in approval.

"Well, these sheep have had their fill of grazing. While they rest, I believe it is time for us to have a bite of food."

Nicodemus and Benjamin both brighten up at the prospect of food. They sit waiting eagerly for Michael to draw out food from his basket in the cart.

"Shall we wash our hands in this handy stream?" Michael bends over the stream and Benjamin follows.

Nicodemus rolls over to join them, grateful for at least this act of obedience restored.

When they circle around on the grass again, ready to eat, Michael lifts up his head to pray. "Thank you, Oh, Lord, for your protection and your provision. Amen."

"Amen," says Benjamin.

"Amen," echoes Nicodemus. He is beginning to have a sense of family with these two.

After they eat, Nicodemus notices that the sun is slipping lower in the west. "Will we go back to our sheep pen or is there another pen?"

"No, we will have to stay here on the hill tonight. Tomorrow afternoon we will be home."

Home. It had a comforting ring to it, but at the same time, it made Nicodemus nervous to think about yet another time of adapting to something unknown

CHAPTER 21
Heading for "Home"

Surely goodness and love will follow me all the days of my life.
Psalm 23:6

Nicodemus has a restless night, half sleeping and half watching Michael and Benjamin as they take turns keeping watch over the sheep. From time to time, they walk quietly around the sheep, careful not to disturb them while looking out into the night, searching for possible predators.

At last, Nicodemus is awakened by the morning rays of sun. Michael and Benjamin are already up, filling the water skins and preparing food to eat. The aches in Nicodemus' muscles remind him of the reality of his fall. *Will I ever be well again?*

He manages to lift himself up on one elbow and then to a sitting position, grunting and groaning with every move. He scoots himself over to the water to wash his hands one last time before they leave this beautiful spot. While they eat, the sheep rouse one by one until they are all up and grazing.

"They like the morning dew on the grass," Michael comments as he coaxes one would-be stray with his staff. "As soon as they have their fill we will move on. We better begin the task of getting you back in the cart. I don't believe you're ready for walking these hills yet."

Nicodemus lowers his head, shaking it with a "you're-right-about-that" expression on his face.

Michael bends over the low end of the cart to check the supports behind the cart wheels, loads the baskets in the cart, straightens the wool skin, and adjusts the rolled blanket for Nicodemus' back.

All the comforts of home, Nicodemus satirizes in his mind. *Lord, help me be grateful for what I do have.*

"Remember how you pivoted on your good foot before? Let's try it once more." Michael turns to his son. "Benjamin, you tend to Master Nicodemus' bad leg."

With that, Michael gets behind Nicodemus to lift him up, pivot, and sit him on the edge of the cart. Benjamin lifts Nicodemus' injured leg while Michael helps him slide further into the cart. After much effort, Nicodemus is back in the cart, propped up with the rolled blanket at his back. He eases with a great sigh into the blanket; sure that he has done a full day's work.

Suddenly, the cart begins to give way. Michael catches a back corner trying to hold on to it as it swerves around.

"Benjamin," he calls out. "Help me!"

Looking up, Benjamin shouts, "Oh, no! I'm coming!"

Nicodemus rolls to the side of the cart that has swung around. It's about to tip over. Nicodemus' heart is in his throat as once again he feels totally out of control. Benjamin runs quickly to that side of the cart. He and his father push and shove. Their sandaled feet slide in the wet grass. Michael shifts around to the corner with Benjamin. With one more shove together, they finally steady the cart. Michael holds it in place while Benjamin rolls the stones back in place and secures them with his foot. They all heave a sigh of relief.

The sheep, startled by all the commotion, commence with their baa-ing and butting.

"Benjamin," Michael says with a deliberately calm voice. "Tend the sheep. You can lead them down the hill *slowly*. We will follow."

Benjamin lingers until he is sure the cart is steady, and then picks up his staff.

"Curly, Brown Boy, Trouble, come with me. We're off to new pasture. You will like it and tonight we will be home. Wayward, over this way." He taps the stray sheep with his staff and continues calling out their names to calm them.

"Cripple, you can make it. Scabby, Morning Dove, come along. This way, Tag-a-long."

Benjamin's voice drifts down the hillside as he corrals all of his charges back into their routine.

"And now, my friend, it is your turn." Michael picks up Bramble and places her in the cart with Nicodemus. Nicodemus is about to complain when Bramble nuzzles her head under Nicodemus' side. *Oh, great. This sheep thinks I'm its faithful companion.* But right now, Nicodemus is more worried about descending the hill in this cart. He watches with wrinkled brow while Michael pulls him up the hill and gradually slants to one side. Nicodemus grabs the sides of the cart in an effort to do his part in stabilizing it.

Michael pulls this way and that making slightly horizontal lines across the hill so as not to have a run-away cart. Once Nicodemus realizes the plan, he is able to relax a bit and endure the bumpy ride down. Bramble jerks her head back and forth as though trying to figure out what is going on. When Nicodemus relaxes, Bramble also relaxes and puts her head on his good leg.

In spite of himself, Nicodemus smiles and scratches her head. She has won him over. "Perhaps we'll both be walking again someday soon, old girl. Someday soon."

In all the excitement, he quite forgot about his leg and head. Fortunately, neither seems to be any worse. In fact, Nicodemus is rather pleased with the healing of his head injury. There's nothing to do now but try to enjoy the ride.

Bramble's head bounces up and down as they hit a rocky patch. She gives up on resting and peers out of the cart, then turns to look at Nicodemus with questioning eyes.

"I fear we will have a day of it ole girl. You'll just have to get used to it."

Bramble turns away with a resolved, "Baa."

Their path gradually leads east, right into the morning sun. Their descent is not so steep now. Nicodemus tilts his head to the sun, allowing the warm rays to knock off the morning chill and to heal his wounded head.

As he and Bramble go bumping along, Nicodemus ponders all that he's experienced in the last three days. He thinks about the pain of the fall, the helplessness that overpowered him as he laid there on the ground, the rescue by the shepherd, the nights outside the dirty sheep pen, the taste of water and food when thirst and hunger were about to overtake him, and the care of his shepherd. But, the one memory that has most haunted him is the first sound of his shepherd's voice. He will never forget the comfort of that voice. *No wonder the sheep follow him and trust him. His care is complete; his devotion unquestionable.*

Nicodemus looks down at the sleeping Bramble. *Except for you, little lady. You have not learned to follow and now you are being forced to learn a hard lesson.* Nicodemus slowly gazes up to fluffy clouds floating in the blue sky above. *And perhaps I'm being forced to learn some hard lessons as well.*

⌘✿⌘✿⌘✿⌘✿

After a brief nap, Nicodemus is roused when the cart comes to a stop. He is sweating from the noon day heat. Michael is wet with perspiration from pulling the cart all morning.

"We'll stop under this tree while we eat and drink," he says. He takes Bramble out of the cart. "Let's see if you can find some grass to your liking, Bramble-girl." He places her in the rich green grass. She nibbles at the patch that is near her nose. Motivated to graze beyond her reach, she struggles to get up on her three good feet. She totters and falls back into the grass. Michael and Nicodemus spontaneously groan as they watch her.

Shortly, she tries again, a bit wobbly at first, but maintaining her stance. She even manages to stagger a step or two to reach the next spot. The two men smile at each other. Michael winks with delight. He sits on the ground and rests his back against the tree trunk. "We only have about three more hours before we make it to my house."

Nicodemus hadn't really thought about Michael's house or his family. His only concern had been for himself. *Michael has done so much for me. I wonder what his life is like at home. I don't even know if he has other children. What of his wife? Does he have other animals? What is his house like? Where will I stay?*

Nicodemus finally asks, "Michael, do you have other children?"

"No, just Benjamin. But he's a fine boy, a joy to his father."

143

"Indeed, a fine boy."

"My wife has been with child two other times, but she lost both in childbirth."

"I'm sorry."

"That's why Benjamin is so special to us."

"I understand." He pauses, realizing he had tread on a tender experience. He continues. "You have parents living nearby?"

"Papa died several years ago. My mother lives with us."

"Then I will be a burden to you."

"No, we actually live in her house. I had a brother and sister growing up. There will be room for you. My mother is a midwife and she knows much about different ailments. She will be able to take care of your injuries better than I have."

"You must have learned from her. You have cared for me well. I'm very grateful."

Michael smiles, for words of gratitude have been grossly lacking. Nicodemus feels embarrassed that these words have been so long in coming. He considers how easy it has been to think of shepherds as dirty good-for-nothing wanderers when you see them from afar. They have no names, no families, no lives, no virtues. It is different when you know their names, experience their care, and see their qualities. *How haughty I have been. The great teacher is being taught.*

Up on the hill, Benjamin perches on a flat rock as he watches his sheep grazing. He continuously rotates his head from one side to the other, checking the mood of his wooly "munchers." Satisfied that all is well, he slides his hands behind him on the rock, stiffens his arms, and leans back with his face to the sun. His chest raises and lowers as though breathing deeply to relish a moment of rest and relaxation. He closes his eyes, the picture of peace.

Nicodemus studies Benjamin for a moment, hypnotized by this quiet scene. Shortly, Benjamin opens his eyes, lowers his head, and once again checks on his sheep.

He has learned the instinct to be ever vigilant. Nicodemus glances around to see Michael with his head propped up by the tree, eyes closed. *This good father has been a good teacher.* The scene causes Nicodemus to muse once again about his own father.

Papa was always so busy with his physician duties; working with patients, piddling with his medicines, or studying his books. I suppose that's where I learned to be faithful to my studies. But he always had time for good talks to answer my questions. Nicodemus' eyes squint as he grins. *And I did have many questions.*

He watches Bramble who is now resting from her victorious labor and surveys the meadow of grazing sheep with their young shepherd. A sparrow takes flight from the tree top—only to return minutes later with food for her young. A wave of something very nostalgic washes over Nicodemus. He hasn't felt this sense of calm, this sense of peace in quite a long time.

He tries to whisper the noontime daily prayer, but the words fall empty from his lips. Instead, a psalm comes to mind.

> "How lovely is your dwelling place,
>   O LORD Almighty!
> My soul yearns, even faints
>   for the courts of the LORD;
>   My heart and my flesh cry out
>   for the living God.
>
> Even the sparrow has found a home
>   and the swallow a nest for herself,
>   Where she may have her young—
>   a place near your altar.
> O LORD Almighty, my king and my God.
> Blessed are those who dwell in your house;
>   they are ever praising you."

Nicodemus closes his eyes as he hears the plucked strings of the gittith in his mind, its haunting tune drawing him back to his beloved Temple in Jerusalem.

Suddenly a couple of old sheep vie for a patch of grass with butted heads and noisy declarations. It jerks Nicodemus from his reverie. Michael jumps to his feet, but Benjamin is already on the go, with staff in hand, to take care of the stubborn old sheep. Michael watches for a moment until he sees that Benjamin has everything under control. Satisfied, he fetches Bramble and returns her to her place beside Nicodemus.

Michael trudges around the cart and picks up the handles to pull it once again. Bramble's head jerks this way and that. She baas her displeasure at being interrupted from her rest. Without thinking, Nicodemus rubs Bramble's back and pats her. She soon settles into the old familiar spot next to her fellow crippled friend.

CHAPTER 22
Home

A contentious woman is like a constant dripping on a rainy day;
restraining her is like restraining the wind or grasping oil with the hand.
Proverbs 27:15

Nicodemus notices that they have been on flatter land for a while. He catches a faint whiff of fish from time to time. *We must be close to the sea.* But the smell of an olive press soon overpowers the air. A few travelers walk by with their donkeys laden with pots of oil. They greet Michael with a hearty "Shalom," but pass Nicodemus with questioning stares. Nicodemus nods trying to set them at ease. He is aware, for the first time, how disheveled he must look—dirty, dusty, and yes, smelly while being hauled in a cart like a pile of sheep skin. *Thankfully, they don't know who I am.*

Soon, signs of a village are all around. On this side of the road, a girl is busy pulling wool into strands. Next door, a woman stirs a steaming pot of dye. Several strips of cloth lay across her stool, waiting to be dipped. On the other side of the road, a carpenter hammers away in his shop. It looks like he is working on a cart much like Michael's. Beyond the carpenter, a farmer plows extra rows beside his planted field. Two women draw water at the well. Most are too busy to notice Michael and Nicodemus. A few give a wave or a glance but continue their work.

At last, Michael pulls the cart up to a medium-sized stone house. An attractive woman stands in the door adjusting the kerchief on her head. She smiles in anticipation when Michael lowers the cart handles and strolls her way.

She steps back in the door as Michael greets her. She gives a welcoming hug to her shepherd. He proceeds to share all the news. Nicodemus can't quite hear what Michael says, but he is fairly sure that Nicodemus' mishap is the topic of conversation. The woman peers around Michael to catch a glimpse of Nicodemus. Nicodemus isn't quite sure whether to nod or speak, so he looks away pretending that he doesn't hear them. He busies himself with adjusting the sheep skin under him, and then sees Benjamin coming over the hill with the sheep. He smiles as he watches his young friend.

Everything feels so awkward. He's gotten use to Benjamin and Michael, but now there are townspeople, a house, and the Galilean women in this home to get used to. About then, he turns and Michael has come up beside him with his wife.

"Nicodemus, this is my wife, Abigail."

"Shalom. It is good to meet you," Nicodemus says cordially.

Abigail nods her head shyly.

Benjamin has come near enough to shout from the hill behind the house. Abigail waves and calls back to him.

"You have a fine son. He learns his trade well."

"Yes, we are pleased with him. Welcome to our home. Michael tells me you had a bad accident on the mountain. We will have you cleaned up in no time and my mother-in-law will tend to your wounds."

"That's very kind of you."

Meanwhile, Michael has been busily putting together a kind of contraption with two branches and sheep skin on which to carry Nicodemus into the house. Michael goes around to the side of the house and calls to Benjamin. "When you get the sheep in, come help me."

Michael finishes his project and turns back to the cart. "Master Nicodemus, we must remove you from your great throne. Let's see if we can get you out of this cart one more time. If you can scoot forward onto your good foot and pivot as before, I will lower you onto this pallet so that Benjamin and I can carry you into the house."

How humiliating. Now some of the town's people are gawking from down the road. But what can he do? Refuse to go in? Stay outside in his cart? Oh what he wouldn't give to be able to jump up and walk away.

Reluctantly, he begins to push himself forward as he has done before. Benjamin runs up in time to hold his bad leg and Michael helps him to balance on his good leg. He pivots, and then Michael eases him down to the pallet.

There he is flat on his back. From this vantage point, he looks up at the house. A window in the second floor comes in view. Abigail and another woman are gazing down on him. More humiliation. He closes his eyes and wishes he were back in Jerusalem teaching his students at the Temple.

Ha, students indeed. If they could see me now, they would never want to sit under my teaching again. Lord, why have you done this to me?

Michael and Benjamin pick him up with a slight jostle as they attempt to coordinate their balance. Nicodemus hears footsteps as the two women hurry down the steps to tend to their visitor.

"Take Master Nicodemus into that room," Abigail points to a small room at the front of the house.

The other woman rushes into the room. "No, no, not on the bed," she says. "Lay him on the floor beside the bed." Father and son heave very audible sighs as they bend over to lower Nicodemus down to the floor.

"I'll need two bowls of water. Abigail, can you steam it over the fire? I'll get my medical supplies." And off goes the woman who must be Michael's mother. Michael glances at Nicodemus, reading accurately his reaction.

"She will take good care of you. My father was a physician and she helped him often in his practice. She still keeps herbs and medicinal supplies on hand. Many in the village come to her for aid."

"And does she have a name?" barked Nicodemus, quite indignant, as he lay flat on the floor.

"Sorry I didn't introduce you. My mother's name is Ruth. She gets very serious when her services are needed. She always hurries about to meet every need."

"Apparently! I've gone this long with your good care. My needs aren't *that* immediate."

"Mama is like that. She'll settle down shortly."

In comes "Mama" again in a flourish. She kneels down beside Nicodemus with not so much as a glance at his

149

face and opens her case of remedies. "Now let me have a look at this wound."

"Mama, let me introduce our guest. This is Nicodemus. Nicodemus, my mother, Ruth."

"Pleased to meet you," she says, still eyeing his leg.

Nicodemus raises his eyebrows to Michael, who gives a shoulder shrug back to him. Nicodemus doesn't bother to answer, sure that she would not even hear him. He isn't quite sure he wants a woman touching him. *But what laws have I kept this whole week?* He sighs softly.

Ruth squeezes a bit of water out of a rag. "I'll need to soften up these bandages so they won't pull the skin or damage the wound further." Gently she begins peeling away the poultice and the strips of cloth made from Nicodemus' spare tunic. She bends his leg slightly to undo the bandage from under his leg. "You made an excellent splint, Michael," she comments as she continues to squeeze drops of water and peel away the cloth.

Nicodemus closes his eyes; fearful of what the *doctor* will find when she gets to the bare wound. The more she unwinds the more tender it becomes.

"You've kept it free from the dust and dirt, Michael. That's good." At last she casts the strips aside and leans in for a closer look. Her presence makes Nicodemus tense. He is aware of a tightening in his shoulder muscles.

"Hmm," she says. He tries to relax, not sure if her observation holds more compliments for Michael or concern about the wound. She takes out some kind of instrument and begins to probe around lightly.

Finally she gives her assessment. "It seems to be healing, but there is some slight oozing around the edges. Abigail," she calls out. "Abigail, do you have that water warmed yet?"

"Yes, Ruth, I'll be right in." Ruth leans this way and that as she scrutinizes the condition of the wound.

"Thanks, dear." She dips a finger in the water. "Perfect, Abigail. Help me slide this other bowl under his leg."

"His" leg? I do have a name you know.

Doctor Ruth scoops up the warm water and gently pours it over Nicodemus' wound, allowing it to drip in the empty bowl. She presses slightly on the edges of the wound, pours more water, and presses again. She repeats this procedure several times.

At first, the water feels soothing, but with all that pressing, Nicodemus starts to feel nauseous.

"How long must you do that?" he finally blurts out.

Both women jerk in surprise. Michael's eyes dart to Nicodemus' face. Nicodemus heaves an audible breath.

"Sorry, I have to drain all the yellow pus out. I think that will do for now."

Ruth pats the area dry with a cloth. "Now we need to clean up the rest of you and find some clean clothes."

Nicodemus flashes a deadly stare at Michael.

"Uh, Mama, you find some clean clothes and I'll see to helping Master Nicodemus with his bath."

"As you wish," she says, as she grunts and groans in an attempt to get herself back up on her feet. "It's hard to get these bones and muscles working again after being all bent over on my knees."

Michael gives her a hand. "Thank you, Mama. I think our patient will be well soon."

Ruth dips her head to have one last look at the wound. "A few weeks perhaps."

Weeks? I'll be laid up like this for weeks? Not with that *woman around.*

She ambles out the door. "I'll find a fresh tunic," she calls from the next room.

Michael pulls a cloth curtain across the doorway and gives a side glance to Nicodemus to see if that seems to give him comfort. Nicodemus rises up on his elbow. "Now what?"

"I'll help you sit up and slide back to the wall."

"I can do it myself," Nicodemus retorts. He pushes himself up and balances on the palms of both hands, and then slides himself back. He reaches back with his hands and slides a bit more, grunting all the way, partly from so much exertion and partly from disgruntlement with his situation. Finally, Nicodemus feels the wall at his back and lets out a breathy, "Ah."

Michael moves the clean water closer to Nicodemus and gives him a wet cloth and dry towel. "Would you like for me to help pull your tunic out from under you?"

"Yes, I suppose so." Nicodemus balances on his hands and lifts his bottom up, while Michael pulls Nicodemus' tunic out. "I thought that woman was getting me a clean tunic."

"I'll check on it."

For the first time, Nicodemus is able to give his wound a good inspection. The looks of it almost brings on another wave of nausea. He looks away and inhales a deep breath of air. To distract himself, he examines the room: stone walls, stone floor, a squatty bed beside him with a small table and stool across the room. *It isn't much, but at least it's clean and much better than the sheep pen or that rickety old cart.*

He leans his head back against the wall and closes his eyes. *How did I ever end up like this?* He relives the accident: the rocky hill, the jutting stones under foot, and his twisted ankle. He remembers the feel of the donkey with its warm, hairy side and the donkey's struggle to hold its stance when Nicodemus had lunged full force against the beast. But it is at this point that Nicodemus' mind always goes blank. Ever so faint in his memory is the flash of rolling over piercing rocks, but the most vivid memory is still the voice, the voice of his shepherd. The voice of Michael.

"We have clean clothes for you, sir," calls that voice that he has come to know so well.

Nicodemus opens his eyes, feeling somewhat repentant for his belligerent behavior since coming into this good shepherd's home. "Thank you."

"Is there anything else you need?"

"No. Nothing."

Michael pauses, tilts his head, and smiles, apparently noticing a slightly different attitude. "Benjamin and I will come back in to help you into the bed after you have bathed and dressed."

Nicodemus nods his head and Michael departs.

❦❦❦❦

Nicodemus scrubs himself as much as he can and puts on the clean plain tunic. It doesn't compare to the fine clothes he is used to wearing. Once again, he has been brought down to the place of a commoner.

He imagines his old friend Joseph walking into the room. Joseph's eyes would squint to see if it was indeed his friend, Nicodemus. He would say, "Nicodemus, my brother, is that you in those peasant clothes? Is that you sitting on the floor? And what is this gash in your leg? What a sight you are!" He would throw his head back in laughter and then shake his head back and forth as his laughter simmered down.

Or what if Argus should walk in the room, what would he say? Nicodemus could see the smirk on his face immediately. "Too bad, Nicodemus. Oh, what a ghastly wound. Love the tunic. I suppose that's what *Galileans* wear." His voice would spew with delighted venom.

Oh, I must think better thoughts. What is it Papa used to say? "You are what you think."

About that time, Nicodemus hears Benjamin's voice in the next room. "Papa, Papa, one of the sheep is missing. I have counted three times just as you taught me, but I only come up with 49. I can't seem to find Tag-a-long. I think she is the one who's missing."

"I will go."

"Let me go with you, Papa. Please. It was all my fault. Please let me help."

"It is late. It may mean another night out."

"I don't care. I must go. Please let me go."

There is a pause. Nicodemus can hear Abigail's soft voice, but he can't quite make out what she is saying.

"Very well, but there's one thing we must do before we leave."

153

Benjamin follows Michael into Nicodemus' room. Michael is all business. "Have you cleaned up, sir?"

"Yes, I feel much better."

"Benjamin and I will lift you up and you can scoot over onto the bed."

Nicodemus slides back down on the pallet. Michael grabs the end of the pallet under Nicodemus' head while Benjamin lifts the lighter end.

Benjamin's usual smile has disappeared. He is obviously worried about his lost sheep.

"Can you not wait until morning to find your sheep?" Nicodemus asks.

"That might be too late. We must go tonight," Michael says.

Benjamin's eyes stare at the floor. Tears beg to be released, but he holds them back. Nicodemus wants to ask why one lone sheep would be so important. After all, Michael has 49 more, but by the look on their faces and the mood of the room, he thinks better than to question any further.

Father and son quickly take their leave and once again, Nicodemus lies alone. *Those sheep seem to constantly demand more attention than I do.* He reflects on the long days, where he sat hungry and thirsty by the sheepfold, waiting for Michael to return.

His thoughts are interrupted when Ruth comes swishing into the room to check on things. "Well, it looks like they managed to get you into bed before they hurried off. Those sheep. Always something! I declare, they left you without a cover. I'll go fetch one. I imagine you are ready for something to eat as well." And off she goes.

Nicodemus shakes his head. *I'm going to be left with that woman all evening?* Something about her take-charge attitude reminds him of Aunt Leah. With the thought of Leah and Laban and his mother, Nicodemus suddenly realizes that they are going to be terribly worried about him. He has been gone much longer than expected. They would certainly anticipate his return before Sabbath. When is the Sabbath? The days have been a blur. He's not even sure what day it is.

Ruth scurries back into the room with a pillow under her arm, a blanket over the other arm, and a tray with a bowl and a cup. She places the tray on the small table across the room, while she pulls the pillow out from under her arm. "If you can sit up and scoot back, I'll prop the pillow behind you."

If I can? Of course I can, you imbecile. Do I wish to? Maybe I do and maybe I don't.

She doesn't wait for an answer. She spreads the wool blanket across the foot of the bed. "It will soon be getting chilly. This blanket will feel good in the night." With pillow in hand, she stands by the bed waiting for Nicodemus to get ready.

I may as well sit up. She'll stand there until I do. Besides, I am hungry. It would be impossible to eat on my back. Nicodemus goes through what has become his regular routine; prop up and push back. She is ready with the pillow.

The smell of the soup entices him, so he willingly accepts the tray. Ruth exits the room mumbling something about light and lanterns.

Nicodemus recites a quick blessing and relishes the warm flavor of the lentil soup. Bread and nuts never tasted so good. He eyes the pear which will add a sweet ending to his meal.

Food, a dry house, a bath of sorts and clean clothes, humble though they be, all go together to bring a certain contentment over his soul in spite of this woman. The fading light through his high window spreads evening shadows across the room.

In comes Ruth once again with two lanterns and a wad of yarn under her arm. "I'm sure you are exhausted after your hillside experience. Michael is always so tired when he comes in from the pasture. Oh dear. We need another table in the room—one by your bed."

She sets her yarn on the stool and both lanterns on the table. As she hustles out of the room, yet again, she mumbles about having to think of everything.

155

Returning with the table, she sets one of the two lanterns on the new table by the bed. "Is the soup to your liking?"

"It's fine."

While he eats, she lights both lanterns, picks up her yarn, and sits down to do her needle work. "What brings you to the Galilee?"

She plans to stay? What am I to do with her? And what business is it of hers why I'm here?

"You were in a remote part of our fair country," she continues, when he doesn't answer right away.

If you must know, "I came to visit relatives."

"You must not have planned to stay long."

"And how would you know that?"

"You didn't bring much with you."

"Some of my belongings went down the hill with me," he retorts, disgustedly.

She looks at him over her stitching, eyebrows arched with a slight smirk. She returns to her work. "Benjamin was glad to have a reason to join you. He loves working with his Papa."

"He is a fine boy." Nicodemus' tone softens a bit. He pops three nuts at a time in his mouth, crunching them vigorously.

"Yes, he fancies himself a shepherd just like my son."

"Your husband, was he a shepherd?"

"No, he was a physician. He did his apprenticeship in Capernaum, but he chose to work in the small villages around here where he grew up. 'They need physicians, too' he always said."

"How is it that Michael...?"

"Didn't become a physician? My husband died when Michael and his younger brother and sister were small. I had no man to marry who wanted three young children."

She laid her partial yarn creation in her lap and looked up at the walls. "I had this wonderful house and a few coins. That was it. Oh, a few people came to me for healing because I had helped my husband, but with the children, I couldn't go from village to village like he did. The coins became fewer and fewer. Some friends gave me food supplies, but they had their own families to feed."

Suddenly interested, Nicodemus ponders what his mother would have done had his father died much earlier. "So what happened?"

"My uncle was a shepherd. He was getting up in years, so he asked Michael to help him. At first, Michael learned to shear the sheep and care for them in the pen. Later, he asked to go out in the fields with my uncle. It provided food and wool and hides. We managed. I also cared for my ailing father who lived with us. He had been a priest." With slight melancholy, she adds, "Michael was fifteen when my father died." She returns to her sewing. She seems at ease talking about her past, but it appears that the reminiscing has opened a tender place in her heart.

Nicodemus finishes his last bite of pear and studies her in the lantern light. A priest and a physician in this family of shepherds. How strange. How uncharacteristic. She knows the pain of the loss of a father. For a moment, Nicodemus feels an awkward connection with this Galilean woman. He is drawn into the conversation.

"My father died a few years ago. He too was a physician. My mother has been very lonely, even though I live with her. We live in Jerusalem."

Ruth looks up with a smile and a nod as though she had already figured that out.

"I came to Capernaum to bring my mother for a visit with her sister. I had planned to visit another uncle on the other side of the mountain. I think I crossed the wrong mountain and then, well, you know…"

"Yes, the accident."

Why does she keep finishing my sentences?

Ruth gathers up her sewing and blows out one lantern. "Well, I'm sure you are tired and ready to rest now. Can I get you anything else?"

"No, the food tasted good to me." She picks up his tray and leaves.

Nicodemus moves back into a reclining position, props the pillow behind his head, and maneuvers his tunic underneath him.

Ruth returns. "I have a salve that I need to put on your wound." She brings the lantern over to have another look at his leg and then sets it back on the table. Gently, she smoothes the salve on his wound and wraps one strip of cloth around it

"This will protect your wound in the night. Do you wish to keep the pillow?"

"Actually, I rather like it."

She pulls the cover up far enough for him to reach it and carries the lantern out of the room. "Shalom. Goodnight."

CHAPTER 23
Days of Healing

Suppose one of you has a hundred sheep and loses one of them. Does he not leave the ninety-nine in the open country and go after the lost sheep until he finds it? Luke 15:2

The morning sun beams through the window onto the wall above Nicodemus' bed forming a square patch of light. He opens his eyes, disoriented for a moment. He glances around the room and down at his cover. *Michael's house.* Michael, Benjamin, Abigail, and—Ruth. *Ah yes, that woman. She'll probably be flitting in here any minute to bother me again.*

He says his morning prayer, wondering where his phylacteries have ended up. He stares at the ceiling. No more hard ground. No cart, jostling him this way and that. The house is quiet. While he finds Ruth annoying, he rather wishes for company. He remembers that Michael and Benjamin went looking for a lost sheep last night. *Are they back?*

Nicodemus peers through the doorway, looking for movement, listening for any human sound. The sheep are up. He can hear their low baa-ing, a sound he knows all too well. A neighbor's chickens cluck next door. A cart rolls by. He recognizes the thumpity-thump of the wheels.

He closes his eyes. *Thus is my temporary new life—sheep, chickens, and carts. How long will I be imprisoned in this land? This house? That woman?*

He hears clanging of pots and shuffle of feet. Hunger pangs stir in him. Food, something to think about. Something to look forward to.

Shortly, he hears the flip flap of sandals coming toward his room. *It's her.*

"And did you sleep well, sir?"

"Favorably."

"I suppose you are ready for breakfast?" she says as she plops a basin of water on the table.

"Hm," he grunts. Even though he doesn't welcome her, he does welcome the food.

He struggles to sit up, but the pillow is in his way. She takes it out from behind him while he sits up and pushes back against the wall. Quickly, she inserts the pillow, and then offers him the basin of water to wash his hands. She carries it out and comes back with a tray of food.

"Michael and Benjamin are back," she reports, as she positions the tray on his lap. "They came in sometime during the night."

"And the sheep?" Nicodemus asks.

"They found Tag-a-long *cast down* at the bottom of the last hill."

"Cast down?"

"Tag-a-long is about to have a lamb. When a mother gets so heavy, she often loses her balance, falls over, and can't control herself. She ends up on her back and can't roll back over on her feet." Ruth demonstrates with her hands straight up.

While Nicodemus eats, she sits on her stool and continues the story. "Michael has to gently roll the sheep on her side to relieve the pent up gases in her system and then set her up on her feet. He straddles her and rubs her legs to get feeling back into her limbs." She demonstrates on her own legs as she talks. "Good thing he got to her. If a sheep doesn't get relief, it can die in that position."

"You seem to know a lot about it."

"I saw him do it once. There's a little hollowed out place in the back pasture behind our house. One day, one of the sheep was napping there on its side and lost its balance. It rolled over on its back with all fours in the air. It frantically flailed about, but once it is cast, it can't get itself upright. I happened to be outside when it happened. Heard that sheep bawlin' all the way to the house. Michael had told me about this before, but it was the first time I saw it for myself. You hear a lot of sheep talk when you live with a shepherd."

160

"I've learned a good bit about shepherding myself—more than I care to know." He rolled his eyes toward Ruth. She smiled and nodded her head knowingly.

"Is the porridge to your liking?"

"Yes, it's quite good."

The day drug on, but Nicodemus relished the cleanliness of his room. Ruth had gathered a few wild flowers and put them in a container beside his bed. He caught a whiff of their fragrance every now and then as a pleasant breeze passed through his window. What a change from the dung-filled sheep pen, the scorching sun, and the dusty cart, laden with old sheep skin.

Sheep. Poor Tag-a-long. He hoped she was better. Yet another example of Michael's unfailing care of his sheep. He found himself thinking of the other names he could remember.

Let's see, there's Cripple and Curly. What's the big one with all the scabs? Of course, Scabby. And the little one, the one that tended to stray—Wayward. Yes, Wayward, Bramble's lamb. The lamb was always straying because of its mother. Hmm, Bramble. I wonder how she's getting along. No more brambles for her. She has surely learned her lesson.

At that thought, Nicodemus considers again whether *he* is being taught a lesson. *What am I to learn? I've been a faithful son and friend. I have been dutiful to the law and my teaching responsibilities.*

It dawns on him that he hasn't thought of the law for days. Even now, he is thinking of sheep, even sheep *names* of all things!

He tries to roll to one side, but his leg is still too tender. Upon inspection, he deems it not to be as swollen. *Perhaps I can put weight on it soon. I'll ask Ruth.*

✦❧✦❧✦❧✦❧

In the next couple of days, Ruth continues to give him "treatments" as she calls it. At least the treatments are becoming less painful. He sees her at meal times and the mid-morning and mid-afternoon treatments. Perhaps she's not so bad. She has been very attentive, unlike Michael and Benjamin. *Where have they been? Working, I guess. After all, the work must go on in spite of my condition. I remember that well!*

Nicodemus manages an afternoon nap. When he awakens, he hears the familiar flip flap of sandals coming to his room.

"Was your nap restful, Nicodemus?"

He is aware that this is the first time she has called him by his name. Before, she used "sir" or just didn't call him anything.

"Yes, very restful," he yawns, pretending not to notice.

"We need to do one more treatment before sundown."

Nicodemus pushes himself into his sitting position. He has become quite proficient in handling it himself, pillow and all.

She proceeds with her routine: washing with a cloth, applying pressure to relieve any remaining pus, washing again, and anointing with her special salve.

"The wound is looking much better and the swelling has gone down considerably," she observes.

"Do you think I'm ready to put weight on that leg?"

"Ah, the anxious one, aren't you?" She raises her eyebrows and smiles with her eyes. "Well, we shall see."

That isn't what he wanted to hear. She is already gathering her supplies and on to her next task before Nicodemus can pursue it further. He huffs a bit.

When Ruth returns, she has brought in two candles which she sets on the table beside her stool. She drags the table to the middle of the room. *What is she up to now?*

"Tonight is Sabbath. I'm bringing the candles in here so you can participate with us." She places a pitcher and basin on the table beside Nicodemus' bed.

Soon, the smell of chicken soup waifs its way into his room. He breathes in the delightful aroma which reminds him of his walks through Jerusalem streets on his way home from the Temple. His heart stirs as he looks at the preparations for Sabbath.

Sabbath. He hadn't realized that a whole week had passed. Time had seemed to be at a standstill. Sabbath—something else to look forward to.

Nicodemus closes his eyes, remembering his father's voice from past Sabbaths.

"The Shabbat is the first among our holy days,
and a remembrance of our exodus from Egypt.
Indeed, You have chosen us and made us holy
among all peoples and have willingly and
lovingly given us Shabbat for an inheritance.
Blessed are You,
who sanctifies the Shabbat. Amen."

Before they ate their meal, Papa would go to the basin to wash his hands. He would pour water from the pitcher into a cup and pour the water over the palm and back of his right hand and then the palm and back of his left hand. Before he wiped his hands on a towel, he would recite the blessing:

"Blessed are You, Lord, our God,
King of the Universe,
who sanctifies us with his commandments,
and commands us concerning washing
of our hands."

Nicodemus, Jeremias, and their mother would each take a turn to repeat the hand washing and blessing. When they finished, Papa removed the cloth from the challah loaves and lifted the bread while reciting the blessing:

"Blessed are You, Lord, our God,
King of the Universe
who brings forth bread from the earth. Amen."

They would sit down to eat their Sabbath meal. Nicodemus would always envision his oldest brother, Neziah, continuing these traditions with his family across town.

And now, here he is in a strange house in Galilee preparing to celebrate Sabbath with another family, a shepherd's family.

CHAPTER 24
Sabbath in Michael's Home

The people were amazed at his teaching, because he taught them
as one who had authority, not as the teachers of the law.
Mark 1:22

Sabbath Eve. Ruth enters with a lantern; Abigail is behind her with a stool, and Michael has a stool as well. Benjamin bounces into the room and shines a bright smile at Nicodemus. Nicodemus holds out a hand and Benjamin grabs it in both of his as he kneels beside the bed.

"Are you healing well, Master Nicodemus?"

"Very well, Benjamin. I have a good physician." Nicodemus glances to the side, but Ruth continues to scurry around the room in preparation. "And your little Tag-a-long, is she doing well?"

Benjamin tilts his head and lowers his eyes; his face falls. Nicodemus realizes this is a painful subject. Evidently, Benjamin still feels badly that he did not keep all his sheep in tow.

Nicodemus reaches over and places his free hand on Benjamin's as he speaks gently, "I was amazed that you realized one sheep was missing out of the entire flock and that you knew it was Tag-a-long. You really know your sheep,"

A smile returns to Benjamin's face. "Tag-a-long is okay now. She will have a lamb soon."

"How exciting."

Michael steps toward them. "Benjamin, we're ready to begin."

Benjamin slides over to sit on the floor beside his mother.

"You're looking well, Master Nicodemus." Michael leans in to have a look at Nicodemus' leg. "I believe the swelling has gone down considerably. Perhaps you can put some weight on that leg soon."

Nicodemus flashes an "I-told-you-so" look at Ruth, who totally ignores him.

She asks, "Michael, shall we begin?" She already has the lantern ready to light the candles.

"Of course," he says as he slips over to his stool.

"To remember and observe," Ruth says as she lights the two candles. She covers her eyes just like Nicodemus' mother always did. As she lowers her hands, she recites the blessing:

> "Blessed are you, Lord, our God,
> King of the Universe,
> who sanctifies us with his commandments,
> and commands us to light
> the candles of Shabbat. Amen."

Michael leads out in the singing of the psalm:

> "Ascribe to the Lord, O mighty ones,
> ascribe to the Lord glory and strength,
> ascribe to the Lord the glory due his name;
> worship the Lord in the splendor
> of his holiness."

Nicodemus enjoys the old familiar psalm sung with these new voices. He has heard Michael singing on the hillside, but now he enjoys Abigail's gentle tones and Benjamin's childlike voice.

Ruth sings with strong crystal clarity. It seems strange somehow to hear her sing. She has been only his caretaker. She looks younger than her apparent age. Can she possibly have a son the age of Michael? The sweet expression on her face reveals her joy in the Lord. He notices her high cheek bones and bright eyes. Her dark brown hair, pulled back in a bun, shows no sign of graying. Her face seems to glow in the candle light.

What is this I'm feeling, this strange sensation? His voice joins in but he has trouble focusing.

The song concludes:

"The Lord gives strength to his people;
  the Lord blesses his people with *peace*."

*That's it. I just have such peace to be here and not out in the
dark of night with the smell of sheep and the pain of a sprained leg. Yes,
that's it—I feel gratitude that things are better. That's what I'm feeling.*

Michael and his son, Benjamin, hold the Kiddush
cups of wine as Michael recites the blessing:

"And there was evening and there was morning,
  a sixth day.
The heavens and the earth were finished,
  the whole host of them.
And on the seventh day God ended his
  work which ...."

Nicodemus' mind wanders once more. He blinks
moist eyes as he remembers the joy of Sabbath with his
family. An unexpected tender memory of his father touches
his heart. Was it so long ago that he stood with his father,
holding the cup and listening to his father recite the blessing?

Michael goes to the wash basin, pours the cup of
water over the back of each hand and recites the blessing.
Each member of the family takes a turn. Ruth brings the
basin to Nicodemus. There's that rush of emotion again. The
more she bends close to him, the more his face flushes. He
takes his turn, thankful that her body shadows him from the
candlelight so that she can't see his red face.

Michael removes the callah loaves from a plain cloth–
–not like the fancy cloth at Nicodemus' house.

In spite of any differences, Nicodemus begins to see
that the common thread of their Jewish core binds them
together. These new friends have saved him from death itself.
They have opened their home to him and are mending him
back to health. Yes, they have become his friends, these lowly
Galileans, this smelly old shepherd.

Nicodemus listens to their chatter in the kitchen as
they eat the Sabbath meal. Their laughter and stories sound
so inviting.

166

Who would have thought that my shepherd had this lovely family awaiting him? He has become the head of his household. I became head of my household when father died, a household with only mother and son. Doesn't seem as complete as this household.

He suddenly feels very lonely. The candles continue to flicker. Instead of a warm glow, it looks like the light is sending shadowy darts around the room. He leans his head back on the pillow and closes his eyes. He wants to walk again and know the freedom of going where he wishes to go. He yearns to see his mother and go back home.

Just as he is about to doze, in comes Ruth with that delicious smelling chicken soup.

"Aye, you must eat before you sleep."

"I must admit, it does smell good."

"Abigail made it this afternoon."

"Hmm. Tell her that it is delicious." Nicodemus lifts the bowl to his lips again. He has learned to eat from the bowl rather than with a utensil as he did in Jerusalem.

"I'll tell her. Tomorrow, we will be going to the synagogue. Perhaps by next Sabbath, you can go with us."

Go to the synagogue. That does sound wonderful. How he longs to hear the Scripture read again. It seems like he's been away for months.

Ruth continues. "Last month, the teacher came to our village. His teaching was amazing. We had people from all the surrounding villages."

"The teacher?"

"Yes, Yeshua—Jesus. Have you not heard of him?"

"No," Nicodemus snaps.

"He teaches us God's truth in wonderful new ways, ways we can understand."

"And exactly who is this 'Jesus'?"

"We believe he is the one of whom John the Baptist spoke. We heard that John called him the 'Lamb of God who takes away the sin of the world.'"

"You believe everything that John says?"

"Why yes, he is a prophet of God."

"He claimed not to be Elijah or the prophet."

"You know him?"

"No, I don't *know* him, I only met him once… and again on the way to the Galilee." His voice trails off as he remembers, with regret, passing by John and his gullible followers.

"Besides his wonderful teaching, Jesus heals people, too."

"Do you *know* that they were healed? Perhaps they were not ill to begin with."

"Why are you so doubtful?"

"Realistic is more like it. We have had many would-be Messiahs already."

Ruth stands to take his tray. "You haven't heard him. You haven't seen him."

With that, she exits. *What is wrong with that woman? I thought she was smarter than to believe an imposter.* He eases back down onto his bed, not wishing to have further conversation with her tonight. He remains with his head turned to the wall when she comes in to put out the lantern. No more words are spoken.

❦❦❦❦❦

After bread, cheese, and goat's milk, the family prepares to go to the synagogue the next morning. Nicodemus can hear Benjamin's voice pleading. "But I want to hear more stories from Master Nicodemus and I have to work every day, helping with the shearing."

Nicodemus hears Michael and Abigail's voices in soft discussion and then a squeal of delight from Benjamin.

"But don't wear him out," Michael warns as they leave.

Nicodemus notes that he did not have a treatment this morning. *Perhaps because of Sabbath,* he conjectures.

Benjamin peeks in the door to be sure Nicodemus is not resting. Nicodemus motions to him. Benjamin's whole face turns into a wide grin. "Did you rest well, sir?"

"Yes, and you?"

"Very well. Master Nicodemus, can you tell me more stories from the Torah? More shepherd stories."

"Why of course, we can do that."

Benjamin turns to the stool that Ruth has been using. He pulls it over next to the bed. Dark brown wisps of hair dart in every direction across his forehead. His big brown eyes open wide with anticipation. "Ok, I'm ready."

Nicodemus contains his amusement at this enchanting boy, but he has to admit that he is just as eager to teach, as Benjamin is to listen and learn. Even though his student is quite young, he is more enthusiastic than all the Jerusalem scholars put together. Benjamin has won his heart.

"Another shepherd story you say?"

"Yes."

"Let me see, who have we talked about so far?"

"King David, Abraham, Isaac, Jacob, and uh..." Benjamin tries to think of another.

"Moses?"

"Yes, Moses. He was a shepherd after he left Egypt the first time."

"Yes, yes, you have a good memory." Nicodemus adjusts the pillow behind his back. "Well, then, let's talk about one of Jacob's sons, Joseph."

"Oh, I remember him. His father made him a coat with many colors. And I think he became a ruler in Egypt, second only to the Pharaoh."

"Very good. Who told you that story?"

Benjamin sat a bit straighter. "My father," he beams proudly.

"Your father is a good man, Benjamin." Nicodemus leans forward, "and your mother makes wonderful soup."

They chuckle softly together.

"My grandmother teaches me stories from Scripture, too."

Ruth. The smile fades from Nicodemus lips as he remembers their encounter last night. Moving on, he says, "So, Joseph it is. Do you remember how Joseph's brothers felt about Joseph's many-colored coat?"

"They were very jealous. They didn't like him. In fact, they wanted to kill him!"

"You're right. Some of the brothers wanted to kill him, but one brother had another idea."

"I know. The oldest brother wanted to throw him in an empty cistern."

"He still would have died if they had left him there," Nicodemus reminds him. "He would have starved to death or been eaten by animals."

"Yeah, that's what Grandmama Ruth said. But she also said that Reuben thought he could come back later and rescue Joseph."

Trying to ignore the reminder of Ruth, Nicodemus pushes on. "Well, before the incident with his brothers, what had Joseph been doing?"

Benjamin's face scrunches into a deep-thinking frown. Nicodemus gives him a moment.

"Oh, I know, he was a shepherd!" he shouts with delight.

"Exactly. Once again God used a shepherd to help his people. Now Joseph's gifts weren't like David's. Joseph didn't kill a giant with the sling or write music or serve as a warrior. No, Joseph had the gift to interpret dreams and he had great leadership skills. He could organize."

Nicodemus can see by the serious look on Benjamin's face that his mind is spinning. Nicodemus pauses to give Benjamin time to absorb these thoughts.

"So, sometimes God takes shepherds and does something else with 'em," Benjamin declares.

Nicodemus suppresses his delight by quietly nodding his head. "Yes, Benjamin, sometimes He does."

By the time the rest of the family returns from the synagogue, Benjamin and Nicodemus have exhausted the entire life of Joseph with lessons of forgiveness and thanksgiving to God for the powerful way God used Joseph to accomplish His purposes.

Benjamin runs to greet everyone and excitedly conveys the highlights of the morning. Nicodemus chuckles in his room as he listens to the hurried synopsis of his teaching lesson.

Later, Benjamin comes in carrying a tray. "Grandmama Ruth said I could bring lunch to you. Do you need anything else?"

"No, I think you have fixed me up just fine."

Another wide grin. Benjamin sits on his stool again. Nicodemus drinks from his cup.

"Master Nicodemus, did you tell your little boy these stories, too?"

Nicodemus lowers his eyes and shakes his head slowly. "No, Benjamin. I've never had children."

"You haven't?"

"No, not even a wife."

"Oh," Benjamin hesitates. "I'm sorry."

"Not to worry. I've been very satisfied with my life." Nicodemus nibbles on a fig while watching to see if Benjamin is ready to let that conversation go.

"Papa says Wayward may deliver tonight."

"You have seen this before?" asks Nicodemus.

"Oh, yes, many times."

"Well then, you have had an experience that I've not had."

"Really? You've never seen a sheep deliver?"

"No, never." Nicodemus chews his bread.

"Then…" Benjamin sticks out his chest. "Then, I've done something you haven't done."

Nicodemus nods thoughtfully. "That's right." He bites into a slice of cheese.

Benjamin goes on. "I wish you could walk. I wish you could come out to the barn to watch."

"Well, I don't know about the barn, but I sure would like to do the walking part. Maybe you could ask your Grandmama Ruth about that."

Michael comes to the doorway. "Benjamin, you must not wear out our guest."

"He is no trouble, Michael. Benjamin helps the time pass and reminds me of my teaching duties in Jerusalem."

"Benjamin, I think your mother needs help in the kitchen."

Benjamin snorts and scrunches his mouth to the side as if to say, "Oh, alright, if I must." He rolls his eyes at Nicodemus and leaves obediently.

Michael smiles at Nicodemus and sits on the stool. "He's done more talking with you here than I've ever heard him before."

"Well, he's a delight to an old man."

"May I ask, what *do* you do in Jerusalem?"

"I'm a teacher of the law."

"A Pharisee?" Michael asks with a slight edge.

"Yes, indeed"

"So that explains the phylacteries."

"Yes, do you still have them?"

"I suppose they are still in the basket. Would you like for me to get them for you?"

"I would like that very much."

"I'm sorry they got rather beaten up during your fall."

"I'm surprised you even found them at all."

Michael gets up to examine Nicodemus leg. "Let me have a look." He unwinds the bandage which is much less thick than before. "I wasn't sure that wound would ever heal. The swelling around your knee is about gone."

"This family has served me well. I'm very thankful."

"You probably need to strengthen that leg to prepare for walking later on."

"How do you suggest I strengthen it?" Nicodemus asks.

"First, tighten the muscles in your leg—right here." Michael touches the upper part of Nicodemus' thigh. "Tighten and release. Try it. Tighten." Michael pauses. "Release." Michael continues, "Tighten." He pauses. "Release."

After a few more rounds of that routine, Michael says, "Now see if you can tighten, and then lift your leg a hand's width above the bed."

172

Nicodemus looks wide-eyed at Michael, but he sees that Michael is serious. He takes a deep breath, tightens his thigh and lifts with all his might. His leg barely rises. He painfully releases his leg with an equally exasperating release of air.

"I suppose I'm not ready for walking yet."

"That leg has had injury and inactivity for many days. It will take a while to regain strength. Keep working on it." Michael re-bandages the leg. "Are you finished with your food?"

"Yes, thank you."

"You'll be needing some rest now, after your busy morning of teaching." Michael grins and takes the tray of food.

Yes, he is right. He's been sitting up a long time and the "tighten, release" routine was rather exhausting. Nicodemus slides down and lays his head on the pillow.

A lovely afternoon breeze passes through his room. Sleep comes quickly. Soon he is dreaming. He hears the bawl of a newborn lamb. His eyes search for the sound. There it is nestled close to the ewe. *Why that's Wayward! I'm in the barn. Wayward has just given birth.*

Nicodemus is standing and someone is by his side holding him up. *It's so dark in here. Who is that holding me up?* The person is shorter. His eyes adjust to the lantern light. He looks again. It's Ruth. How did she get him out here?

"We must go back," she says.

They walk from the barn. She holds him up as he steps with his good leg and she supports the side with the injured leg. Three awkward steps and he is about to fall. He's falling and falling. When will he stop falling?

Suddenly, Nicodemus wakes up. His eyes dart around the room. *Ah, only a dream.*

He lies there thinking through the activities of the day. He remembers his good talk with Benjamin. What a delightful boy. He thinks about Benjamin's question. "Have you told these stories to your little boy?" No children. No wife. Very satisfied with my life.

173

A wave of sadness sweeps over him. *Satisfied with my life.*

He rolls his head toward the wall. He feels imprisoned. *When will I be released? I must work my leg.* Tighten——release. Tighten—release. It takes his mind off the dream, off of Ruth.

Michael enters. "Everything alright in here? I heard you calling out."

"Just a bad dream. I've been working my leg."

"Good, the more the better. Oh, wait, I'll be back."

Wait? Well, I'm sure not going anywhere.

Shortly, Michael returns and hands Nicodemus something bundled up. His phylacteries.

"Thank you, Michael." He holds them close to his chest. "Thank you."

"Certainly." He starts to leave the room. Nicodemus wants someone to talk to.

"Benjamin says you are shearing the sheep this week."

"Yes, it will take us a few days. They don't like the shear, but they like being cooler."

"Has Wayward had her lamb?"

"No, we're still waiting. A few other ewes are ready as well."

"Always work to do."

"Yes. Do you need anything else?"

"No. Thank you for bringing these." He holds up the phylacteries. Michael nods and leaves.

CHAPTER 25
A New Week

We know that suffering produces perseverance,
perseverance, character, and character, hope.
Rom. 5:3-4

Nicodemus wakes up the next morning to the sound of sheep, but it is a different sound, not their usual "waking-up" sound. *Are they all having lambs? No, that can't be. Ah, yes. I remember, they're being sheared today. What a racket!*

Nicodemus listens for the sound of Ruth's sandals, but only hears Abigail's light humming. Shortly, he hears the patter of Abigail's bare feet coming toward his room. She peeks in.

"Shalom. Good morning, Master Nicodemus."

She waits while Nicodemus sits up for his breakfast, sets the water basin in his lap, and hands him the towel from her arm. When she returns, she sets the food tray on the stool.

"I hope you rested well."

"Very well, thank you."

"Sorry for all the noise. The sheep get fussy waiting their turn for the shearing."

"They evidently don't like being sheared."

"Oh no, they are quite silent while they are sheared. They're just noisy waiting their turn."

"I see."

After Abigail removes the water and hands him the food tray, she stands awkwardly, not knowing what else to say. Nicodemus takes up the slack. "I enjoyed your delicious chicken soup last night."

Abigail drops her head embarrassed. "Oh, I'm glad you liked it." Nicodemus takes a bite of the eggs. "Is there anything else I can get for you?" she asks.

"No. Nothing. Everyone has cared for me well."

She smiles, nods her head, and takes her leave.

Alone again. Where is Ruth? No one to talk to. Benjamin is helping his father; Abigail has her work, but where is Ruth? *Still mad about our discussion of that would-be Messiah. Doesn't she know I must warn her?*

Nicodemus chews slowly, making the meal last longer. He looks toward his window. *The neighbor must be feeding the chickens, all that clucking and pecking.* At least it serves as a temporary distraction.

What about my wound and my bandages? Isn't Ruth going to check them today? She didn't come in at all yesterday. But even with concentrated listening, all he hears is Abigail. She comes back in to take his tray. He can stand it no longer.

"Where is Ruth today?" he asks, as casually as he can muster.

"She's gone to Capernaum. She said she needed to get some supplies." Abigail notices Nicodemus' questioning look. "Medical supplies," she adds. "She goes about once a month. Many people depend on her."

"How far away is Capernaum from here?"

"About a two-hour walk."

"Oh, I wish I had known. I need to send word to my family that I'm doing well. They don't know about my accident."

"I'm sorry. Ruth should be back later this afternoon."

"She doesn't travel by boat?"

Abigail smiles and picks up the tray. "Oh no, that would be too much bother." As she leaves, she looks over her shoulder adding, "and expense."

So, he must wait until late afternoon to truly have any attention again. *Will she still refuse to come and see me? Well, maybe her "medical duty" will bring her in.*

Nicodemus sulks. He holds his face in his hands. He runs his fingers up through his stiff, dusty hair, a reminder that he hasn't had a good thorough cleaning yet. *I probably smell. No wonder Abigail doesn't stay long. No wonder Ruth doesn't want to be near me. Benjamin and Michael don't notice because I smell just like they do.*

He studies his leg. Time for exercise. *I must walk again. I must get out of here—back to my normal way of life.* Tighten–release. Tighten–release. *Oh to dip in my warm bath at home.* Tighten–release. *Ten times this morning. I must add two more each time.*

Now, to lift my leg. His hands grip the side of the bed. He slowly fills his chest with air, focusing all his attention on the wounded leg. He tightens the muscle, willing his leg to move. Up, up, a little more. His strength gives out and the leg thumps to the bed as he blows out all the pent up air. He grunts as his leg pulsates from the drop. *At least I'm making progress, such as it is.*

He lays his head back against the wall and relaxes from the ordeal. With his head tilted up, he realizes that he hasn't said his morning prayers. He remembers the phylacteries wrapped up on the table beside his bed where he left them yesterday.

Delighted with the thought of doing something from his real life, he reverently reaches for this one piece of himself that is left. He places the box on his left hand and wraps the leather strap between his fingers, around his hand, and up his arm, 5, 6, 7 times around. Now he places the second box to his forehead, runs the straps around his head and over his shoulder. It all comes back so easily. *No prayer shawl, but that's all right, I'm just glad to have something of the past.* He says his morning prayer with renewed energy.

Slowly, he unwinds the straps, folds the tools of his prayers, and places them on the table. He slides down the bed to rest, tired from the morning duties, and weary of waiting.

Lunch is uneventful except that it provides a short lapse from hearing the bleating sheep, while Michael and Benjamin come in for lunch. Shortly, they are back out to continue their shearing. No time for greetings. No time for listening to his stories. No time to notice their guest.

How long into the afternoon will Ruth be gone? I should have asked. But will she even come in to see me once she returns? Deep sigh.

Time for more exercises. Tighten–release. Tighten–release. 3, 4, 5... *I did ten this morning. I must do twelve.* He is pleasantly surprised at how much easier it is now. Good sign.

Oops, I spoke too soon. He huffs and puffs and grunts and groans. 11, 12. *Whew!* Certainly that deserves an afternoon nap. Perhaps when he awakens, Ruth will be back.

CHAPTER 26
Ruth Returns

A cheerful look brings joy to the heart,
and good news gives health to the bones.
Proverbs 15:30

Nicodemus has grown accustomed to the noisy sheep voicing their protest over the change in routine. In fact, it lulls him to sleep.

He is on the hillside enjoying the fresh air away from the sheep pen. The gurgling brook runs beside him; a blue bird flies overhead; the sheep graze lazily just down the hill from him while Michael plays that haunting tune on his flute.

Suddenly, Nicodemus is in the Temple area bumped this way and that by busy festival goers. *What festival is this?* Some are carrying sheep they brought from home; others hurry to the pens just inside the Sheep Gate, looking to purchase an unblemished lamb for the sacrifice.

"No, you can't take these sheep," Nicodemus shouts. "They must be kept for shearing. We need their wool. Go away. Leave them be!" Nicodemus flails his arms to shoo away the pilgrims and Temple helpers.

One of the shepherds in charge yells back at Nicodemus. "Who do you think you are? We brought these sheep for the sacrifices. Get out of our way. We're doing the work of the Lord."

Nicodemus is pushed to the side and then shoved another way. He loses his balance and is about to fall. Falling, falling down the hill. Rolling over sharp rocks. Falling, falling.

"Help," he hears himself cry out. He opens his eyes. The room seems to be spinning for a moment. Then he realizes he is in his bed. There's the window, the stool, the tables.

I've been dreaming again. What a crazy dream. I've been around these sheep too long.

Nicodemus becomes aware that the sheep have ceased their bleating. *The task must be accomplished.* He hears voices in the kitchen. His ears perk up for he recognizes the voice he's been waiting for. *It's Ruth.*

But will she come? Is she still upset with him? Ruth and Abigail are talking, but he can't quite make out their conversation. Ruth sounds excited.

Shortly, he hears the familiar flip flop of sandals. Quickly, he brushes his hair back with his hands. She pokes her head in the door. "Is anyone awake in here?"

"Just barely. A bad dream woke me up."

"Well, I have surprises." She bustles into the room with her medical case. "I have a new salve that was brought in from Laodicea across the great sea. It is actually an eye salve, but many say it has wonderful healing properties for injuries."

Her face is aglow with excitement and hope. Nicodemus can only smile and bask in her joy.

Ruth carefully removes the precious salve from her bag and holds it triumphantly before him.

"Well, let's see what miraculous effects it will have," he says, chiding her just a bit.

She goes to work, unwrapping the cloths around his wound. "What is this?" she exclaims. "I'm only gone a day and it looks better than ever."

"Two days," he states flatly.

Anxious to try her new find, she ignores his comment completely. "Well, it can't help but make it heal even more." She carefully spreads a thin layer of her valuable salve over his wound. "There now, let's see what that does." She sits back on her stool, staring at the wound as though waiting for it to suddenly heal.

Finally, her eyes brighten again. "Oh, I nearly forgot. I have another surprise for you, but that will have to wait until later."

"You tease me unmercifully."

She laughs, enjoying her secret. "I must get your supper for you. You need strength for the next task." And off she goes to the kitchen, bag of salve in hand.

He smiles contentedly. All seems right with the world again. What is this strange power she seems to hold over him? *I'm only in need of her medical help*, he tells himself. *That is all.* But all his self-talk can't deny the contentment he feels in her presence.

Nicodemus looks at his leg and smiles again at the new wonder salve she applied and her comment about how well his wound is healing. *Maybe all my exercising has helped.* He scoots back down to proceed with his routine. He'll try to make it to sixteen this time.

13, 14, 15, 16. *I think I can do two more.* "17, 18," he says out loud in great triumph. He blows out his breath and continues huffing until his breathing returns to normal. All of a sudden he remembers Ruth's last words. "You need strength for the next task." Feeling energized, he tries lifting his leg again and is amazed how easily he gets it up a hand's width off the bed.

He hears Ruth coming and pushes back up in a sitting position. Once settled with his tray, he asks, "And just what is this new task?"

Unable to contain her *surprise* any longer, she says, "I think it is time to see if we can get you up." She goes outside the door and brings in a pair of crutches. He grins broadly.

"Well, I have a surprise for *you*," he says. "I have been doing an exercise that Michael taught me, to strengthen the muscles in my upper legs. I can lift my leg a hand's width."

She drops her chin with a how-about-that kind of look. "So my shepherd son is taking over the doctoring duties, huh? Well, he has always had a knack for helping. Look how he wrapped you up and cared for your wound out there on the hills."

"Yes. It was a rough few days, but he kept me alive got me here in one piece." Nicodemus ponders that journey for a moment. "But I never thought I would ever be hauled into town in a cart with a crippled sheep in tow."

He looks up to see Ruth covering her mouth. She is hardly able to hold in a mounting snicker. Unable to contain it any longer, she giggles and then bursts out laughing. In between heaves of laughter, she spits out a phrase or two. "Oh, I know," she says. "You were such a sight." More cackles. "You were trying to look so dignified." Her shoulders shake with giddiness.

Her laughter is contagious. Nicodemus chuckles and sputters, caught up in her fun and laughing at her laughter. "And when I saw that sheep all cuddled up next to you..." She cackles so hard that tears come to her eyes. "I thought, 'what in the world has that son of mine drug in from the hills?' "

Nicodemus is getting so tickled that he nearly spills his soup which makes both of them laugh all the harder.

Abigail comes running in. "What is going on?' she asks breathlessly. Nicodemus and Ruth look at each other and burst out again. Abigail can't get a thing out of them. She finally shakes her head and leaves, apparently satisfied that there is no catastrophe.

Finally, after several deep sighs, they each settle down into pleasant smiles. Nicodemus pops a couple of olives in his mouth. "I suppose you *were* anxious about having this intruder in your home, knowing that it might take a long while."

Ruth raises her eyebrows. "Yes, I did consider that this would be a long-term ordeal." She picks up the stool and brings it beside his bed. "But I must say that I rather enjoy our talks," she says, as she sits.

Nicodemus puts his bread down, fearful that he will choke if he tries to eat it. That strange wave of emotion he had before sweeps over him again, warming him from his toes all the way to the top of his head. "Uh, yes," he stammers, afraid to look into her eyes. "I have enjoyed the company as well."

As if aware of his discomfort, she moves on to another subject. "I had a good trip to Capernaum today.

Besides my purchases, I had opportunity to visit some friends."

Glad for the change in subject, Nicodemus joins right in and tries to continue his meal. "I wish I had known you were going there because I have an aunt and uncle in Capernaum. I need to get word to them that I am healing from an accident."

"Oh, really? What is your uncle's name?"

"Laban."

"Laban and Leah?"

"Why yes. Do you know them?"

"I talked with them today! Leah's sister is visiting from Jerusalem." Suddenly the connection dawns on Ruth. "Why, Leah's sister must be …"

"My mother. Yes! Did you tell them I was here and that I'm all right?"

"No… I mean, I didn't know. I had no idea that they were related to you. I'm sorry."

"I'm afraid that they are getting worried about me. I had planned to be back before last Sabbath."

"Surely there will be someone going to Capernaum in the next day or two. We can send a message by them. I will check on it for you."

"That would be good. Thank you."

"Well, tomorrow we will try out your new crutches and see if we can get you upright."

"Maybe I'll get to see Tag-a-long deliver her lamb after all. Has she had it yet?"

"I don't know. I'll have to ask the boys. I'm not sure you'll be ready to make it all the way to the barn."

"A little bit at a time, eh?"

"One step at a time. Well, I will take your tray and let you rest up for your big day tomorrow."

She puts her stool back and picks up his tray. "I'll be back to blow out your lantern."

He is snuggled down into his bed when she returns. She straightens his blanket and extinguishes the lantern. "Good night, Nicodemus."

"Shalom. Good night, Ruth."

He is glad that the subject of the "Galilean preacher" did not come up. He smiles when he remembers Ruth's laughing spell. *Her presence always seems to fill the room.*

Tomorrow, tomorrow I will walk again. He drifts off to sleep with a smile still lingering on his face.

CHAPTER 27
Walking Day

Walk in the way that the Lord your God has commanded you.
Deut. 5:33

Nicodemus awakens as the first rays of sunshine creep into his room. He gazes at his small window, awash with the light of promise for this special day. His heart beats with excitement.

I must do my exercises to prepare. I'll wake up those muscles—get them ready!

He begins his routine. Tighten, release–one. Tighten, release–two. *Much easier now.* 15, 16–*I must pass the last goal.* 17, 18–*almost there.* 19 and 20–*I did it!*

He relaxes a moment and then tries to lift his leg. Tighten, lift. Up, up, up—straight up in the air. Victory! He has been lifting the other one, too, just to keep them both in good working order.

Energized, he sits up, leans forward and stretches his hands toward his toes. Not quite. He leans forward again and again, fingertips edging closer. He sits tall, rolling his shoulders backward, forward, and backward again. He rolls his head around slowly, stretching out the tension in his neck.

He eases back down to rest, his heart throbbing in his chest. *I mustn't overdo.* His heavy breathing subsides.

Nicodemus is hungry and anxious to get on with the task for the day, but he doesn't hear the slightest activity in the kitchen. He closes his eyes, trying to be patient. Suddenly his eyes pop open when he hears the click of a clay bowl. *Porridge, breakfast, action.* He smiles. By the time Ruth walks in with his tray of food, Nicodemus is propped up.

"Well, I see the patient is ready for the day."

"More than ready. I've been waiting for this day a long time."

"Let me guess, you've already been doing your exercises this morning," she teases.

185

She knows him so well. A bit embarrassed, he admits, "Well as a matter of fact, I have, and with greater ease than ever, I might add."

Suddenly, Benjamin comes rushing in the room. "I got up early to do all my chores. Have I missed it? Oh, I do want to see Master Nicodemus walk. Have you tried yet?"

"Whoa, hold on there." Ruth hugs Benjamin's shoulders. "Let the poor man have his breakfast. No, you haven't missed a thing. Have the mama sheep had their lambs yet?"

"Four of them have, but Tag-a-long is still, well, tagging along." They all laugh.

Benjamin notices the crutches in the corner of the room. "When will you try to walk?"

Ruth pats Benjamin on the head. "After a good breakfast, if you'll just give him time to eat."

One side of Benjamin's mouth turns up as he tilts his head for a sideward glance at Nicodemus. "Sorry," he says.

"I'm just as anxious as you are, but we have to do whatever the doctor tells us." Nicodemus rolls his dancing eyes at Ruth.

Ruth looks from one to the other. "You two would rush the chicken to have her eggs if you could." They both laugh, wondering what chickens have to do with anything, but knowing that they are being gently chastised.

"Ok. See, my bowl is clean." Nicodemus holds his bowl up for inspection. He gobbles down the last piece of bread and finishes the last drops of goat's milk. "All done."

Ruth shakes her head and smirks at the two of them as she takes the tray from the room.

Benjamin eyes the crutches again. "Mind if I try them?"

"No, maybe you can teach me. I've never used crutches."

Benjamin puts the top of the crutches under his arms. "I had a crippled friend who used them all the time. I watched him, but I never tried it myself. Let's see." He points the other end to the floor in front of him, but they stretch way out. He tries to swing himself forward, but falls sideways.

Nicodemus' eyebrows arch. "Are you all right?"

Ruth comes storming into the room when she hears the crash. "What's this?"

Benjamin scrambles to get up. "I was just trying them out."

"If you were a man, they might work for you. These weren't made for the height of a boy."

Benjamin drops his chin. "Oh, I didn't think about that."

"If you're not careful, I'll have two patients."

"Sorry, Grandmama."

Ruth ruffles his hair lovingly. "Are you in one piece?"

Benjamin nods his head silently.

"Well, now, let's see to the real patient. Nicodemus, see if you can swing your legs around and bring your feet to the floor."

Nicodemus tightens his legs and slowly shifts them to the side of the bed, bending his knees as his feet ease on down to the floor.

"Any pain?"

"No."

Ruth holds the crutches in one hand. "Benjamin, you stand on that side of him and I'll stand on this side. Nicodemus, you can put one arm around my shoulders and lean the other hand on Benjamin's shoulder."

They both lean down to support Nicodemus as he tries to stand. All three grunt a little in the effort, but soon have Nicodemus up on his good foot.

"Now, just stand here a moment to get your balance."

Even in the midst of this great effort, Nicodemus is well aware of the feelings inside of him as he stands there touching, no, almost embracing Ruth. His face is closer to her than ever before. He shakes his thoughts away and focuses instead on the task at hand.

"Are you feeling balanced?" she asks.

"Yes."

"Put just a little pressure on your injured leg. Not full weight, just half of your weight."

He feels only slight discomfort, more born out of fear that it might begin to hurt than any actual pain.

"Now release the weight." He stands with full weight on the good leg.

"Look straight ahead instead of down at your feet. Balance yourself. Breathe deeply."

After a few moments, she says again, "Put half weight on your other foot again." She waits.

"How is that?" she questions.

"Good."

"Release the weight."

Nicodemus allows only his toe to dangle on the floor without any weight.

"Release your hand from Benjamin's shoulder and balance on this crutch." She eases the crutch under his arm and he re-shifts his balance to the crutch.

"Balanced?"

"Yes," he answers.

"Look straight ahead again."

Nicodemus straightens his shoulders which eases him away from Ruth. He feels vulnerable, as though he is losing a crutch. *Fancy that.*

Ruth slides the crutch between them, anchoring it under his arm. "Steady. Steady." She steps forward so his hand is free to slide down to the crutch. "Take hold of the crutch. Steady. Steady."

She remains close to him and gradually backs away. "Very good. You are on your own. Upright!" She says in triumph.

Benjamin's eyes are wide with excitement. He's never looked up at his friend before. "You did it, Master Nicodemus."

"Now, let's see if we can reverse the process. Put your arm around my shoulder while I move the crutch away."

Nicodemus is partly disappointed that he isn't going to try to walk with the crutch, but partly grateful because he is getting weary and fearful of being unstable.

"Benjamin, when Master Nicodemus puts his hand on your shoulder, remove the crutch." Benjamin follows directions, delighted to be a helper.

"We will ease you back down to the bed." They all grunt collectively as Nicodemus sits on the side of the bed. Ruth lifts his bad leg as Nicodemus moves his good leg back onto the bed.

"Ah, a good morning's work," she says. "Now you must rest." She motions to Benjamin.

As they exit the room, Nicodemus calls out, "Ruth." She turns. "Thank you." She nods and smiles.

Nicodemus sighs out loud with exhaustion. He thought he was so ready for the job, but realizes that he is still rather weak from all this time in bed. He welcomes the rest, but is disappointed that they didn't accomplish more.

Possibly an hour later, Ruth reappears. "Are you strong enough to try our routine a second time?"

"Certainly," he responds with the enthusiasm of a little boy.

"I'll go fetch Benjamin to help us."

Benjamin is delighted that his services are needed. They all move with more assurance this time after their practice round. Nicodemus moves with confidence up to his good foot, crutches in place, standing straight.

"Try half weight again," Ruth coaches. It feels better this time as he knows what to expect. "How do you feel?"

"Great, let's do more."

"Alright. Place the crutches about a foot's length in front of you." He complies. "Now, hop forward on your good foot." Benjamin and Ruth stay very near as Nicodemus hops forward with only a slight falter.

"Good. Good. Let's try it again. Crutches forward." She pauses. "Then a hop." Smoother this time.

"I think I have the feel of it."

"Ok, try two steps." His helpers remain very near. "Great. Let's stop and focus on balance for a moment. Are the crutches at a comfortable height for you?"

"They're perfect. How did you figure out the length I needed?"

"One night while you were sleeping, I measured you with a strip of cloth from armpit to heel."

Nicodemus grins and shakes his head. "You think of everything, don't you?"

"See if you can make a slight turn toward the stool this time. Two steps."

He maneuvers well.

"Now two more turns back toward the bed." He starts to lean too far sideways. Ruth quickly catches him as he regains his balance. "That's okay, you're doing well. You probably have four more steps back to the bed. Can you do four steps and stop?"

Nicodemus hops steadily, relieved to have a straight path.

"Can you pivot yourself around?" He works at it and hands off his crutches as he sits on the bed. "Great work this morning," Ruth encourages.

"Thank you. I have good helpers." Nicodemus pats Benjamin's back and receives a big smile.

"We'll let you rest until lunch."

Twice more that afternoon, they practice their walk/hop routine, each time going a few steps farther.

"Perhaps you can join us at the table in the kitchen for our evening meal."

"That would be nice," he says, as he eases himself down on the bed.

Energized by his good progress for the day and the prospect of sitting at a table for a meal with this good family, he dozes for what seems only a short while, when two male faces peer around the doorway. Benjamin has brought his father, Michael, to show off Nicodemus' accomplishments for the day.

When Nicodemus opens his eyes, Michael steps into the room. "I hear you have had a victorious day, sir."

"Shalom, Michael. Yes, we've made great progress today."

"I've been sent to be the new assistant."

Nicodemus winks at Benjamin. "Do you think he will know what to do?"

Benjamin joins in with the fun. "Maybe he can learn."

Nicodemus swings his legs around with surprising ease. Michael notices. "My, you *have* improved."

Benjamin grabs the crutches and hands one to Michael. "Let him put his arm around your shoulder to help him up," Benjamin instructs, as he bends his shoulder down for Nicodemus to support himself.

All three heave themselves up and Nicodemus balances himself with the crutch Benjamin hands him.

"Give him the other crutch, Papa." Michael looks a bit unsure.

Nicodemus assures him. "It's okay, Michael, I'm ready."

With only one turn to maneuver, Nicodemus heads for the door. He realizes he has never been nor even seen beyond this point except for the day he arrived. He aims in the direction where he has heard kitchen voices the last week and a half. Even now he can hear the dishes thumping on the table and wonderful smells floating through the room. A few more steps and there he sees Ruth and Abigail putting on the final touches of their meal. The table is spread like a huge feast with roast lamb in the middle.

"Are we inviting the neighbors in?" Nicodemus asks in awe of what he sees before him.

"We're celebrating your victory today!" Ruth exclaims.

They seat Nicodemus beside Benjamin. Michael offers the blessing and the bowls are passed around. For the first time in a long time, Nicodemus feels like a person again instead of a patient. He enjoys the chatter around the table and notices the humble but well-kept surroundings. This feels like family. He looks over at Ruth. She responds with smiling, knowing eyes.

"Is everything to your liking?" she asks.

"Yes, everything is wonderful," he says, gazing into her warm eyes.

Michael glances at Nicodemus, then his mother, and then at Abigail as if to say, "What is going on here?"

Abigail raises her eyebrows and lifts her shoulders as if to say, "I don't know."

Benjamin begins to tell about Tag-a-long, which distracts them all from their previous thoughts. "I think she may give birth tomorrow!" he concludes.

"Abigail, Ruth, you have prepared a wonderful feast and I feel quite celebrated. Thank you for caring for me so well. I believe I need to make my way back to my bed, now."

Nicodemus relishes rolling back in his bed. It has been an eventful, gratifying day, but he is more than ready to rest. He drops off immediately and enjoys a good sleep.

⸎⸎⸎⸎

The next morning, Nicodemus is startled awake by Benjamin's excited voice from the kitchen. "But he's never seen the birthing of a lamb, Mama. It could happen any time now. Please let me wake him."

"Benjamin, Master Nicodemus hasn't even had his breakfast yet. Besides, the barn is a long way. It would be too far for him to try to walk."

"I know. I've already thought about that. He walked to the kitchen yesterday. We can bring the cart to the kitchen door and then he can ride to the barn. I have a bale of hay for him to sit on. Please Mama, please."

Nicodemus shouts from his room. "It sounds like a great plan to me. Who will come and bring me my crutches?"

Benjamin's eyes brighten. Ruth hugs Benjamin. "I'll help," she calls loud enough to be heard in Nicodemus' room.

"Me, too," Benjamin exclaims as he scrambles after her. Abigail just shakes her head, knowing she's been out-voted.

Nicodemus doesn't relish climbing into that cart again, but Benjamin has stolen his heart. He would do anything for him and he doesn't want to miss sharing this special moment with him.

Bumping along in the old cart brings back a host of unpleasant memories, but Nicodemus tries to focus on the mission at hand. Michael comes running from the barn. "I'll pull the cart, Benjamin. You better tend to Tag-a-long."

Nicodemus' heart flutters with excitement as they reach the barn. This is so important to Benjamin, and Nicodemus is anxious to share in his joy.

Just as Nicodemus hobbles into the barn, Benjamin cries out, "She's ready, Papa!"

Michael helps Nicodemus sit on the bale of hay and they watch together as Tag-a-long raises her nose in the air and emits strange bleating sounds. She paces around in a circle as the bleating grows louder. Finally, she lies on the straw.

Michael bends over Tag-a-long. "She's struggling, Benjamin, I believe you better help her."

Benjamin immediately eases his hand into the birth canal, clutches the lamb and gently pulls. The nose slides out and then two front feet. Tag-a-long's body contracts in and out in an attempt to birth this new life. Little by little, Benjamin pulls in time with the contractions. At last, the new lamb is born! Nicodemus is more wide-eyed than Benjamin.

The lamb lies very still. Nicodemus holds his breath. *Is it alive?* Finally, the lamb wiggles around and makes a feeble attempt to stand, but falls back down. Tag-a-long looks around at her little prize and nudges it with her nose. The new lamb responds as they rub noses with each other. Nicodemus is mesmerized by the natural way they connect to each other. The ewe begins licking the lamb.

"What is Tag-a-long doing now?" Nicodemus whispers to Michael.

"She's cleaning her lamb."

Cleaning for sure! She licks the lamb's nose, the legs, and the body. Soon, Tag–a-long urges her newborn to begin sucking.

Benjamin slips over to sit on the hay bale next to Nicodemus. Nicodemus was impressed with Benjamin's calmness during the birth and his lack of fear. *His father must have taught him how to do this several times.*

"Papa always says that he is amazed at the new life God brings us," Benjamin says reverently. "Isn't he a fine lamb?"

"A fine lamb indeed," says Nicodemus as a tear escapes down his cheek. *What a picture this is; a thoughtful young man beholding an innocent lamb. He's been taught to see the heart of the Lord Almighty. Blessed be the name of the Lord.* "And you are a fine shepherd, like King David himself."

As Nicodemus lies in bed that night, he is once more made aware how the members of this family have endeared themselves to him. A part of him would like to stay here indefinitely. *A teacher of the law happy to be in a shepherd's home— how could this have possibly happened?*

CHAPTER 28
Back to Capernaum

In his heart a man plans his course,
but the Lord determines his steps.
Proverbs 16:9

As each day passes, Nicodemus grows stronger at the home of Michael, the shepherd. Ruth encourages him, Benjamin delights him, and Michael and Abigail graciously host him. Word has been sent to the home of Uncle Laban that Nicodemus is well and will be joining them soon. He also asked for word to be sent to Joseph in Jerusalem that he will be delayed for a while.

Now that Nicodemus is no longer bedfast, he can more easily bathe himself and wash his hair. What a relief! In the evening, he sits with the family in the gathering room. Usually, Michael's family goes to bed early, leaving Nicodemus and Ruth to have additional conversation before turning in for the night.

He barely needs his crutches these days. In fact, he has used only a cane recently.

"Will you take your crutches with you tomorrow when we go to Capernaum?" Ruth asks.

"No, I think I can manage with my cane."

"It *is* fairly flat, but we will have some rough terrain at times."

"I understand. We may have to stop occasionally, but I think I'll be fine. What time do you suggest we leave?"

"Shortly after sun-up. It would be best for you not to have the unforgiving rays of the mid-day sun."

Ruth sits with her head down. She smoothes her skirt out and fiddles with her hands. Nicodemus watches her, then lowers his eyes to the floor. In the unusual, awkward silence, they both are facing the fact that their time together is coming to an end. They will walk together to Capernaum in the morning, but tonight is their last private time alone.

195

"I will..." he begins to say. "Will you be staying..." she begins to say at the same time.

"Go ahead," he urges her on.

"I was just going to ask if you will be staying at your uncle's house for a while."

"Yes, until I can walk without this cane. I will need more stamina for the journey back to Jerusalem. Have you been to Jerusalem?"

"Oh, yes, many times, mostly at Passover. It's quite a trip."

"Indeed. And Michael, does he go as well?"

"Yes. I may travel alone to Capernaum, but I would never make the journey to Jerusalem by myself."

"Of course."

Another awkward pause. *What is this? We always talk so freely. No pause in our conversation. Why are we so short with words tonight? Perhaps it is sadness.*

"Ruth ..."

"Yes ..." More awkward silence.

"Uh, I suppose we need to rest for our journey tomorrow."

"Yes, I'm sure you're right."

They stand, look at each other, and hesitate for a moment.

"Do you need anything?"

"No, nothing. Goodnight, Ruth."

"Shalom."

Somehow that oft-used word seems so final tonight. Nicodemus lies awake for a time. He is excited about seeing his family and eventually returning to Jerusalem, to his work and his friends. After all, this is what he has been working toward, right? But a weight lingers with him, robbing him of rest in his soul. He shakes the feeling, rolls over, and eventually falls asleep.

The next morning after breakfast, he begins packing the new bag Ruth had bought him to replace the dirty, battered one. Michael had given him one extra tunic and an extra pair of sandals. Abigail had packed food for the journey.

He packs these gifts and the one remaining possession he has with him, his phylacteries. He loops the straps of the bag over his head with the bag hanging at his side.

When Nicodemus comes out the front door, Michael is standing there with Bramble. "I thought you might like to say 'goodbye' to your old friend."

"Baa," Bramble says as she walks on four good legs to Nicodemus. He chuckles as he bends down to pat his old traveling companion.

"And 'baa' to you, Bramble. Looks like you have a good leg too. Perhaps we have both learned some lessons."

Benjamin hangs around looking quite forlorn. "Master Nicodemus, will you come back to see us again?"

Nicodemus glances at Michael, who nods.

"I'm sure of it. It may be awhile though."

Michael asks, "Are you sure you don't want me to go with you?"

"No Michael, you have your work. You have done quite enough for me. You saved my life, my friend." They embrace. Nicodemus does not let go until he is able to get his emotions under control.

"We will miss you," Michael whispers as he holds his friend.

Nicodemus takes Abigail's hands in his. "My dear Abigail, you have been most gracious to this old man. May your house be blessed."

"Thank you, Master Nicodemus. We have been honored to have you."

Benjamin hangs his head, waiting his turn for the good-byes.

Nicodemus ruffles Benjamin's tossed hair. "Benjamin, my son..." Benjamin cannot wait for words. He grabs Nicodemus around the waist and clings to him, tears spilling down his cheeks.

Nicodemus fights for composure as he holds him close. "You are a fine shepherd. You must continue to be a good help to your father." He feels Benjamin's head nod against his abdomen. "And take care of all those stinky sheep." Benjamin giggles as he continues to hold on.

"I have an idea," says Nicodemus, bending down to look him eye to eye. "Maybe you could come to Jerusalem at Passover and stay at my house. Would you like that?"

Benjamin musters a slight smile as he nods his head.

"We must be off. Ruth says we should arrive before the mid-day sun shines its unforgiving rays." He smiles at Ruth and they walk together down the path.

Nicodemus turns after several steps to see his three dear friends and one stray sheep still standing in front of the house. "Shalom, my friends," he calls over his shoulder.

"Shalom," they answer, as they wave.

Glad to have that difficult departure behind him, Nicodemus begins to chit chat with Ruth. They seem to be back to themselves again as conversation flows freely.

In the next town, they approach a well. The last woman is just leaving as they come near.

"Hello, Ruth," she calls as she goes about her day.

"Good to see you, Miriam. Is Silas doing better?"

"Yes, very well, thank you."

Ruth explains to Nicodemus how she had cared for Miriam's husband with his medical needs last month.

Nicodemus nods his head knowingly. He, too, knows the care of this dear woman.

"Let's rest here at the well. We can have a drink of water," she suggests.

Nicodemus doesn't have to be asked a second time. He is ready to stop. Perhaps this trip will be more strenuous than he thought.

A full olive tree shades them well and a light wind provides a pleasant breeze for their rest.

They travel for another hour focusing more on breathing than talking. In another small town, they stop to enjoy something tasty from Abigail's food supply.

"With all our stops, we may not make it in two hours," Nicodemus sighs.

"That's why we left early. We'll still make it before noon." She pauses and then comments casually, "Perhaps Jesus will be back in Capernaum when you are there. You will be able to see him for yourself and hear his teaching."

Nicodemus can't believe his ears. She hadn't mentioned this man's name since that day she went to Capernaum. He thought it was a subject put to rest. His anger flares as before.

"Ruth, I have no intention of seeing or hearing that man."

"But he heals the sick and he teaches in amazing ways. He has a compassionate heart and teaches the people about God's love."

"Ruth, I will hear no more of this."

He speaks with such force, she is immediately silenced. She has never seen this side of him before. She shrinks like a whipped puppy.

Nicodemus realizes how forceful his words sounded, and is embarrassed, but he will not back down on this subject. She must understand that.

"Perhaps we should continue our journey," he says at last.

They walk along in silence.

Soon he sees the seashore and begins to recognize familiar townspeople, familiar fruit stands and houses. "We're getting close, aren't we?"

"Yes, Capernaum is just around the bend."

At last, he sees all things familiar. Why, he can even lead Ruth now. The thoughts of being with his mother and family overwhelm him. It seems like a life time since he has seen them instead of a few weeks.

"There it is!" Excitement fills his voice. "There's the street where my family lives."

"Yes, I know," she smiles, glad to see his sudden enthusiasm.

His tired legs take on renewed energy. She can hardly keep up with him.

Laban is sitting on a stool in front of the house. He catches a glimpse of Nicodemus and squints his eyes to make sure. He stands and shades his eyes from the brightness of the day.

Nicodemus waves his hand like a school boy. Ruth laughs at his excitement. "I'm sure he sees you, Nicodemus."

Laban waves back and darts into the house. Immediately, Martha and Leah rush out the door. Nicodemus lumbers as fast as he is able while his mother, Martha, runs to meet him.

"Nico!" She embraces him. "Oh, Nico, I was so worried about you. Let me look at you. You're walking with only a cane?"

"Yes, mother, I'm almost good as new."

She embraces him again and he hugs her warmly. "It's so good to see you, Mother."

"We just couldn't imagine why you were gone so long." She looks him over once more. "My, that's an interesting looking tunic." She grins.

"May a tired old man come in and take a rest?"

"Of course. I'm sorry. I'm just so glad to see you."

Leah and Laban saunter over to give their greetings as well. "Come, come, you must be exhausted from your long walk on a crippled leg." Leah shoos them toward the house.

"Not so crippled now, Aunt Leah."

Laban leans over to Nicodemus and whispers, "Rebecca is waiting to see you. She's been very anxious." Nicodemus nods his head.

They enter the house and Nicodemus walks straight to Rebecca's room. "Where's my favorite cousin?"

"Oh, Nicodemus, thank the Lord you are here. We were all worried sick about you."

"Well, I'm here, safe and sound. I'm not sure I can carry you though."

"That's all right, I'm just glad to see you."

"Everyone, come to dinner," Leah calls out. She has quickly put a meal together.

"Can a traveler wash his hands first?"

After they gather around, Laban asks Nicodemus to say the blessing. As Nicodemus looks around the table at these wonderful familiar faces, his emotions once again come to the surface. He clears his throat and prays a sincere blessing over the food and these dear ones. For a moment, no one speaks.

Trying to overcome the awkwardness, Leah chatters. "Now just pass whatever is in front of you. There's plenty, and what you don't see, we'll find more. Ruth, I can't believe you didn't tell us about Nicodemus when you were here last month."

"I would have, if I had known he belonged to you. I was amazed when Nicodemus and I were talking and discovered that he was your nephew. You had mentioned that your nephew had come, but I never made the connection."

Nicodemus hastens to save Ruth's good name. "Ruth was kind enough to send word to you through an acquaintance. Who was it, Ruth?"

"It was the shepherd that helped Michael when they found you on the hillside."

"Oh, I remember, the one who shared the sheep pen that first night with Michael's sheep. Well, I guess he told you the whole morbid story."

"He told us enough to know you had a rough time. We're amazed how well you have fared," Laban responds.

Nicodemus looks lovingly across the table at Ruth. "Well, I had a good physician, a wonderful caregiver." Ruth blushes and lowers her eyes. "I will say one thing. I certainly know a lot about sheep now." They all chuckle. "In fact, not long before we left, my little friend, Benjamin, that's Ruth's grandson, took me to the barn to witness my first birthing of a lamb. He was so proud and did a good job helping the little lamb along." He pauses. "I'm going to miss that little fellow."

"He's going to miss you, too, Nicodemus." Ruth looks earnestly at Nicodemus. He returns her smile. Martha looks at one and then the other, her mind whizzing while everyone else is busy eating.

"And then there's shearing time. You never heard such a racket as when those sheep wait their turn for shearing. I can tell you about the chickens next door as well." Everyone laughs again at Nicodemus' uncharacteristic chatter. He's usually the very serious, almost stoic guest.

After dinner they continue their conversation while catching up on the events of the last few weeks. Eventually, Ruth stands and announces that she must be on her way.

Leah protests. "Surely you can stay the night, Ruth. It's such a long trip."

"Oh, I'm used to it. I will pick up a few things while I'm here, but I must get back. I have a new mother due in a few days. These little ones can come early, you know."

"You're welcome any time, Ruth."

"I know. You're most gracious."

Laban walks outside with Ruth. "Is he really doing as well as he seems, Ruth?"

"Yes, he's doing well. He's worked very hard. He was in sad shape when he came to us." She looks down the road thoughtfully with moist eyes. "We will all miss him."

Laban cocks his head, taking note.

"Jesus is coming back to town next week," he continues. "Perhaps you would like to come back."

"No, I don't think so, and it would be best if you don't say much about that to Nicodemus. He doesn't take too kindly to the mention of the Master's name."

"I see. You have discussed this with him?"

"Yes."

Nicodemus approaches behind them, carrying Ruth's basket. "Leah has replenished your food basket with enough to take you to Jerusalem," he laughs. Laban slips back to the house to give them time alone.

"Your Aunt Leah is quite a woman. You have a wonderful family, Nicodemus."

"I have two wonderful families."

"You know you are welcome any time," she says sincerely.

"Even if I'm not a patient?"

202

"Even if you're not a patient."

He hands her the basket and places his hand on hers as she clutches the handle. "You have been a great help to me, Ruth. I will miss our talks." He swallows hard. "I will miss you."

She looks down and then looks up into his eyes. A tear all but slips out. She nods her head, but no words will come. She places her other hand on top of his and squeezes.

"Good-bye, Nicodemus. Shalom."

"Shall I walk with you to the edge of town?"

"No," she says quickly. "No," she says gently. She turns and leaves and does not look back.

"Shalom," he mumbles, almost to himself. He watches her for some time.

Martha and Leah stand in the doorway taking in this scene a short distance away. "I see many changes in my son," Martha says.

"Changes?" spouts Leah. "Why that old man has turned into a young man in love, my dear sister!"

"You noticed too?"

"Couldn't help but notice. Written all over his face."

"I never thought it would happen. A shepherd's mother is not what I had in mind, but she seems very nice."

"Ah, that's for sure. Ruth is the salt of the earth. A caring heart. She doctors most everyone around these parts. Her husband was a doctor before he died. Highly thought of."

"But how did her son... I mean, why wouldn't her son...?"

"... take up doctoring? Well, he was pretty young when his father died. The boy spent a lot of time with his uncle. He learned the ways of shepherding from him and just took it up. They all live in Ruth's house. Nice big one for that village. She's a good one, that Ruth."

Laban returns to the house. "And what might you two old ladies be talking about, huddled over here in the doorway?"

"Talking about a young man in love," Leah declares.

"I don't know about the "young" part, but I believe you have the rest of it right."

Martha looks surprised. "*You* noticed too?"

"Written all over him."

"Shush, he's coming. Let's go in."

When Nicodemus reaches the door, he mutters, "I'll take my things up to my room." With no further word, he climbs the stairs.

Nicodemus gazes out his north window, but wishes for a west-facing window. Perhaps he could still see her walking away. He lays aside the tunic Michael gave him. Just touching it takes him back to the life he has known for the past few weeks. *My shepherd.*

He places his phylacteries on the table and sits down on the side of the bed with his elbows on his knees and one hand holding his bent forehead. His thoughts are a mixture of here, there, and what's to be. He suddenly feels exhausted. *A tiring trip.*

He falls back on the bed and has a fitful nap. When he awakens, he looks out his window once more. *It looks to be about the ninth hour. Afternoon sacrifices are proceeding at the Temple about now. It is time for me to move forward. I must focus on getting stronger so I can make the trip home.* He sees a stray chicken cross the yard. He shakes his head with a smirk. "Wherever *home* is."

❧❧❧❧❧

Leah hears him coming down the stairs. "Well, he *is* alive."

"Can a hungry man get something to eat?"

"Just like a man, always looking for food," she mumbles as she putters in the kitchen. "Here, eat these grapes your mother picked this afternoon. That will hold you until I get something ready. Tell me more about that boy. Was it Benjamin?"

Just the mention of his name is all Nicodemus needs to go off on a lengthy description of how Benjamin looks, things he says, and things he does—which leads to Michael, Abigail, and Ruth. By the time he finishes, they know all about his four friends.

Days later, he feels strong enough to carry Rebecca out to their favorite tree. He shares even more special detail with her.

"Oh, Nicodemus, it is so lovely out here. Just like old times."

They sit in silence enjoying the gentle breeze, the sun, and the shade. Then they begin their flow of conversation. *Kind of like talking to Ruth.*

All of a sudden, she notices his new tunic. "You went shopping I see." He has acquired a Capernaum-style tunic that can be used for travel back to Jerusalem.

"Yes, I will be leaving for Jerusalem soon. I have been away far too long."

"You love your work there, don't you?"

"Of course," he says, with only slight enthusiasm.

"Nicodemus, I haven't told you about the new teacher."

"Teacher?" he questions, skeptically.

"Yes. His name is Jesus. He was born in Nazareth, but we believe he has been sent by God." Nicodemus puffs up and turns away. She continues, "He heals in miraculous ways and his teachings are amazing. One day he talked to a group out on the road close to the house. I could hear…"

"Rebecca, how can you be taken in by this imposter? Don't you know that these 'miracles' are but a hoax? By whose authority does he speak anyway? Besides, can anything good come from Nazareth?"

The force of his words and the tone of his voice take Rebecca back. She has never heard him explode so angrily.

He realizes immediately that he has crushed her spirit. He softens his tone. "It's just that I don't want you to be deceived like the others in this town."

"But have you heard him teach?"

"I think I know plenty about teaching. I don't wish to hear any more about this… this… this man."

Thankfully, Nicodemus hears Leah calling. "We need to go in," he says abruptly. Frustrated, he carries her back in. *When will I stop hearing about this deceiver?*

A few days later, Nicodemus is sitting on Laban's stool in front of the house. Laban brings another stool out to sit beside him.

"It looks like you are recovering well, Nicodemus."

"Yes, I'm thinking of returning to Jerusalem after the Sabbath. Do you think mother will go back with me?"

Laban shakes his head slowly. "Oh, I don't know. She seems pretty fixed right here. I did hear her and Ruth talking about going together to Jerusalem for Passover. Maybe she'll be ready to stay in Jerusalem then."

"Ruth was here?"

"No, it was the day when she came here with you."

"Oh." After a pause, "I thought maybe…" his voice trails off.

He watches three children running down the road while another chases after them. A man saunters by, leading a donkey the other way. The donkey sparks a memory. "Oh, dear me, Uncle."

"What is it?"

"I completely forgot about the donkey, the one I had on that trip over the mountain. When I fell, the donkey went tumbling down the hill, too. I think Michael told me that the donkey died. I had borrowed the donkey from a trusting man over in Magdala who said he knew you. I must find him and pay him."

"Do you remember his name?"

'I think he said, 'Old Bones' or something like that."

Laban grins. "Ah, yes, my old friend. We go way back together…"

Nicodemus' mind is already turning in a different direction. "Actually it might be a good trial trip for me to see if I'm up to making the long journey home. I'll leave in the morning."

"Are you sure you want to go that way again?"

"I'll just go across the Sea to the other shore and return in the afternoon. No mountains for me."

Laban chuckles.

"Nicodemus, I would like to talk to you about something."

"Yes?"

"I know you have no use for the teacher, Yeshua, but…"

"Rebecca's been talking to you, hasn't she?"

"Nicodemus, you are a man of reason. You study to know the truth. The least you can do is listen to the man, see him for yourself."

"I will think about it. That's the best I can do for you."

CHAPTER 29
No Escaping the News

Jesus went into the synagogue and began to teach.
The people were amazed at his teaching, because he taught them as one
who had authority, not as the teachers of the law.
Mark 1:21-22

Early the next day, Nicodemus boards a small boat to set sail for Magdala. The crisp morning air refreshes him. He is ready to be out in the open, out of the house, away from the constant reminder that he should "see the teacher" who seems to have everyone in his power.

The uneventful ride brings him to the shore where his adventure had begun weeks ago. There, in almost the same spot, stands the man from whom Nicodemus had borrowed the donkey.

"Good morning, may I speak with you?"

"And who might you be? You look familiar."

"I'm the nephew of Laban of Capernaum."

The man thinks a moment. "Ah, yes. You borrowed a donkey from me a while back." He looks around behind Nicodemus. "And where is my donkey?"

"That's why I'm here. You see, I had an unfortunate accident on the mountain over there. The donkey and I went rolling down the side of the mountain. I have finally healed from my injuries, but I'm afraid the fall killed your animal. I'm here to pay you for your donkey."

"I see. You're a man of honor, I must say. Out of good stock like your Uncle Laban."

"Thank you."

"Well, I tell you what. That old donkey was getting awfully decrepit. I'm not too surprised he couldn't hold his own. Just give me a denari. That should take care of it."

"As you say." Nicodemus digs in his money bag to pay the man. "It seems like there are fewer people working here today. Is something going on?"

"Oh, they've all gone around the shore, up your way, as a matter of fact. Gone off to find that teacher who goes around healing everybody. Has quite a following, he does."

"Yeshua? Jesus?"

"Yes, that's what they call him. You know him, too?"

"Why haven't you gone chasing after him?"

"I'm too old for chasing. Kind of like old Hemlock, the donkey." The old man chuckled.

"Tell me, do you actually *know* anyone this "healer" has supposedly healed?"

"Well, there's a young man here who was deaf. Jesus came along one day, touched his ears, and he could hear for the first time. He jumped for joy. The whole town was excited. That's why they've all gone off to hear more from him."

"Are you sure the young man was deaf?"

"Aye, I've known the lad all his life. Couldn't hear a thing. When Jesus healed him, his eyes bulged out in surprise. He looked in every direction, hearing sounds he had never heard before. It was really somethin'. He tried to say some words, too. Never had said a word before. I guess it was because he couldn't hear the words. Had the whole town talkin'."

"Humph. Well, I'll be on my way. Sorry about the donkey."

"Have a safe trip."

Nicodemus glances northeast, imagining the townspeople traipsing around after the imposter. *He and that John the Baptist are of like ilk. Full of tricks. Still, the people seemed to have known this young deaf man, known his background. Maybe he just never spoke and decided to start speaking. Maybe he could hear all along but never revealed it until now. Away with these thoughts; I must find another boat. Ah, there's the one that brought me here. Maybe he will take me back.*

As Nicodemus floats along the Sea of Galilee, he scans the shoreline with appreciation for its beauty and serenity. Rocky mountains beyond, lush green hills toward Capernaum. Reluctantly, he considers the healer. *I am bombarded on every side by talk of this man. Perhaps Uncle Laban is right. In any other matter I would study, investigate, discuss rationally. Maybe I will surprise them all and go to hear the man.*

⊘✦⊘✦⊘✦⊘✦

As the boat draws near to the Capernaum shore, Nicodemus notices several groups of people gathered in clumps talking excitedly.

He overhears bits of their conversations as he heads back to Laban's house.

"I couldn't believe it. We had our fill all right," one says.

"And baskets left over," says another.

"Where?" questions a third man.

"Just over the hill there. We had spent all afternoon listening to him, but we were getting hungry. He took a few loaves of bread and a couple of fish, blessed them and broke them. The fish and bread just kept coming. It was a miracle."

"Why did you stay so long?"

"He taught us there on the hill. New ideas. Amazing things."

"He'll be in your synagogue on the Sabbath. Hear him for yourself."

Nicodemus steps up beside those who are in discussion. "Excuse me. Who are you talking about?"

"Why, Jesus of Nazareth of course. Have you not heard of him?"

"Yes, I've heard of him." With that Nicodemus stomps away in disgust.

When Nicodemus heads down the street toward Laban's house, he encounters more little groups of people buzzing about the "great miracle on the hill." Even Laban and three of his friends stand huddled together in front of the house waving their hands about and babbling all at once.

When Laban spies Nicodemus, he touches their arms and gestures with his head. They suddenly fall silent.

210

"Shalom, gentlemen," Nicodemus nods as he marches straight into the house.

"Shalom," they mumble all around.

The men continue their rousing discussion in softer voices.

Martha greets her son gladly. "Did you find the man you were looking for?"

"Yes. I took care of the debt I owed," Nicodemus states in a flat tone.

"Did you find yourself with enough stamina to endure the trip? You must be tired."

"I fared very well, but I am hungry. All this talk around town of food multiplying has worked up my appetite."

"I see you have heard about the Mast…, I mean the teacher."

"Who couldn't? The whole town has heard."

"We are told he will teach in the synagogue on the Sabbath."

"Yes, yes, I've heard that too."

As the family gathers for the meal, they chit chat nervously, aware of Nicodemus' sullen attitude. He goes to bed early with the excuse of needing rest after his long day of travel.

Nicodemus stares at the ceiling from his bed trying to say his evening prayers, but the words seem meaningless, monotonous. *What choice do I have but to attend the synagogue on the Sabbath?* He sleeps fitfully, tossing this way and that through the night.

◆◆◆◆◆◆◆

The dreaded Sabbath arrives and Nicodemus dresses in his Pharisee robe. He's grateful he had left it here so that it didn't become a dirty torn mess like all his other things. He looks down at his sleek, well-tailored, garment. It makes him feel staunch and pious and back to his old self. *I will have some pertinent questions for this man. We'll see just how much of a "teacher" he is.* Nicodemus is aggravated that the leaders preferred to have this stranger teach instead of him.

Laban's family joins others in Capernaum as they walk to the synagogue. Nicodemus glances around in anticipation of seeing the "great" teacher. They settle on the bench where Laban always sits in the synagogue. Nicodemus is glad to be sitting so that his slight limp is hidden. He straightens his back and takes note of who notices him. No one does. Instead, they all seem consumed with anticipation as they stretch their necks this way and that searching for the healer and questioning each other, "Have you seen him?"

Suddenly, a slight murmur ripples through the crowd and eyes turn to the rear of the synagogue. In spite of himself, Nicodemus breathes deeply to overcome his own tinge of emotion at finally seeing this all-too-famous person.

Jesus walks unpretentiously to the front of the room to take his place. He quietly nods to a few familiar faces. Peter, James, and John along with other of his followers stand against the wall. Others crowd in and around the doorway.

Nicodemus studies the teacher for a moment, confident of his judgment of character. *Hmm, quite ordinary looking, I must say. Not the hero I expected. Just another common Galilean.*

A blessing is pronounced; a verse recited. The congregants sing a Psalm. Nicodemus joins in, singing confidently, comfortable with the routine.

> "Oh God, you are my God, earnestly I seek you;
>   my soul thirsts for you,
> My body longs for you, in a dry and weary land
>   where there is no water."

For a moment, the drama of this scene suddenly shifts in Nicodemus' mind to another. He remembers the agony of the days and nights outside the sheep fold. What he would have given for a drink of water. He doesn't remember crying out to God. He just remembers grumbling and complaining and cursing the shepherd who saved his life because he went off to do his shepherd duties and left him to suffer alone.

"I have seen you in the sanctuary
     and beheld your power and your glory.
Because your love is better than life,
     my lips will glorify you.

I will praise you as long as I live,
     and in your name I will lift up my hands."

    Disturbed by this unplanned interruption in his thoughts, Nicodemus shifts his position slightly and glances around only with his eyes as though checking that no one is privy to his reflections. Again he studies Jesus, who sits with his head slightly bent. He seems to be in deep thought or even prayer.
    Laban stands to read from the holy scroll. A younger man lifts the heavily adorned scroll from the ark and places it on the bimah, the reading table. Laban unrolls it reverently. The young man lifts the scroll for all to see and returns it to the bimah. Laban retrieves the long-handled pointer and begins to read.

The Israelites set out from Elim
     and came to the Desert of Sin.
In the desert the whole community
     grumbled against Moses and Aaron.

The Israelites said to them,
  "If only we had died
     by the Lord's hand in Egypt!
There we sat around pots of meat
     and ate all the food we wanted,
     but you have brought us out into this desert
     to starve us to death."

Then the Lord said to Moses,
  "I will reign down bread from heaven for you.
The people are to go each day
     and gather enough for that day."

Then Moses told Aaron to speak to the people.
While Aaron was speaking to the people,
> they looked toward the desert, and there was
> the glory of the Lord appearing in the cloud.

The Lord said to Moses,
> "I have heard the grumbling of the Israelites.
Tell them: at twilight you will eat meat,
> and in the morning you will be filled with bread.
Then you will know that I am the Lord your God."

Laban lays the pointer down and slowly rolls up the scroll. With quiet anticipation, the worshippers turn to Jesus. He gazes over the congregation and begins to speak.

"Many of you were on the hillside with me two days ago. Some of you have come today, not because you saw miraculous signs but because you ate the loaves and had your fill."

Yes, that's about the truth. Feed them and they will believe anything. He has them figured out all right.

"I tell you, do not work for food that spoils, but for food that endures to eternal life, which the Son of man will give you. On him, God the Father has placed his seal of approval."

What is this? Does he claim that he gives eternal life?

One man humbly asks, "What must we do to do the work that God requires?"

Jesus answers, "The work of God is this; to believe in the one he has sent."

Another man who evidently wasn't at the miraculous feeding asks, "What miraculous sign then will you give *us* that we may see it and believe you?"

Another man, even more skeptical, questions, "Yes, what will you do? As we heard in our reading today, our ancestors ate manna in the desert. Moses gave them bread from heaven."

Quickly, Jesus responds, "I tell you the truth; it was not Moses that gave the bread but my Father who gave the

CHAPTER 30
Back to Judea

Pay attention and listen to the sayings of the wise.
So that your trust may be in the Lord,
I teach you today, even you.
Proverbs 22:17, 19

It had not been the best of departures. Martha cried. Leah was upset because Martha was upset. Laban had tried to reason with Nicodemus, but Nicodemus' anger at Jesus' words would not be abated. Dear Rebecca's face was filled with sadness as she and the others waved goodbye.

Moving on, Nicodemus steps into the boat that would carry him the length of the Sea of Galilee. He has become rather used to this mode of travel and used to this beautiful sea.

He finds a place for his belongings in the bottom of the boat and settles himself on a cross bench. As the boat sets sail, he welcomes the delightful breeze on his face. He lifts his closed eyes to the morning sun and cries out in his soul, *Blow, oh wind. Blow away all that I leave behind. Blow me back to my life.*

In spite of his desire to forget and look forward, he cannot help but reflect. Everything reminds him of the life he has lived here these past weeks.

In his mind's eye, the water's edge to the west reminds him of the "donkey man" and the mountain behind it where he had his ill-fated fall. North of that lay the grassy hills where he suffered and grew accustomed to his shepherd and sheep. He can't help but smile when he thinks of Bramble and their bumpy ride together in the cart. It's funny how things like that can be amusing later. It certainly wasn't at the time.

His gaze shifts past the grazing hills to the area of Michael's home where he finally had a bed to sleep in, plentiful food and water, and loving care to promote healing. He pictures Michael even now hovering over a wounded sheep and Benjamin ready with a bucket of water, Abigail busy in the kitchen, and ... Ruth. A pang of heartache unexpectedly rises up in him. Unforeseen tears creep into his eyes. He briskly wipes them away and intentionally tries to wipe away any thoughts of Ruth by turning his attention to Capernaum to the north.

He has enjoyed seeing his family again. His mother seems happy there in her hometown. How he wishes things had turned out differently at the end. All the more reason to feel bitterness toward that charlatan. *How in the world did Simon, James, and John get mixed up with him?*

Nicodemus turns back to the south to behold the sea stretched out before him. It is as though a fresh new path lay ahead. The monotony of the waves lapping against the boat lulls him into a drowsy stupor, so he curls up on a blanket and drifts off for a welcomed nap.

Nicodemus is on shore when he hears an excited voice calling his name. "Nicodemus. Nicodemus, you forgot something." He turns to see someone running toward him. It's Ruth! He rushes toward her, but he can't seem to get there quick enough. His legs are moving but he isn't getting anywhere. She holds her arms out to him, but he can't reach her. "I'm here," she calls. "I'm coming," he calls back.

Abruptly, Nicodemus is jerked awake by the excited voices of the other two men in the boat.

"He's there," says one.

"Where?" says the other.

"Over there, due east." He points. "I'm sure it's Jesus and his disciples with him."

Nicodemus is well aroused now. He mounts his bench once again and spots the boat and crew that has caused enough excitement to interrupt his sleep.

"Do you see it, man?"

"Yes, I see the boat," Nicodemus moans half-heartedly.

"Have you seen the healer before?" asks the boatman, excitedly.

"Yes, I have seen the one who makes blasphemous claims."

Ignoring Nicodemus' comment, the man rambles on. "I saw him two weeks ago in Capernaum. He healed a man, crippled from birth. I saw it with my own eyes. Those gnarled old limbs were as straight as they could be. And he walked. He walked right down the street. He jumped; he ran, he danced."

Nicodemus turns his head the other way. *There seems to be no escape from this healer.*

"I heard him teach on the hillside," the other man chimes in. "It was amazing teaching. Not like the usual we hear from the rabbis."

Where have I heard that before? You would think the King of Israel was passing by. But what do these mere fishermen know? A few sorcery tricks and they'll listen to any teaching.

For the next while, he is forced to listen to their ongoing conversation of what Jesus did and how he did it, what Jesus said and how wonderfully he said it. Nicodemus tries to block out their conversation with his own thoughts, but he is held captive by their enthusiasm.

Finally, they settle down and decide to change the sails so they can drift and catch a few fish while they are out in the middle of the sea. Frustrated by yet another delay, Nicodemus is left to his thoughts. He watches them unenthusiastically for a while and then turns his attention to a flock of sheep on the hillside.

This scene reminds him of his days lying in the green grass by the stream as the sheep grazed. He remembers the sheep's names. He can almost hear Michael calling them one by one. That first night, the two flocks spent the night together in the sheep fold. He recalls that when the other shepherd, the one with the nasally voice, called his sheep the next morning, Michael's flock stayed in the pen. Michael explained that sheep follow only the voice of their shepherd. Michael knew his sheep and they knew his voice.

I cannot believe this. I'm thinking of sheep again! I should be reviewing the laws. I should be planning my lessons. I'll be teaching again soon.

But before Nicodemus can revisit the laws in his mind, the fishermen are ready to maneuver the gear for sailing. The boat has drifted near the eastern shore. Nicodemus spots a noisy crowd gathered near the water's edge. They seem to be walking together further inland, up the slope. The fishermen take notice as well.

"If I were a betting man, I'd say they are gathering to see Jesus. Maybe this is a good time to stop for lunch."

Lunch? I brought food with me to eat on the boat, didn't they? Not another delay. I'll never get home at this rate.

Most of the band of followers has moved on by the time they reach the shore. The fishermen lose no time in catching up with the crowd. *No telling how long they'll be gone.*

◦✿◦✿◦✿◦✿◦

Nicodemus finds an inviting rock to sit on as he rummages through his bag for the food Aunt Leah prepared for him. The boisterous crowd soon grows subdued as a strong voice addresses the listeners. As Nicodemus finishes his lunch, the wind blows in such a way that he can pick up a word or two here and there, but not enough to discern the whole teaching.

Against his better judgment, he decides that if he has to wait, he might as well hear what is going on. *It will help me have more examples of his heresy to report to the Sanhedrin.*

He brushes the crumbs from his tunic and meanders in the direction of the group.

Most are seated on the ground, their full attention on Jesus. A few children play quietly under a tree. Jesus is seated up the hill on a large stone so the people can hear and see him. Nicodemus lingers at the outside edge of the crowd.

"In the same way, let your light shine before men that they may see your good deeds and praise your Father in heaven," Jesus is saying.

Nicodemus notices that several are nodding their heads in approval.

"The Father has sent me," Jesus continues, "so that you might better understand his ways and the kingdom of heaven."

Oh no, here we go again.

"Do not think that I have come to abolish the Law or the Prophets. I have not come to abolish them but to fulfill them."

If only that were true.

"I tell you the truth, until heaven and earth disappear, not the smallest letter, not the least stroke of a pen, will by any means disappear from the law until everything is accomplished. Anyone who breaks one of the least of these commandments and teaches others to do the same will be called least in the kingdom of heaven, but whoever practices and teaches these commands will be called great in the kingdom of heaven."

Nicodemus arches his back as though proud to be one of those who "teaches others these commands and will be called great."

But before Nicodemus can blink an eye, Jesus goes on to say, "For I tell you that unless your righteousness surpasses that of the Pharisees and that of the teachers of the Law, you will certainly not enter the Kingdom of heaven."

Nicodemus glares at the blasphemer. The same anger he felt in the synagogue at Capernaum boils up in him once again.

"You have heard it said to the people long ago, 'Do not murder,' and 'anyone who murders is subject to judgment.' But I tell you that anyone who is *angry* with his brother will be subject to judgment."

Nicodemus' anger turns to embarrassment. He glances around to see if anyone has noticed his angry red face, but every eye is still fixed on Jesus.

"Therefore, if any of you are offering your gift at the altar and there remember that your brother has something against you, leave your gift there in front of the altar. First go and be reconciled with your brother, then come and offer your gift.

"You have heard that it was said, 'Do not commit adultery.' But I tell you that anyone who looks at a woman lustfully has already committed adultery with her in his heart."

Nicodemus notices several men shift uncomfortably. *Hmm, interesting teaching. Indeed, the Lord looks upon the heart, but I have never heard it expressed in quite this way before.*

"Again, you have heard that it was said to the people of long ago, 'Do not break your oath, but keep your oaths that you have made to the Lord.' But I tell you, do not swear at all, either by heaven, for it is God's throne; or by the earth for it is his footstool; or by Jerusalem, for it is the city of the Great King. And do not swear by your head, for you cannot make even one hair white or black. Simply let your 'Yes' be 'Yes' and your 'No,' 'No;' anything beyond this comes from the evil one."

Reluctantly, Nicodemus can see the wisdom in these words.

"You have heard it said, 'Love your neighbor and hate your enemy.' But I tell you: Love your enemies and pray for those who persecute you, that you may be sons of your Father in heaven."

By the expressions on their faces, Nicodemus sees that a few men feel as he does—this is a hard saying.

"He causes his sun to shine on the evil and the good, and sends rain on the righteous and the unrighteous. He loves all men. If you love those who love you, what reward will you get? Are not even the tax collectors doing that? And if you greet only your brothers, what are you doing more for others? Do not even pagans do that?"

Nicodemus notices that several men lower their heads. *Are they thinking or repentant?*

"Therefore, be mature. Be complete. Be perfect, even as your heavenly Father is perfect. Again I say, I have not come to do away with the Law; I have come to fulfill it. This is the will of my Father."

"My father." There it is again. These words may be all well and good, but what of the insinuation that he comes from heaven, sent by God. He's a mere man. I'll ask him how he explains such blasphemy.

But before Nicodemus can speak out, Jesus continues.

"It is good to give to the needy, but be careful how you do it. Do not do your acts of righteousness before men to be seen by them. If you do, you will have no reward from your Father in heaven.

"So when you give to the needy, do not announce it with trumpets, as hypocrites do in the synagogues and on the streets, to be honored by men. I tell you the truth; they have received their reward in full. But when you give to the needy, do not let your left hand know what your right hand is doing, so that your giving may be in secret. Then your Father, who sees what is done in secret, will reward you.

"Likewise, when you pray or when you fast, do not be like the hypocrites who want to be seen of men, but do these things in secret and your heavenly Father who sees what is done in secret, will reward you."

Jesus stops his ongoing flow of words as they all try to take in the things he has said. No one stirs. No one asks questions.

Jesus' eyes drift to the hillside just beyond. All eyes turn in the direction Jesus is facing. A shepherd is leading his sheep to the next pasture. The sheep follow obediently.

"Many will try to deceive you," he begins again. "Behold the shepherd and his sheep. Tonight, the shepherd will lead his sheep to the sheep pen. He will sleep by the gate and no one can go in through the gate to harm his sheep because the shepherd lies at the gate. If anyone climbs in another way, he is a thief and a robber."

Jesus turns to face the crowd. "I tell you the truth; I am the gate for my sheep. All who ever came before me were thieves and robbers, but the sheep did not listen.

"I am the gate. Whoever enters through me will be saved. He will come in and go out and find pasture. The thief comes only to kill and destroy. I have come that they might have life and have it to the full."

Jesus turns back toward the shepherd. "In the morning, the shepherd will open the gate and the sheep will listen for his voice. He calls his own sheep by name and leads them out. When he has brought out all of his own, he goes on ahead of them, and his sheep follow him because *they know his voice*. They will never follow a stranger."

Jesus stands and faces the crowd. Nicodemus is so confounded by now that he hasn't been able to voice any questions. Jesus scans the faces who stare back at him. He pauses when he sees Nicodemus.

Even at a distance, Nicodemus feels the teacher's penetrating gaze. Jesus declares, "*I am the Good Shepherd.*"

Nicodemus is paralyzed. He cannot move. He cannot speak. His heart feels like it will leap right out of his chest.

"I know my sheep and my sheep know me—just as my Father knows me and I know the Father. And I lay down my life for my sheep."

He knows. He knows what I have been through. How does he know? How can he possibly know? What does this mean?

✴✴✴✴✴

Bewildered, Nicodemus turns and limps away. Whether Jesus continued or the crowd dispersed, he does not know. In a daze, he somehow makes it back to the shore. He takes his basket of food and wanders back and forth along the shore waiting for the fishermen to return.

His mind whirls. Strange, conflicting emotions well up in him. He can't think. He can't reason. No law comes to him to be of any help. The one thing that washes over him again and again is the thought that he must talk to Jesus— alone, in secret.

He continues pacing back and forth, sure that he is going insane. *How can I disrupt my plans and stay here to talk to him? I'm on my way home. I can't be delayed further. Even if I did stay and talk to him, what would I say? How could I have a private hearing*

224

with him? I must pull myself together. What would I tell the fishermen? How can I find out where Jesus is? Where will he be staying tonight?

Soon the people disperse, going this way and that. Nicodemus spies the fishermen lumbering down the slope. He waits for them.

"Ready to go?" one of them shouts to Nicodemus.

Nicodemus gestures. He waits until they are closer.

"I have decided to stay here for the night," he tells them.

"Here? Well, suit yourself."

Nicodemus pays the boatmen their due and they sail off. As Nicodemus stands there watching, he has second thoughts. *What am I doing? There goes my assurance of a ride to the south shore. What am I thinking? Am I thinking? Jesus and his followers may head off as well. Then where will I be? Have I been deceived like all the others?*

He scans the hill for the shepherd and sheep that Jesus had pointed out earlier. *Gone around to the other side. Gone--like the boat that would have carried me on my journey home. What madness is this that has overtaken me?*

Nicodemus sits on the rock that had been his resting place for lunch and searches through his bag for something to eat. Tucked in one corner and wrapped in a cloth lies a cluster of grapes. A faint smile crosses his face. *Mother.* The tight muscles in his back relax as he recalls the journey from Jerusalem with his mother when she wanted him to approach the vine arborist. *She does love her grapes.*

A cold, lonely, empty chill comes over him. When he returns to Jerusalem, she won't be there. Only the one servant will be left in the house. He looks back the length of the sea toward the direction of Ruth's house and stares, too exhausted to think or feel.

The shout of a fish vendor brings him back to reality. He looks down at the grapes in his hands and chews a few. If he is determined to see Jesus; he must find out where he is or where he is going. Thankfully, Nicodemus is more anonymous in his traveling clothes than he would have been in his Pharisee garb. To do his investigating, he will have to talk with the commoners. He decides to start with the fish vendor. Surely a local man will know what goes on around here.

"How much for your dried fish?"

"You want dried when you can have fresh?"

"Yes, I'll be traveling." Nicodemus didn't want to tell the man that he had never built a fire for frying out in the open. They make the exchange. As nonchalantly as possible, Nicodemus asks, "I guess you heard the teacher this afternoon."

"Of course. Didn't everyone?"

"I wonder where he has gone, now."

"Over to the next village, I'm told. He will probably return tonight and set sail in the morning. That's their boat right there, the one he and his followers came in. Belongs to Zebedee's fleet."

Nicodemus can't tell that it is any different from the other boats bobbling along the shore. "Zebedee, from Bethsaida?"

"Somewhere from up north. You're not from there, are ye?"

"No, but I have relatives in Capernaum. I'm familiar with James and John, Zebedee's sons." He remembers that it was quite the talk when James and John left their father and started following after Jesus. "I've known the boys from the time they were very young." Nicodemus had noticed James and John in the throng of people, but without his Pharisee robe, Nicodemus assumes James and John probably hadn't spotted him.

"Aye, and ye probably know Simon and his brother Andrew as well. I hear Simon's mother-in-law lives in Capernaum. Big house and all."

"Yes."

It dawns on Nicodemus that with all Jesus' disciples around him, it may prove quite impossible to have a private hearing with him. He walks away from the vendor.

This is all such foolishness. I've never done anything so spontaneous before. Everything is always well thought out. Researched. Planned. Think, Nicodemus, think.

He turns back to the vendor. "Is there an inn around here for a night's lodging?"

He motions. "Down that way a short walk." Nicodemus reasons that since he is here, he will have to make the best of it.

The "short walk" turns into quite the long distance. He makes arrangements in the less than desirable dwelling. At least this will give him time to think. While sitting on the bed, he dreads the thought of lying in it. Granted, it is a step up from the dirty ground outside a sheep pen. *Oh well, this is the least of my worries right now.*

Nicodemus revisits the teachings he heard on the hillside. *Different ideas they were. Deep concepts.* Dare he admit it, even to himself; they were "amazing."

But it is those last statements that he turns over and over in his mind. "I am the Good Shepherd. I know my sheep and my sheep know me, just as I know the Father and he knows me." *He speaks to me out of my own experience with Michael, but I cannot get past the idea that it is blasphemous to compare such a relationship between himself and Almighty God. Unless...unless, he is the Promised Messiah...forgive me, Holy One of Israel, for even thinking such thoughts.*

Enough of this emotional stuff, he must confront this mere man and put him in his place.

CHAPTER 31
A Night Talk with the Teacher

*I tell you the truth; no one can see the kingdom of God
unless he is born again.*   John 3:3

Determinedly, Nicodemus leaves his dingy room and marches back the long "short-walk" to where he left the fish vendor. *Possibly Jesus and his followers will return somewhere near their boat for the night. That's what the vendor said.*

The pinks and purples of the fading sun spread across the evening sky sending a beautiful glow over the sea. The vendor is gone. Fishermen and boatmen have returned to their homes or have already set off for night fishing. All is quiet along the shore.

In the stillness, Nicodemus ponders the beauty and majesty of the creation of the Almighty God he serves. Lovely, open, peaceful moments like these are rare in Jerusalem. He watches the gentle waves rolling in one after the other and stands mesmerized by their consistency. So like the faithfulness of the God of Israel, one generation after another.

Nicodemus sits on what has become "his" rock and feels content to patiently take in this scene. He considers the questions he wants to ask Jesus and the laws he would like to discuss to see if this teacher really knows anything. Just as the sun falls behind the western hillside, he hears voices in the distance. Not far away, he sees a group of men building a fire and gathering around it.

Could it be them? If so, there still remains the question of how I can speak to him privately.

With uncharacteristic boldness, Nicodemus forges ahead in that direction. *This would be so easy for Joseph. He is the bold one. He would know just what to say and how to say it.*

What am I thinking? I'm a great teacher of Israel. I speak to my students every day. We discuss; we debate. This should be no different.

By the time Nicodemus approaches the group, they have cooked their evening meal. Several notice him and turn in his direction. One large, burly man stands and ambles down to meet him.

Simon. Nicodemus has seen him several times in Capernaum and recognizes his walk.

"Can I help you?" he asks, in his deep, gruff voice.

"I have come to speak with... Yeshua," Nicodemus says, as assuredly as he is able.

Simon glances back at Jesus, who signals to Simon that it will be all right. Simon motions for Nicodemus to come.

The pungent aroma of fried fish penetrates the air. A few of the followers have moved away from the hot flames to eat their meal. They appear to be used to strangers coming to see Jesus and pay him little attention. But those from the Capernaum area, particularly young John, know the Pharisee, Nicodemus. They cautiously watch Nicodemus and glance around behind him to make sure no more "enemy" forces have followed.

"I have come alone," he assures them. "I wish to speak with Yeshua," he repeats.

Jesus remains seated near the fire but nods to his men. They gather their things and move away from the fire, still within earshot, but far enough away to give Nicodemus a sense of privacy.

The healer squats and slowly pokes a stick at the fire without looking up at Nicodemus. Nicodemus perches on a log nearby, sitting as straight and regal as one can sit on a log on the ground.

"Rabbi, we know you are a teacher who has come from God. For no one could perform the miraculous signs you are doing if God were not with him."

There. That should be a good beginning. Before Nicodemus can even ask the first question, Jesus turns to look at Nicodemus with those penetrating eyes, much like he did earlier in the afternoon. Jesus continues, "I tell you the truth–

–the truth you seek; no one can see the kingdom of God unless he is born from above, unless he is born again."

Miffed that Jesus has interrupted his speech, and surprised with such a comment, he spouts back, "How can a man be born when he is old? Surely he cannot enter a second time into his mother's womb!"

"I tell you the truth," Jesus answers, "*no one* can enter the kingdom of God unless he is born of water *and* the spirit. Flesh gives birth to flesh, but the Spirit gives birth to spirit. You should not be surprised at my saying, 'You must be born again.'"

Jesus pauses, but Nicodemus is at a sudden loss for words. A slight breeze causes the fire to flicker. It draws their attention.

"It is like the wind," he says. "The Spirit is like the wind. The wind blows wherever it pleases." Jesus looks up at the leaves in a tree as they flutter. "You hear its sound, but you cannot tell where it is from or where it is going. So it is with everyone born of the Spirit."

Nicodemus has not heard this kind of talk before. He is a factual man. He has come to question Jesus, not be taught strange ideas.

"How can this be?" Nicodemus questions.

Jesus turns to him, "You are Israel's teacher and you do not understand these things?"

Nicodemus juts out his wounded Pharisaic chin.

Jesus stares at the fire as he goes on, "I tell you the truth, we speak of what we know, and we testify to what we have seen, but still you people do not accept our testimony. I have spoken to you of earthly things and you do not believe; how then will you believe if I speak of heavenly things? No one has ever gone into heaven except the one who came from heaven—the Son of Man."

Jesus stands up and walks a few steps toward the water. Nicodemus wonders if Jesus is already signaling the end of the conversation. He stands as well and feels a slight breeze whip around his robe.

Jesus speaks again as he stares at the sea. "Just as Moses lifted up the snake in the desert, so the Son of Man must be lifted up, so that everyone who believes in him may have eternal life."

He turns to Nicodemus with those intense eyes. The moonlight reflects on Jesus' face with a glow-like radiance. His voice is gentle now, tender. "Nicodemus, God so loved this world that he gave his only Son, so that whoever believes in him shall not perish but have eternal life. For God did not send his Son into the world to *condemn* the world, but to *save* the world through him. Whoever *believes* in him is not condemned, but whoever does *not* believe stands condemned already because he has not believed in the name of God's one and only Son."

Jesus turns his gaze back to the sea. Without those eyes focused on him, Nicodemus feels he can breathe again. Jesus continues, "This is the verdict:" He raises his hand toward the moon. "Light has come into the world, but men love darkness instead of light because their deeds are evil. Everyone who does evil hates the light, and will not come into the light for fear that his deeds will be exposed." Jesus faces Nicodemus and touches his shoulder, "But, Nicodemus, whoever lives by the *truth* comes into the light, so that it may be seen plainly that what he has done has been done through God, not through man."

Then, with almost a "thank you" in its tone, Jesus says, "Shalom, my brother." He turns and walks back to the fire.

"Shalom," Nicodemus mutters as he stumbles on down the slope to the shore.

Why is it that he cannot seem to find the words he wants to say in Jesus' presence? His mind and emotions are spinning even as they did after the earlier teaching session.

I started well—acknowledged his acts of healing. I had questions, but he kept telling me what he wanted to say. What about what I wanted to say?

Born again, Moses and the snake lifted up—what does that have to do with anything? Who is his teacher? By what authority does he speak these things? What is his opinion of certain details of the law? Now that is where I have knowledge. I'm sure I could have tripped up this uneducated Galilean.

Nicodemus makes it to his rock and slumps down.

Very well, I shall think this through logically, thoroughly. He seems to imply that he is the Son of Man who has come from God, as though He has been with God Himself. Blasphemous! There are those who know of his hometown and his mother and father. He is from Nazareth, and our Scripture says Messiah will come from Bethlehem, the town of David. This simply does not…

Suddenly, recollections come to him that he has not thought of in years. Another night long ago when he was out walking, a light from Bethlehem drew his attention. He never told anyone, not even Joseph. The next day, merchants brought a report from a few Bethlehem shepherds who claimed they had seen a visitation of angels, proclaiming Messiah's birth. Nicodemus had dismissed such a proclamation coming from lowly shepherds.

But then, over a month later, a young Galilean couple carried their baby to the Temple when the mother came for purification. My friend, Ethan, came out muttering the words of old Simeon. What was it he always said? Something about not dying until his eyes beheld the Messiah?

Nicodemus sat in solitude for several moments, trying to reach back in his memory for any tiny bit of remembrance that could help him put the pieces together.

The couple was from Galilee or at least I thought they were. I remember questioning why they were in Jerusalem at that time. What was it? A festival? A celebration? The census? Yes, that's it, the census. I reasoned that she bore the child during the census and would not have been able to return until later. That might explain a Bethlehem birth, but what of Herod's soldiers storming into Bethlehem to kill the babies? Would that baby not have been killed as well? Ah, more questions.

The waves of the sea continue their monotonous lapping onto the shore. He hears the waves but doesn't really see them. He relishes this physical peace, but his mind is still in turmoil.

Shepherds. Hmm, perhaps I need to make a visit to those old Bethlehem shepherds.

He ponders what his friends in the Sanhedrin would think of that. But then, what would they think of him scrounging around in sheep pastures and riding in a cart with a crippled old sheep by his side?

A gust of wind blows through his beard reminding him of Jesus' comparison of the Spirit to the wind.

"It comes and goes as it will," he said. *"You don't know where it is going or where it has been. Thus it is with the Spirit."* *Was it this same Spirit that sent me sprawling down the mountain side? And nearly starving me to death? And leaving me lame for weeks? A humbling experience to be sure.*

He languishes in disgust of those memories and stares up the sea in the direction of the despised mountain, reliving the experiences that led him to this moment.

Perhaps… perhaps that is it. All this was to humble me?

Giving a deep sigh, he decides he had better make his way back to the room he has rented for the night. The chilly night air reminds him of Jerusalem, but coming off the water it seems all the more penetrating. He pulls his robe around his shoulders. His bad leg aches a bit. The darkness makes him cautious as he stumbles along the rocky shore with only the moon to light his way.

Physical exhaustion and the emotional burden of these encounters have left him bedraggled. He simply has no mental strength left to sort through the events and conversations of the day. *Unpleasant as it is, that meager bed will prove inviting to this weary worn traveler.*

CHAPTER 32
On to Jerusalem

I rejoiced with those who said to me,
"Let us go to the house of the Lord."
Our feet are standing in your gates, O Jerusalem.
Psalm 122:1-2

The morning sun sends a beam of light across Nicodemus' dingy room, but it is the boisterous voices of fishermen that rouse him from sleep. He rubs his sleep-filled eyes, trying to gather his senses about him. Through the tiny window, he spies the noisemakers outside who have apparently just come in from a night of fishing. He throws his robe around his shoulders and picks up his bag. He must secure a boat for traveling south.

All the men on the shore sit mending nets and sorting fish. The strong smell of fish reminds him in an uncanny way of the overwhelming stench of dirty dew-laden sheep in the morning.

None of these rough fishermen appear to be preparing to push out again, but Nicodemus inquires about any outgoing boats.

One man speaks up. "Mishua will be taking baskets of our fish down to a market later in the morning." He looks Nicodemus over and breaks into a toothless grin. "If you don't mind sailing with the fish, you can probably ride with him." The other fishermen burst out with haughty laughter at Nicodemus' expense. At this point, Nicodemus really doesn't care how he travels; he just wants to get out of this place.

Eventually, "Mishua" strolls down the shore and agrees to take Nicodemus who thankfully sails away from this detestable territory.

Nicodemus is glad he had eaten some figs and nuts before the voyage, because he certainly has no appetite now with the overpowering stench of fresh fish, a few still jerking in their baskets. Fortunately, the trip only lasts about an hour, an hour too long for his liking.

On shore at last, Nicodemus secures a donkey to ride. He notes with satisfaction that the donkey appears to be younger and healthier than the last one he had.

He gazes down the long stretch of the Jordan River and begins the two-day walk to Jerusalem.

As the sun blazes on his shoulders, His mind wanders back to the things Jesus had told him. *"You must be born again,"* he said. *"Flesh gives birth to flesh, but spirit gives birth to spirit." Strange talk.*

Nicodemus' attention is diverted across the way where two boys argue over some object one is holding.

"It's mine," one of the boys yells.

"No, it's mine."

"Yours is back in the house."

"No it isn't. I brought that one out from under my bed."

"It's mine," the other screams and takes off running with whatever it is.

"I hate you," the other says as he grabs a stick and chases the thief over the hill.

Nicodemus finds the scene slightly amusing, but the bitterness and hatred he hears are disturbing. He remembers Jesus words, "You have heard it said, 'Do not murder for anyone who murders is subject to judgment.' But I tell you anyone who is angry with his brother will be subject to judgment."

Other things Jesus said keep coming to Nicodemus' mind— "If you are offering your gift at the altar and remember that your brother has something against you, go and be reconciled first, then come and offer your gift." *That certainly has merit. Come before the Lord in purity.*

What was it he said about adultery? Ah yes, "The law says, 'Do not commit adultery.' But I tell you anyone who looks at a woman lustfully has already committed adultery in his heart."

All these teachings have to do with the condition of the heart— the inner man. It was said of King Saul in his tall handsome array that

235

the Lord looks upon the heart not the outward appearance. But what of our many laws? We study faithfully and work diligently to keep the law "with all our hearts."

Jesus words come to him again— "When you pray or when you fast, do not be like the hypocrites who want to be seen of men. Instead, do these things in secret and your Father, who sees what is done in secret, will reward you." *Hmm, this is not the way we look at things.*

The tinkling of a sheep bell across the Jordan draws his attention. He watches a shepherd coaxing a wayward sheep to keep up with the others. Nicodemus smiles as he thinks of Wayward and Bramble. He's glad that Bramble's leg healed before he had to leave. Strange how he can detest and yet care about those sheep at the same time.

What might Michael be doing today? Is he out on the hillside with the flock? Are they lazily munching grass? Is Michael playing his flute? Has Benjamin joined him on this grazing trip? Ah, dear Benjamin—such a delight. And Ruth. Dear Ruth. What might she be doing today?

Nicodemus has a pang of heartache as he remembers her sliding her stool over to his bed to have a talk. He misses her already. How surprised she would be to know of his encounters with Jesus. If only she were with him. He would be able talk to her about the things Jesus said. She could help him sort through his thoughts.

About that time, he hears the shepherd call out to his sheep. Nicodemus squints his eyes in an attempt to see the shepherd's face, but he is too far away. The voice is different from Michael's. He knows Michael's voice as well as Michael's sheep do.

Jesus words suddenly penetrate his heart as he recalls him saying, "I am the Good Shepherd. My sheep know my voice and they follow me." An emotional wave sweeps over Nicodemus again just as it did when Jesus stared at him in the crowd and talked about the sheep and shepherd. He had felt so exposed, as though his life was an open book. He felt sure Jesus knew about his experiences on the hillside. But how? How could he know?

Nicodemus finds a tree he can sit under to eat lunch. It's amazing how much cooler he is, shielded from the sun. The grapes have shriveled, so he nibbles on a piece of bread and the dried fish he bought from the fisherman earlier. The figs are still fairly tasty.

He observes a couple of questionable-looking characters on the banks of the river. They don't notice Nicodemus, but they look around as though they are up to no good. They go deeper into the tall grass near the river and seem to make an exchange.

Hmm, have to hide their misdeed.

Nicodemus stays perfectly still so they don't spy him. Who knows what they might do if they think he has caught them.

After a lengthy conversation, they come out of the grass, looking this way and that. They slink away in opposite directions. Nicodemus reminds himself that, when he travels from Jericho on the narrow treacherous path up to the Mount of Olives, he must set out with a group of travelers. Robbers often take advantage of hiding places along the winding path. He will be sure to go through there in the light of day.

Truly, Yeshua is right when he said, "Men love darkness rather than light because their deeds are evil. Everyone who does evil hates the light for fear that his deeds will be exposed."

Nicodemus sits quietly for a time. *Where have I heard these words before? It was a very long time ago. I remember thinking that it was a different way to put it.* He wrinkles his forehead and closes his eyes. His shoulders hump as he concentrates. *It seems like Hillel was alive then and commended the person who said it. When? Where? Who? Hillel, the Temple, the courtyard?* It won't come to him.

He finally opens his eyes. Just then, a boy, maybe twelve or thirteen years old, walks to the river. Nicodemus idly watches the boy. *That's it! The boy. It was the boy at the Temple that amazed the teachers; even old Hillel was impressed.*

How long ago was that? Let me see I was just about to become a member of the Sanhedrin. It must have been some twenty years ago. The boy would be around thirty years old now.

A wave of heat surges through Nicodemus when he reasons that Jesus might be about that age. *Can the boy who so amazed us long ago be the man who amazes all who hear him today?*

No, I'm imagining things; making too much of this. Pure coincidence.

He reflects on other words of Yeshua. "Whoever lives by the truth—*the truth*—comes into the light, so that it may be seen plainly that what he has done has been done, not through his own deeds, but through God."

His father's words come to him. "Seek the truth, Nicodemus." *Am I seeking the truth in this matter? Are my deeds done to please men rather than God? Oh, to emulate David, a man after God's own heart.*

Nicodemus raises his eyes and looks to the sky through the leaves that shade him. "Oh, God, help me to have a heart for truth."

❧❧❧❧❧

Weary from all his thinking, he gathers his belongings and proceeds on the journey. He makes great effort to think of other things as he rides his donkey or walks along. He stops for the night and travels again the next day.

As he draws near to Jerusalem, he focuses on the tasks ahead, people he will need to see, and lessons to be taught. The rest of his journey proves uneventful.

Finally, the Mount of Olives looms in sight. *Almost home.* He offers a prayer of thanks for the safe journey, then sells his donkey so that he might enter the city unencumbered. He trudges up the mountain, glad that it is not rocky. Already weary from the days of travel, his leg begins to ache, but anticipation mounts as he rounds the path for the descent.

And there it is—his beloved Jerusalem! Nicodemus stops. He presses his hand to his chest and closes his tear-filled eyes. *Jerusalem, oh my Jerusalem.* He opens his eyes to be sure it isn't a dream. With a deep sigh, he says, "Home. Home at last."

He will never tire of this thrilling view. This is the view many pilgrims see first as they come to Jerusalem, white-stoned houses and palaces nestled inside the expansive wall. But the Temple—ah, the Temple—all who behold it are dazzled by its brilliance. It towers high above the wall and can be seen from anywhere in or outside the city.

He pulls his Pharisee robe from the bag and proudly dons it along with his phylacteries before he enters the eastern gate and walks the length of the Temple court.

❧❧❧❧❧❧

"Rabbi Nicodemus, you have returned," exclaims one of his eager young students of the law.

"Yes, my son. How have you been?"

"May I carry your traveling bag for you?"

"Yes, thank you."

"Will you be resuming your teaching, rabbi?"

"Yes, indeed."

"Some of us have been studying with Rabbi Argus and some of your other students with Rabbi Pethahiah."

"I see." He had wondered what his students would do while he was gone. Since he has been away so long, he will need to explain his extended absence.

He speaks to the blind beggar and drops a coin in the beggar's cup. "Thank you, Rabbi Nicodemus."

It's even good to see the blind beggar again.

He nods to other students and friends along the way who stop their conversations to wave. He gazes up at the magnificent columns of the Temple towering above him and the massive doors at the top of the steps. His spirit soars with delight at all things familiar.

Merchants, priests, students, rabbis—all nod... or are they practically bowing as he strides by? On the far steps, he recognizes a cluster of rabbis. They all turn. Argus, with his back to Nicodemus, glances over his shoulder then turns back to the others to say something. As Nicodemus approaches, they stroll toward him. Nicodemus is suddenly aware of his injury and makes every effort to walk as naturally as possible—no limp.

Taking it upon himself to be the spokesman, Argus inquires, "Well, Rabbi Nicodemus, we wondered if you had left us permanently."

"Oh no, I would not forsake my students. I simply had a delay. I understand you and Rabbi Pethahiah substituted for me. Thank you for your assistance."

"Indeed. And what was the cause of your delay?"

"Just some family business. Everything seems to be going on as usual here. Is there anything new I should be aware of?" Nicodemus tries to redirect their conversation.

Another rabbi answers. "Mostly the usual. It is good to have you back, Nicodemus. We have missed you."

"Thank you. I have missed Jerusalem."

Argus pipes up again. "Yes, well, I'm sure anyone would be glad to be out of the Gilgal. And did you run into the new teacher who has everyone in an uproar? He tantalizes the crowds with his healing displays."

"Yes, I've heard of him."

"Well, we have sent another group to check him out. Just more riff raff like that Baptizer. Maybe this one will have his head chopped off as well." Argus makes that annoying gurgle-like sound in his throat.

"What do you mean?"

"Oh, haven't you heard? Antipas had John beheaded at the wish of his wife, Herodias."

"I see. No, I didn't know about that. Well, I've had a long trip and I must get home to clean up and rest." He turns from Argus and looks directly at one of the *friendly* rabbis. "Good to see you."

The student carrying Nicodemus' bag continues walking by his side. "Rabbi Nicodemus, it will be very good to have you teaching us again."

"Thank you. And thank you for assisting me with my bag. I will take care of it now. I'll see you tomorrow."

They part ways. If it weren't for the encounter with Argus, this would have been a perfect return to Jerusalem. He reminds himself that Argus is Argus and always will be.

The familiar market stands, vendors, townspeople, children, streets and houses all feel so comfortable and yet strange at the same time. It is like stepping back into a world of the past.

At last he comes to his own home. The summer flowers are still blooming, emitting a fragrant welcome. *Mother would be pleased.* He opens the door to an empty house. "Marida?" he calls. "Where is that servant girl?" He checks each room, but no answer. He peers out into the courtyard and sees her tending the grapevines. "Marida."

"Oh, Master Nicodemus, I didn't know you were coming. I'm having such a time with these vines. I can't do it like your mother does. How is she? How are you? You must be tired. Your room is clean. And hungry, you must be hungry. Oh dear, I'm such a mess. I will clean up right away and prepare your dinner." She quickly gathers dead vines into a basket and flits by him, then turns with a slight bow. "So nice to have you back sir." She hurries away.

"Yes, nice to be here," Nicodemus says to the empty courtyard. He shakes his head and smiles. *Marida is a young version of Aunt Leah.*

He glances at the grapevines in disarray. *Yes, they do need mother's touch.* Plucking a handful of the best plump grapes, he munches them on the way back inside. He is particularly aware of the large rooms and luxurious furnishings as he climbs the stairs to his bedroom, which looks four times the size of the one he had at Michael's house. This big old house served his family well with mother, father, and three sons, but now it seems grandiose and excessive.

Nicodemus gathers clean clothes and a towel and proceeds straight to the bathing room. After firing the bricks to warm the water, he sinks down into the relaxing pool and

241

relishes having a warm bath from head to toe for the first time since he has been gone. How wonderful. He leans against the wall and absently swirls his hands through the water.

His mind wanders back to that first day when Ruth insisted that he be washed. He didn't like her much then. He smiles as he ponders the way their relationship changed over the weeks he was with her.

Perhaps she's delivering a baby right now or maybe applying a poultice on a wound like mine. Could she be sitting with the family... and thinking of me?

Eventually, Nicodemus leaves his warm reverie and meanders through the big empty house. After a quick meal, he settles in for a long night's rest in his own bed.

CHAPTER 33
Teaching Again in Jerusalem

*The arrogance of man will be brought low
and the pride of men humbled.* Isaiah 2:17

The next morning, Nicodemus opens his eyes and immediately remembers that he is home. *Thanks be to the Almighty One.*

He dresses quickly, says his morning prayers, and heads out for his first day back. Everything feels wonderfully familiar. Suddenly, he remembers Joseph.

In my haste to get home yesterday, I didn't visit my good friend. I'll stop in on my way to the Temple. It will be good to see him and he can fill him me in on what has happened while I was away. Ah, there's his house up ahead.

"Nicodemus, my friend. I heard you were back." They hug enthusiastically.

"It's good to see you, Joseph. What's been going on?"

"Well, I've been gone myself." Joseph explains that he has been on a journey to a beautiful land far beyond the Mediterranean Sea. He mentions the tin mines he saw there and how profitable it would be to his father's business. "When I returned," Joseph concludes, "Argus had most of your students following him."

"Yes, I heard. And Pethahiah took the remaining ones. I'm sure Rabbi Judah will help me straighten this out when I see him this morning."

"Let me see, I think the other rabbis continue with their disciples as usual. Gamaliel has quite the dynamic follower in Saul of Tarsus. Headstrong, to say the least."

"I remember him commenting on the young man before I left."

"The most disruptive turmoil has been over the new teacher-healer in Galilee. The Sanhedrin is even more upset with this one than they were with John the Baptizer."

"I understand Herod Antipas had John beheaded."

243

"Yes, what would you expect from the likes of Herod? He is his father's son for sure."

"What are the issues with Yeshua of Nazareth?" Nicodemus asks nonchalantly.

"Oh, you've heard of him? Did you see him while you were away?"

"Yes, briefly."

"What did you think of him? Did you see him perform a miracle?"

I must not divulge too much about my encounters with Yeshua, even to Joseph, until I have an idea what the talk is like around the Temple. Besides, I'm still trying to decide for myself what I think of the teacher.

"No, I saw no miracles. What are the other Pharisees saying about him?"

"Well, they have to acknowledge some of the very convincing stories of healing, but they are more caught up in the matter of blasphemy."

"Blasphemy?" Nicodemus pretends innocence.

"The healer speaks of himself as the Son of God and tells people they are forgiven of their sin."

"Sounds as if he thinks of himself as the Messiah." Nicodemus hints.

"Hmm. Could be. Like John, he has a huge following. Personally, I think that is why the leaders have such a problem with this man. They don't want anyone to take their place."

"Perhaps so, although blasphemy *is* something to be concerned about. Well, it's time I go see about reclaiming my disciples."

Nicodemus assures Joseph that his mother and his aunt and uncle are doing well and he promises to talk later about all his other experiences while he was in Galilee.

Marching on to the Temple, Nicodemus is so glad to be in comfortable surroundings. He meets with Rabbi Judah. Nicodemus' students seem more than willing to leave Argus and Pethahiah to once again follow Nicodemus. He gathers them on the steps in his old familiar place to get reacquainted, for some of them are relatively new.

He checks to see which laws they have covered. They respond rather unenthusiastically when he questions them about their discussions of these laws. "We had plenty of debate," one student emphasizes, negatively.

"I see." Nicodemus is silent for a moment. He looks toward the hills of Bethlehem stretching out beyond lower Jerusalem and imagines that he can almost make out a shepherd with a flock on one of the hills. He remembers the enthusiasm of young Benjamin when he told him stories of heroes of the faith.

Nicodemus looks into the expectant faces of his twelve students. "Before we move forward with the discussion of our laws, let's consider our second king of Israel, King David. You may well remember that before he was king, David was a shepherd boy."

Several students look a bit puzzled, but interested.

"We might assume that David had many experiences on the hillside. No doubt he had ample time to practice his skill at the sling. Maybe he aimed at a particular bush in the distance until he mastered that shot, and then tried his skill aiming at a small rock. Perhaps he kept stepping back until he could hit it every time, even at greater distances."

Nicodemus notices a few smiles; as though they had never considered the mighty King of Israel routinely practicing with the sling.

"A shepherd must also give earnest attention to his sheep; caring for them, leading them to the right grasses and water, and protecting them with his very life. He saves them from wild animals, poisonous weeds, and thieves. He finds them when they go astray. He binds their wounds when they are injured."

More students appear mildly interested, but their furrowed brows show question. A few look at each other as though wondering where all this is leading? What does it have to do with the law?

Nicodemus gazes again at the Bethlehem landscape, the very place where David would have done his shepherding. "David loved his sheep. He wanted them to feel secure and rested so he played the harp for them. He had many hours to practice his skill on the harp until he could play beautifully and with ease. No doubt he sang songs on the hillside and made up new psalms. At some point, the prophet, Samuel, anointed him as the next King of Israel, but while patiently waiting for the Lord's timing, David went back to his shepherding duties. This provided him with many hours in the evening to meditate on the Holy Torah and offer prayer to the Almighty, his source of strength."

Nicodemus can see from their expressions that his words are provoking thoughts. Perhaps they are picturing the shepherd king in a fresh way.

"Now I ask you: what did David do with these experiences?"

The students sit in silence. Nicodemus waits.

Finally a younger student speaks up, "Well, his practice with the sling certainly stood him in good stead with the giant, Goliath."

The others chuckle softly.

Another student adds, "His experience with wild animals gave him strength to face the giant, for he said, 'The Lord who delivered me from the paw of the lion and the paw of the bear will deliver me from the hand of this Philistine.' "

"Yes, yes, that's right," Nicodemus urges them on.

"One might say that his harp skills gained him entrance into the palace to see what life was like as a king," another says.

Others chime in.

"His fearlessness served him well as a warrior."

"His songs have been our psalms for years."

"His care of the sheep prepared him to be shepherd for our people."

"Yes, yes, yes, my dear students." Nicodemus declares in victory. He pauses and then leans forward to look each of them in the eye. "You see, just as the Lord prepared David, he also prepares you. This time of study is your preparation ground. We study the law that we might better know how to love the Lord our God with all our hearts, and all our souls, and all our strength."

Nicodemus appraises the faces of these young men as their eyes beam brightly back at him, full of hope and thirst for learning. He is as rejuvenated as they are.

"That will be all for today. I look forward to seeing you tomorrow."

Slowly, as though wanting more, the young men disburse with parting comments: "Thank you, Rabbi Nicodemus," "So good to have you back," "Good lesson, Rabbi," "Shalom."

❧❧❧❧❧❧❧

Nicodemus remains seated on the steps for a while. His heart is stirred by his own spontaneous lesson. *Where did that come from? Why did I say all those things?*

"You must be born again—born from above. Flesh gives birth to flesh, but Spirit gives birth to spirit."

A slight wind brushes across his face. *"You hear its sound, but you cannot tell where it comes from or where it is going. So it is with everyone born of the Spirit."*

Nicodemus is drawn to the study room down the tree-lined pathway. When he arrives, he pulls out the ancient scroll of Isaiah's prophecies. Spreading the scroll reverently across the table, he adjusts the lanterns so as to have the best lighting, and sits down to begin his study.

> "God said, 'Stop bringing meaningless offerings!
> Your incense is detestable to me.
> I cannot bear your evil assemblies.
> Your New Moon festivals and
>   your appointed feasts my soul hates.
> When you spread out your hands in prayer,
>   I will hide my eyes from you.
> Wash and make yourselves clean!'

247

I'm reminded again that the Lord does not look on the outward appearance but on the heart.

> 'Stop doing wrong, learn to do right!
>   Seek justice, encourage the oppressed.
> Defend the cause of the fatherless,
>   plead the case of the widow.'

Care for the helpless sheep of Israel.

> "Come, let us go to the mountain of the Lord,
>   to the houses of the God of Jacob.
> He will teach us his ways,
>   so that we may walk in his paths.
> The law will go out from Zion,
>   the word of the Lord from Jerusalem."

Yes, yes, my beloved Jerusalem.

> "Come, O house of Jacob,
>   let us walk in the light of the Lord."

Hmm—walk in the light…the light.

> "The eyes of the arrogant man will be humbled
>   and the pride of men brought low;
>   the Lord alone will be exalted in that day."

…arrogant man humbled …pride brought low

> "The Lord Almighty has a day in store
>   for all the proud and lofty,
>   for all that is exalted
>   and they will all be humbled."

Humility again–

Nicodemus' reflects on his sheep pen experience. *Humbled and brought low… that is for sure.*

He continues to read of the prophecies of Isaiah and Judah's captivity by Babylon. *How easy in hindsight to see the sin and arrogance, the disobedience and idolatry of our forefathers. Oh Lord, do we stand guilty before you in our generation as well? Do I?*

He searches on in the Isaiah scroll…

> "The virgin will be with child
>   and will give birth to a son,
>   and you will call him Immanuel."

God with us.

> "In the past he humbled the land of Zebulon
>   and Naphtali,
>   but in the future he will honor
>   Galilee of the Gentiles,
>   by way of the sea along the Jordan–"

Honor Galilee?

> "The people walking in darkness
>   have seen a great light;
>   on those living in the shadow of death
>   a light has dawned…"

There it is again—the light. Yeshua said, "…whoever lives by the truth comes into the light."

> "For unto us a child is born, to us a son is given,
>   and the government will be on his shoulders.
> And he will be called Wonderful Counselor,
>   Mighty God, Everlasting Father,
>   Prince of Peace…."

> "He will reign on David's throne
>   establishing and upholding it
>   with justice and righteousness
>   from that time and forever."

Forever?

"A shoot will come up from the stump of Jesse…"

David's father.

"…from his roots a Branch will bear fruit."

"Nazareth" means shoot or branch. Nazareth—the Nazarene.
He reads on.

> "The Spirit of the Lord will rest on him –
>   the Spirit of wisdom and understanding,
>   the Spirit of counsel and of power,
>   the Spirit of knowledge
>   and of the fear of the Lord–
>   and he will delight in the fear of the Lord."

Nicodemus stares at the flickering fire of his lantern.
He deliberates about that evening at the fire with Jesus.
Though everything Jesus said was not perfectly clear,
Nicodemus did sense a spirit of wisdom, counsel, power, and
fear of the Lord.

> "He will not judge by what he sees with his eyes,
>   or decide with what he hears with his ears;
>   but with righteousness he will judge the needy,
>   with justice he will give decisions
>   for the poor of the earth.
>
> He will strike the earth with the rod of his mouth;
>   and with the breath of his lips
>   he will slay the wicked.
> Righteousness will be his belt
>   and faithfulness the sash around his waist."

*Can this be Yeshua, Jesus of Nazareth? Only if he is the
Promised One can he make the statements I have heard from his lips.*

Nicodemus' eyes are weary. He has read from morning into the late hours of the afternoon—right through his noon meal and on through his prayer times.

After rolling up the sacred scrolls, he raises his slumped shoulders and pulls his prayer shawl over his head. Rather than praying his rote prayers, he cups his up-raised hands and cries out, "Almighty One of Israel, hear my prayer. Open the eyes of your servant. Illumine my mind. Prepare my heart for truth. May I be your righteous …humble servant."

CHAPTER 34
What Next?

The fear of the Lord teaches a man wisdom,
and humility comes before honor.
Proverbs 15:33

The next day, Nicodemus leads his students in discussion of one of the laws of Sabbath preparation. They bat questions, ideas, and technicalities back and forth. Nicodemus pulls the basic truths out of the law. On one hand, he feels contentment in his old setting, but he also feels restlessness in his soul.

He hasn't paid a visit to his older brother's family since his return from Capernaum and decides he should report on his mother and relatives, so they plan a family get-together.

Neziah and his family greet him enthusiastically, eager to hear all the family news. Nicodemus' niece and nephew join them for dinner. Their young children give Nicodemus hugs around his legs before he can scoop them up in his arms. The older great nephew is about Benjamin's age. In fact, he reminds Nicodemus of Benjamin.

As they sit around the table, Nicodemus fills them in on the trip to Capernaum – the grape incident, Aunt Leah's fussing around, and Uncle Laban's steady good humor. Nicodemus reports that his mother is very happy to be in her home town with her sister and wants to stay until they come for Passover next spring. Neziah is glad to hear that she is content but disappointed that he will not see her for so long.

"Did you get to see Uncle Zeriah?" Neziah asks.

Hesitantly, Nicodemus mentions that he wasn't able to see him which, of course, doesn't make much sense given the length of time he was gone. Nicodemus is still fighting bruised pride about the fall, so he quickly moves the conversation in another direction, asking about Neziah's medical practice.

Nicodemus watches Neziah and his wife interact playfully with one another. Why had he never noticed that before? The children and grandchildren talk and laugh. The house is filled with good food, good smells, and the warmth of family. His heart aches for Michael, Abigail, Benjamin, and... Ruth.

When Nicodemus returns to his empty house, the quiet rooms are deafening, the loneliness over-whelming. His mother isn't there to fill the house with her presence. Ruth is not there to have their good discussions and make him laugh.

He remembers the night when Ruth muffled her amusement telling about the day when she first saw Nicodemus hauled in on that cart. "What a sight you were," she had said. She could contain herself no longer and soon she and Nicodemus were both laughing uproariously together. He grins as he remembers that evening. It was the first time he laughed at himself. She always made him feel comfortable, happy, and accepted. Oh, how he longs to be with her again. *Get a hold of yourself, Nicodemus; you're acting like some lovesick school boy.*

He washes his face and prepares for bed. *I must think about more important matters. What am I to do about this Yeshua situation?*

He spots the tunic Michael had given him before he left Capernaum. Instinctively, he holds the tunic up to his face to smell it. Maybe it would smell like Michael and his memories. But, alas, he only detects a faint whiff of fish from the boat ride across the Sea of Galilee. Disappointed, he puts the tunic back on the shelf. *No shepherd smells.*

Hmm. Perhaps I should investigate the Bethlehem shepherd claims of long ago. Let's see, I figured that to be at least 30 years ago. Who would be left among the shepherds to remember the event? How could I go unrecognized among the shepherds? They might be fearful or threatened if a Jerusalem rabbi came calling.

He looks at the tunic on the shelf. *That's it. I'll put on Michael's tunic.*

He finds another piece of fabric and throws it over his head. *This will partially hide my face. I'll cancel my class on the day before Sabbath and leave early that morning before everybody is up. I'll have time to get there, find a shepherd, talk to him, and return before Sabbath evening begins. I'll take a bag to carry my regular robe for my return into the city.*

Satisfied that he has a good plan, Nicodemus teaches through the rest of the week, eats the not-so-tasty meals that Marida prepares for him, reinstates his two days of fasting, and continues thinking about his plan.

At the Temple, he watches with interest as the Bethlehem shepherds bring their unblemished lambs through the sheep gate. After all these years, he realizes it is as though he is capturing this scene for the first time.

He scans the shepherds, looking for any who might be older. It certainly would be more convenient to talk with one of them here, but far too risky. A teacher of the law cannot be found fraternizing or even speaking with a shepherd. No, his previous plan will be best.

Anticipation of this clandestine meeting keeps his mind occupied all week.

CHAPTER 35
The Shepherd's Testimony

An angel of the Lord appeared to them,
and the glory of the Lord shone around them.
Luke 2:9

Nicodemus retires early the night before his investigative trip and awakens before sunrise. Clothed in his plain garb with a walking stick in hand, he sets out for Bethlehem. Providentially, the moon provides sufficient light as he passes undetected through lower Jerusalem while sleepers still dream in their beds.

As he continues down the hill, he sees the first hint of daylight to his left. When the sun finally peers over the hill, its rays streak across the small town of Bethlehem.

Nicodemus spies a secluded spot where he can leave the bag with his traditional Pharisaic robe, headpiece, and phylacteries. He will change into these on his return trip. Carefully, he bends over to tuck the bag under a bush.

When he straightens up, he notices a shepherd over on the hill to the right. Nicodemus watches the shepherd as he appears to be pulling weeds and setting them up on rocks. *Ah, yes, pulling up all the poisonous weeds to get the pastureland ready for the day's feeding.*

Nicodemus breathes in deeply, treasuring the smell of early morning out in the open fields. He descends his hill as the shepherd ambles down his own grazing hill. When the shepherd reaches the sheep pen, Nicodemus stops to observe the shepherd calling his sheep out of the pen. He listens for the names, but the shepherd is too far away.

The shepherd leads and the sheep follow. Nicodemus finds it surprising that he feels as at home in this setting as he does with his disciples at the Temple. Somehow, he doesn't worry about how he is going to find the right shepherd with whom to talk. He has a sense that it will all work out. *I've never done anything so spontaneous and daring, other than my night visit with Yeshua. Getting bold in my old age, I guess.*

As Nicodemus walks into the town, he passes three large courtyards with rooms all around for sleeping and stables for keeping animals. He surmises that during Jerusalem festivals these rooms are packed with visiting pilgrims from all over Israel. Nicodemus finds it amazing that he has lived in nearby Jerusalem all these years and yet he has never been to Bethlehem, except to the outskirts for the census.

All is quiet except for the baaing of new lambs behind one of the inns. A young boy, already up for the day, tends to three of the lambs and their mothers. Nicodemus observes the boy with a stray lock of hair dangling on his forehead. *Just like Benjamin.* As Nicodemus approaches, he hums one of Michael's flute tunes in an effort not to startle the young boy. The boy glances up when he hears Nicodemus. "Did the ewes give birth recently?" Nicodemus inquires.

"Just last night," the boy answers. The boy gently strokes the smallest lamb.

"I suppose the rest of the flock is up there on the hill," Nicodemus continues.

"Yep, they been out four days, but they'll be back this afternoon."

"Is that your father I see up there with the sheep?"

"Yes sir." He covers one of the lambs with a woolen blanket.

"I suppose you will be going out in the fields in a few months too."

"Oh, I have already," the boy says proudly. "I just stayed back this time to take care of the newborns."

"I see that you are a big help to your father."

The boy grins shyly. "Where are your sheep?" he asks.

Nicodemus smiles. "Well, I'm not a shepherd, but my good friend is. I wonder if you could help me with some information."

"I will if I can." He stands tall, trying to look very important.

"Years ago, there was a report that shepherds from around here said they saw angels appearing to them in the sky. Do you know anything about that?"

The boy's eyes brighten. "Oh, yes sir, I know all 'bout that. The angels proclaimed the coming of the Messiah. My grandpa was one of them shepherds who saw it all."

"Well now, I'm sure that's quite a story."

"Ain't no story, mister. It's the actual fact. You can ask him 'bout it yerself."

"I see. You mean your grandfather is here?"

"Yes, sir. He's over there in the house. I'll go get him."

And off he goes before Nicodemus can say another word. This is easier than he had imagined it would be.

From across the yard, Nicodemus sees the old man come to the back door and peer out. Nicodemus turns his side to the door so as not to be too intimidating. Perhaps if the old man looks him over, he'll feel more at ease.

"The boy says you want to speak with me," the man calls from the house.

"Yes, if it is convenient for you."

"What is it you want?" he says, still standing in the doorway.

"Perhaps we could sit out here under this tree for a while."

Hesitantly, the man takes a couple of steps out the door and glances around.

"I have come alone. I simply want to talk to you about something that happened long ago."

Nicodemus saunters over to the tree where a couple of upturned logs have apparently provided a place for discussions through the years. He hopes the man will follow.

The man edges that way. "Where are you from?" he asks apprehensively.

"I live in Jerusalem, but I have a friend who shepherds in the Galilee."

The man doesn't move.

257

Nicodemus speaks again. "You have a fine grandson. It seems that he is preparing to follow in your footsteps."

The man ruffles the boy's hair. "Yes, he's a fine one. That he is." A broad grin on the grandson's face prompts a slight smile from the grandpa.

The shepherd meanders over to the tree to join Nicodemus and sits beside him. He motions to his grandson. "Aram, you can go on and tend to your lambs now."

"Oh," Aram responds, in a disappointed tone. Nicodemus figures the boy wanted to be in on the talk too. Aram shuffles away kicking a stone as he goes.

Sitting here near the old shepherd, Nicodemus remembers having seen him before at the Temple with his sheep. Nicodemus looks at the ground as he talks, hoping the man doesn't recognize him. *Quite a change for me. Usually I want to be noticed.*

Nicodemus jumps right in to his reason for coming. "I heard a story years ago about a vision seen by some Bethlehem shepherds. I rather dismissed the story back then, but things have happened in my life that caused me to think about this incident again. I just wanted to hear the story for myself from an eyewitness."

"Well, first of all, it wasn't a vision and it wasn't a story," the old shepherd states emphatically. "It really happened. I was right over there on that hill." He points with a leathery, tanned finger.

"I was helping my nephew and my uncle that night with their flock. We had settled the flock down for the night in the pen. I had walked up the hill a short way playing my flute. The other two had checked the sheep and were closing the gate, when out of nowhere a bright light appeared and a man startled us. The light glowed all around him and lit up the whole sky. We could see each other plain as day. My flute went dangling at my side and I fell to the ground, covering my face, same as the other two. We were scared half out of our wits. The strange man said, 'Do not be afraid because I bring you good news of great joy that will be for all the people.'

258

"I looked out carefully from behind my hands. I thought I must be dreamin' or somethin'. I blinked my eyes, tryin' to get use to that light. There was a strange odor, a pleasant smell, somethin' I had never smelled before. Now you can't dream a smell, you know."

Well, no, Nicodemus had never thought about that before, but he couldn't ever remember "dreaming a smell."

"The man in the light was so excited and yet comforting all at the same time. I wanted to hear more. I tried to listen real careful, knowin' this must be somethin' very important. The man said, 'Today in the town of David a Savior has been born to you: he is Christ the Lord.' Then I *knew* it was important! By this time, I figured that this was an angel of the Lord speaking to us. What else could it be?

"The angel said, 'This will be a sign to you: You will find a baby wrapped in cloths and lying in a manger.' Before we could take all that in, suddenly there was a great company of the heavenly host appearing with the angel. It nearly took my breath away.

"The whole sky was lit up with all of them singing and praising. They said, 'Glory to God in the highest, and on earth peace to men on whom his favor rests." Yep, they said, 'Glory to God in the highest and peace to men. Hmm, Glory to God and peace.' " The old shepherd sits there looking up in the sky as though he can see the heavenly host even today.

Was this the light I saw that night so long ago?

"We were absolutely awe-struck by it all," he whispers as he continues staring at the sky.

Nicodemus waits until the old man is ready to go on with his story.

"When the angels went back into heaven, we stood there in amazement. We couldn't speak, couldn't move. Finally, my nephew said, 'Let's go to Bethlehem and see this thing that has happened, which the Lord told us about.'

"We didn't stop to think about the sheep. Guess we thought the Lord would take care of them since he gave us such important business." He stops and chuckles softly.

259

Nicodemus is so caught up in the story that he urges the shepherd on.

"Well, we hurried off down the hill and around the bend. We couldn't believe any mother would have a baby in a stable, but we looked in every stable in town. They were all full because of the census, you know. Finally, we came to one with a lantern lit. Sure enough, there was the baby all swaddled up tight in his strips of cloths, lying in the straw— his mother and father sittin' beside him.

"In the quiet, we realized how loud our panting sounded. We finally caught our breath and whispered, 'Shalom.' The baby's mother—her name was Mary—she invited us to come closer. Can you believe a nice lady like that would let us dirty old shepherds get close to her new baby?

"Her husband welcomed us too. We spoke real soft to them, so we wouldn't wake the baby, and told them about the angel and what he said and the host of angels and their song and the light and everything. But Mary and Joseph didn't seem the least bit surprised. I guess it was because they knew it was all true.

"Well, we looked at the baby a long time. Almost like looking at a newborn lamb all full of life. We knew deep in our hearts that this was a special baby. The angel had said, 'He is Christ the Lord.' You don't get any more special than that."

The shepherd's flow of words gives out as he sits there thinking about all he has shared. Nicodemus is overwhelmed by the account. His eyes moisten. He wants to speak but can't find the words.

Finally, the shepherd muses softly, "I haven't told these things in a long time." Then he goes on, "That next morning the three of us told it over and over to all who would listen."

Nicodemus remembers the merchants, who had been in Bethlehem, telling the story "over and over" as well.

Nicodemus' voice trembles as he asks, "And what name did they give the baby?"

"Oh, I remember that well. They named him, Jesus."

260

Nicodemus anticipated this but still, he is stunned. "Yeshua—the Lord saves," he says softly.

The shepherd continues, "Mary and Joseph stayed on for several months in Bethlehem. One of our families moved away, so Mary and Joseph lived in their house. Joseph made many things for the people of our town. He was handy with wood and stone. And everybody loved Mary.

"One day we couldn't believe our eyes. Some men from the East came riding into town with their camels and their fine clothes. They brought expensive gifts. Said a star led them to our town. Mary told my wife that the men went into their house and bowed down before Jesus, kind of like they were worshipping him. Mary showed my wife the gifts the men brought—gold, frankincense, and myrrh.

"The men were concerned about King Herod. Rightly so. I could have told them a thing or two about that man."

Nicodemus nods. He remembers the tyrannical Herod well. He also remembers the strangers coming into Jerusalem looking for the new king.

The old shepherd adds, "So the plan was that these eastern men were going to avoid Jerusalem and go back to their land another way."

Ah, so that was what happened to them.

"In the middle of the next night, Mary knocked on our door and said her husband, Joseph, had been warned in a dream that they should flee and off they went. We were heartbroken."

The old man pauses to remember and then continues. "Within the week, after Herod realized these men weren't coming back, he went into one of his tirades and decided... he decided to kill all the babies in our town who could possibly be close to Jesus' age."

The shepherd looks to the ground for a long time. Nicodemus can't tell if the old man is through talking or still thinking. After a few deep sighs, he wipes his eyes and continues, but in a broken voice. "Herod's soldiers came storming into Bethlehem as though they were fighting a legion of enemy soldiers. They went door to door looking for babies and stab…"

The old man cannot finish his sentence. His elbows fall to his knees and he holds his face in both hands. His back trembles as he muffles the pain of remembrance.

Nicodemus wants to hold this dear man to comfort him, but isn't quite sure what to do.

Finally, the man raises his head and tries to gain control of himself. "Our first-born baby…"

He lowers his head and shakes again, weeping audibly. Finally, he wipes his nose with his sleeve and wipes his eyes with the back of his hand. He breathes in and out with great gulps of air trying to steady his emotions.

At last, he tries to speak again. "Our first-born baby was one of those taken by Herod's soldiers. It was a day of horror. Screams and wails all over our little town. I'll never forget it."

"I'm so sorry," Nicodemus offers, helplessly.

After a couple of minutes of silence, the shepherd concludes his recollections. "We didn't hear from Joseph's family for several months. When they finally did come back to Bethlehem, we told them that Herod had died but Herod's son, Archelaus, was reigning as the new king. He was about as bad a ruler as his father had been. Mary and Joseph only stayed a few days and told us they were going on to their hometown of Nazareth. We haven't heard from them since."

Nicodemus reaches over and pats the old man's shoulder. "You have been very kind and most helpful. Thank you for telling me your stor…er, your experiences." Nicodemus remembers the shepherd's insistence that it wasn't a *story*.

"Why do you come asking about these things?" the shepherd questions.

"There is a man called Jesus, who is going about the country healing people and teaching about the Lord. He is a young man, maybe thirty or so. Perhaps he is your Jesus."

"Have you heard him? Have you seen him," the man asks excitedly.

"Yes. He calls himself the Son of Man sent from God."

"You believe him to be our Messiah?"

Startled by this direct question, Nicodemus splutters, "I... I am trying to determine that. It is why I have come to you today."

Nicodemus stands and the old shepherd follows suit. For the first time he looks into Nicodemus' face.

"I have seen you before—in Jerusalem, but you were dressed..." It dawns on the shepherd who he is. "You're a teacher of the law, a rabbi. But why...?" He looks at Nicodemus' clothes.

"I felt the need to come... uh, unnoticed."

"Couldn't be seen talking to a shepherd, eh?"

"As I told your grandson, I have a good friend in Galilee who is a shepherd. He taught me many things about sheep and shepherding, and life. It has been a pleasure talking with you. Thank you."

"It has been good to remember the angel's message and the babe of hope."

"Shalom, my friend."

As Nicodemus turns to leave, he glances over at the boy. "Don't let those lambs go astray."

"Yes, sir. Good-bye." He waves.

Nicodemus smiles at the old man who winks back at him.

♪❦♪❦♪❦♪❦

As Nicodemus walks along the road, he finds it interesting that in a short hour with this stranger, he feels closer to him than to some of his rabbi friends. He looks back. The old man is sitting on the stump. *Still reminiscing, I guess.*

Nicodemus thinks through the whole story, piece by piece, and is more amazed than ever at what he has heard. *This old man has nothing to prove. He simply tells the story, hmm... the "experience" as he vividly remembers it. It certainly explains many things, but what do I do now?*

Nicodemus finds his bag of clothes where he left them. He dons his robe and adjusts his phylacteries and headpiece. He feels slightly disturbed about his need for disguise and sneaking around like this. *Bound by my traditions.* He shakes his head at himself.

Squaring his shoulders, he marches into Jerusalem as though nothing unusual has happened. Nicodemus' mind is abuzz as he tries to process all he has heard. He realizes that he must discuss his thoughts with someone. Who else, but Joseph. *I will go to Joseph's house right away.*

On the way, he notices members of the Sanhedrin clustered in little groups. Gamliel spots Nicodemus and breaks away from his group to greet him.

"Do you know of our meeting this afternoon?" Gamaliel asks Nicodemus.

"No, what is the urgency?"

"More about the Galilean."

Nicodemus wrinkles his brow in question.

"The healer again," Gamaliel sighs with dread.

Nicodemus nods. "Do we meet at the seventh hour?"

"Yes. Surely we will be finished before the afternoon sacrifice at the ninth hour."

Nicodemus hurries on to Joseph's house. Maybe they will still have time to talk. Joseph's wife, Deborah, comes to the door.

"Shalom, Deborah."

"Nicodemus," she nods. "Joseph said you had a good trip with your mother. Is she well?"

"Very well, thank you. She loves being with her sister."

"I can imagine so," Deborah smiles.

"I was wondering if Joseph is at home."

"No, he had some business in the market. He said he would return shortly before the meeting with the Sanhedrin."

Seeing that Nicodemus is notably disappointed, Deborah adds, "May I be of help to you?"

"No, no, I will just see him later."

CHAPTER 36
The Sanhedrin Meeting

*Does our law condemn anyone without first hearing him
to find out what he is doing?*
John 7:51

Disappointed to have missed Joseph, Nicodemus plods along to his house and later on to the meeting place in the Temple, dreading the brow-beating discussion to follow. He spies Joseph across the way and they both walk briskly to meet one another.

"Nicodemus, Deborah said you were most anxious to see me. Is something wrong?"

"No, I just have a great many things I want to talk to you about. Let's meet soon so I can catch you up on everything."

"I thought there was more to your trip than the little you told me," Joseph says with a knowing twinkle in his eye.

"Oh, there's even more than my trip to tell you about," Nicodemus tantalizes.

As they approach the steps, Joseph mumbles under his breath, "First we have to wade through this ranting and railing about the teacher."

Several have gathered in the room of hewn stone while others linger outside the entrance.

"Argus, Pethahiah." Joseph nods as he and Nicodemus enter. Argus and Pethahiah return the nod.

Joseph leans over and whispers to Nicodemus. "Counting for a quorum, no doubt."

The room hums with multiple discussions. Pharisees, which includes most of the teachers of the law and some of the elders, gather in one area. Sadducees, including several priests and most of the chief priests, gather in another area. They may disagree on political and religious issues, but they all seem to share like views about Yeshua. The longer they complain to one another, the louder their voices.

At last, Annas, the previous high priest, enters the room and they move toward their benches to be seated. When Caiaphas, the present high priest, approaches his place, the room falls quiet.

Caiaphas begins. "Men of the high court, it seems that we have ongoing concerns about this teacher from Galilee."

He has a name.

Caiaphas continues in his cool serene tone. "It has been reported that he healed a lame beggar just yesterday—on the Sabbath."

One by one, outbursts come from around the room:

"Yes, and he told the man to pick up his mat and walk. Pick it up. On the Sabbath!"

"I've heard that he and his followers have picked grains of wheat on the Sabbath."

"I know for a fact that this man and his followers eat with sinners and publicans."

Perturbed at being interrupted, Caiaphas breaks in, "Yes, yes, I know. We have sent the Temple guards even now to arrest this imposter. He says that he is like the bread sent from heaven when our forefathers wandered in the wilderness. Imagine comparing himself to the holy manna." Disgusted murmurs float around the room.

From one side of the room someone declares, "The other day, he had the gall to claim that he *did* come down from heaven." A collective gasp punctuates the comment.

From the other side, "Well, when we went to Galilee and saw him heal a lame man, he told the lame man his sins were forgiven. Blasphemous!" Hisses and clicking of tongues fill the room.

A sudden commotion outside the door draws their attention. Argus steps into the room. "The Temple guards have arrived. *Empty handed,*" he adds sarcastically.

"Bring them in!" Caiaphas demands. They enter and stand just inside the doorway.

"Come. Come, come," Caiaphas shouts at them. "Why did you not bring him in?"

"No one ever spoke the way this man does," one of the guards says sheepishly.

Standing near the guard, Argus is beside himself. "You mean he has deceived you also?" He motions toward others in the room. "Have any of the rulers or any of the Pharisees believed in him? No! This mob that knows nothing of the law—there is a curse on them."

The Sanhedrin is in a state of stunned silence. Caiaphas seems not to know what to do next as his anger seethes at the disobedience of his own guards. He heaves out a disgusted sigh.

Nicodemus rises. All eyes dart to this respected member of their ruling body. He speaks calmly. "Does our law condemn anyone without first hearing him to find out what he is doing?"

Argus' right eyebrow arches in a cunning smirk as if the adder has finally trapped his prey. "Are you from Galilee, too?" he sneers. "Look into it, and you will find that a prophet does not come from *Galilee*." He spits out the word with contempt.

Nicodemus sits. His face is flushed to the point that he feels slightly dizzy. The discussion continues. Condemnation of the teacher builds layer by layer, but Nicodemus can hardly hear for the pulsating, pounding in his head.

How could I ever tell them all I've experienced? How could I ever explain that he was born in Bethlehem, just as was prophesied? But a shepherd's word is not trusted—a shepherd is not even allowed to testify in this court. These rulers would never believe that Yeshua could actually be the promised Messiah. I'm not sure myself, but I want to seek the truth. I want to know the truth. Oh, Holy One of Israel, lead me to the truth.

Joseph touches Nicodemus' hand in a gesture of support. It brings Nicodemus back to the comments at hand, but his stomach turns at the venom and hatred that spews from these "religious" leaders.

Their minds are made up. There's nothing Yeshua can do to redeem himself. There is no turning back.

267

Nicodemus and Joseph make a hasty retreat from the meeting amid questioning glances from the other members. As soon as they clear the doorway and descend the steps, Nicodemus heaves a sigh of relief. *Who am I? What is my place? I'm becoming a stranger even to myself.*

Joseph senses his need to talk. "Would you like to stop at my house so we can discuss things?"

"Yes, thank you, my friend."

They greet Deborah and walk through the house to an inner courtyard. The afternoon sun is shadowed by one wall but shines warmly on the opposite wall. Sitting on a bench in the shade, the two catch up on Nicodemus' many adventures of the past weeks.

Nicodemus begins with his trip to Capernaum; where he passed John the Baptizer, visited Aunt Leah, Uncle Laban, and Cousin Rebecca, and had the fateful fall and injury on the hill. Emotions surface along with the flow of words as Nicodemus describes his frustrations, his pain, as well as those tender moments of self-realization. He talks about Michael's family and Ruth—Ruth's service and care, Ruth's talks with him, Ruth's nature, the way Ruth looks—Ruth, Ruth, Ruth.

Joseph smiles. The more Nicodemus chats away, the more Joseph grins; he chuckles, and then he laughs out loud. "Why, Nicodemus, you old man, I believe you have finally found the love of your life." Nicodemus blushes.

Joseph slaps him on the back as they have a hearty laugh. Nicodemus is glad to release some of the weight he has been carrying. Laughter is good.

But Nicodemus has so much more to tell. His mood becomes serious again as he tells of his encounters with Jesus. Joseph can hardly believe that Nicodemus had a private hearing with Jesus and begs to hear all the details. Nicodemus has reviewed that conversation hundreds of times in his mind, so he can easily relate every word.

By now, the courtyard is totally shadowed with only the top of the wall still in the sun.

"Oh, Joseph, the best is yet to come. I know how it is possible that Yeshua was born in Bethlehem, as our Scripture foretells." Nicodemus tells of his visit to Bethlehem and the shepherd's story.

Joseph lets him tell his story and then he shares how *his* family knows Zechariah and Elizabeth, Mary's relatives. He knows Mary's story; the birth and the escape from Bethlehem. He has followed Jesus' growing up years, all the time wondering.

Nicodemus' eyes brighten with relief and delight. Can this possibly be? Yet another sign of affirmation.

"Oh, but there is more, Joseph. When I returned to Jerusalem, I reread Isaiah's prophecies. I'm wondering if Yeshua could possibly be our promised Messiah. I know he doesn't come as a king or a warrior as we may have expected, but I see the possibilities in our sacred Scripture. I hope this doesn't upset you."

"Nicodemus. Nicodemus, my brother, I have come to this same conclusion."

"But why did you not tell me these things long ago?"

"You wouldn't have believed me."

Nicodemus stares at him for a moment and then hangs his head. "You're right, I wouldn't have. I was too proud, too steeped in the law, too busy, too rigid. I would never have believed a dirty, smelly old shepherd either."

269

CHAPTER 37
Questions for Jesus

Why do your disciples break the tradition of the elders?
Matthew 15:2

Jesus has escaped the scrutiny of the Sanhedrin in their meeting place, but the members continue to actively pursue and question him. Though they may complain vehemently *about* him with each other, their encounters in public are cloaked in measured diplomacy. His popularity with the people will not allow for anything more daring.

Week by week, the Jewish leaders add to their list of questions. Surely one of these questions will trip up the popular teacher.

One afternoon, Argus corners Nicodemus. "Nicodemus, your new disciples seem to be faring well under your teaching."

"We have thorough discussions. There are many bright ones among the group."

"And what have they to say about the miracle worker?"

"I am a teacher of the law, Argus. We dwell on obedience not political opinions."

"Oh, but the healer speaks of our law. Surely you want to help your students defend it."

Before Nicodemus can counter, Argus issues an invitation. "You haven't joined us on any of our trips to question the man. We leave tomorrow afternoon to see him just beyond the Jordan in Perea where he is teaching. You can see for yourself how he continues to mislead the people."

I suppose I must join them in order to speak intelligently about their complaints. It is hard to defend what I have not heard.

"Very well, I shall join you tomorrow."

"Excellent!" Argus breaks into that cunning smile of his.

As Argus struts away, Nicodemus closes his eyes and shakes his head. "Lord of heaven and earth, give me patience," he mutters. *What was it Yeshua said? "Anyone who is angry with his brother will be subject to judgment." Tame my temper. O Lord.*

The next day, after a hasty lunch, Nicodemus begrudgingly gathers his things for another trip outside the walls of Jerusalem. Joseph is off on one of his business trips so Nicodemus is left to the company of Argus and Pethahiah. Fortunately, a couple of other friends from the Sanhedrin are going along as well.

As Nicodemus and his companions approach the large assembly, they hear outbursts of joy popping up from one portion of the crowd to another. Apparently miracles of healing are occurring as Jesus circulates among the people.

For some time now, the action appears to center in one particular area, so the Pharisaic scholars push that way to find the healer. By the time they arrive, Jesus is teaching. He is seated on a rock while those gathered around him are seated on the ground. Jesus seems to be drawing some conclusions, but before he can move to his final point, Argus speaks up.

"Sir, some have noticed that your disciples do not wash their hands before they eat. Why do they break the tradition of the elders?"

All heads turn to this one who has interrupted.

Jesus' gaze flies across the heads of those at his feet and lands like an arrow on Argus. "And why do you break the command of God for the sake of your tradition? For God said, 'Honor your father and mother.' He also said, 'Anyone who curses his father or mother must be put to death.' But you say that if a man says to his father or mother, 'Whatever help that you might have otherwise received from me is a gift devoted to God.' You say he is not to 'honor his father' with it. Thus you nullify the word of God for the sake of your tradition."

Argus falters for a moment. He, in fact, has been one of those who has said this very thing. His father squandered much of his inherited money, so he apparently questioned why he should give his father money in his old age. "It is Corban," Argus had declared— "dedicated to God."

"You hypocrites!" Jesus calls out. "Isaiah was right when he prophesied about you. 'These people honor me with their lips, but their hearts are far from me. They worship me in vain; their teachings are but rules taught by men.'"

Jesus turns away from Argus and speaks again to the people, "Listen and understand. What goes into a man's mouth does not make him 'unclean,' but what comes out of his mouth; *that* is what makes him 'unclean.' For out of the heart comes evil thoughts, adultery, sexual immorality, theft, false testimony, slander. These are what make a man 'unclean'; but eating with unwashed hands does not make a man 'unclean.'"

Argus juts out his chin and looks down his nose at these simple people. Sneering, he hisses to Pethahiah, "Sly he is. These ignorant people take it all in. What do they know?"

Nicodemus notices the scowls from those nearby. They tip their heads to one another with muffled whispers. Nicodemus hears one man whisper, "He and his kind don't belong here." Argus appears oblivious to all this as he looks up at the sky seeming to plot his next question.

"Do not judge," Jesus is saying, "or you too will be judged; for in the same way you judge others, you will be judged, and with the measure you use, it will be measured to you. Why do you look at the speck or sawdust in your brother's eye and pay no attention to the plank in your own eye?" A few rumbles of agreement float among the listeners. They catch his obvious exaggeration. Three or four glance around at Argus.

Jesus presses on. "How can you say to your brother, 'Let me take the speck out of your eye,' when all the time there is a plank in your own eye? You hypocrite, first take the plank out of your own eye, and then you will see clearly to remove the speck from your brother's eye. In everything, do to others what you would have them do to you."

Nicodemus glances at Argus. *In spite of himself, Argus is drawn in by Jesus illustration. Like it or not, Jesus' teachings are, as they say, "amazing."* Nicodemus contains his smile.

Jesus continues. "I have come to seek and to save those who are lost. Suppose one of you has a hundred sheep and loses one of them. Does he not leave the ninety-nine and go after the lost sheep until he has found it?" Jesus glances at Nicodemus with a sparkle in his eye. Nicodemus smiles his acknowledgment.

Jesus looks again at the people. "And when he finds his sheep, he joyfully goes home and calls his friends and neighbors to rejoice with him. I tell you that in the same way there will be more rejoicing in heaven over one sinner who *repents* than over the ninety-nine who feel they do not *need* to repent."

Argus wrinkles his forehead. *Argus doesn't seem to know how to take these words. He probably rationalizes that Yeshua is rebuking these people and not us—certainly not himself.*

Argus starts to raise his hand in an effort to capture the teacher's attention so he can ask another question, but Jesus moves right on with his teaching.

"One day two men went up to the Temple to pray."

Hmm, another story.

"One was a Pharisee, and the other a tax collector."

Uh-oh. Argus isn't going to like this one.

"The Pharisee stood up and prayed about himself. 'God I thank you that I am not like other men—robbers, evildoers, adulterers—or even like this tax collector. I fast twice a week and give a tenth of all I get.'

"But the tax collector stood at a distance. He would not even look up to heaven, but beating his breast, he said, 'God, have mercy on me a sinner.' I tell you *this* man, rather than the other, went home justified before God."

Jesus casts his eye directly at Argus from across the crowd. "For everyone who exalts himself, will be humbled, and he who humbles himself will be exalted."

Argus has had enough. In a huff, he turns around dramatically as if to shake the dust of his feet from this commoner. "I can see that there is no reasoning with this man. It is plain that he knows nothing of the law and certainly has no respect for our authority. He will find himself in big trouble and very soon. I will speak to Caiaphas about this."

Nicodemus is reluctant to be associated with this group; nonetheless, he follows Argus and the other Pharisees away from the crowd. At the edge of the crowd, he sees John, Zebedee's son, just a short way off. Nicodemus cannot answer the questioning look on John's face. His response is but a regrettable shake of the head, his eyes downcast. How can he possibly explain all that has taken place since he spoke to Jesus that night months ago.

Nicodemus is glad to be away from the crowd, but he is not glad to listen to Argus' continual ranting and raving about Jesus. *He heard nothing that the teacher was trying to tell him. He has no idea what humility is. But then, neither did I until the trip to Capernaum.*

Animosity toward Jesus grows among the leaders. Nicodemus finds calm only with Joseph. The meetings in the Sanhedrin are consumed with condemnation of Yeshua. Their anger has turned to rage. Plots to kill Jesus brew constantly.

The breaking point comes when rumors surface that Jesus has raised Lazarus of Bethany from the dead. The chief priests and Pharisees call a meeting of the Sanhedrin.

"What are we accomplishing?" one red-faced chief priest practically screams at the gathering. "Here is this man performing all kinds of trickery. If we let him go on like this, everyone will believe in him, and then the Romans will come and take away both our place and our nation."

In that order. That's what they're worried about—their "place," themselves, their political connections—not whether they are seeking truth.

Caiaphas, the currently Roman-appointed high priest, stands to his feet. With his usual haughty disdain, he addresses the group.

"You know nothing at all! You do not realize that it is better for you that one man die for the people than that the whole nation perish." Caiaphas goes on to declare that the leaders shall put out an order to the people. If anyone finds out where Jesus is, they are to inform the leaders so that Jesus might be arrested.

Well, there it is. They are determined to kill him.

A heavy darkness looms in Nicodemus' heart. *What are we doing? Where will all this lead? Is it possible that this is fulfillment of prophecy with or without the will of this daunting assembly?*

Nicodemus retreats to his study place where copies of the sacred scrolls are kept. Once more he will seek out the prophet Isaiah.

CHAPTER 38
Isaiah's Prophecy

We all, like sheep, have gone astray;
each of us has turned to his own way.
Isaiah 53:6

Nicodemus pulls out the scroll of Isaiah and unrolls it carefully. It opens to the same place where he left it days before. *Evidently, no one else has been reading the prophet's words.*

Hmm, another servant song:

"See, my servant will act wisely;
  he will be raised and lifted up
  and highly exalted."

That is what Yeshua said the night I went to see him. "Just as Moses lifted up the snake in the desert, so the Son of Man must be lifted up, and everyone who believes in him may have eternal life." Lifted up. What does it mean? Exalted? Put upon a throne? Made to be the king?

He reads on.

"Just as there were many who were appalled at him—
  His appearance was so disfigured
    beyond that of any man
    and his form marred beyond human likeness."

What is this? Surely not that of a king.

"So will he sprinkle many nations,
  and many kings will shut their mouths
    because of him.
For what they were not told, they will see,
  and what they have not heard,
    they will understand."

Sprinkled—cleansed maybe? Shut their mouths—astonished at his suffering and exultation?

276

"Who has believed our message
     and to whom has the arm of the Lord
     been revealed?
He grew up before him like a tender shoot,
     and like a root out of dry ground."

From the stump of Jesse.

"He had no beauty or majesty to attract us to him,
     nothing in his appearance
     that we should desire him."

Yes, I remember thinking that he looked quite ordinary.

"He was despised and rejected by men,
     a man of sorrows and familiar with suffering.
Like one from whom men hide their faces,
     he was despised and we esteemed him not."

*The Sadducees, the elders, the scribes, the chief priests, even my
fellow Pharisees, most have despised and rejected him.*

"Surely he took up our infirmities
     and carried our sorrows,
Yet we considered him stricken by God,
     smitten by him and afflicted,
     but he was pierced by our transgressions,
     he was crushed for our iniquities;
     the punishment that brought us peace
     was upon him,
     and by his wounds we are healed."

With each word, tears sting Nicodemus eyes. *Pierced?
Crushed? Wounded? No, Lord, no. This cannot be. Why must he die?*
And as soon as the question leaves his lips, the answer
returns—*our* infirmities, *our* sorrows, *our* transgressions, *our*
iniquities. The punishment that brought *us* peace was upon
him. By *his* wounds, *we* are healed.

"We all, like sheep, have gone astray…"

Nicodemus cups his face in his hands as he weeps. The mental picture is too much; the memory of his pious attitude too vivid, his own emotionally humbling experience too real.

"Oh, Lord, like those straying sheep, I too have strayed. I have concentrated so intently on the letter of the law, worried so about pleasing men, and have indulged in self-exaltation that I am far from you. My mindless, routine prayers are of little account. My heart is cluttered with laws and man-induced rules. There is little room for truth, mercy, grace, love. And like a sheep that has gone astray, I have caused others to stray as well. Forgive me, oh Lord. Forgive me."

Through tear-stained eyes, Nicodemus finishes the passage.

> "We all, like sheep, have gone astray,
>   Each of us has turned in his own way,
>   and the Lord has laid on him
>   the iniquity of us all."

...*laid on* him *the iniquity of us all*. Nicodemus stares at the flickering flame of the lantern. *Is he to become our sacrificial lamb?*

Nicodemus leans with his elbows on the table, his face in his hands. The words tumble over and over in his mind. This is not his picture of the Messiah.

Is our repentance greater than military strength? Are his wounds greater than political freedom? Is sacrifice greater than victory? Or indeed, will our repentance, his wounds, and his sacrifice bring us victory over our sin?

It is more than Nicodemus can bear. In anguish he rolls up the scroll and replaces it on the shelf.

CHAPTER 39
Family and Friends Come to Jerusalem

Bless the Lord, O my soul: and all that is within me,
bless his holy name. Psalm 103:1 KJV

Nicodemus' heart is heavy for days. Allowing his students to argue over insignificant details of the law seems vain and mundane. Daily, he trudges from home to Temple, Temple to home, still mulling over the prophecies of Isaiah.

Some days, he has doubts about what he read. Did he read into it more than was there? Could Isaiah have been speaking of someone of his day? Was he talking about Israel as his servant rather than Messiah as the servant? But Nicodemus kept coming back to the conclusion—*no one has borne the iniquity of us all.*

The only thing that brings joy to Nicodemus' heart is the hope of Passover. He will see his mother again and Michael and Benjamin and... Ruth. Dear Ruth. How much should he share with her? Certainly she will want to know of his change of heart about Yeshua.

He remembers Joseph's observation. "Nicodemus, I do believe you have found the love of your life." A contented smile grows on his face. He begins counting the days.

Surely they will come before Sabbath so that we might have a full week together before Passover. I wonder if mother will stay or will want to return to Capernaum.

At last, it is the day before Sabbath—one week before Passover. Nicodemus reminds Marida to gather in ample food supplies in anticipation of the arrival of family and friends. He even helps her tidy up the vineyard. *New vines are greening up, just in time for the mistress of the garden.* Nicodemus makes sure the old dead vines are cleaned out. He grins. His mother, "Martha the Inspector," will be sure to check.

Oh, and I need to examine the flowers in the large vases at the front of the house. Must have a good entrance.

279

Nicodemus cuts short his next morning at the Temple. He doesn't want to miss their arrival. As it turns out, however, he may as well have stayed longer. He paces back and forth; checks the vineyard, glances at the front flowers, inspects the bedrooms, examines the cupboards. Yes, ample food. He meanders out to the gate to look down the street. A few visitors here and there, but not *his* visitors. He doesn't really *know* that they are coming today. What if they decide to arrive *after* Sabbath?

He comes in to freshen up a bit; washes his face in a basin of water and combs his hair. Suddenly he turns his ear toward the front door. *Are those voices I hear?*

His heart skips a beat and he feels sudden warmth rushing to the top of his head. As he bounds to the front door, he recognizes the voices.

He flings open the door and there stands his mother with Laban, Leah, and Zilia.

"Mama! Oh, it is so good to see you," Nicodemus says, as he takes her bags.

"And what a welcome sight you are, my son," Martha exclaims as she hugs him tightly. "I've been gone way too long."

Hmm, perhaps she does plan to stay.

"Laban, I'm surprised to see you. I didn't think you would be up for the trip?"

"Well, I've been feeling better and thought I would try to come one more time. I'm sure ready for one of your beds though."

"Well, come right in and we'll find you one."

"Aunt Leah, so good to see you."

"And you Nicodemus."

She must be tired. So few words.

After hugs all around, they move their baskets and bags from the doorway.

"Zilia, come in, come in. Welcome back."

"Thank you, Master Nicodemus. It's good to be back."

Laban adds, "Michael and Abigail are on their way."

280

Just then Michael rounds the doorway with Benjamin by his side.

"Ah, two of my favorite men. Welcome to Jerusalem," Nicodemus stretches his hands out to Benjamin who runs to him. Benjamin clings tightly to Nicodemus' waist and Nicodemus holds him lovingly as he kisses the top of his head and ruffles his hair.

Benjamin has lots of tales to tell. "We rode the boat all the way across the Sea of Galilee and then we walked and walked and walked. It's a *long* way to Jerusalem."

Nicodemus and the others laugh. "Yes, my boy, it *is* a long way, but you are here and that is the important thing. Later, you can tell me all about your trip."

"Michael, my friend, I'm so glad you came."

"We're honored to be in your home, Master Nicodemus." Michael stands awkwardly, gawking at the surroundings as though he doesn't quite know how to act in this elaborate house.

"I hope you will find my home as welcoming as yours was to me."

Nicodemus helps Michael bring his things in. Everyone is chatting. Martha greets Marida and gives her instructions on where everyone will sleep. Leah says she wants to see the grapevines. Zilia and Marida greet each other. Laban and Benjamin talk of the things they will do and see while in Jerusalem.

When Nicodemus turns around, there is Ruth. His heart jumps to his throat. He croaks out, "Ruth."

"Nicodemus." She looks at him with longing and yet question in her eyes.

He holds both hands out to her and she offers her hands to him.

"I've missed you so much, Ruth." He pulls her to him and puts both arms around her shoulders. She is a bit hesitant, but quickly melts into his embrace.

"I missed you so much," he whispers again. "I have many things to tell you. We will have a good long talk."

281

"That sounds wonderful," she says, cradled in his arms.

Nicodemus and Ruth are suddenly aware that all the chattering has stopped. Nicodemus releases Ruth and they look around, a bit embarrassed at all the smiling faces.

"Well, this is a good sight indeed," he sputters, his face flushed. "I'm glad everyone has made it here safely." Nicodemus looks around. He realizes someone is missing. "And Abigail, has Abigail not come with you?"

Martha speaks up with special warmth in her voice. "Yes, Nicodemus. Abigail has come and she has a surprise."

They all look toward the doorway. Nicodemus turns to see Abigail standing just inside the door, but someone else is just outside the door. Bright sun rays from behind, shadow the other person. Nicodemus wrinkles his brow trying to make out the identity of this other woman. Everyone is breathlessly quiet. He walks closer and grows wide-eyed with disbelief.

"Rebecca, is that you?" He leans forward. "Is it Cousin Rebecca?"

"Shalom, Nicodemus. Yes, it is me."

He rushes forward as if he must help her stay on her feet, but she is standing, standing on her own.

"But how... what... when...?"

"It was the healer, Nicodemus," she says softly. "He came to our house and touched me. He healed me. He told me to stand up and I did. Jesus healed me, Nicodemus. He healed me."

"I... I can't believe it." Everyone stands motionless. All eyes are on Nicodemus to see how he will receive this news.

"Believe it, Nicodemus." She prances all around him. "Believe it, Nicodemus. Believe it!"

"I do believe. I *do* believe. Bless his Holy Name, I do believe!"

If ever Nicodemus needed confirmation, this was it.

"Rebecca, my dear cousin, you look wonderful. What a blessing this is." He hugs her warmly and backs away to look at her, then hugs her again.

"Praise to the Lord Almighty of Israel," he lifts both hands in the air. "And praise to the healer and teacher, Yeshua. Oh, my dear family and friends, I left you in such an unloving way. So much has happened. We will have many hours for explanation. Just know that I share your joy for this miraculous victory.

"Dear Rebecca, you have traveled a long way to share your wonderful news. And your first time to our beloved city of Jerusalem. Can my heart hold anymore? But come, you will all want to bathe… and eat. Marida, let's prepare a feast. Tonight we will have a Sabbath feast like none other." He reaches out to Ruth and squeezes her hand.

With that, everyone scrambles to take their belongings to their rooms, bathe themselves, rest a bit, and prepare for Sabbath.

❦❦❦❦❦

Candlelight and a lone lantern provide a beautiful glow around the room as Nicodemus, his family, and these dear friends celebrate Sabbath together.

When they gather around the table for the Shabbat meal, Nicodemus gently squeezes Ruth's hand under the folds of her skirt.

Benjamin beams his delight at getting to sit on Nicodemus' other side. He is in a prime spot to have Nicodemus' full attention so that he might tell many more stories of his journey to Jerusalem. Nicodemus listens to his tales and wonders, could life be any sweeter than this?

Nicodemus shares bits and pieces of his run-ins with Yeshua. Michael listens intently to Nicodemus' story, especially when Nicodemus tells of the stirring in his soul when Jesus said, "I am the Good Shepherd." Benjamin is wide-eyed with interest when Nicodemus shares about his discussion with the Bethlehem shepherd and his grandson.

283

A tear slips down Martha's cheek signaling her gratitude for the change that has come over her son. Laban wears a perpetual smile and can't keep from nodding his head in approval. A quiet joy fills the room as they all cherish the holiness of this moment.

Laban shares with Nicodemus that many travelers along the way spoke of rumors that Jesus would be entering Jerusalem on the first day of the week. "They all want to be here to greet him."

"Indeed," says Nicodemus, not daring to tell them of the danger lurking ahead for Yeshua. *This is not a good time to tell these sweet innocent ones that Yeshua's very life is being threatened by the religious leaders of the Temple. They will learn all too soon about the hostility of this bitter group.*

The next morning they go to the nearest synagogue to worship. Nicodemus is glad to have his family and friends with him.

"There are so many people in your synagogue, Master Nicodemus," Benjamin exclaims with wonder.

"You are in Jerusalem now, my friend." Nicodemus grins from ear to ear. "Wait 'til we go to the Temple tomorrow."

CHAPTER 40
Benjamin Visits the Temple

How lovely is your dwelling place, O Lord Almighty.
Psalm 84:1

The following morning, Nicodemus proudly marches Benjamin to the Temple. They pass through the narrow streets with all the houses lined up side by side. Benjamin gawks from one side to the other.

When they enter the market place, Benjamin exclaims, "There's more fruit and vegetable stands here than I have ever seen in one place."

Greedy vendors squabble with stingy customers who want more for their money. A mother boxes her two misbehaving children on their ears when they try to snatch figs from a merchant's basket. Benjamin giggles.

At last, no more houses, no more markets. They climb massive steps and there, spread before Benjamin, is the Temple shining in the morning sun. Benjamin's eyes are big as donkey's hooves. His mouth hangs open. "Look at that," he finally manages to say as his eyes span from one end to the other. They walk closer, and Benjamin's head rolls back to take in the breathtaking height of the Temple. Nicodemus puts his hand to Benjamin's back for fear he will fall backwards.

"Well, what do you think, my boy?"

"I never seen anything like it."

Nicodemus is amused at Benjamin's wonder. *How delightful to see through new eyes.* "Ah, we are just in time to see the Temple doors open." Five Levites at one door and five at the other pull the massive doors open.

"They're gigantic," Benjamin marvels.

"That's why it takes five men to open each door."

They stroll to the Nicanor gate. "Do you see the Levites gathering?"

"The ones with the puffy white head pieces?"

285

"Yes, those would be the ones," Nicodemus smiles. "They form the choir of singers. Some have musical instruments. See the ten-stringed instruments? And over there are the lyres and the flutes."

"None of those look like Papa's flute."

"Sh-h, they're about to sing and play."

The choir to the right sings forth in brilliant tones. The choir to the left responds, answering the first choir. Back and forth they go with their antiphonal singing accompanied by the harps and lyres. The trumpets provide an interlude.

"Are those harps like the ones King David used?" Benjamin asks.

"Very possibly—especially like the ones he might have had in the palace of King Saul."

Nicodemus hears the music he has heard for so many years through new ears. The chief priests take turns proclaiming the Word of God from the Torah and projecting their long prayers with loud voices.

"Ah, look, the lambs are being brought in for the sacrifices."

"Sacrifices? You mean they will be killed?"

"Yes, Benjamin, but they must be spotless—only the very best."

"Why?"

"Because we want to offer only the best to the Lord."

"No, I mean, why must they be killed?"

"It is our way of offering our sin to God to receive forgiveness."

"But a lamb is innocent."

"Yes, that's true. It is as God taught us in the Torah. We bring our worship to God through the blood sacrifice we make to him on the altar."

"Is it for the sin of those men who are taking the lambs up to the altar? What have they done?"

"Well, yes, it is for them and for all of us."

It becomes obvious to Nicodemus, as he watches Benjamin's questioning face, that this concept is not very clear.

"Perhaps we better return to the house now. Marida will have lunch ready for us soon."

As they walk, Benjamin continues to ask questions which cause Nicodemus to re-examine his own understanding of the sacrificial lambs. *It can become so commonplace to us that we lose sight of its meaning,* Nicodemus considers thoughtfully. He remembers John, the baptizer, calling the people to repentance.

Before they leave the Court of the Women, they hear a crowd gathering at the other end. They spontaneously turn to see what is happening.

"What's going on?" Benjamin questions.

"I don't know. They seem to be shouting or singing."

"Some of the people are waving branches in the air. Can we go and see?"

It appears to be a friendly excited crowd, so Nicodemus gives his approval and they head back across the courtyard of the Temple.

"I can't see, Master Nicodemus."

"There's a little fig tree up ahead. Can you climb a tree?"

"Oh, yes, I've climbed many-a tree."

Benjamin runs ahead and scampers up the tree. Nicodemus huffs and puffs trying to catch up to him. "See anything up there?" he asks, when he finally reaches the tree.

"The people are facing toward the gate where we saw the Levites singing. It looks like they're laying branches in a path for someone to come through. Could it be a king?"

"Possibly, but I can't imagine who....

"I see him! I see him! He's riding on a donkey."

"A donkey? Who is it? Is he wearing a royal robe?"

"No..." He stretches his head this way and that. "He looks like Jesus. I know it is, Master Nicodemus, it's Jesus! Just like Laban said, the people were all getting here early to see Jesus come into town. Isn't this exciting?"

"Indeed." But Nicodemus can only think how the leaders are going to balk at this display. *They will be livid with jealousy.*

Nicodemus doesn't want to spoil Benjamin's enthusiasm, but he also doesn't want him to witness an ugly scene between the people and the leaders. Besides, it wouldn't be too advantageous to Nicodemus for a fellow Pharisee to see him with a boy who is vocally excited about Jesus. He gives Benjamin a little more time and then encourages him to come down so he can tell the others at home about his exciting morning.

⚜⚜⚜⚜⚜

Nicodemus shares in the excitement as Benjamin tells his young-boy view of his morning visit to the Temple, but when Benjamin culminates his story with the "best part," Nicodemus draws within himself at Benjamin's description of the joyful crowd.

With slumped shoulders, Nicodemus lowers his eyes to the floor. He gazes out the door to the garden. All he can think about is the wrath of the leaders which will surely intensify. Laban notices and makes eye contact with Nicodemus. Laban's tilt of the head and questioning wrinkled brow causes Nicodemus to lower his eyes once again as if to ignore or dismiss Laban.

Later in the afternoon, Laban confronts Nicodemus in the courtyard near the grapevines.

"Nicodemus, I am overjoyed at your openness to Jesus and your pursuit of truth. It is what we have prayed for. But at lunch I had a distinct impression that you are troubled. Am I correct?"

"You have always been very discerning, Uncle Laban. Yes, yes I'm troubled. You have not seen the bitterness, well... even the hatred, which I have seen among our "religious" leaders. This grand welcoming entry into Jerusalem will not set well with the Temple rulers. If they had their way, Yeshua would already be dead."

"Dead?"

"Yes, Uncle Laban, it has come to that point."

"I see." Laban strokes his beard the way he always does when he is mulling over a situation. "Then, this puts you in a very difficult position, does it not?"

"You see the picture well."

"But why? Why would they despise him so?"

"*You* understand his teachings. You see his heart, Uncle Laban. You have benefited from his miraculous healings. You believe in him. All they see is a threat to their positions. They despise his popularity with the people. My fellow Pharisees say they long for Messiah, but they do not open their eyes to the possibility that he is here among us. Had I not had that humbling experience on the hillside in Galilee, I would likely be right there with them. You saw my anger before I left Capernaum."

Laban nods his head.

Nicodemus continues. "Even Caiaphas, the high priest, declares that one must die for the good of all. If the truth be known, his concern is not for the good of all, but for the good of himself. No, Uncle Laban, it is not the glorious time in Jerusalem that you had hoped for."

"But the people are so joyful, so welcoming of Jesus. They listen to his teachings and rejoice in his miracles. Many believe in him."

"But those with influence and power do not."

"What do you predict then?"

"I don't know, Uncle Laban. I don't know."

Martha enters the courtyard with a bright smile. "Come, come, you serious men, let's have a good meal together. No time for these long faces." She floats back to the dining area.

Laban pats Nicodemus on the back as they leave to join the family. "Well, my son, we must eat. No sense borrowing trouble."

CHAPTER 41
Nicodemus and Ruth

...for your love is more delightful than wine...
your name is like perfume poured out.
Song of Songs 1:2, 3

That evening after everyone has slipped off to bed, Ruth and Nicodemus remain to continue talking. Ruth stitches away at the wooly fabric she brought with her.

"And what are you making now, Ruth?" Nicodemus inquires, with an admiring smile.

"Why, it's a warm cloak for your cool night walks. You told me you like to walk in the evenings, so I thought you would need some good wooly protection provided by our sheep."

"How could you have possibly known that my cloak is wearing out?" he grins lovingly.

"Well," she smirks back, "I asked your mother."

He nods his head as he chuckles.

They sit in silence for a moment, a comfortable silence that only two people who feel at home with each other can have.

"It is good that we are here together, just like we were in your home. It is even better that I'm not speaking to you from a bed." He grins.

"And it is also good that you are not frowning at me because of my belief in Jesus," she chides.

"Yes, yes." He nods pleasantly, but his smile soon turns to a thought-provoking frown as he stares at the floor, reminded once again of the danger that lurks ahead.

Ruth glances up two or three times and finally puts her work in her lap. "Nicodemus, I see the same look of concern that I saw this afternoon when Benjamin talked of Jesus' grand entry into the Temple. What is troubling you?"

He gazes into her eyes lovingly. The lantern light glows around her face as it did that night so long ago—the night when strange feelings came over him in her presence. "I have missed you so much."

He stands and awkwardly shuffles to the sofa where she is sitting. She offers her hand to him and he gladly holds it as he settles in beside her.

"I felt like part of me was missing when I came back here," he confesses.

"I felt the same. I didn't know what to do with myself in the evenings when everyone went to bed. All I could think of was our talks, our laughter, our times of sharing."

He puts his arms around her and she willingly nestles her head on his chest. "Oh Ruth. Hmm, Ruth—your name means companion. Are we too old? Too old for second opportunities?"

He loosens his embrace. She lifts her eyes to his. He caresses her cheek with his hand.

"We are never too old to follow our hearts," she whispers.

They smile and slowly lean in to each other. Their lips meet.

Nicodemus experiences even more new sensations. His heart is racing; his spirit soars to new heights. "Dear Ruth, I never want to be without you again."

"I know, Nicodemus, I know."

Their foreheads meet as he holds her hand to his heart. "We have many things to work out," he says.

She straightens up and looks at him again. "Nicodemus, you didn't answer my question."

"What question?"

"What is troubling you?"

"Nothing for you to worry about."

"Nicodemus, we must be honest with each other."

He folds his hands in his lap and taps his thumbs up and down as he weighs what to tell Ruth. She waits patiently.

"It's the Temple leaders, Ruth. Most of them are very opposed to Yeshua. They dislike his teachings; they doubt his miraculous signs, they find fault with the healings because he heals on the Sabbath. They criticize him because of the people with whom he associates and they are jealous of his popularity with the people. Most of all, they fear losing their places of leadership and losing the nation. I fear for his very life, Ruth. The people rejoice and follow him, but the leaders are plotting against him."

"And how do you respond to them?"

Nicodemus hangs his head. He is quiet for a moment. "I tried once to temper their hatred, but they only turned their bitterness on me, so… I don't respond, Ruth. I sit in silence. I wish I could tell them all that has happened to me, but they would turn deaf ears. They would cry 'blasphemer' to me as well."

"Your heart is heavy." She touches his cheek and looks into his eyes. "If we are to share our lives with each other, we must share the heavy burdens as well."

His tense eyes relax. "Yes." He touches her hand on his cheek. He closes his eyes and nods his head. "Yes, you are right."

When he opens his eyes, they share one more, tender kiss. As they embrace, he whispers, "I love you, Ruth. I need you."

"I'm so happy," she sighs.

When they release one another, they reflect each other's smiling faces.

"And now," she says as she gathers up her things, "I think we both need a good night of rest."

"I suppose you're right."

They stand and give clasped hands one more squeeze as they part ways.

❧❧❧❧

The next morning, Nicodemus asks Ruth to join him in paying a visit to Joseph and his wife, Deborah. As they walk, Nicodemus reminds Ruth of some of his life experiences with Joseph.

When they arrive, a servant comes to the door. "Master Nicodemus."

"So good to see you, Astra. We have come to see Joseph and Deborah."

Joseph and Deborah come quickly to greet their guests. After a short get-acquainted time, Deborah whisks Ruth off to the sitting room while the men retire to the courtyard.

Joseph jumps right in to discuss the latest happening at the Temple. "Nicodemus, I assume you have heard of yesterday morning's disruption."

"Yes, Yeshua had quite a grand march through the crowds."

"Well, that *and* the rampage through the Temple."

"Rampage? I don't understand."

"Yeshua went into the Temple courtyard and overturned the tables of the moneychangers, scattering the coins everywhere. He drove out the animals that were there for the sacrifices. It was quite a scene."

"But why would he do this?"

"He said, 'It is written, my house will be a house of prayer.' And then he told them, 'You have made it a den of thieves.' He said, 'How dare you turn my Father's house into a market.' "

Nicodemus sits silently for a moment as he mulls over these words.

"It's true, you know. The Temple leaders benefit from all that money changing. In many ways it does border on thievery. Buying and selling the animals becomes little more than a marketplace atmosphere. If a person wanted to pray, he could not hear himself."

Joseph lowers his head. "You're right. We dishonor the Lord with our marketplace routine. David said,

> "As the deer pants for streams of water,
> so my soul pants for you, O God.
> My soul thirsts for God, for the living God.
> When can I go and meet with God?"

293

"Joseph, we have long sought for a political Messiah, one to rescue us from Rome. I have been reading Isaiah's prophecies again. He gives a different picture of the Messiah—one who will take up our iniquities, carry our sorrows, be pierced for our transgressions, and crushed for our iniquities. Caiaphas may be more accurate than he knows. You remember he said, 'It is better that one man die for the people than that the whole nation perish.' Must Yeshua be our sacrificial lamb, Joseph? Is that how he will save our nation?"

"Is that how he will save our *souls*?" Joseph asks thoughtfully.

"Do you think he will be teaching at the Temple today?"

"Most likely."

"Come, let's go see."

They find the women talking inside.

"Ruth," Nicodemus calls out. Both women look up. "Joseph and I are going to the Temple. Would you like to return…"

"Oh, Nicodemus, do let her stay longer. We are just getting acquainted. Later, we will go to the market and then I'll walk Ruth back to your house. Does that sound good to you, Ruth?"

"Sounds delightful."

"Okay. Take good care of my Ruth." Nicodemus beams.

Joseph and Deborah beam at one another as they watch this late-life love in full bloom.

CHAPTER 42
Jesus Teaches at the Temple

You will know the truth and the truth will set you free.
John 8:31

As Joseph and Nicodemus approach the Temple mount, they are amazed by the huge crowd that has already gathered for the morning. They hear Jesus speaking and are not at all surprised to see that the listeners are giving him rapt attention.

Nicodemus overhears one man saying to his friend, "How did this man get such learning without having studied?"

A few leaders mill about on the pavement near the Temple steps, but most of the people are seated on the ground beyond the outer courtyard. Nicodemus and Joseph move in as close as they dare and find an inconspicuous spot partially hidden by a tree.

"My teaching is not my own," Jesus is saying. "It comes from him who sent me. If anyone chooses to do God's will, he will find out whether my teaching comes from God or whether I speak on my own. He who speaks on his own does so to gain honor for himself, but he who works for the honor of the one who sent him is a man of truth; there is nothing false about him."

Jesus continues, "Has not Moses given you the law? Yet not one of you keeps the law. Why are you trying to kill me?"

A murmur rises up through the crowd. One shouts out, "You are demon-possessed, who is trying to kill you?"

"Consider this." Jesus responds. "I did one miracle and you were all astonished. Yet because Moses gave you circumcision, you circumcise children on the Sabbath. Now if a child can be circumcised on the Sabbath so that the Law of Moses may not be broken, why are you angry with me for healing the *whole man* on the Sabbath? Stop judging by appearances and make a right judgment."

295

About that time, a couple of chief priests, some elders, and a few teachers of the law make their way over to Jesus. Nicodemus nudges Joseph and nods toward the intruders. "Trouble."

One of the chief priests serves as the spokesman. "Tell us by what authority you are doing these things. Who gave you this authority?"

Jesus answers, "I will ask you a question and then I will answer your question. Tell me, John's baptism—was it from heaven, or from men?"

As the leaders discuss it among themselves, Joseph whispers to Nicodemus. "Good question. If they say, 'from heaven,' he will ask them why they didn't *believe* John. If they say, 'from men,' they will incur the wrath of the people because most believe John was a prophet."

Finally the chief priest turns back to Jesus. "We don't know where it was from."

"Neither will I tell you by what authority I am doing these things."

Nicodemus and Joseph look at each other with slight smirks.

Jesus goes on to tell a parable about a man who plants a vineyard and leaves tenants to tend it. At harvest time, the owner sends a servant to get fruit from the vineyard, but the tenants beat him and send him away empty-handed. He sends a second and third servant, but each time they are treated badly.

Joseph mutters, "Much like our ancestors treated the prophets."

The parable concludes—"Finally, the owner sends his own dear son in hopes that the tenants will respect him, but since this is the heir, they decide to kill him and claim the inheritance for their own."

Jesus asks, "What then will the owner do to the tenants? He will come and kill them and give it to others."

Some in the crowd call out, "May this never be!"

Jesus stares directly at the Temple leaders and asks, "Then what is the meaning of that which is written: 'The stone the builders rejected has become the capstone.' Everyone who falls on that stone will be broken to pieces, but he on whom it falls will be crushed."

Nicodemus comments, "The leaders know Yeshua is talking about them. Look, they're eyeing the Temple guards. They probably want to have him arrested right now."

Joseph grunts a "no." "Too many people believe in Yeshua. I don't think the leaders will try anything rash."

Frustrated, the leaders slither away.

"Look over there." Nicodemus points in another direction. Argus and a couple of men of Herodian persuasion are head to head planning something. "Can you believe Argus is consorting with the likes of them?"

"Common enemies make strange accomplices. Anything to get their way."

One of the Herodians, who supports the rule of Herod Antipas and thus the power of Rome, approaches Jesus nonchalantly. "Teacher, we know you speak and teach what is right, and that you do not show partiality but teach the way of God in accordance with truth." Joseph and Nicodemus roll their eyes at one another recognizing the hypocrisy. "Is it right for us to pay taxes to Caesar or not?"

"Hmm," Nicodemus reflects, "tricky question. If he says 'yes,' the people will be upset. If he answers "no," the Herodians will report him to the Roman authorities."

Jesus seems unaffected by the question. He asks them to show him a coin. He turns it over in his hand. "Whose portrait and inscription are on it?" he questions.

"Caesar's, of course," they reply.

"Then give to Caesar what is Caesar's and give to God what is God's."

Argus and his "friends" are immediately silenced as an admiring murmur can be heard through the crowd.

Some of the Sadducees head toward Jesus. *Now what will they come up with,* Nicodemus wonders. "Seems like they *all* want to test him," he says to Joseph who shakes his head in disgust.

The spokesman approaches Jesus. "Teacher, Moses wrote for us that if a man's brother dies and leaves a wife but no children, the man must marry the wife and have children for his brother. Suppose there were seven brothers and the first one marries a woman and dies childless. The second marries her and dies. Likewise, the third marries her and dies, and in the same way, the seven die leaving no children. Finally, the woman dies too. Now then, at the resurrection whose wife will she be, since the seven were married to her?"

"Can you believe that?" Joseph gasps. "The Sadducees don't even *believe* in resurrection. What a farce."

They listen for Jesus' response.

"You are in error because you do not know the Scriptures or the power of God. Those who are considered worthy of taking part in the resurrection of the dead will neither marry or be given in marriage, and they can no longer die; for they are like the angels. They are God's children, since they are children of the resurrection. In the account of the bush, even Moses showed that the dead rise, for he calls the Lord 'the God of Abraham, and the God of Isaac, and the God of Jacob.' He is not the God of the dead, but of the living, for to him all are alive."

"Well said, Rabbi," one of the teachers of the law responds, giving a knowing look at the Sadducees, for the teachers of the law often talk of resurrection.

No other factions try to question him.

Nicodemus scans the people and sees the same response that he saw on the mountainside by the sea. One near him says, "He speaks the truth." Others nod their heads in approval. Many seem to put their faith in him but show visible signs of their disgust at the leaders.

Jesus fixes his eyes on the people. "If you hold to my teachings, you are really my disciples." He turns Nicodemus' way. "Then you will know the truth, and the truth will set you free."

Nicodemus swallows; he no longer sees the crowd. Instead, he is transported to a night months ago when he heard the Master say, "Whoever lives by the truth comes into the light." *These critics may test Yeshua, but he is the true one. He is the light.*

✒ℰ✒ℰ✒ℰ✒ℰ

The next day, the people gather again to hear Jesus. As Joseph and Nicodemus reach the edge of the crowd, Nicodemus spots Zebedee's son, John.

Nicodemus approaches John cautiously and nods his head. "Shalom John."

John nods back. "Shalom Nicodemus."

Glancing around nervously, Nicodemus pauses beside John. "You know, of course, that the leaders are more than upset with Jesus' teachings?"

John looks at the ground. "Yes."

"Be careful, my son."

"Yes sir." John looks away, and then turns back to Nicodemus. "Thank you, sir."

Joseph and Nicodemus hasten on to the spot they had yesterday. They pass a couple of other Pharisees who have appeared to be sympathetic to Jesus' teachings.

"When a man believes in me," Jesus is saying, "he does not believe in me only, but in the one who sent me. When he sees me, he sees the one who sent me. I have come into the world as a light, so that no one who believes in me should stay in the darkness.

"As for those who hear my words but do not keep them, I do not judge them. For I did not come to judge the world, but to save it. I do not speak of my own accord, but the father who sent me commands me what to say and how to say it. I know that his command leads to eternal life. So whatever I say is just what the Father has told me to say."

Argus is back today with a group of teachers of the law. They whisk past Nicodemus and Joseph. To Nicodemus' surprise, he notices that Hakkoz is with them.

"What is Hakkoz doing here?" Nicodemus whispers to Joseph.

"Haven't you heard? He is now a student of Argus."

"Surely not."

With a bit of prodding from Argus, Hakkoz calls out to Jesus, "Teacher, which is the greatest commandment in the Law?"

Jesus answers, "'Love the Lord your God with all your heart and with all your soul and with all your mind.' This is the first and greatest commandment. And the second is like it. 'Love your neighbor as yourself.' All the Law and the prophets hang on these two commandments."

Argus and the other teachers seem satisfied with Jesus' answer and begin to drift away. But before they depart, Jesus declares, "The teachers of the law and the Pharisees sit in Moses' seat. So you must obey them and do what they tell you."

Argus and the others proudly pause to face Jesus and give an agreeing nod.

Jesus continues. "But do not do what they *do*, for they do not practice what they preach. They tie up heavy loads and put them on men's shoulders, but they are not willing to lift a finger to move them."

Argus' pride turns quickly to indignation. He lifts his arm and opens his mouth to protest, but Jesus hastens on with rapid fire.

"Woe to you, teachers of the law and Pharisees, you hypocrites! You clean the outside of the cup and dish, but inside, the dish is full of greed and self-indulgence. Blind Pharisees! First clean the inside of the cup and dish, and then the outside also will be clean."

Argus plants his hand on his hip; his mouth opens wider, his eyes bulge.

"Woe to you, teachers of the law and Pharisees, you hypocrites! You give a tenth of your spices—mint, dill and cumin. But you have neglected the more important matters of the law—justice, mercy and faithfulness. You should have practiced the latter, without neglecting the former. You blind guides! You strain out a gnat but swallow a camel."

Argus let's out an audible gasp and finally closes his mouth. For once, he is speechless.

"Woe to you, teachers of the law and Pharisees, you hypocrites! You are like whitewashed tombs, which look beautiful on the outside but on the inside are full of dead men's bones and everything unclean. In the same way, on the outside you appear to people as righteous, but on the inside you are full of hypocrisy and wickedness."

Jesus' denouncement grows stronger with more woes and accusations. Nicodemus is so stunned he can hardly breathe. Joseph whispers, "He seals his fate."

Nicodemus glances at Argus and the other Pharisees. They are livid. Argus whips around in disgust. "Come, come, let us leave these foolish accusations. I will hear no more," he barks to his companions. Then with suppressed rage, "He will regret this."

As Argus marches ahead of his men, he catches sight of Nicodemus and throws him a look as if to say, "Surely you will join us in leaving this imposter."

Nicodemus avoids eye contact with Argus for his mind is spinning, his emotions racing. On the one hand he thinks, "How dare Yeshua speak to us like this!" On the other hand, he knows Jesus' accusations are all too true. Nicodemus feels all eyes are on him—questioning eyes from Argus; judgmental eyes from Jesus, and condemning eyes from the people around him. He feels anger. He feels remorse. He feels confusion.

Argus does not wait for Nicodemus to make a move. Instead, he storms out with his entourage of like-minded friends, while Jesus continues with his blistering condemnation.

"Everything they do is for men to see: They make their phylacteries wide and the tassels on their garments long; they love the place of honor at banquets and the most important seats in the synagogues; they love to be greeted in the marketplaces and to have men call them 'Rabbi.' The greatest among you should be your servant. For whoever exalts himself will be *humbled* and whoever humbles himself will be exalted."

Humbled. There it is again. Oh Lord Almighty, how much more humility must I go through?

The next few teachings are a blur to Nicodemus as he turns the words of the last few moments over and over in his mind.

A man in the crowd asks a question. Everyone's attention is drawn to the man who is at the other end of the crowd. It seems to be a good time to leave—escape is more like it. They ease slowly away from the listeners.

Nicodemus doesn't feel he can breathe deeply until he is out the Temple gate. The two men walk in silence for some time, each trying to sort through their thoughts.

Finally, Nicodemus speaks, his voice broken. "What are we to do, Joseph?"

"I don't know. It is becoming very dangerous."

"All I can think of is that night I went to him. He said, 'You must be born again—born of the Spirit.' He said that God loved the world so much that he gave his only Son and that whoever believes in him will not perish but will have eternal life. He said men love darkness where they can hide their evil deeds, but he has brought light to expose them."

"He certainly did that today. Such boldness."

"He speaks to us as well, Joseph. We have been blind Pharisees, hypocrites."

"I know. I know."

"That night when I went to talk to him, he said, 'whoever lives by the *truth* comes into the light so that it may be seen plainly that what he does has been done by God.' We have lived as though everything depended on us and our teachings. He is right; our bowls have been scrubbed and clean on the outside, but we are unfit on the inside."

"Our fellow Pharisees don't see this, Nicodemus. Their eyes are closed; their ears do not hear."

"I fear they will not allow this much longer. Their disgust and anger is turning to rage. Isaiah is right; he will be pierced, crushed, and wounded for our iniquities—led like an innocent lamb to the slaughter."

"And where does that put us, Nicodemus?"

302

"I don't know, Joseph. I don't know."

They arrive at Joseph's house.

"Would you like to come in?"

"Thank you, but no, I must think this through."

✒❧✒❧✒❧✒❧

Nicodemus finds his family and Ruth gathered in the kitchen in lively, happy discussion. Their voices are a comfort in one way, but they don't match his mood, and so he slips quietly upstairs to his bedroom. He removes his headpiece, robe, and phylacteries. Jesus words of accusation come to his mind again as he fingers his phylacteries.

Did God not command us to bind his words on our foreheads and on our hands? He looks out his window where he has a view of the Temple. *Perhaps the Lord meant that we are to put his words in our minds and apply them to the things we do with our hands. We are so literal. Have we missed the inward meaning and focused only on outward symbols? Oh, Adonai, forgive me. Forgive me.*

A tear trickles down Nicodemus face. He lies across his bed in mental and emotional exhaustion and falls into a deep sleep.

"You are one of them too," Argus yells at Nicodemus. "He has fooled you just like these ignorant people. Stone him. Stone him!"

Suddenly Nicodemus is aroused by the opening and closing of a door. He hears loud voices downstairs. When he glances out his window, he realizes that it is already sunset.

Michael and his family have returned from visiting friends. "Have you seen Nicodemus?" he hears his mother ask.

Nicodemus struggles to his feet and goes down to join them. He tries to be congenial with the family and these dear friends, but it takes great effort.

That evening, Ruth confronts him again. He shares the struggles of the day with her. She provides the listening ear he needs.

The next two days, Nicodemus stays in. It is unbearable for him to face his fellow Pharisees or the crowd, even Jesus. Finally, on the second afternoon, he journeys down the path to the reading room where he unrolls the scroll of Isaiah to reread earlier passages, but nothing seems clear or helpful to him.

That evening they celebrate Passover together. For Benjamin's sake, Nicodemus tries to stay fully engaged, but he has a deep unrest in his soul, a heavy burden that goes beyond the happenings of the last few days.

CHAPTER 43
Scripture Fulfilled

... and the Lord laid on him the iniquity of us all. Isaiah 53:6

Nicodemus tosses and turns in a restless, fitful sleep. As the sun peers in his window, he hears a loud rapping at the door. He looks out his window and sees Joseph below. The knocking persists, so he runs down the stairs to answer.

"Joseph, what is it?"

"Nicodemus," Joseph says breathlessly as he pants for air, "the leaders arrested Yeshua in the night and tried him before Annas and Caiaphas, and then they took him to Pilate. When Pilate heard Yeshua was from Galilee, he sent him to Herod. Now they have taken Yeshua back to Pilate at the Antonia Fortress."

"I will put on my clothes and come immediately."

As they trek at a fast pace, Nicodemus questions why the Sanhedrin would hold trial during the night. "Our law says it must be done during the day. And why were we not informed of this meeting?"

"No rules apply here. They are determined to have him crucified."

"Crucified? Not stoned?"

"No, that's why the leaders have taken him to Pilate. *Our* leaders certainly can't have him crucified. They do have to obey *Roman* law, even if they don't observe our own laws."

"Dear Lord in Heaven, how has it come to this?"

A crowd has gathered by the time they arrive at the Antonia Fortress. Pilate seems frustrated and impatient as he speaks to the religious leaders. "Herod found no charge against this man and I tell you again; *I* find no basis for a charge against him."

Joseph comments to Nicodemus, "Pilate can see through them. He knows they are jealous of Yeshua."

Just then, Pilate's wife comes out and whispers something in Pilate's ear. The color drains from Pilate's face.

"I wonder what that's about," Nicodemus mumbles under his breath.

Glancing around the crowd, Nicodemus notices small groups of Sadducees and Pharisees lurking among the people, talking to them, and rousing them. He touches Joseph's arm and nods toward the infiltrators.

Joseph responds, "They're fanning the flames of their own hatred."

Someone shouts, "He stirs up people all over Judea with his teaching."

From another part of the crowd, "He subverts our nation."

And yet another, "He opposes payment of taxes to Caesar and claims to be Christ, a king."

"A king?" Pilate questions. He turns to one of his men to say something, and then to Jesus, apparently asking him a question.

Pilate calls back to the crowd, "I find no basis for a charge against this man. He has done nothing to deserve death. Therefore, I will punish him and release him."

"No," the crowd roars. They continue shouting random statements. Soon one phrase gains momentum. "Crucify him! Crucify him!"

Pilate turns fearfully from one of his men, then to his soldiers, and then to the crowd in apparent panic. He has an idea and holds his hands up to quiet the crowd. "It is your custom," he says, "for me to release to you one prisoner during the time of the Passover. Do you want me to release the King of the Jews?"

Quickly, almost as if anticipating this question, someone shouts, "No, not him! Give us Barabbas!" "Yes, Barabbas," others chime in.

Nicodemus is astounded. "That rebellious murderer?"

"What then should I do with the one you call the King of the Jews?" Pilate calls out.

"Crucify him!" the shouts erupt again.

"Why? What crime has he committed?"

One of the leaders yells, "If you let this man go, you are no friend of Caesar. Anyone who claims to be a king opposes Caesar."

Pilate is visibly shaken. He turns toward a bowl of water on a table and ceremonially washes his hands. "I am innocent of this man's blood. It is your responsibility."

"Let his blood be on us and our children," someone shouts. All those around this man repeat the cry. "Let his blood be on us and on our children!"

"They have gone mad," Nicodemus gasps.

Pilate tries to speak, but his words are swallowed up as the people bellow all the more, "Crucify him! Crucify him!" Hundreds pick up the refrain with total abandon.

Nicodemus lowers his shaking head and holds his ears. "No," he utters, "this cannot be happening." *Why is Pilate so weak? Surely he sees through the hypocrisy of these religious rulers. He has the authority to release Yeshua. Why does he not act courageously?*

It is too late. Pilate gives instructions to his soldiers. They take Jesus away.

Joseph puts an arm around Nicodemus. "I'm sure this will mean a Roman flogging." Nicodemus sighs deeply and sadly nods his head in agreement.

Groups of women huddle together weeping. Men, who agreed with Jesus' teachings, now bow their heads in stunned agony. Their eyes glaze over with disbelief.

Others, who have been roused by the leaders, boisterously brag about their triumph. All mill about to see what will happen next. Joseph and Nicodemus stand helplessly, observing the people, their own thoughts turn inward. The morning sun beats on them with an intensity to match the flame of their emotions.

After the reality has settled in, Nicodemus tells Joseph that they will need to prepare their families for this dastardly turn of events. Joseph agrees. They trudge back to their homes with heavy hearts.

Nicodemus gathers his family and loved ones around him as he tries to find the words to prepare them for what is about to happen.

As his dear ones listen, they all remain silent, stunned, and frightened.

Finally Ruth speaks. "We must go to him, support him," she says, passionately.

"Ruth," Nicodemus says gently, "a Roman crucifixion is an ugly sight. In addition, he will have been flogged. It is bloody, grotesque, and inhumane."

"But he was there for me," Rebecca says, with a quiver in her voice.

In spite of Nicodemus' pleading, they all agree that they must go. Abigail tells Nicodemus quietly that she will keep Benjamin at the house with her. Michael agrees that it would be best.

They all put on clothes of mourning and follow the crowds as they make their way outside the city gate. Ruth expresses her disgust at the frivolous atmosphere, but soon they come upon groups of mourners wailing their sorrow. Drops of blood mark the path where the soldiers must have led Jesus. Martha winces and holds her stomach. Nicodemus grabs her arm to support her.

As they come near the scene, they hear the pounding of the Roman hammer driving Roman nails into a Roman cross. Soon, the despicable sight is laid out before them—three crosses, two men already hung. The soldiers lift the heavy cross bearing the body of Jesus. Nicodemus was right; Jesus' beaten body is grotesque beyond recognition. Martha and Rebecca fall to their knees weeping audibly. Ruth kneels and bends over, spreading both arms around them, tears flooding her face. Leah folds into the arms of her husband, Laban. Michael turns his head to the side, unable to bear it.

Nicodemus swallows hard and closes his eyes. He wants to scream, "No, you cannot do this. Take him down. You have pierced his head and beaten his back raw. It is enough. Take him down!"

He edges through the crowd of mourners, closer to the horrific scene. Perhaps, he fantasizes, he can persuade the soldiers. But as he draws near to the cross, he spies some of the Pharisees and Sadducees who had tested Yeshua earlier in the week. Argus is among them, along with Hakkoz. They are shouting insults.

"You saved others; save yourself if you are the Christ."

"Look at the Chosen One now." They sneer and burst into haughty laughter.

"Cast yourself down, and then we will believe you."

Nicodemus sees a man near the cross comforting a woman. The man stands to glare at these accusers. *It is John.*

John locks eyes with Nicodemus. Nicodemus shakes his head slightly, trying to convey that he is not a part of these accusations. John hangs his head and turns back to comfort the woman.

Nicodemus' eyes are drawn to the gruesome nails, the bloody body, and the heartless crown of thorns piercing Jesus' brow. Above Jesus' head is a sign. "King of the Jews," it proclaims in three languages.

Jesus' eyes open slightly as he looks down at John and the woman beneath him. His mouth moves as though he is speaking to John. John nods his head. Slowly, painstakingly, Jesus gazes at his accusers as they jest with each other, oblivious to his stare. One eye is mostly swollen shut. With his other eye, Jesus surveys others in the crowd and rests on Nicodemus. For one painful moment, Jesus looks deep into his very soul. Nicodemus cannot breathe. Thankfully, Jesus' eyes lower and close.

Nicodemus can take it no longer. He backs away, not wanting to be part of this travesty any longer. He wants to throw off his Pharisee headpiece and robe, even his phylacteries, but he slinks away trying not to draw attention to himself.

When he returns to Michael, Laban, and the women, he urges them to return home. Reluctantly, they agree.

They reenter the city, but just as they are about to reach the house, a veil of darkness falls over them. It is the middle of the day, but they cannot see their hands in front of them. Tears of sorrow become cries of fear in the streets.

What is happening? Even the sun itself is hidden from our eyes. Nicodemus is reminded of Yeshua's words. *Men love darkness where they can hide their evil deeds.*

His family finally makes their way into the house and on to the kitchen where someone lights a lantern. They huddle around the light and talk in whispers. With only the small bit of shadowed light, Nicodemus feels his way out to the courtyard to be by himself.

He sinks onto the nearest bench and curls his head down into his arms. "Oh Mighty One of Israel," he prays, "What are we to do? Please lift this darkness from our eyes. Open our hearts to your truth." He clutches his head and shakes uncontrollably as he weeps.

Suddenly the ground begins to tremble; the lantern flickers out in the other room. *Earthquake.* Pots jiggle on the shelves; the bench on which he sits rumbles. A loud cracking sound rips from the vicinity of the Temple. Screams and cries from the street punctuate the turmoil. *What more is to come?*

When the shaking stops, the people fall silent as though holding their breath wondering what will erupt next.

In the dark silence, Nicodemus sees the horrific scene of the cross play out in his mind once again. His thoughts turn to the words of Isaiah:

> "He was despised and rejected by men,
>> a man of sorrows,
>> and acquainted with suffering.
> Like one from whom men hide their faces
>> he was despised and we esteemed him not.
>
> Surely he took up our infirmities
>> and carried our sorrows,
>> yet we considered him stricken by God,
>> smitten by him and afflicted.

But he was *pierced* for *our* transgressions,
  he was crushed for *our* iniquities;
  The punishment that brought us peace
  was upon *him*,
  and by his wounds we are healed.
We all, like sheep, have gone astray,
  each of us has turned to his own way;
  and the Lord has laid on him
  the iniquity of us all."

It seems like hours before the darkness lifts, but at last the light of day seeps into the courtyard. Nicodemus feels the need to find his friend, Joseph, so he trudges out the door toward Joseph's house.

Joseph's wife tells him that Joseph is not there. Nicodemus wanders in the direction of the Temple and sees Joseph coming toward him. Joseph's walk is staggered, his shoulders bent. Slowly, solemnly, Joseph speaks. "He's dead. They pierced his side. He is dead."

Nicodemus embraces his weary, worn friend, practically holding him up.

Joseph straightens. "Nicodemus, the Romans won't be letting family members take his body. I will not stand by and let him be tossed in a pauper's grave. You remember that I recently prepared a tomb near Golgatha? I'm going to go to Pilate and request permission to take his body down from the cross."

Nicodemus is horrified. "Joseph, if the Sanhedrin learns of this, they will throw you out or worse yet, imprison you. Besides, it is too close to Sabbath, you would desecrate yourself with the handling of a dead body."

"Nicodemus, it is the least I can do for my Savior."

His words penetrate Nicodemus' heart. *I have hidden in the shadows long enough. I, too, must stand my ground. He is the way, the truth, the light for our lives. Lord, make me as bold as this dear friend.*

"Joseph... I will get the spices and the linen and meet you at the tomb."

"Thank you, my friend."

311

CHAPTER 44
The Burial

Taking Jesus' body, the two of them wrapped it
with the spices in strips of linen. John 19:40

The two men part to prepare for their committed tasks.

Nicodemus knows that the storage room at home still holds many spices and the extra linen he and his brothers had purchased before his father's death. The last time they used any of the linen was for his father's burial. As he walks along, memories of his father flood his mind.

"Always seek truth," he said. Like King David, I have tried to have a heart for truth. I have found it in Messiah, Yeshua. Oh, Lord, Holy one of Israel, give me strength for this task. Help me be as bold as my friend Joseph.

Nicodemus rehearses in his mind the procedures his brother taught him as they prepared his father's body years ago.

When he arrives home, he locates a small cart from the courtyard. He loads two buckets of water into the cart, and then searches through the storage room for myrrh and aloes. After he has nearly filled the cart with spices, he steps back into the storage room. Reaching up to the top shelf, he carefully removes the container that holds the precious linens. *Yes, they are still here.* He packs the linens in a flat basket and carefully places the basket on top of the spices.

Laban comes walking in. "What are you doing, Nicodemus?" Surprised, Nicodemus straightens up from his task. "I heard that squeaky cart and couldn't imagine what was going on!" Laban exclaims.

"It's just me." Nicodemus faces the temptation to deny his intentions. He boldly admits, "I'm preparing for a burial, Uncle Laban."

At first puzzled, Laban frowns. Then his eyes open wide in horror. "Surely, you're not…"

"Yes, I'm preparing for Yeshua's burial," he states resolutely.

Laban looks at the cart, full of spices. "That's enough for a king's burial!"

"Exactly."

Laban nods his head with a half-smile. "Yes," he contemplates. "Yes, I suppose that would be appropriate." He pauses. "Can I help you?"

"No, I can make it—but thank you."

"You've considered the risk?"

"Yes."

"I never imagined his life would come to this." Laban says sadly.

"He has become our sacrificial lamb. Isaiah told us that he would be led like a lamb to the slaughter."

"Hmm." Nodding his head, Laban ponders the thought and then raises his eyes to Nicodemus. "And I never dreamed you would come to believe in him. May the Lord Adonai be with you, my son."

"Thank you, Uncle Laban." They embrace.

"Shalom," Laban whispers.

ᏩᏋᏩᏋᏩᏋᏩᏋ

Nicodemus finds Joseph's tomb and pulls the cart through the opening. A shelf-like ledge, long enough for a man, has been hewn out of the rock. The cave is noticeably cooler than out in the sun and not very musty since it is a relatively new tomb.

Nicodemus empties the spices on the floor and lays the basket of linens and one bucket of water beside the spices, leaving one bucket in the cart. He grabs a large sheet from the basket which he thought to put in at the last moment.

Nicodemus stands clutching the sheet, astonished that he has gotten himself into this unbelievable situation. He contemplates the things that have happened since he walked up that shore many months ago to talk to Jesus at night. So many times he has reviewed Yeshua's words in his mind. Unexpectedly, a new memory comes to mind. He remembers that, as he was departing that night, Yeshua touched his shoulder almost as a gesture of gratitude. *Strange that I haven't thought of that intimate touch until this moment.*

He looks down at the sheet he is clutching in his hands. *He knew. Yeshua knew I would be here in this final act.* Nicodemus slumps down on the ledge, tears flowing. *Oh, Adonai, help me. Help me to carry this through to the end.*

He wipes his eyes with his sleeve and stands with determination to tend to the task at hand. *Sheet, water, cart; I think I have everything we will need.*

He pushes the cart back out into the afternoon light. The brightness contrasts with the dark tomb. When his eyes adjust, Nicodemus gazes in the direction of the cross and he sees the frame of Jesus still hanging there. He takes a deep breath and slowly guides the cart that way.

About half way there, he catches sight of Joseph approaching.

When Nicodemus draws near to the cross, he has a difficult time looking at the tortured body of Jesus. His stomach turns; the back of his throat clogs up. He gasps for a gulp of air, fearful that he may get sick. *Help me Lord, Adonai.*

Breathlessly, Joseph arrives at the cross and shows his letter of permission from Pilate to the soldier still on duty. The soldier studies the two of them, apparently questioning why the likes of them would want Jesus' body. He looks again at the paper and shoves it back into Joseph's hand.

"I'll help you," he says, gruffly.

They finally manage to remove the bloodied body from the cross. Empowered by the task at hand, Nicodemus tells Joseph and the soldier to lay Yeshua on the ground. Nicodemus pours part of the water from his bucket over Jesus to wash away the worst of the blood. He tries to remove the crown of thorns that had been forced on Jesus' head, but it is so embedded that he cannot budge it. Nicodemus breathes deeply to fight his anger and repulsion at the torture Jesus had to endure.

The soldier comes around and takes hold of the thorns with his strong rough hands. He pulls the crown loose and tosses it aside. Nicodemus nods appreciation and gently pours more water over Jesus' head.

The soldier stands quietly as he watches Nicodemus work tenderly over Jesus' body. "He never spoke a word of hatred," the soldier states flatly.

Nicodemus motions to Joseph to help him spread out the sheet.

The soldier speaks again, "It was really unusual to have all that darkness in the middle of the day. Kinda scary."

"Let's lay him on the sheet," Nicodemus says to Joseph.

Joseph picks up Jesus' ankles and Nicodemus tries to lift the shoulders, struggling under the weight. The soldier comes to the rescue and easily lifts the body onto the sheet.

Joseph and Nicodemus wrap the sheet around Jesus. The soldier grabs up the cocooned body and gently places it in the cart.

"Thank you," Nicodemus says. The soldier nods.

"Wait," the soldier darts back to the cross. He yanks the sign loose that had been attached over Jesus' head. He hands it to Joseph. "Do you want this?"

Joseph hesitates. "Yes, thank you."

Together, Joseph and Nicodemus guide the cart back to the tomb.

Already, the tomb is filled with the aroma of the spices. They remove the sheet-wrapped body of Jesus from the cart, place it on the floor of the tomb, and unwrap the blood-soaked sheet. Nicodemus tears strips from the sheet and soaks them in the half bucket of water. They wash away as much dried blood as possible with their limited time before Sabbath begins.

Nicodemus begins the Tahara, the cleansing ritual, just as he and his brother had done years before. He pours water over one arm, then another, and on around the body. Nicodemus recalls and quotes many of the Scriptures his brother spoke when he had performed the ceremony for their father.

They lift the body to the ledge and begin to anoint it with the generous amount of spices. They wrap him with linen strips. With their task complete, Nicodemus lays the final linen shroud over Jesus' body and stands in a moment of silence.

As if in a daze, they mechanically gather the buckets, the basket, and the bloody sheet and place them in the cart. Nicodemus picks up the slab of wood which declares Jesus "King of the Jews." He gently lays it in the cart and turns to look at the massive amount of spices they used; indeed, fit for a king.

When they come out of the tomb, Joseph motions to the large stone standing near the entrance. It takes the two of them to roll the rounded stone along its trough until it forms a closure over the entrance to the tomb.

As they turn to leave, they notice some of the women followers of Jesus watching from a ways off. The women bow deeply in gratitude to Joseph and Nicodemus. The men return the acknowledgement with a nod and pull the cart away.

They walk in silence; the rickety cart humming a rhythm as they plod along the path with snatches of the spice aroma still lingering from the cart. Each man is deep in his own thoughts and emotions.

When they arrive at Joseph's house, Joseph places his hand on Nicodemus shoulder. "Thank you, my friend. You always know just how to do things right."

Nicodemus clasps Joseph's outstretched arm. "And you always have the boldness to do it."

CHAPTER 45
The Resurrection

Remember how he told you while he was still with you in Galilee: "The Son of Man must be delivered into the hands of sinful men, be crucified, and on the third day be raised again." Luke 24:6-7

A somber veil hangs over the home of Nicodemus and his mother, Martha. The loved ones gathered there, speak in hushed tones. No one disturbs Nicodemus who spends most of the next day in his room or in the courtyard staring into space. He has washed himself and is waiting the required time to be cleansed from handling a dead body.

Laban ventures out to the market on the first day of the week. He hears rumors that Jesus' body has been stolen from the grave. A merchant tells that Roman soldiers have spread the word that some of Jesus' disciples came and took him away, but there is no report that the soldiers were punished.

"The whole thing smells fishy to me," Laban mumbles as he ambles back to the house. He hesitates to tell Nicodemus about this rumor, but after the next Sabbath, when Nicodemus becomes more settled, Laban finally shares what he has heard. Nicodemus closes his eyes and drops his head with a sigh. Slowly he shakes his head back and forth unable to reason this thing through.

That night he talks with Ruth. As usual, she helps him put things in perspective.

When they stand to part ways for the evening, he holds her hand and looks into her eyes. "I think it will be best for you and the others to go back to Galilee. Things are so uncertain here. You must prepare to leave tomorrow."

"But..."

He presses his finger to her lips to stop her. "It will be best." He kisses her forehead and embraces her. She folds into his arms and clings tightly. "We *will* be together again. I promise you," he whispers.

He releases her. "And now, sleep well, my love. You will have a long journey tomorrow." He kisses her lovingly and they part for the night.

It is difficult for Nicodemus to see his loved ones leave the next day. His mother decides to stay, refusing to leave him alone.

Shortly after they depart, Nicodemus hears a knock at the door. He pulls open the door, and to his amazement, there stands John.

"Shalom, Master Nicodemus, I hope I have not disturbed you."

"No. No. Come in."

"I bring you great news. But first I want to thank you. The women tell me that you were a helper to Joseph of Arimathea in burying our Master. Regrettably, we were all too frightened and upset to take care of this. Besides, the authorities would never have allowed us to receive his body. So we are grateful that you helped with his burial. It was a very bold gesture on your part."

Nicodemus nods his head and then gestures toward a nearby bench. "Please sit down."

John continues. "Now for the good news. The women also reported to us on the first day of the week, that they saw an angel at the tomb. The angel reminded them of what Jesus had told us when we were in Galilee. Jesus had said, 'The Son of Man must be delivered into the hands of sinful men, be crucified and on the third day *be raised again.*' In our stubbornness and fear, we found this hard to believe. Even when Peter and I ran to the tomb and found it empty, we could not understand what was happening."

Confused, Nicodemus asks, "Then you didn't steal the body from the tomb?"

"No, of course not. That is simply a story concocted by the Temple leaders. Anyway, later that morning, Mary Magdalene said she had seen the Lord alive. And last night, two followers came to us to report that they had been with Jesus and had a lengthy conversation with him on the road to Emmaus. I confess, we still had our doubts."

John lowers his head and heaves a big sigh so as to hold back his emotions. He swallows and takes another deep breath.

With shaky voice, he continues. "While we were talking, Jesus appeared to *us.*"

"Surely this cannot be."

"It is true, Nicodemus. We saw him for ourselves. We could hardly believe our eyes. We thought it must be a ghost or something. But he showed us his hands and feet where he had been pierced; he ate with us, he opened our minds so we could understand the Scriptures. We felt the power of his presence as never before while he commissioned us to bear witness of these things."

Nicodemus' eyes fill with tears as he, too, feels the power of the Lord's presence in hearing this good report.

"Thank you, John. Thank you for coming to me with this news. My heart has been so heavy." Nicodemus pauses to regain his composure. He gazes out the window. "We say we believe in resurrection." He pauses in thoughtful meditation. "Indeed the Lord has demonstrated it before you."

Nicodemus studies John a moment. He is no longer the impish young boy from the shores of Galilee. He has become a favored young man, full of life experiences with the Master Teacher. John's eyes seem to show relief that Nicodemus has believed him.

"I must go now," John says. "It may be dangerous for you to be seen with me. Shalom."

"Shalom, John. Peace be with you."

CHAPTER 46
And so...

Jesus did many other things as well. If every one of them were written down, I suppose that even the whole world would not have room for the books that would be written. John 21:25

The disciples of Jesus once again become obedient to him. In the fullness of their faith, they speak boldly in the Temple area. Thousands come to believe.

Members of the Sanhedrin maintain their bitterness toward the believers. When Simon, now called Peter, and John heal a crippled beggar, the Sadducees, priests, and captain of the Temple Guard arrest Peter and John. The next day, the leaders are baffled by Peter's boldness as he blatantly preaches to *them* in the Sanhedrin gathering. Nicodemus takes particular note of Gamaliel's reaction and determines to have a conversation with him.

The leaders have no real reason for holding Peter and John as prisoners, so they release the disciples but warn them not to continue their preaching. Peter speaks up again, "Judge for yourselves whether it is right in God's sight to obey you rather than God." John adds, "We cannot help speaking about what we have seen and heard."

✿✿✿✿✿✿✿

Not long after, Nicodemus visits with Gamaliel. They discuss Jesus and the momentum of his followers.

Gamaliel paces back and forth, slips over to the window, and leans on the sill, looking out as though assuring himself that no one is eavesdropping. Turning to Nicodemus, he folds his arms in defiance. "There have been others like this, you know," Gamaliel retorts. "Do you remember Theudas and his band of followers? About four hundred men rallied to him, but he was killed and his followers dispersed. They soon faded away."

Nicodemus acknowledges with a nod. "Yes, and there was Judas of Galilee who led a band of people in revolt during an early census. He too was killed and his followers were scattered. His movement gave way as well. But those two men came with swords, not with words of truth. In this movement, thousands have come to believe *and* to repent."

"What if they are fooling the people with their tricks of *'miracles'* and healings."

"Gamaliel, you know some of those who have been healed. You have seen it for yourself. You have passed by the crippled beggar at the gate day after day. You saw him leaping for joy."

"Why do you defend this movement, Nicodemus? Have you become one of them? Do you not remember that the man claimed to be the son of God? How can you tolerate such blasphemy?"

"Gamaliel, we have waited for centuries for Messiah to come to redeem us. What if Yeshua was indeed our Redeemer?"

Gamaliel frowns. "Like the others, he too is dead. Hung like a criminal. Did he free us from Rome? Did he bring freedom to Israel?"

"Isaiah the prophet tells of the suffering servant who would take up our infirmities and carry our sorrows; who would be pierced for our transgressions and crushed for our iniquities. Was it by Yeshua's wounds that we are healed? Did the Lord lay on him the iniquity of us all? Instead of a *political* redeemer as we have thought, were we given a *personal* Redeemer?"

Gamaliel deliberately turns his head away as though shunning these words and strange thoughts.

Nicodemus' voice softens. "Gamaliel, my brother, if this movement is of human origin, it will fail just like the others. But if it is of God, you and the whole Sanhedrin will not be able to stop these men; you will only find yourself fighting against God."

With that, Nicodemus leaves the room. He walks out into the refreshing spring air, energized by his own boldness to speak truth.

He reflects back to his last conversation with Joseph. Joseph felt he must leave Jerusalem and carry the message of the Good News to a land far away, the land he visited many years ago. "A beautiful lush green land," he had said, "with copper and tin mines. I will proclaim the truth to them."

Perhaps it is time that I move on as well. Before I know it, this illustrious band of judges will want my head. I'm sure there are many young men in Capernaum who could use my services as "Israel's teacher." Ah, but I have so much more to teach now.

Nicodemus and his mother have packed as many of their earthly goods as possible and now Nicodemus stands on Mt. Olivet to gaze back over his beloved Jerusalem.

More of Isaiah's words come to Nicodemus' mind:

> "These people come near to me with their mouths
>   and honor me with their lips,
>   but their hearts are far from me.
> Their worship of me is made up only of rules
>   taught by men."

A slight breeze blows over Nicodemus and flutters his robe. He smiles as he remembers the Master's words— "You should not be surprised by my saying, 'You must be born again.' The wind blows wherever it pleases. You hear its sound, but you cannot tell where it comes from or where it is going. So it is with everyone born of the Spirit."

~Final Thoughts~

In this second book of the series of stories about "unlikely believers," I had one burning question about Nicodemus. What would cause a staunch Pharisee like him to come to the point of turning to Jesus when most of the Pharisees and teachers of the Law condemned Jesus?

Scripture gives us a three-part progression of Nicodemus' journey. First, he seeks out Jesus privately at night, but there is no commitment at that point. (John 3:1-21) Next, we find him speaking before the Sanhedrin in an attempt to diffuse their anger; however, it is not a true defense of Jesus. (John 7:50) Finally, we see him at the tomb to participate with Joseph in the burial of our Lord. He is willing to desecrate himself with the handling of a dead body right before Sabbath and to risk his reputation, his position, even his life. It is, at last, an amazing commitment indeed! (John 19:38-42)

As you can see, the apostle John, and only John, is our biblical source for these three glimpses into Nicodemus' life. One can surmise that John knew Nicodemus well in order to have this information and to deem it worthy to mention.

Again I asked, what could have turned Nicodemus in this direction? It seemed to me that only an extremely humbling experience could shake up this stoic Pharisee. Was it a fall on a Galilean hillside? Did a shepherd rescue him? Did he become incapacitated for a while? I don't know. But I do believe that the Lord used some kind of experience to teach Nicodemus humility so that his heart was open to the truth.

Did Nicodemus hear the rumor of the Bethlehem shepherds' story? Possibly. He lived in nearby Jerusalem. Was he privy to the twelve-year-old Jesus' discussions at the Temple with the teachers? Very possibly. Nicodemus was a teacher. The Temple was the center of his life. I find it quite conceivable that he could have been there. Do we know what the boy Jesus said or asked? No, but we do know that his words amazed the teachers. Conceivably he said some things at that time that he would come to say later as an adult.

We may read portions of Scripture and think of them as isolated events, but they are often connected. Seeing these connections, helps us immerse ourselves in the reality of the people's lives and their understanding.

As a side note, the reader may be interested to know that Glastonbury, England has historical documentation claiming that Joseph of Arimathea settled there, establishing the first Christian witness in that country. The Glastonbury Abbey boasts of roots tied to Joseph. It is said he brought the Lord's cup with him, the cup of the last supper—the Holy Grail. I find it fascinating that all the legends that grew out of the search for the Holy Grail, with the likes of King Arthur and such, had their roots in Joseph of Arimathea. England is the land I had in mind when Joseph departs from Israel.

I could find no further history on what happened to Nicodemus in his later years. One source claimed that he died in 54 A.D. and that he was buried in the same cave as Gamaliel. Some historians believe Nicodemus and Gamliel were related.

I ask again, "What did it take for a Pharisee like Nicodemus to turn to Jesus?" The proud, the pompous, the arrogant do not see the need of something beyond themselves. Even the one who is religiously devoted to the rules can be blinded by his rituals and meaningless routine.

May we all learn from Nicodemus' story that it is not enough to be clean on the outside. We must be humble enough to give attention to the inside in order to have clean submissive hearts where God's truths can take root.

Joyce Cordell

Appendix

Verses Used in the Background of the Story

Account of the angel appearance to Zechariah, father of John the Baptist

Luke 1:5-25 The angel of the Lord said, "Zechariah, your wife will bear you a son and you shall call him, John."

Purification in the Temple

- Luke 2:22-24 Every firstborn male is to be consecrated to the Lord.
- Luke 2:25-35 Simeon took the baby in his arms and praised God.
- Isaiah 42:6-7 Simeon quotes Isaiah's words.

Jesus' possible conversation with the rabbis at age 12

- Isaiah 60:1 Arise, shine, for Thy light has come, and the glory of the Lord rises upon you.
- Isaiah 59:20 "The Redeemed will come to Zion, to those in Jacob who repent of their sins," declares the Lord.
- Luke 6:45 The good man brings good things out of the good stored up in his heart, the evil man brings evil things out of the evil stored up in his heart. For out of the overflow of his heart his mouth speaks.
- Jeremiah 49:16 The pride of your heart deceives you.
- Isaiah 29:13 The Lord says, "These people come near to me with their mouth and honor me with their lips, but their hearts are far from me. Their worship of me is made up only of rules taught by men."
- Deuteronomy 6:4 Hear, O Israel: The Lord our God, the Lord is one. Love the Lord your God with all your heart and with all your soul and with all your strength.
- John 3:19 Light has come into the world, but men loved darkness instead of light...

Verses written in the phylacteries
(small boxes that are tied to the forehead and to the left arm.)

- Exodus 13:1-10 Instructions to observe Passover every year.
- Exodus 13:11-16 Instructions to give the firstborn of your animals to the Lord at Passover and share the reason for the celebration with your son.
- Deut. 6:4-9 Includes the *shema* – "Hear, O Israel: The Lord our God, the Lord is one. Love the Lord your God with all your heart, and with all your soul and with all your strength." Instructs to impress the commandments upon your children.
- Deut. 11:13-21 If you faithfully obey, God will provide for your needs. Don't be enticed by other gods. Teach these words to your children. (All of these verses also include instructions to tie these words on your arms and bind them on your forehead.)

Scripture used for Nicodemus' teaching in the synagogue in Capernaum

- Deut. 13:1-4 Beware of a prophet who comes with signs and wonders, but tries to lure you to worship other gods. "Keep [the Lord's] commands and obey him."
- Psalm 86:11 Teach me your way, O Lord, and I will walk in your truth; give me an undivided heart that I may fear your name.

Crowds around John the Baptist include tax collectors and soldiers

- Luke 3:12-14

Psalm quoted on the shepherd's hillside

- Psalm 22:1-6a, 14-15, and 19, Psalm 23

Scripture about sheep—good grazing land; drinking good water, butting heads
- Ezekiel 34:15-22.

Jesus' teachings at Capernaum
- John 6:1-15 Lessons at the feeding of the five thousand
- John 6:25-59 I am the bread of life

Jesus teachings on the hillside
- Matthew 5:17-20 Do not think I have come to abolish the Law
- Matthew 5:21-26 You have heard that it was said, "Do not murder" ...But I tell you anyone who is angry with his brother will be subject to judgment.
- Matthew 5:27-30 You have heard it said, "Do not commit adultery." But I tell you that anyone who looks at a woman lustfully has already committed adultery in his heart.
- Matthew 5:33-37 You have heard, "Do not break your oath." ...But I say do not swear ... Simply let your "Yes" be ""Yes," and your "No" be "No."
- Matthew 5:43-48 You have heard "Love your neighbor and hate your enemy." But I tell you: Love your enemies and pray for those who persecute you.
- Matthew 6:1-4 Be careful not to do your acts of righteousness before men, to be seen of them.
- John 10:1-18 I am the good shepherd. The sheep follow him because they know his voice.

Nicodemus' night time discussion with Jesus
John 3:1-21

Nicodemus' readings in Isaiah
1:13-17, 2:3, 5, 11, 12, 17, 7:14, 9:1, 2, 6, 7, 11:1-5, 52:13-15, 53:1-7

Pharisees criticize Jesus for eating with sinners. Parable of the lost sheep
Luke 15:1-7

The old shepherd's account of the appearance of angels
Luke 2:8-20

The visit of the Magi from the East
Matthew 2:1-12

The escape of Mary, Joseph, and young Jesus to Egypt
Matthew 2:13-15

Herod's slaughter of baby boys
Matthew 2:16-18

Jesus' family returns to Nazareth
Matthew 2:19-23

Temple guards come back empty-handed, Nicodemus speaks in the Sanhedrin
John 7:45-52

Descriptions of Joseph of Arimathea
Matthew 27:57-61, Mark 15:43-47, Luke 23:50-55, John 19:38-42

Pharisees question Jesus about why his disciples do not wash their hands
Matthew 15:1-11, 18-20

They come near to me with their mouths and lips, but their hearts are far from me.
Isaiah 29:1

Jesus teaches about judging
Matthew 7:1-5, 12

Parable of the Pharisee and tax collector
Luke 18:9-14

The Sanhedrin and Caiaphas plot to kill Jesus
John 11:47-50

Jesus' Teachings at the Temple
- John 7:15-24 My teaching is not my own but from the one who sent me.
- Luke 20:1-8 By what authority are you doing these things?
- Luke 20:9-19 Parable of the tenants
- Luke 20:20-26 Paying taxes to Caesar
- Luke20:27-40 The Resurrection and marriage
- John 8:31-32 You will know the truth and the truth will set you free

The Trials
- John 18:12, 13 Jesus taken to Annas
- John 18:24 Jesus taken to Caiaphas
- Luke 23: 4 Jesus taken to Pilate. "I find no basis for a charge against this man."
- Luke 23:6-11 Taken to Herod and back to Pilate
- Matthew 27:15-26 Pilate's wife warns him of her dream. Pilate offers Barabbas. The crowd cries for Jesus to be crucified. "Let his blood be on us and our children."

The Crucifixion
- John 19:19-20 A sign on the cross read, "This is the King of the Jews"
- Matthew 27:41-43 Mocking insults from the religious leaders
- Mark 15:33 Darkness came over the land for three hours
- Matthew 27:50-54 An earthquake and the Temple curtain torn in two

The Burial
- Matt. 23:55 The women follow Joseph to the tomb
- John 19:38-42 Joseph and Nicodemus bury and anoint Jesus
- Luke 24:1-12 The women come to the tomb and see the angel
- John 20:1-9 Peter and John go to see the empty tomb but do not understand that Jesus is risen

The Resurrection
- John 20:10-18 Mary Magdalene sees the risen Lord
- Luke 24:13-35 The two on the road to Emmaus talk with Jesus
- Luke 24:36-49 Jesus appears to the disciples in the upper room

The Aftermath
- Acts 4:1-22 Peter and John arrested. Peter preaches to the Sanhedrin. They are released.
- Acts 5:12-16 The apostles heal many.
- Acts 5:27-39 They are brought in again before the Sanhedrin. Gamaliel defends them.

Other Resources

The New American Commentary
Commentary on John 3, John 7:50-52, and John 19:38-42 (by Gerald L. Borchert)

The Interpreter's Bible
Commentary on John 3

www.Chabad.org
"The Tahara" by Rabbi Maurice Lamm

Dialogue with Rabbi Malkie Janowski about burial
practices
www.jewishvirtuallibrary.org/jsource/Judaism/tal
Talmud/Mishna/Gemara
Tractate Shabbat, Chapter 1
Mishna I
Mishna III

www.law.umkc.edu/faculty/projects/ftrials/fesus/sanhedrin.
html
"The Sanhedrin"
What Is the Sanhedrin?
Verdicts in Capital Trials Only to Be Reached
in Daytime
Requirements for Conviction

www.keyway.ca/htm2002/pharisee.htm
"Who Were the Pharisees?" (by Wayne Blank)

www.intouch.org/mighty/nicodemus_78037.html
"Illuminated By Love" (observations of Nicodemus
from Scripture)

www.elvenministrel.com/kontext/nicodemus.htm
"Connecting the Dots in John 3"
(by David J. Finnamore)

www.searchgod'sword.org/enc/isb/view.cgi?number=T6393
"Nicodemus" (by C. M. Kerr)

***A Shepherd Looks at Psalm 23* by Phillip Keller**
Zondervan Publishing House, 1970

***A Shepherd Looks at the Good Shepherd and His Sheep*
by Phillip Keller**
Zondervan Publishing House, 1978

From Amer Nicola (Nazareth Village Research and Curriculum Dept)...

Water skin was called "hemet" or "nod" in Hebrew. It was a whole animal skin that was removed as one piece. The skin would be tied at the hand and feet, but opened at the neck.

When the traveling skin stored water or milk, it was called hemet. The word comes from the Hebrew word "hemaah" which means butter. When the skin held wine, it was called "nod."

Shepherds would have had water, oil, and wine for injuries. Herbs – balm (Jeremiah 8:22, 46:11, 5:8) and myrrh (Genesis 37:25, 43:11)

About the Author

Joyce Cordell, a graduate of Georgetown College, makes her home in Louisville, Kentucky with her husband Jim.

Through the years, Joyce taught public school music and directed children's choirs while writing scripts, Bible studies, and short works for publication. Now in retirement, she has turned in a new direction to fulfill the passion God has given her to write about lesser known Bible characters.

Joyce's first novel, *Ears to Hear*, was published in 2007 by OakTara Publishing. The book told the story of Malchus, an unlikely believer. It was the first in this series of unlikely believers.

A Heart for Truth, the second novel of the series, explores the life of another Bible character, Nicodemus.

Joyce's desire is to help readers see these characters as the very real people they were—facing challenges, struggling with their vices, striving to follow God's will, and rejoicing in His blessings just as we do.

What about the third book of the series? "I'm thinking about three people in the Bible whose stories will intertwine," Joyce says. Her goal, as before, is to discover what might have been the rest of the story for these characters and to tell it with as much authenticity as possible, staying true to the culture and to Scripture.

For more information on Joyce Cordell:
www.joycecordell.com
joyce@joycecordell.com

Made in the USA
Columbia, SC
11 October 2023

24306224R00207